LAND MINE!

Schramm could feel the front of the jeep suddenly lift up off the road, the force of the floorboards against his boots, and the pressure against his leg muscles as the ground disappeared.

The jeep somersaulted, throwing him clear.

He could feel his right hand clutching at the strap of his M-16, the pain as he flew up into the air, and then the rifle slamming against his arm just as the earth raced toward him again and he crashed roughly back into the dirt.

It was then that he saw the three figures rising from the gully. One of them was pointing an RPG at him. . . .

THE BLACK EAGLES
by Jon Lansing

#1: HANOI HELLGROUND (1249, $2.95)
They're the best jungle fighters the United States has to offer, and
no matter where Charlie is hiding, they'll find him. They're the
greatest unsung heroes of the dirtiest, most challenging war of all
time. They're THE BLACK EAGLES.

#2: MEKONG MASSACRE (1294, $2.50)
Falconi and his Black Eagle combat team are about to stake a claim
on Colonel Nguyen Chi Roi—and give the Commie his due. But
American intelligence wants the colonel alive, making this the
Black Eagles' toughest assignment ever!

#3: NIGHTMARE IN LAOS (1341, $2.50)
There's a hot rumor that the Russians are secretly building a
nuclear reactor in Laos. And the Black Eagles are going to have to
move fast—to prevent the nuclear fallout from hitting the fan!

SAIGON COMMANDOS
DINKY-DAU DEATH

#3

JONATHAN
CAIN

ZEBRA BOOKS
KENSINGTON PUBLISHING CORP.

ZEBRA BOOKS

are published by

Kensington Publishing Corp.
475 Park Avenue South
New York, N.Y. 10016

First printing: May, 1984

Printed in the United States of America

Dedicated to the brave Americans of Vietnam's 716th Military Police Battalion, both living and dead, who were always cops first, despite the motto. Especially Sergeant K. Miller, who took out the sniper above Thanh Mau Street but failed to save me from the girls of Tu Do.

DINKY-DAU DEATH is a novel based on several true stories the author swapped with other MPs at Mimi's Bar in Saigon where he was assigned to the 716th Military Police Battalion.

"Saigon Commandos" was a derogatory term invented by infantrymen in the field to refer to any soldier stationed in the "rear." But some of the military policemen—fighting snipers, sappers, and other hostile hooligans across the Saigon underworld—affectionately adopted the title, proud to be lawmen battling crime in the toughest beat in the world.

Jonathan Cain
July, 1983
Singapore

1. THE DAY DEATH ROLLED IN WITH THE MIST

Constantly shifting shafts of sunlight pierced the high ceiling of trees, filtering down through the mist and gun smoke like falling angels, lost in the rain forest. The firefight was over; men were busy going from body to body, checking for IDs and documents.

A gunship dropped suddenly from the dark afternoon skies and hovered briefly above a break in the dense triple canopy, its pilot inspecting the detachment of U.S. military policemen. A squad sergeant on the ground gave the "all's well" sign— thumb and forefinger cupped in a circle, the other three fingers extended out straight—and the chopper banked sharply to the left and disappeared beyond the treeline, its rotors beating dully at the hot, sticky air, thick with the stench of death and the licorice taste of cordite.

Pvt. David Schramm popped the empty banana clip from his M-16 and replaced it with a fresh thirty-round magazine, then surveyed the valley trail. Their MP jeep had been totaled. One American was critically wounded—already on his way back the seven miles south to Saigon and Third Field Army Hospital. Schramm knew that when the man woke from his morphine-induced stupor he'd wish he were dead: The "family jewels" had been snatched from his battered body and thrown to the monkeys in the trees.

The squad sergeant was busy photographing the dead Viet Cong down in the gulley beside the trail. It was a mystery to

7

Schramm where the NCO had come up with a pocket camera, complete with flash—especially on a jungle patrol on the outskirts of South Vietnam's capital city—but he soon dismissed the man's antics and concentrated instead on the propaganda leaflets littering the wet and rotted floor of the forest. He didn't read Vietnamese that well—only enough to understand "Halt!" and "Drop your weapon!"—but there was no mistaking the drift of the shredded paper in his hands. It depicted the likeness of an American army captain, and above the picture was a reward in piasters: five million.

"Hhmmph," Schramm muttered beneath his breath with disgust as he scanned the unfamiliar text for some hint the bounty would be paid whether the officer was brought in dead or alive. After a moment of unsuccessful study, he told himself, "I been watching too many westerns," and hastily folded up the thin poster, quickly forgetting about the captain as he rejoined the other MPs.

Artillery rumbled in the distance just then, silencing the noisy tree monkeys as all eyes turned to the storm that was moving slowly across the horizon. The thunder of the afternoon showers often mingled with the outgoing cannons north of Gia Dinh, until it was nearly impossible to tell them apart. But Schramm suspected the shrieking limb-dwellers were not fooled, merely curious as the clouds of black smoke from distant explosions met and merged with the lightning-laced gloom.

The squad sergeant wiped off the thick layer of sweat coating his forehead—scouts from the swarm of mosquitoes above him had already landed in it and were swept aside with the grit—and ordered Schramm and his partner over to the three lifeless guerrillas.

"Gather up those AKs and what's left of the RPG launcher and hustle it back to headquarters. Take Harker's jeep."

Schramm looked down at the soldiers in the black calico trousers and shredded, camouflaged fatigue shirts. Their tire-tread Ho Chi Minh sandals had been blown off their feet when they had tried to ambush the twelve-man, four-jeep convoy of cops, and their rocket-propelled grenade had detonated the instant it was launched. "What about them?" The private's

8

eyes remained glued to the buzzing haze of horseflies that had descended on the pile of entrails lying wet and sticky beside the Cong in the middle.

The sergeant, a stocky buzzard in his forties with close-cropped hair and a Combat Infantryman's Badge on his left chest—a sure sign he was a burnt-out grunt who had re-enlisted for 95-Bravo and wasn't to be messed with—grumbled something about "Don't worry your green cherry ass about *them*" and started over to inspect the jeep lying on its top, all four tires nearly disintegrated and the floorboards charred black as coal by the land mine.

"Yeah, newbie." One of the six-month-plus vets had emerged from the shadows behind the carnage and lowered icy blue eyes down on the slender, bespectacled private. "We'll stay behind and take care of the paper work. And the *dirty* work. You and Barney get them weapons in the jeep and skate back to Pershing, so the bossman'll stay happy and keep off our butts!"

Schramm tried not to squint as he moved slightly to center the towering MP on the hillside above him against a sliver of sunlight that had lanced down through the floating steam. The man appeared almost giantlike as he stared down at the private—hands on his hips, the muscles on his tanned forearms rippling back and forth against the rolled-up sleeves of his tiger-stripe fatigues—successfully intimidating the rookie.

Schramm couldn't understand what it was with these guys. Always looking down on him and razzing him about being new in-country. He could still remember the group of MPs he had met at the in-processing center at Camp Alpha. Down from a year in Danang, they had received the royal shaft and were being sent to Thailand—all four of them—to complete another thirteen months in Asia before returning stateside. When those vets had learned he was being assigned to "easy REMF duty" in Saigon they had angrily risen from the table at the bar and stormed out into the street, cursing his luck and the unfairness of it all—especially after the four of them had weathered over a year of daily rocket and mortar barrages from the VC of Quang Nam Province.

Schramm had followed their departure with a hurt look in his eyes—it wasn't *his* fault Personnel had seen fit to assign him to the 716th. Hell, he had volunteered for Vietnam duty, for Christ's sake, had told them to send him where the bullets were flying and the flak was thickest! Could he help it if his "green cherry ass" ended up in the rear? Now, he gazed up at the clean-shaven, razor-cheeked, unblinking ogre on the hillside and decided to swallow his pride.

"Let's go, Barney," Schramm began gathering up the AK47 automatic rifles, feeling ashamed with himself for having backed down from the Spec. 4 with the tropical tan and the country-club muscles. Barney, who had been with the 716th MP Battalion three years but was still a private and comfortable taking orders from even the newbies, shrugged his shoulders and stooped to pick up what was left of the grenade launcher. Private First Class Harker, his jeep now commandeered by the squad leader, resigned himself to helping drag the Cong bodies up out of the gulley. Schramm frowned in disgust and turned quickly away when he noticed the wild dog emerge from the treeline and follow cautiously behind Harker, lapping at the trail of thick, mirrorlike blood with its tongue.

"Why do they call you Barney?" Schramm asked later, as their jeep turned onto Highway One-A and headed south, back to Saigon.

A leaf-colored Phantom jet swooped down from the cloud cover just then, drowning out the big soldier's answer as it passed low overhead, barely visible above the ceiling of tangled trees. A stomach-jerking sonic boom followed the waving of wings and it was gone that quick.

". . . And ever since then," Barney continued, more like he was talking to himself than Schramm as he ignored the intrusion of the fighter plane into the silent world of the jungle. "Ever since I failed to qualify at the target range and accidentally winged the instructor in the control tower, they been razzing me that I cain't hit the side of a barn. So now it's 'Barney' instead of Felix."

Schramm wasn't sure why he had bothered to ask the question in the first place. He already knew the answer—knew that Barney had just made up the story about his terrible aim back at boot camp. The men had already warned him about Barney—told him to stay away from the big oaf if he ever got moody and exhibited that far-off look in his eyes. And started conversing more like he was talking to himself than the man sitting beside him.

But, hell, Barney was his partner! And the one thing they drilled into you back at The School in Fort Gordon was you always stood by your partner. No matter what. You *never* abandoned your partner, regardless of the circumstances. You went to hell if you did, plain and simple.

Besides, Schramm was intrigued by Barney's past. How could a soldier as big as he—gentle and easygoing as he was—complete three tours in the 'Nam and still have mosquito wings for rank on his arms? Surely there had to be something besides that story the platoon captain told him when he was assigned as Barney's rook partner. Something besides the time Charlie Company was involved in house-to-house fighting in Cholon and big Barney was in charge of the lead gun jeep. The captain told Schramm how the Cong had shot the tires out from under Barney and how the jeep had rolled down into the Ben Nghe canal. But the big MP had emerged from the muck with the monstrous M-60 blazing, cradled in both arms like an angry baby. How he had kept firing until the VC were routed, the machine gun's barrel was melted, and two buildings in south Cholon had been reduced to a pile of rubble. And ever since then, the men had called him Barney. Barney Rubble.

"So what are they gonna do with these weapons?" Schramm asked as he took off his wire-rimmed glasses and began cleaning them with the cuff of his blood-stained fatigues. "They're all shot to hell." But the newbie was really wondering how many enemy Cong Barney had smoked during that firefight in Cholon.

"Documentation, Davey boy," the three-hundred-pounder steered the jeep with his knees for a few seconds while he scratched at his crew cut with thick fingers to free the flakes

11

of mud and whatever was crawling in it from his scalp. "Documentation. You see, all these tools of warfare carry identifying marks of origin." The senior partner returned his fists to the steering wheel but never once looked Schramm in the eye. "Chinese AKs, Russian AKs, whatever. The boys in MI love to substantiate U.S. claims that the Soviets are supporting not only the NVAs, but the insurgents here in the South."

"But everyone already knows *that*." Schramm frowned as he noticed how his forearms still stuck out like sore thumbs: bone white, with hundreds of little red mosquito bites everywhere, making them look like he had the measles. It was a wonder he hadn't contracted malaria. He was sure he'd never forget that first night in Vietnam, only last week, when the company clerk—a goofy corporal with a pet rat that enjoyed nesting amidst the curly locks of his blond afro—had initiated him quite properly into the notorious Saigon nightlife by getting him so drunk on Ba moui Ba beer that the newbie had passed out on his barracks cot without remembering to spread out a mosquito net. Some joker had walked by and turned off the noisy electric fan, and the swarm of hungry pests had descended from the rafters and proceeded to feast on his exposed arms until he awoke from a restless nightmare of bargirls with bamboo slivers between their legs and old mama-sans with black betel nut smiles to find he was covered with countless bite marks that sent his heart pumping and the hangover throbbing even harder against his temples.

"Yeah, if it weren't for the fucking Ruskies in Moscow, we'd have had this little police action wrapped up years ago," Barney continued, his eyes on a graceful magpie now instead of the road. Schramm wanted to ask why he kept returning to Vietnam if he felt that way, but the eighteen-year-old already knew the answer. Barney was just like Schramm's older brother Dennis had been: frustrated upon his return home to The World, bored with his old friends and a life that seemed alien to him. An existence he vaguely remembered but had no desire to return to. Barney had lost his innocence in the 'Nam. He had lost part of his soul, if not all of it, but, worse, that contentment he had had in Saigon had failed to follow him back to America.

There was no job satisfaction in pouring concrete or erecting bridges or roofing new homes. Only in tearing them all down. No excitement in a nine-to-fine workday. No one shooting at you, firing up the adrenalin pumps, forcing you to live on the edge. No one to shoot back at. No one, that was, if you wanted to stay out of the cages, free of the bars. The Military Police Corps had trained him to exist in the jungle, or survive on the street. It was training that did not pay wages back in the real world—only made him fall in with the bad crowd, the back alley denizens. The same scum he fought so hard in the side streets of Saigon.

So Barney had returned to Vietnam, again and again. To the only place he really felt at home, valuable, needed. Just like Schramm's brother, Dennis.

Four years older than him, Dennis had never even come home for R&R. Stayed in Saigon twice, and took one vacation in Hong Kong, where a prostitute in Wanchai stabbed him over a wrist watch. The letters were regular, brief and modest—with no mention of the knifing until an army captain visited Schramm's mother. His father had died in a car accident the year before, yet Dennis's unit was so deep into the jungle at the time, MACV Command was not even sure of their exact location, and Dennis missed the funeral.

Twice the infantry sergeant wrote long letters home to his younger brother. They were filled with exciting stories about pursuing the VC through mist-enshrouded rain forests or hunting tigers on R&R on the outskirts of the rubber plantations with only one round in the thirty-bullet clip—it made the hunt more challenging and the risks greater. It was while anxiously awaiting that third letter—Dennis had written his squad was due to ride some choppers west toward the Cambodian frontier on a low-profile mission of some sort—that the family received the telegram from the government. Advising that Dennis was missing-in-action and presumed dead after an intense firefight with NVA forces north of Saigon, outside of Gia Dinh.

Presumed dead. Killed and buried in the muck of some

13

steaming battlefield, twelve thousand miles from his homeland. In the jungle he had come to love and now called home.

Schramm shook the visions from his head just as Barney swerved suddenly to the left in an attempt to run down one of the countless wild dogs as it ventured out into the roadway. The animal emitted the briefest of yelps as it was bounced around beneath the undercarriage and dragged along for several yards before tumbling to a stop in the dust. Barney imitated a crying canine with a high-pitched whine that caused Schramm to do a double take, but the smile never left the big MP's face as he concentrated now on staying right behind a huge turquoise dragonfly that had appeared inches in front of the vehicle's windshield.

As Schramm pulled the folded Wanted poster from his thigh pocket, the dragonfly detected the metal predator on its tail and veered off abruptly into the sky. "Whatta ya think of *this*?" Schramm held the reward flyer proudly, like a war trophy, but Barney's eyes remained on the dragonfly—now only a dark dot against the castlelike clouds leaning ominously out from the vast blue skyline—and Schramm marveled at how the man could keep the jeep on the road without paying any attention to his driving.

"Oh, we get those leaflets around here all the time," Barney dismissed the poster with a wave of his hand. "Don't mean nothin'. Just the Cong puttin' the fear into another U.S. Army officer. Don't usually see a bounty that high though. Let's see . . . five million p," and once again he took both hands from the steering wheel as he began calculating on his fingers just how many greenbacks five million piasters converted into. Schramm closed his eyes tightly as they narrowly missed an old man pulling his water buffalo along the side of the road. Barney was still counting his finger tips a few seconds later when they were almost struck head-on by an ARVN deuce-and-a-half. "Yep, that comes to about ten thousand dollars. Not bad for a lousy captain."

"Whatta you think he did to make them so angry—to put up so much money?" Schramm closed his eyes voluntarily this time, as he leaned out the side of the jeep slightly to feel the hot, humid Asian air slapping at his mustache. Yes, a few

14

more days under the tropical sun and the red dots would merge with his sunburn and vanish.

"Aw, there's no tellin' about that. Them grunts are always pissin' off the dinks. I doubt Charlie's even got ten grand to back the bounty, but it's good propaganda, and, like I said, puts one hell of a scare into the officers. Hell, for ten grand, *I* might even take up the offer. Of course, it's always possible old man VC didn't even put out the ... well ..."

Barney's smile faded for the first time and he started drumming his fingers on the steering wheel as he finally began concentrating on his driving. "Didn't put out the what?" Schramm persisted.

"Forget it."

"Put out the what?"

The military radio attached to the side of the rear seat blurted out a sudden storm of static and unintelligible jargon but both MPs ignored the outburst when it drifted off the net and failed to return.

Barney's attention shifted to the floorboard beneath the gas pedal about that time, and as he reached down to pull an old newspaper out from between the sandbags that filled the bottom of the jeep they drifted across the center line again and were almost clipped by a bus, loaded down with riders clinging to the running boards and door handles. The huge vehicle soon disappeared beyond a cloud of dust in the opposite direction as its driver swerved over onto the dirt shoulder of the road, but Barney didn't seem to hear the profanity and insults being yelled by the slowly fading, fist-waving Vietnamese.

"*Stars & Stripes!*" A grin automatically returned to his features as he recognized the tattered remains of the official American newspaper overseas. And as he opened it up wide, completely obscuring his view through the windshield, Barney made no effort to stop the jeep and change seats but merely suggested, "You drive for a while," and leaned over on his left elbow as Schramm frantically reached for the steering wheel just before the jeep started onto a bridge.

"Look at this shit!" Barney suddenly shifted the newspaper in front of Schramm's eyes, forcing the newbie to sit

15

up in his seat in order to peer over it.

A full-page photo showed American marines torching a village. Several huts were in flames, but although a full platoon of soldiers was evident, there was not a single Vietnamese in the picture. On the bottom, right-hand corner of the page, a smaller photograph—depicting a refugee mother cowering in a filthy gutter with her malnourished infant—had been superimposed over the first, and the caption read, "Search And Destroy has come to mean SAD."

"Nowhere in here do they tell you those marines are just burning down a VC training center or an ammo cache," Barney groaned, and Schramm could feel the anger boiling over in the big man. He wondered what the participants of a bar fight would look like after Big Barney was unleashed on them. "Whose side are these guys on, anyway?"

"Hey man, don't let the press get to ya," Schramm offered the only words of comfort he could come up with, but he was ignored.

"What's the fuckin' date on this rag, anyway?" he asked the sticky afternoon air rushing through the jeep, and Schramm could see that the thirty-year-old private was incensed, ready to burst.

Barney finally found enough left of one page to read the date. "It fucking figures." He tossed the newspaper to the wind. "June 1965. Exactly two years ago. Age of the limp-wristed, bleeding-heart Aquarians! Shit, I feel like going out and killing something!"

"Don't look at me." Schramm grinned, but Barney saw no humor in the remark.

"You go and join the armed forces to protect your country, and some wimp with a pen and camera tears down everything you've sacrificed for, just to put out commie trash like that!"

As they approached a burned-out, abandoned tank on the side of the road the big man behind the wheel ordered the private doing the steering to pull over.

After the jeep coasted to a stop, Barney stepped out, chambered a round into his M-16, then let loose with thirty

16

rounds on full automatic right at the rusting turret on top. Sparks and tracers ricocheted against the backdrop of dark thunderclouds racing toward them and the incredible noise sent Schramm sinking lower in his seat as he looked about nervously to see if any of the nationals had seen what occurred.

"Aw, that felt better than taking a hearty shit, ya know what I mean, Davey boy? Better than a hearty shit!" Big Barney jumped back into the jeep and set the gears to screeching as he spun tires back onto the highway. After they pulled away from the tank, several Vietnamese children who had been playing inside the turret jumped to the ground and scampered off down the road at high speed, in the opposite direction.

The sound of sporadic automatic-weapon fire reached their ears as the jeep's straining engine pulled the vehicle up onto high ground, and at first Schramm thought it might just be an echo of Big Barney's rock and roll show, but the waves of heavy machine gun shooting and high-caliber discharges quickly merged into one drawn-out roar that sent a chill down Schramm's spine.

"It sounds like someone is catching some godawful shit back there," he told the big MP, his tone suggesting they might return to check on the men back at the ambush site.

"Fuck it," Big Barney's answer came as a sarcastic lament to his priorities in the 'Nam. "We've put in our twelve hours. Those boys can handle themselves. Besides, that don't sound like it's anywhere near where our jeep bit the dust. Just sit back an' relax: It's time to pay homage to little ole mama-san downtown."

"But what if—" Schramm continued to protest, and just then another garbled transmission broke across the airwaves. But Big Barney, anticipating the rookie's concern, quickly reached back and turned off the radio. He had spent too many double shifts in the past responding to half-ass shoot-outs that always fizzled out before he got there, leaving the bulk of the ensuing paper work for those MPs unlucky enough to arrive late. And he couldn't remember the last time genuine VC had been involved—it was usually

17

disenchanted bandits from one of the religious sects, just out to pop off some poorly aimed rounds at the imperialists.

Barney reached down and flicked on the AM radio Harker had taped to the bottom of the jeep's dashboard, turning the volume up full blast until the Sunrays' song, "I Live for the Sun" drowned out the reports of distant gunfire. "Sit back and enjoy the music!" he said, suddenly pleased with himself at having found the American Forces Radio Network frequency so quickly—it usually took forever.

Schramm gritted his teeth, hiding the clenched fists beneath his seat as he endured the helpless feeling silently. He forced his eyes closed and leaned back against his flak jacket, feeling the thick fiberglas dig into his neck. He tried to concentrate on the words of the song—he wasn't sure if it was about beachcombers or Aztec sun gods—but the clatter of machinegun fire kept drifting back to his ears, and soon his mind was re-creating the events of earlier that afternoon.

It had started out as routine as any of the busy-work patrols, mainly a high-profile, let-the-Cong-see-the-MP-jeeps type strategy, designed to reduce the increasing incidents of daylight terrorism in the suburbs. Schramm and Barney had been in the lead jeep, choosing the worn-down trails, hoping to make an uneventful sweep and be back in town by lunchtime.

Barney had even let Schramm drive that day, and it was only their second day together. It was the senior partner's belief your average green rook didn't really get to know the streets or the countryside well enough unless you gave him the wheel and free reign to patrol on his own. Of course, Barney still had to point the way now and then, but for a newbie he was catching on faster than most.

Schramm had always thought he'd be struck with a certain feeling before experiencing his first encounter with Charlie Cong—a chill, or tenseness in the air, a twisting of his gut. But nothing except an ominous silence preceded the land mine blast. Even the multicolored parrots in the trees overhead had watched the whole affair without uttering a single shrill chirp or whistle.

Perhaps that was the signal, he thought later. The

uncharacteristic quiet of the birds. He had spotted them while they were still far down the bumpy trail—it was hard to miss the red and yellow feathers contrasting against the brilliant shades of green jungle spread out below the thundering skyline—and he should have taken notice of the way they followed the approach of the jeeps, utterly silent, bowing their heads now and then to eyeball a spot in the road where the land mines had been planted, almost as if they had watched the VC dig the holes a thousand times before and had been conditioned to expect the disruption of jungle life that always followed.

The sandbags piled along the floor of the jeep had saved the two privates. Their jeep was one of the few that didn't have metal planks welded to the undercarriage, but the sandbags had done the job—despite the force of the explosion having flipped the vehicle completely over and throwing the men into the path of the patrols following fifty feet behind.

Schramm could still feel the front of the jeep suddenly lift up off the road, the force of the floorboards against his boots, the pressure against his leg muscles as the ground disappeared—almost like the roller coaster rides back home—and the jeep somersaulted, throwing him clear. He could feel his right hand clutching at the strap of his M-16, the pain as the ground was left below and the rifle sprang back, slamming against his arm just as the earth raced back up at him and he crashed roughly back into the dirt, the rotted floor of the jungle and the slimy things that slithered through it.

It was then that he saw the three figures rising up from the gulley, one man pointing the RPG at the second jeep. His first impulse was to bring up his own weapon, spray the trio with automatic-weapons fire before they could launch the grenade. The blinding flash of light that erupted where the guerrillas had been took him totally by surprise, and it was the concussion from the accidental explosion that flattened him against the reeds, not his training.

The men would later joke about their luck at having the terrorists' own RPG blow up in their faces, but at the time

19

Schramm had never been so scared in his life.

Not at the prospect of exchanging shots with the communists, nor even the probability that he'd be killed or captured once the ambush was completed and the patrol was terminated. It was the wrath of the drill sergeants back in Georgia that kept racing through his mind like tracer rounds. Damn, if word ever got back to The School that he had screwed up and allowed an entire MP convoy to get wiped out there'd be four or five DIs sure to hop the next flight to Saigon just to jump in his shit and tear off his head for making *them* look bad.

Schramm was just beginning to relive the anxiety he had experienced at facing his first encounter with hostile forces when the three MP jeeps raced past in the opposite direction, lights flashing and sirens screaming as they roared down the highway in the direction of the shooting. Barney was just starting to slow their own vehicle when a fourth unit barreled by, its driver glancing back at the two bewildered privates with intense irritation in his eyes. The anger on the buck sergeant's face clearly read: Why aren't you men pointed in the right direction?

As the big MP jerked down on the steering wheel and brought the vehicle around in a controlled slide, Schramm shook the daydream from his head and reached back to turn up the military radio.

"All units proceeding to Delta Seven's last known location, code zero: shots fired!" the dispatcher back at Pershing Field droned on in an unemotional tone, "I repeat: exercise caution. Delta Seven reports shots fired, MPs down. A secondary ambush from the north and east."

"Suggest all units approach from the south!" came a scratchy voice over the airwave static. Schramm instantly recognized Harker's voice.

There was only gun smoke and the stench of death in the air when the two privates finally arrived, ten minutes later. No bullets flying, no flak to dodge. No Cong to chase down. No brother MPs to fight alongside.

They were all dead. Wiped out. Pulverized.

The buck sergeant they had passed back on the highway was on his radio, switching frequencies as he attempted to make contact with the ARVN gunship that had appeared above the triple canopy and was now hovering over the silent battlefield. "Victor Charlie escaping to the north-by-northeast, north-by-northeast!" he repeated as his fingers slowly moved the radio dial from notch to notch, allowing mere seconds for a response. The only answer from the Cobra helicopter was the dull thump-thump-thump of its rotors beating at the thick, humid air. The men in the three other jeeps had scattered on arrival at the ambush site and now attended to the bodies, searching for survivors.

"Victor Charlie escaping to the—" the sergeant was still yelling against the whir of the rotors beating down on the tangled canopy overhead, but the chopper was suddenly banking sharply to the right, and then it was gone, skimming low over the treetops in the direction opposite to that of the fifty fleeing VC.

"Fuckin' Arvins! Fuckin' Arvins!" the sergeant screamed as he watched the shadow of the craft disappear across the domelike roof of the rain forest, refusing to remain in the area long enough to draw sniper fire. He threw the useless microphone back in the jeep when he caught sight of Big Barney and his rookie partner. Schramm was running toward one of the burning MP jeeps, determined to rescue the first corpse he could find from the angry jaws of the fire. Barney dismounted his unit more slowly, moist eyes glued on one of the other jeeps that had been destroyed by incoming HE rounds from the dozen captured M-79s.

"Fairchild!" the sergeant yelled at Barney, "get back in your unit and start up the trail! We're gonna have to beat feet to catch up with . . . Fairchild! Listen to me, boy!" But Big Barney was ignoring the E5 as he walked like a zombie toward the wreck that had crushed one of his few friends into the dead flora littering the jungle floor.

Sgt. Mark Stryker shifted his attention to the MPs from the three backup units briefly, ignoring Big Barney as he went from man to man, pulling them sometimes forcefully from their fallen comrades and propelling them back to their jeeps. "After the Cong, goddamnit!" he was directing the teenagers, feeling unforgivably foolish in knowing any enemy marksmen that had been ordered to remain behind the retreating guerrillas could easily pick him and his men off with ease, choosing with extreme prejudice the closest exposed targets.

The flames licking at his hands had jolted Schramm from the daze, and he turned to face Stryker just as the sergeant was about to grab him by the shoulders. "I know! I know!" Schramm screamed, recoiling both from the sting of heat and the enraged NCO bearing down on him. "The chase," his mind told him as he turned to sprint back to his jeep. "The chase is always Priority One. Get the suspects first. Reinforcements will tend to the wounded officers. But get the damn suspects. Without them, your gunned-down brothers will have died in vain." And his mind's voice took on the tone of the DIs back at The School: "Get the suspects. Get the goddamn suspects, no matter how great the pain and indecision!"

"Good boy!" Stryker slammed the private on the back, knowing the kid knew what to do, reading his voices—the electricity of the battlefield and the death all around channeling through Stryker's icy blue eyes a power almost telepathic that *told* the men what had to be done. Even if the rooks, in their confusion, rationalized that the men they chased were back-alley criminals and not hardened jungle fighters.

Schramm and the other privates were aware they were not pursuing a street gang in downtown Cholon. They were painfully mindful of the fact you didn't chase down fifty heavily armed VC with jeeps. You took to the trails on foot, carefully tracking them through *their* backyard, aware that even if you survived all the booby traps that were sure to be left behind, crafty Mr. VC would most likely vanish into some murky tunnel complex built deep into the bowels of the earth.

The MPs fired up their jeeps, already mentally exhausted, pausing long enough to watch Stryker run up to Barney

22

Fairchild and boldly slam both open palms against the big man's chest in an attempt to halt his march toward the overturned jeep. Barney tottered back on his heels briefly, still unaware the sergeant had struck him, then started again toward the charred forearm sticking out from beneath the crushed side panels.

"Move out!" Stryker turned toward the three jeeploads of men when he sensed they had yet to leave, and as the first vehicle's tires sent dust flying the sergeant shook his head at the sight of all those MPs on wheels. "Damn, where'd they learn field tactics, anyway!" he thought to himself as he decked the three-hundred-pounder with both hands, clasped together and directed at the giant's left temple.

Stryker caught the private as he tumbled toward the ground and began dragging him by the shoulders toward the only jeep at the scene left in operating condition.

After several unsuccessful attempts at lifting Barney up into the jeep, Stryker dumped him beside it, then rolled him as far under the chassis as his bulk permitted.

The military police sergeant then unslung the upside-down M-16 from his shoulder, paused briefly as he surveyed the blanket of mist creeping in on the scene of devastation, and slowly disappeared in the breeze-swept sea of elephant grass, starting after the communists on foot.

2. GUNSHIPS THROUGH THE TREES

Five miles east of An Linh, in Military Region 3 . . .

Capt. Louis Moast, his hands clutching the sturdy wall racks protruding from the thin inner skin of the Bell UH-1D helicopter, leaned out through the open side of the craft and surveyed the lush carpet of jungle racing by below. The doorgunner beside him, Spec. 4 Randy Nelson, took his eyes off the countless huts spread out between the rice paddies and grinned at the prospect of his "fearless leader" tripping out through the gaping hole and plummeting down through space to his death. An accident. Turbulence. A jolt to the left, a stray sniper round from the ground. Anything could happen in a war zone. Anything could tempt fate and award that ten thousand dollar prize into the hands of the deserving soldier. But actually collecting the bounty might be another matter.

Captain Moast turned to face Nelson suddenly, his own smile now ear to ear as the fleet of gunships approached LZ Python, and the doorgunner's eyes flashed back to the terrain below, seeking out black-pajama-clad figures in the brilliant collage of blues and greens that extended to the horizon.

"Yes, Specialist, gonna be a hot LZ!" Moast licked his lips as he referred to the landing zone, notorious not only for its VC ambushes but for the occasional man-swallowing snakes that passed through. "A mighty hot LZ! I can taste it in the air!"

The captain leaned back out the portal, his short blond hair forced down even farther by the gust of hot wind and the blast from the rotors overhead. Seconds earlier it had been cold

24

enough that Nelson buttoned up his flak jacket—now they were skimming just above the treetop level and the sweat was trickling down the small of his back again.

"Yes, Captain, another hot LZ," the spec. 4 thought to himself, "just the way you like it. Another skirmish with bad bad Victor Charlie just to clear a lousy hillside that we'll abandon tomorrow. And they'll reclaim, after they emerge from their fucking tunnels." Nelson found his eyes roaming back to his captain's frame in the portal, mere inches from the M-60 sitting ready on its swivel. The urge to just kick the bastard out was overwhelming, and he forced his concentration back down on the hamlets below, pretending the officer was one of those whores in Gia Dinh: irresistible, but a treat you nevertheless avoided, knowing full well the consequences later on.

The combat patch on the man's right shoulder was another reason Randy Nelson refrained from booting his captain out into never never land. The doorgunner felt a deep sense of camaraderie for anyone wearing the U.S. Army's largest unit insignia: the black and gold First Cavalry Division Airmobil emblem. Nelson suffered an unshakable loyalty to anyone wearing the shield-shaped patch with the diagonal bar running top left to bottom right and a horse head in the upper right corner, even if that person happened to be an overzealous infantry captain whose reputation for leading his men into virtual suicide missions was unsurpassed.

Just the week before, Moast had volunteered his company for a mission along the west banks of the Song Dong Na, outside Loi Tan, and after *that* firefight only three squads were left. The company had been completely surrounded by a battalion of North Vietnamese regulars, and seven choppers had been lost. The survivors made it out only because MACV rushed south reinforcements from Nhon Co air base and dispatched a squadron of Phantoms from Tan Son Nhut.

The crazy thing was that Moast never observed the battles from a Charlie-Charlie, or command & control gunship, a mile above the hostilities. He was always in the thick of things, leading the charge. So much so that recently the men—those who survived his insane escapades against overwhelming

25

odds—had taken to calling him Moast the Ghost. Not because he always escaped unscathed but because he was so good at making ghosts of his men. And wherever Moast the Ghost ventured, Mr. Death always followed.

Now they were skimming along the northern boundary of Gia Dinh province, closing in on the "diamond's point" where it met with Binh Duong and Phuoc Thanh, in search of a renegade band of bandits who had terrorized the villagers of An Linh, kidnapped the chieftain's two daughters, and looted the people's temple of all its artifacts and precious statues. Including the bundles of gold leaf that had been buried beneath the Buddhist shrine.

Definitely an ARVN (Army of Republic of Vietnam) affair, Nelson decided. No reason American soldiers should be anywhere near An Linh. But once again Moast the Ghost had come up with brain-storming proposals and of course the colonel had bought it all, hook, line and sinker. Nelson didn't doubt Captain Moast had hidden incentives he failed to tell the colonel about. Such as how nice all that gold leaf would look above Moast's fireplace back in Delaware. No, Nelson feared this was not a sincere attempt at merely improving public relations with the Vietnamese.

The funny thing about Captain Moast was that he knew all about the money his men pooled every payday. The ten, twenty or fifty dollars each man was rumored to put up until the kitty totaled thousands of dollars. A bounty to be turned over to the first soldier who delivered Moast's head to the medevac choppers, telling the dust-off pilots that that was all that was left of their "beloved leader."

But Moast was never in the right place at the right time. Sure, ricochets had slammed into his back on several occasions but his trusty flak jacket had always stopped the slugs. And the one time a grenade had rolled into his command post he had simply jogged out toward the perimeter, all smiles, and disappeared beyond the bushes that served as a latrine until tempers cooled down.

The man never ordered an investigation. Never brought his troops up on charges. Never requested a transfer. Moast the Ghost seemed to thrive on death and danger, appeared to take the morale problem in his unit as an irritant better attended to by the chaplain than himself, told his lieutennats the reward posters were humorous, even a compliment. Nothing to lose sleep over. He was being paid big bucks to elude Mr. VC, and if the rumors were true that it was not Charlie Cong but his own men who were putting out the posters then so be it. Even less sweat. The guerrillas were one thing—they had been at this sort of thing for decades. His teen-age troops were rotated from the field every thirteen months. To Moast, that meant their cunning, skill and technique were considerably less than the commies', increasing his odds for survival and that promotion to major. Thank Buddha an officer's Vietnam tour was only six months.

"And now," thought doorgunner Nelson, "Moast the Ghost is taking us deep into Injun country, on another wild goose chase after Mr. Death, a bad dude you just don't mess with."

Nelson caught the co-pilot's signal out of the corner of his eye: a stiff forefinger directed at the slightest hint of something shiny reflecting up from the ground at their first pass. A silver line that crisscrossed the LZ for only a microsecond and revealed the guerrillas had probably strung wire between two treetops or bamboo poles, hoping to tear off some rotors when the gunships set down.

The choppers on either side of Moast's craft swung out wide of the formation and descended in amongst the tallest palms, strafing the perimeter gullies with 7.62 caliber tracers at six thousand rounds per minute.

Nelson watched the lone UH1C in the fleet off to the right loop up above the rest of the choppers in preparation for covering the first men off the lead bird. The oldest craft out that mission, it was faster and stronger but not nearly as maneuverable as the younger Hueys.

A cheer went up from the crew as the strafers hit an ammo cache, and the underground bunker blew skyward in a bright ball of yellow and orange that tossed limbs and pieces of bark up against the observation windows of the landing choppers. Soldiers were quickly jumping to the ground while the ships hovered less than a meter above the marshlike landscape. Then, their payloads expended, they banked sharply to the left, noses dipping slightly as the rotors strained to push them back away from earth.

Nelson could hear the chatter over the pilot's radio just then: something about zips closing in on the LZ through the trees. Then the guerrillas magically appeared in his own MG sights and his knuckles turned white with pressure as the huge M-60 began barking hot lead.

The bullets flying back at him—it was the first time he had ever seen white tracers used, and they were now bouncing in at him from all angles—made hollow, almost electriclike twanging noises as they sliced through the sides of the gunship and ricocheted off helmets and other metal in the cabin.

For the first time since arriving in 'Nam, Nelson began to feel the fear that comes with a reversal of the odds. He had never seen so many Cong as he did now, emerging from the treeline, rushing like a flood of black-clad demons down the hillside toward the choppers. Suddenly the power associated with the fleet—the doorgunners on every ship, the incredible firepower, the legendary bravery of the troopers, the notorious reputation of the First Cav itself— it all seemed to fade as it became apparent the Americans were outnumbered ten to one.

Nelson felt his own chopper sink in the air slightly as the last soldier hopped off. It should have then shot up skyward, away from the advancing swarm, but Moast was yelling something into the ear of the pilot—Nelson could not hear above the roar of his 60—and both crewmen were nodding, grinning even. And the bird whirled around clockwise, without lifting an inch, so that Nelson was facing the brunt of the attack.

"Now mow 'em down, boy!" Moast had glided back to Nelson's hole in the wall. "Mow Mister Charlie's ass back into the grass!" The captain had produced both of the .45s he kept on his hips and was taking pot shots at individual guerrillas with slow, smooth, unexcited arm movements.

"Yeah, I'm gonna mow 'em down, you cocksucker," Nelson thought, gritting his teeth, knowing full well he intended to also cut Moast the Ghost cleanly in half at the precise moment it looked like the bad bad VC were about to win the odds gamble.

"See that motherfucker with the LAW tube?" Moast asked the spec. 4, not really waiting for an answer as he brought his sights down on the guerrillas now only thirty meters from the gunship and placed four carefully aimed hollow points into the chest of the biggest soldier.

Nelson watched the Vietnamese halt in midstride, as if a taut tripwire had caught him full in the throat and bounced him back to the ground. Only the splash of blood—like the spittle exploding from a boxer's mouth when he's caught with a strong punch, except this was red—signalled the man's true fate. Nelson, despite the mind-numbing effect of the gunfire all around, found himself wondering if the guerrilla's spirit had drifted up to the lush, green treetops and was even then gazing down at his lifeless body, dumbfounded, bewildered, confused about what had gone wrong. He had heard the battlefield tales so often he now wondered if even the despicable Cong practiced enough religion to believe in an existence after their demise. Especially violent death.

"That group! Those!" Moast was slapping him on the shoulder, jarring him from that other world of things-that-might-be and pointing to a squad of sappers off to their right.

Nelson swung the M-60 around, but before he could fire a black Loach swooped down between the trees and dropped, like a basket of mangos, a dozen grenades. The multiple explosions—many completely tearing off the faces of the few stunned teen-agers foolish enough to reach for the bouncing grenades—sent concussions rolling out at the gunships on the ground. Nelson's ship was rocked almost onto its side as gray, smoking shrapnel peppered the craft's skin.

Both pilots were now looking back at Moast, their smiles gone, the anticipation in their eyes sparkling like stars through the dark green shades both men wore.

"Captain!" Nelson's face took on the grim, sallow complexion of a death's head. "We better lift off! Ammo's running dry!"

"Nonsense! Nonsense, I tell you! This is why we soldier! This is why we're here in the fucking 'Nam! To ice Charlie! Now take your M-16 if your 60's out and get to work, *Specialist!*"

Just then two Hueys that had looped back to provide cover fire appeared menacingly above the treetops, their noses tilted slightly down at the swarm still materializing on the jungled hillside. Nelson glanced over at the pilots in his own craft, but they only raised their hands in helpless resignation, unwilling to challenge the Ghost.

Nelson felt a spray of lead pass between himself and the captain just then—the group Moast had fired his pistols into had now zeroed in on his chopper—and he searched again for the hovering green birds through the walls of swirling gun smoke, hoping they'd also seen what was happening.

The helicopters were equipped with two pods on each side, seven two-and-a-half-inch rockets in every pod, fired electronically by the pilot. Nelson could tell the bird on the left had one of the 40mm cannons in its snout. He couldn't actually see the snub-nosed barrel, but painted across the belly of the craft was the inscription, "CUNT CANNON CILLER," and that could only mean a real-heavy-duty burper. Nelson knew each helicopter also sported two XM-21 minigun systems that had ten-degree pivots, allowing them to automatically track from side to side five degrees off center.

But the gunships remained silent, and as they sat there, motionless in the boiling, sticky Asian air, observing the death and destruction like box seat baseball fans munching on their popcorn, Nelson swung the big M-60 around until the muzzle slammed snugly into Captain Moast's belly.

"What's the goddamned meaning of this, soldier!" Moast stammered as he attempted to slap the machine gun barrel aside, but Nelson kept it firmly in place. "Why, I'll have you digging latrines in Khe Sanh, boy!"

"The *meaning* of this is that I don't feel so lucky today, Captain. And I don't plan to go down as a KIA statistic just so you can climb the promotion ladder. My mama ain't receivin' no posthumous Purple Heart and her favorite son in a body bag, care of Uncle Sam." Nelson turned slightly to face the pilot. "Take her away, gentlemen!"

As the rotors gained speed and twigs and dirt began to blind the soldiers rushing down toward the gunships, Moast said, "You might as well pull that trigger, son. 'Cuz when we get

30

back to camp, I'm gonna nail your hide to the cross!"

"You do whatever you damn well please, Captain. I just know I'd rather be judged by six of my peers than carried to my grave by the same men."

As the Huey lifted off and veered out away from the battlefield, the choppers hovering above the treeline unleashed their rockets and deafening explosions tore holes into the hillside as big as jeeps. But the Cong kept coming and Nelson watched one of the birds still on the ground catch an RPG through its open hatch. The craft burst into flames as sections of twisting rotors were thrown out at the arms and legs that were already airborne.

"No, I'm not going to shoot you, Captain," Nelson muttered as he pulled off the smoke-smeared goggles and brushed back his light brown hair with his fingers, "although God knows I should. I could use the ten grand." He looked up so that his eyes drilled into Moast's as he said sarcastically, "I just don't know who'd pay the bounty . . . *sir.*"

Moast was silenced by the reference to the reward posters they had found at every landing zone these last two weeks. His gaze fell to the thick muzzle of the heavy machine gun creasing his web belt then shifted back to the determined eyes of the doorgunner. Obviously, the man meant business. And Lady Luck would not save him from an MG burst at close range from one of his own soldiers. Both men stared at each other in silence after that.

As Spec. 4 Randy Nelson's gunship labored up through the mist to the haze above the treetops the only sounds besides the rotors and the muffled explosions in the distance were faint, crackling radio transmissions in the background as frantic medics on the ground screamed for more medevac choppers.

3. CRITIQUING DISASTER

MACV Headquarters compound, Saigon

Sgt. Mark Stryker slammed the night stick up against one of the red Magic Marker circles on the plastic map of Region Three. The map covered half the wall of the third-floor briefing room, and most of the forty military policemen crowded into that room flinched at the cracking sound. "*This* is where the enemy troops emerged from their tunnel system," then he smacked the stick against another smeared circle, "and *this* is where they were last seen. *After* they went and offed half the goddamn platoon!"

Stryker was fuming. The ambush two days earlier had left seven MPs dead. The six who had initially come to their aid were unsuccessful in routing the guerrillas from their jungle sanctuary. In fact, they had not even located the underground tunnel system until five hours later, after Stryker had spent the entire afternoon crawling through the elephant grass while his men roared from one end of the rain forest to the other, crisscrossing its quiet trails with their screaming jeeps.

"What did you expect, Stryker?" a buck sergeant from the back of the room asked bravely. "We're cops, not grunts."

The ex-Green Beret slid his night stick back into its keeper and squinted against the beam of light from the slide projector, hands on his hips. After a few moments of silence he decided not to confront the NCO in front of the men, although he had instantly recognized Gary Richards's voice, leader of the controversial Decoy Squad. Instead, he said, "We *all* went through boot camp, gentlemen. You had to graduate from basic before being accepted into the Military Police Academy. Granted, some of you 'graduated' by the skin of your teeth. But while there,/ you were supposed to have learned some rudimentary jungle skills, including how to pursue enemy forces through the bush.

"Yet you all acted like typical cops and raced back and forth code three while Charlie sat snickering in his underground penthouse, listening to the Moody Blues on the AFRN. And now we've got seven dead men."

"Aren't you being a little hard on the company, Sergeant?" Richards stood up and walked down the aisle to the projection on the wall. "Those men were dead when Second Squad got there. Sure, there was a lot left to be desired on the tactical end of the chase, but you can't blame anyone here for the deaths."

"What about Big Barney?" Schramm got to his feet finally after endless minutes of indecision. "Nobody's heard from him since the medics brought him down to Third Field."

"Fairchild's suffering his own private little guilt trip." Stryker turned to examine the multicolored coordinates on the map, suddenly feeling nausea and dizziness in the pit of his stomach as he tried to avoid an ugly subject and the probing eyes of his men, hidden in the dark recesses of the blacked-out room. "Last night he tried to hang himself."

"*Tried*?" Schramm's eyes twinkled with hope rediscovered.

"You know how big Barney is," Stryker said, no humor or innuendo in his tone, "the rafters collapsed and he broke a leg in the fall."

Schramm sat back down slowly, his mouth open and his eyes unblinking as all the easy ways of suicide flashed by his mind's eye: sleeping pills, a shotgun under the jaw. Anything but death by hanging. It just seemed so painful. And hadn't he always read that the only honorable way for a cop to pull the pin was with his service weapon against the temple? And Barney was all cop at heart. It just didn't make sense.

"It just doesn't make sense," the private next to him whispered aloud, reading his thoughts.

"Suicide never makes sense." Stryker shook his head then set to rubbing his own temples as he felt another migraine

33

coming on. "Neither does the way we responded to that code one hundred north of Gia Dinh. And MACV's General Harding has been gracious enough to let us borrow his conference room here—use his slides and everything—so we can brush up on our infantry skills. Relief shift has been instructed to remain on the street until I'm satisfied every one of you will, in the future, know how to properly respond to an MP-needs-help call outside the concrete jungle of the city.

"Now don't get me wrong. When it comes to patrolling Saigon itself, I'm confident you men can handle whatever you come up against—even better than the *canh-sats*. But after today, there'll be no doubt in anyone's mind what course of action to take if your duty takes you out into the boonies."

Stryker consulted some notes on the podium, then stared back out at the dark audience, irritated he could not see the eyes of his men or gauge their reactions.

"Hey, uh . . . excuse me, Sarge," came a timid voice from the back of the room, "but, uh, I got an appointment with a Saigon police official down at the Tran Hung Dao station at 1300 hours. So, uh, how long's this gonna take?"

"The lady cop you been screwin' can wait, Thomas," he responded like a whip snapping, but the retort still generated a murmur of laughter across the dark room and some scattered applause. "Anyway, this won't be painful at all. Two films on jungle warfare, fifteen minutes each, and a ten-minute summary afterwards, in which I'll go over the proper responses for ten engagements with the enemy."

"Engagements?" Spec. 4 Tim Bryant frowned innocently at the private beside him as he pulled nervously at the wedding band on his finger. Before they were married, his Vietnamese wife had stabbed him outside a Tu Do Street bar when she saw him going in without her.

"Firefights." Michael Broox shook his head with a pained expression on his face, fully aware even Bryant wasn't that naive.

"But there's a few things we've got to attend to first," Stryker said, grinning, looking the same way he looked when a ten-minute-old bar fight finally crashed into his table, interrupting his peace and quiet.

"Oh oh, sounds like a weapons inspection." Bryant nudged

34

Broox with his elbow and the private punched him back, not in the mood for conversation.

"Got a letter here from Kip Mather over in Georgia. Says he's doing fine—concentrating all his energies on a particular rook who went and *volunteered* for this crazy place!" Stryker didn't bother to mention he himself had re-enlisted specifically for Saigon, and would have it no other way. It was the Orient or out.

"Sounds like that embassy kid we rousted back during the Bis Ky Dong stake-out." Thomas leaned over and grinned at Richards, but the sergeant's only reply was, "That goof," and he closed his eyes tightly again and resumed dreaming about his last R&R to Singapore.

"It's right up here if any of you care to read it," Stryker said, referring to Mather's letter. "For those of you men who are new to the 716th, Kip Mather was an unwilling member of the Decoy Squad who caught a grenade from some Honda Honeys in his lap and lost half his bod. Uncle Sam retired him medically, then hired him on as a civilian instructor at The School. Definitely a Class A copper, in his time."

"I saw him take down four Aussies in a bar fight at the Queen Bee one night," Thomas whispered to the attentive newbie on his other side. "The man could really kick ass. And he loved the street. That's why he never made it past buck sergeant. He loved the street, my friend. Loved the street and the night shift too damned much." The rookie next to Thomas nodded his head eagerly as though he wished he had known the man—just the reaction the senior MP had waited for. It was expected.

"Now, down to serious business," Stryker said, ruffling the papers on his clipboard and ignoring the rubber-band-powered balsa-wood airplane that suddenly took to the muggy air above the fifty black helmets, sputtered around the room a couple of times and then crashed into the red and gold flag of South Vietnam propped in one corner of the huge room. "Two complaints here from the ambassador's wife that some of Madame Kwok's ladies of the evening are wandering over to the BOQs again and hanging out in the lobby. Check out their VD cards if you get a chance and escort 'em back over to the Pleasure Palace. But be gentle."

35

"What was the fuckin' ambassador's wife doing over at the bachelor officers' quarters in the first place?" an anonymous private giggled from the back of the room. When it became apparent Stryker was intent on ignoring the challenge just as he had ignored the earlier interruption a second MP answered, "Exactly *that!*" to another round of scattered applause.

"Like I was saying." The stocky sergeant with the medium-length brown hair and the thick mustache leaned against the podium so that his muscular arms bulged out at the men. "Be gentle on the whores. Madame Kwok has been the source of excellent information in the past. We wouldn't want to sour our working relationship over a lousy complaint. But check it out. Ignore a bitch from Puzzle Palace and next thing you know we'll be posting a foot beat at every BOQ to sign the ladies in and out."

"That could prove interesting," said Thomas with a grin.

"Hot runs," Stryker went swiftly to the next item on the agenda, raising his voice as he spoke—a clear message that the murmurs rising throughout the room were to cease. "I don't wanna see no more hot runs unless the situation warrants it. In other words, no more hitting the siren every time you pass your favorite whorehouse on Le Loi or Tu Do. No more flashing lights every time you come up against heavy traffic while responding to a routine call. No more combinations of any of the above just because the impulse strikes you.

"Last night I saw three units running code to a stupid street disturbance on Cong Ly. And there weren't even any weapons involved. Now, can you really justify *that*, especially if you total out a jeep in traffic, or are the cause of one of the nationals stacking up their own automobiles?"

"But, Sarge, we *were* justified in running code to that fight!" a voice called out from the back of the room.

"Bullshit." Stryker gave the word his most skeptical tone.

"No, really, Sarge," a second anonymous voice came to the defense of the first. "We got that call as a real brawl: two of Saigon's finest girls-of-questionable-virtue tearing each other's clothes off in the middle of the street!"

Several snickers punctuated the claim and the first MP added, "That could've caused a real traffic accident—a bona fide threat to life and property, and we couldn't let *that* happen now, could we?"

"Coffee breaks," Stryker continued, his eyes glued to the clipboard as he refused to look up at the teen-age patrolmen, afraid he himself would start smiling.

"Who the fuck drinks coffee in this climate?" Richards whispered over to Thomas.

"The PM is tired of seeing a dozen units parked outside Mimi's Bar every night just before shift change. And I am too. First of all, you clowns aren't varying your routine—one of these nights some half-intelligent Charlie Cong is gonna wire up every damn jeep on Nguyen Hue and blow 'em sky high.

"Secondly, it's bad public relations: just don't look good to have a fourth of the downtown patrol congregating at one night club.

"Third, the other bar owners have already complained to HQ that you're not affording equal 'protection'—and I use that term lightly—to the rest of the joints on Nguyen Hue. I know, I know: frivolous bullcrap. But, hey: half of police work is keeping the man on the street happy—PR. Therefore, henceforth . . ."

"Such big words." Bryant frowned over at Broox.

". . . The provost marshal is limiting bar checks: four per shift. You *will* note each one on your log. And there will be no more than two units at each establishment at any one time. Understood?"

Several disgruntled comments drifted across the room with the cigarette smoke, but they were kept down to a respectable hush.

"Haircuts. Now we been slackin' off on you guys lately on personal appearance because of all the shit Mr. VC has been throwing at the battalion. But too many of you are taking advantage of our generosity." Stryker held his hands up in the air defensively as the protests rose in volume. "Now I know your shack-ups downtown like it over the collar, but the PM doesn't. And he's the one that hands out paychecks. Right?

"I really should inspect you bums tonight—I know I'd find a whole shitload of dirty .45 barrels and I can see even in the dark half of you didn't even shave today. But we're running late as it is, and I'm sure relief shift would like to hit the showers. So we'll dispense with guard mount today, but consider it fair warning: Sometime this week you can expect a thorough going-over.

"OK, now we come to the sore point of the briefing, a special assignment. Requiring volunteers. I need, as the jarheads say it, two good men," and the sergeant peered into the darkness looking for hands. "You—the last man in the fifth row, by the door," he called out. "Hit the lights. I can't see no hands in the air!"

"That's 'cuz there ain't no dumbfucks stupid enough to volunteer for one of your 'special assignments,'" Thomas whispered just before the fluorescent lights began buzzing and popping on one at a time.

"I'm sure you all read the article about Moast the Ghost in the *Overseas Weekly* yesterday," Stryker said, letting his face sink to one side as if the story soiled the image of the armed forces and bothered him personally.

"The captain with the First Cav who has got a price on his head," answered Craig Davis, one of only two black MPs in the room.

Stryker nodded his head in the affirmative. "Ten thousand greenbacks to be exact. Well, yesterday a doorgunner on one of his own choppers almost blasted the good captain outta his jump boots."

Several mild cheers filled the room, bringing an instant frown to the big buck sergeant's face, which in turn silenced the enlisted men: They were never quite sure when Stryker was serious or not. He had been through so much in the last three months alone—one shoot-out during which a .357 slug was stopped from tearing a hole in his chest only because of hidden body armor, a firefight with the VC at a Green Beret stronghold outside Pleiku where an AK round had pierced an ear lobe for him, and an encounter with a Soviet KGB agent who put three bullets in the MP's gun arm—it was hard to believe he'd let such trivial nonsense bother him.

"Captain Moast has finally filed an official complaint with PMO. And since the incidents come under the jurisdiction of the Eighteenth MP Brigade, CID has decided to play chess with the grunts—using some of us as the pawns.

"I can guarantee an ArCom to the volunteers," Stryker continued. "Perhaps even more if all goes as planned and we

38

make a big bust."

"Yeah, like Purple Hearts," Broox whispered over to Schramm sarcastically.

"Posthumously," the rook replied, a frown masking his face, but intense excitement pulsing through his insides.

"Now you know they don't give MPs Purple Hearts, Mikey," Bryant ribbed Broox with his elbow.

"The plan is to infiltrate Moast's unit." The sergeant grinned. "Keep a low profile just like any other newbies in-country, observe the activities of your fellow grunts, participate in a couple genuine firefights, and eventually determine through the grunt grapevine just who is putting out the bounty on Moast the Ghost." The anticipation on Stryker's face said, Now here's a chance to do some real soldiering for a change. The Green Beret in his gut was showing through.

"These men are policemen, not infantry doggies," Richards came to the rescue. "Uncle Sam don't pay 'em enough to play your kind of 'game.'"

"That's where you're wrong," he replied. "It's time they started earning their combat pay."

"You call a lousy twenty extra a month 'combat' pay?" Thomas challenged, but Stryker ignored him.

"After all, we are *military* policemen. It comes with the territory. And I wager, Sergeant Richards, that I'll get more volunteers than I need. Well, gentlemen? Who wants boonie duty for a couple weeks?"

The room remained silent and still for several seconds until someone in the last row of chairs mumbled, "He's outta his fuckin' tree."

And at the same moment Private Schramm's fist slowly rose into the air.

Both Broox and Bryant jumped to force it back down, and as the private struggled with them good-naturedly, several catcalls echoed back and forth across the room.

"Goofy rook," Richards muttered over to Thomas.

"Yeah, you can always count on them to pull the most *dinky-dau* shit under the sun."

"Well, frankly, I was hoping for someone with a bit more experience." Stryker smiled down at Schramm. "But I appreciate your offer, Private."

Schramm's hand fell as fast as his disappointment rose. Ever since arriving at the slaughter north of Gia Dinh, he had prayed for contact with the communists. Even though he had personally known none of the men killed, they *were* brother cops. And he had promised each of them he would not leave the 'Nam until, in his own way, he had avenged their murders and evened the score. To Schramm, the ambush of seven MPs was not an act of war, but a brutal crime he as a law enforcer would eventually solve. No matter where the chase led him. Perhaps his motivation was that he was still so young—an idealist with an innocent heart who actually thought his tour of duty in Vietnam would make a difference to the Vietnamese and their homeland. The MP motto, "of the troops and for the troops" was lost on Schramm. He had no desire to soldier his way through life, only to be a good cop. To him, the uniform was green only because it blended better with the jungles of both the city and the countryside. In his heart, it was as blue as any policeman's back in The World.

"Come on, you big pussies," Stryker prodded the men. "Just two lousy volunteers. Here's the chance to show Mama the true length of your pecker!"

"*Yo* mama!" Davis called back with a jive accent and half the room laughed along. To the men of the 716th, you weren't white, black or brown. If you wore the armband, the helmet and the badge, you were blue. Schramm's shade of blue.

"Is he talkin' back 'bout my mother?" Bryant leaned over in Broox's face again.

"You never even had a mother," Broox replied.

"And just what does that mean?"

"Oh, shut the fuck up, buttocks breath, before I volunteer you myself!"

A solitary clapping accented the rising volume of catcalls as an MP in the back of the room noticed one of the privates finally folding under Stryker's legendary powers of suggestion.

"My man, Leroy boy!" he exploded, as if he should have expected it all along. "Why, I'm damned proud of you, son! Step on up here—I wanna shake your hand!"

Leroy Crowe, sporting close-cropped curly hair and a dark complexion that made him look Arabian, pushed his wire-rimmed glasses up on his nose and hoisted his short, wide

40

frame up toward the podium as he shook his head slowly, eyes downcast with embarrassment.

"Don't look so modest, Leroy!" Stryker laughed as the private sauntered up to his supervisor. "You're the first real man I've seen tonight, next to Schramm there."

"Show him your pecker, Leroy!" Sergeant Richards called out from the back of the room.

As the briefing hall exploded with laughter Thomas added, "Hell, he ain't got no pecker! Madame Kwok bit the tiny noodle off last week when he couldn't get it up during a sucky-fucky five-dollar session upstairs in the Pleasure Palace. You mean he didn't tell *you* about it?" the Pfc. feigned a look of utter incredulity for Stryker's benefit. "Hell, it was an on-the-job injury. Definitely duty related. He lost it during a routine bar check which the PM now insists we curtail."

"Bullshit!" Crowe began waving his night stick at Thomas good-naturedly.

"I think you oughta put him in for a Purple Heart," Broox suggested in a loud jest. "I'd love to word the citation myself: 'And while in the performance of his official duties as Saigon Commando, Private Leroy joy-boy Crowe did suffer the loss of one shriveled-up vital organ while *sticking* an uncooperative prostitution suspect.'"

Broox had stood up rigidly and held out both hands as if he were reading from an invisible proclamation when Bryant pulled him back down into his seat. "I already told you: they don't give MPs Purple Hearts, goddamnit! When you gonna learn?"

"Awright, awright!" Stryker held up his hands to quiet the men as Crowe, his face now red as a cherry, rushed back to his seat. "Only one more volunteer. Now who's it gonna be? Perhaps one of you awe-inspiring NCOs in the back row?"

The room remained silent until the slender Schramm, his eyes darting back and forth amongst his brother MPs, raised his hand again.

"Jesus H. Christ," Stryker sighed in resignation, and his own eyes raced about the room one last time, hoping against hope. "OK, Schramm. I wanted you to at least experience a little of what Sin City had to offer before giving you a taste of combat and having you lose your cherry by fire instead of between the long, sleek legs of some almond-eyed lady downtown."

"Boy, he do ramble on, don't he?" Richards smacked his chewing gun at Thomas.

The private nodded his head in agreement, "Shoulda been a fuckin' poet, but don't know it."

"I guess that settles it," Stryker ducked just in time as the balsa-wood airplane mysteriously buzzed across the room again and nearly clipped him on the ear. "Crowe and Schramm will be the next heroes of this gutless outfit. I hope you 'veterans' sleep good over this one."

"Like a sack of rocks," Richards remarked sarcastically, his confidence merely a front for the pride he actually felt for the two privates.

"OK!" Stryker clapped his hands once as he lost the grim look on his face and replaced it with a boyish grin as Jake Drake, the company clerk, wheeled in a film projector. "It's show time!"

Two men in the back of the room, Larry Lydic and Calvin Schaeffer—they were both officially classified as mental cases, but since they had "lost it" on the job, they were allowed to stay on in the 716th as unarmed, low-profile maintenance men—fought to restrain their glee as they leaned over on Richards's shoulder and whispered into both of his ears. "We switched the film reels," Lydic giggled, pointing at the projector, "back at the orderly room," explained Schaeffer. "Substituted some of that stuff Raunchy Raul brought back with him from Taiwan."

"You're kidding!" Richards sat up in his seat, suddenly interested in the proceedings. "This oughta be good."

Jake Drake lifted his pet rat out from the depths of his curly, white afro and placed it on top of the projector as he started threading the film. The long, skinny rodent raised itself up on its hind legs as its inquisitive snout followed the balsa airplane that was still circling the room lazily.

"Now the first program is on escape and evasion," Stryker announced. "Just in the event you 'jungle experts' get lost and cornered while tracking the bad bad VC. And I've got a little surprise: since the audio is still out on our projector, this training class will be narrated by Specialist Fifth Class Linda Covert from MACV Psy-Ops, who has so graciously consented to grace us with her presence tonight."

"Oh shit," whispered Thomas as he and Richards both gasped and sunk down in their chairs, trying to disappear behind the other men. The tall, top-heavy brunette in the tailored, figure-hugging uniform who walked in, her bottom bouncing with just the right shake, had just the opposite effect on Lydic and Schaeffer. They both leaned on the shoulders of the MPs in front of them, wrestling for a better look as the lights went out again and the projector came on.

"I guess I shoulda brought a bowl of popcorn," she tittered like a dumb blonde from a fifties movie. "You all look so hungry."

The remark brought numerous suggestive snickers from the men and Crowe whispered over to Schramm, "Dispense with the BS and the brassiere, and I'll show her *hungry!*"

"Yeah, I can see them taut nipples of hers fighting to burst out through that o.d. green at any second. Goddamn, Leroy, she must be a forty-four."

"At least. The nipples alone are bigger'n fried won-tons!"

"Now, first we'll be watching a group of Special Forces men interrogating a suspected VC." She sounded like she was about to curtsy, and the plastic Southern accent was a bit much, but the men loved it. "And I want you to concentrate on the technique they use."

Several of the MPs in the front row burst out laughing as the opening scene depicted a middle-aged European businessman lying on a bed, his pants pulled down around his ankles, and a gorgeous Oriental masseuse with firm, bouncing breasts urgently sucking on his erect penis.

Linda Covert halted her narration in midsentence and turned to look at the screen. The sight of the man's loins exploding in the prostitute's mouth brought Miss Covert's hands to her lips in shock. As the woman on screen struggled to swallow all his juices but failed at the last moment, Linda squealed, "Oh my gooodness!" in embarrassment—just seconds before the sputtering balsa-wood airplane shot across the room and smacked her in the ass.

43

4. THE SCHOOL

Classroom 68, U.S. Army Military Police Academy, Ft. Gordon, Georgia

"You are responding to a report of an armed robbery. You arrive on scene, and the liquor store clerk rushes out the front door to meet you. He's babbling hysterically about two suspects that just blasted his assistant. He tells you they just split in a black pick-up with out-of-state license plates." The drill sergeant was laying out the situation to the class of forty prospective military police recruits. "How do you proceed at this point?"

"Get the numbers of the plate," someone suggested.

"What kind of pick-up truck?" another private asked.

"Have the victim describe the weapon involved."

"What was their direction of travel?"

"OK, OK, fine," interrupted the sergeant, a husky veteran who had been an MP in both Korea and Vietnam, with three tours of duty in each country, and held little patience and much contempt for green rookies. "Once you get all that information, what else do you need?"

He was answered by a classroom of unknowing, but eager stares.

"I said, *what else do you need?*" he roared, momentarily tearing one back-row recruit's attention from the daydream he had been immersed in. Pvt. Nick Uhernik was not often a dedicated or disciplined student, even with his recent transfer after basic training in California to the highly respected

44

Military Police Academy at Fort Gordon. He often found himself bored at the repetition of law enforcement studies and longing for the action and excitement of the streets. He imagined himself racing down some dark back alley in that sleek MP sedan, pursuing felons amid the wail of sirens and hail of flying lead.

"How do you buffoons expect us to make MPs out of you, if you don't pay attention?" The sergeant had drifted to the rear of the concrete classroom and was screaming into Uhernik's ear. Uhernik jumped from his daydream to the position of attention, misunderstanding the question and causing the class to erupt into laughter.

"Sir?" It was obvious to all he was confused and disoriented.

"Got your head up your ass again, *Private*?" he asked more softly, tapping his thigh patiently with a swordlike blackboard pointer.

"Yes, sir!" the recruit answered without thinking.

"Yes, *drill sergeant*!" the DI corrected him. "I'm not a *sir*. I'm a *drill sergeant*! I work for a living, soldier!"

"Yes, Drill Sergeant!"

"Now." He stared the teen-ager straight in the eyes. "After you've got your vehicle description and the direction of travel, what else do you want?"

"Sir? I mean, Drill Sergeant?" Uhernik had no idea.

"What if the suspects ditch their truck and flee on foot?" he hinted.

"Description of the suspects!" someone from the back of the room decided.

"Right!" yelled the drill sergeant, moving away from the recruit with the last name none of the DIs could pronounce.

"That's the last time I hide in the last row," Uhernik whispered to the man next to him.

"Suspect descriptions," affirmed the sergeant as he paced back toward the front of the classroom, patting his palm with the pointer. "Height, weight, hair and eye color, hair length and style, clothing description, and—"

Just then the rear door to the classroom flew open, slamming against the wall and disrupting the session.

A huge Mexican dressed in civilian clothes rushed down the

45

middle aisle of the room, brandishing a handgun. The drill sergeant's eyes almost popped out in surprise. They grew very big as the instructor brought his hands up to protect his face.

"I'll teach you to poke my old lady while I'm out of town!" screamed the Mexican as he pulled the trigger in rapid succession. The roar of gunfire sent most of the recruits scrambling under their desks as their beloved drill sergeant somersaulted backwards over the instructor's platform and flipped to the ground, clutching his chest.

The daring gunman then dashed back out the way he came in. Two of the recruits in the back of the room started out after him, while others were yelling for an ambulance and running to the aid of the wounded DI.

As the two privates started to chase the big Mexican, the drill sergeant was miraculously rising to his feet, unharmed. "Awright! Awright! Take your seats, take your seats!" he was blaring as he dusted off his uniform.

"What the fuck?" several of the privates murmured in unison.

"Now, quickly!" The drill sergeant pointed at a man in the third row. "How old was the suspect that just shot me? How tall? How big? What was he wearing? What kind of weapon did he use? How many shots did he fire?"

The private's jaw was still in the process of dropping to the floor. He was dumbfounded, his eyes still searching the sergeant's chest for any sign of blood.

The two men in the back of the room were still hesitating at the door. They had been caught in midstride. "I said *sit down* back there!" the DI ordered them.

As they took their seats, the class started offering answers. They were all different.

Fifteen minutes later the recruits came to the conclusion that the suspect was either white or Puerto Rican, was fat or skinny, was bearded or clean-shaven, and was either bald or suffered from a receding hairline. They all agreed that he was very tall and spoke with an accent.

"What kind of accent?" demanded the drill sergeant.

"Either Puerto Rican or Spanish, Drill Sergeant," someone offered.

46

"Definitely Latino," another expert decided.

"Naw, da guy was from Brooklyn," declared an anonymous jokester from the back of the room. The DI flashed Uhernik an accusing stare although the private hadn't said a word.

Everyone agreed that five shots had been fired and that a revolver, not an automatic, was used.

When the "suspect" finally sauntered back into the room for their examination, he fitted very few of the descriptions given.

"You rookies got a long way to go," the drill sergeant muttered, circling the room slowly and pulling at his gray hair. The "suspect" turned out to be another drill sergeant.

"Which one of you punks called me a Puerto Rican?" threatened the "gunman" as he pounded his fist down powerfully on a desk top.

No one spoke up.

The skies over Augusta, Georgia were filled with Green Berets, parachuting down into Camp Benning a few miles away, but the attention of some two hundred MP recruits was on the drill sergeant standing stiff and rigid on the raised platform in front of them.

". . . And you'll jog everywhere," he was saying. "To meals, to classes, to the pistol range. Everywhere! But don't misunderstand this to be harassment. It's a vital segment of your training. Eventually, you'll thank us for building up your endurance. You'll need it for that first bar fight or foot chase. Remember: a lot of these punks out on the street work out seven or eight hours a day at their fancy health spas and weight rooms just so they can brag to their peers that they whipped some cop's ass out on the block. So long as you've got that MP armband on, you will *never* allow your ass to be kicked! Now don't forget it."

"Is this guy for real?" a short, skinny private in fatigues three sizes too large leaned over and whispered into Uhernik's ear, but the taller recruit remained motionless at the position of attention.

"Unfortunately, due to the increasing demand for military

47

policemen overseas," explained Senior DI Mills to the vast formation of newly arrived soldiers that spread out before him, "we have run out of living quarters. You men in platoons one through five will be assigned to Brems barracks."

"Alright!" several recruits gave a mild cheer at the news, but quickly fell silent when Mills frowned at the disruption.

"You will find it to be one of the most modern dwelling places offered to soldiers of today's army," he continued.

"Shit," snickered the short, skinny private. He was a member of sixth platoon, having arrived at the honor because the company was divided up alphabetically and his name just happened to start with a V.

"I guess that means we pitch tents," Uhernik replied.

"However," Sergeant Mills raised a finger into the air to gain everyone's attention again. "You unfortunates assigned to sixth platoon will find yourself over at Splinter Village, the old World War II barracks on the other side of camp."

Numerous grunts of complaint drifted over the last group.

"The high command here at Fort Gordon is sorry for the inconvenience," he smiled and Uhernik grinned back, knowing the Green Machine was never sorry about anything. "But, personally, I don't give a fuck. I don't give a fuck because I'm leaving this man's army in seven lousy months! Stomach that, rookies!"

They didn't see Sergeant Mills much after that.

Another DI soon took the podium, just about the time everyone's knees started going out on them. They had been in formation all day, listening to the orientation and philosophies of various drill sergeants.

"You won't find the harassment and brutality here in AIT that you experienced in basic training," he said in a fatherly tone. "We're only interested in making professional police officers out of you—the best the armed forces can offer. Regardless of whether your eventual assignment is Korea or Panama or Germany or right here at Fort Gordon." He beamed proudly down at the privates, ignoring the grumblings from some draftees who had been placed in the MP corps against their wishes. It was amazing how many potential military cops had spent most of their civilian lives trying to elude the long arm of the law.

"Or Vietnam," added Sergeant Mills, returning to the podium briefly to locate his lost cigars. The men started talking softly amongst themselves.

"No, no," the younger sergeant said, grinning, trying to restore order. "No men in this training cycle scheduled to go off to war, Sergeant Mills. No more MPs, anyway. Not that I'm aware of."

Sergeant Mills flashed his subordinate a tolerating set of smiling teeth. "Gimme that fucking roster," he growled, and after spending a few seconds reviewing the list of names he tapped a finger down loudly next to a serial number. "See there! That soldier! We got *one* goin' off to 'Nam."

"Who?" somebody in the crowded formation asked anxiously, but the sergeants went on to another subject. Pvt. Nick Uhernik's eyes dropped to the ground. Here he was building up all this camaraderie with his fellow rooks, yet it now appeared none of them would be crossing the South China Sea with him.

The drill sergeants ignored his searching eyes and droned on, reviewing the procedures on reporting for sick call, but the Saigon bound recruit's mind was wandering again. His eyes saw the Far East out an airplane window, the lush green shores of Vung Tau sparkling beneath the castlelike cloud cover. His daydream was of home, and the Vietnamese girl he had walked along that pearl white beach with a hundred times.

Uhernik had been born in Saigon seventeen years earlier. The son of an embassy consular officer, he had been whisked back to America briefly, at the age of four, during the period of unrest when the French were forced out of their own colony.

Order was quickly restored under the Diem regime, however, and after a couple of years on a government project in the Colorado mountains, his father returned the family to the tropics, thousands of miles from the bitter Rocky Mountain winters.

From an early age, the boy had been fascinated by police, first the courtly demeanor of the palace *canh-sats*, and later the flashy confidence of the arriving American MPs. After graduating from the English-speaking New Asia High School—

49

where he spent four years as the faithful companion to the same Vietnamese girl—he had surprised everyone, including Angi, by enlisting in the U.S. Army.

As a new drill sergeant took the stand, Uhernik was still recalling that hot, humid evening, nine weeks earlier and an ocean away, when he had broken the news to Angi that he was leaving her for the service. He'd never forget how the sixteen-year-old tigress flew into a rage and nearly threw him through a window, her long, black hair in disarray as it clung to the tears streaking her almond eyes. As he looked back on it now, the irony struck him: so many similar scenes must have transpired across America when fiancees nationwide learned their restless boyfriends were escaping to strange lands, overseas.

He had tried to explain to her that their separation would be only temporary: his contract was for Vietnam duty—he'd return to Saigon after four months of training. And, besides, it'd be a chance to see the homeland he had never known, though, in his heart, Vietnam came first—despite his heritage.

"They'll send you north!" Angi had complained. "To Pleiku or Danang. There's no guarantee you'll return to Saigon." He could not explain why he just *had* to begin planning his life out—and what could be more rewarding than a career roaming the dark back alleys of the Orient?

"My name is Sergeant Flowers," the DI introduced himself, jarring the white Vietnamese from his memories, "and the first man who laughs, or offers me some, pulls a week of KP! Got that?" The men understood. They were too tired to laugh anyway. "Good. You GIs have probably noticed a few good marines in your ranks. Let me tell you now: welcome them with open arms! They're your brother soldiers for the next seven weeks. The United States Marine Corps does not have its own police academy, so their men come here to learn how to be cops! Any objections?" he asked.

Nobody voiced any.

"From the army *or* the marines?" he asked specifically, but still no one spoke. "Good," he concluded. "We always seem to have some brawls here between the services. Seems the jarheads have this dislike for you dogfaces, and vice versa. But I can see we're all gonna be one big, happy family."

50

A marine turned and looked at Uhernik like he wanted to eat the private's liver.

"Awright!" snapped one of the other sergeants, "move out for a three-mile run around the ballfield, then line up for chow!"

"What, no showers?" complained Jack Zriny, a short soldier who was nearly as wide as he was tall—but it was all muscle. He occupied the top bunk next to Uhernik. The two were becoming fast friends, though the only thing they had in common was the desire to become good cops and get to work fighting crime in the streets.

"I guess not," Uhernik answered, "but we can't smell much worse than the army food," and Zriny nodded in agreement as they started to trot toward home plate.

Drill Sergeant Flowers was mysteriously assigned to sixth platoon, "because us niggers are used to the rats," he suggested, and he in turn assigned a National Guardsman as platoon leader and a marine as Nick and Jack's squad leader.

"You mean to tell me you get outta Fort Gordon after graduation and you just go home and serve as a soldier on weekends?" laughed Barry Todd, a former Golden Gloves boxer who was also in their squad. He had confronted the platoon leader in a corner after learning the man was a "weekend warrior."

"Christ, if I had known there was such a program, I wouldn't have signed up for four years," frowned Private Valters, who exaggerated his German accent but looked more Italian in appearance.

"Aw, come on, Pete!" replied Andy Smallwood, the only black soldier in the squad. "You know you eat this regular army shit up!"

"Hell, I don't wanna serve under no fuckin' reservist!" Todd grabbed everyone's attention by grabbing the platoon leader's throat. It took the whole squad to wrestle him to the floor. "And I don't want no fuckin' jarhead marine in my squad, neither!" he added for the benefit of the squad leader, who just ignored him and continued spit-shining his combat boots. The marine sat on his footlocker, refusing to wrinkle the cot behind it—the o.d. green blankets across it were tucked in so tight you could bounce a dime off them.

"This is gonna be an interesting two months," Uhernik told Zriny as he struggled to keep just one of Barry Todd's huge arms pinned down.

Sergeant Flowers had been right about the rats.

The recruits peeled the planks off the boarded-up barracks in the middle of Splinter Village and cautiously peeked inside. Wide shafts of sunlight penetrated various layers of floating dust from a gaping hole in the roof. Cobwebs stretched from wall to wall, and the building's furnace lay on its side, disconnected from the termite-infested walls.

A sudden fluttering of wings in the rafters sent Valters tumbling backwards into Zriny.

"What the hell was that thing that just ran across the floor?" gasped Smallwood, the whites of his eyes growing suddenly larger to contrast with his dark skin.

"I told you," reminded Sergeant Flowers. "Rats."

"That weren't no damn rat!" insisted Todd. "*That* was a bear!"

"Naw, I think it *was* a rat, Barry," commented Zriny.

"I just hope it's the only one in there," stated Valters.

"You got your gun, Sarge?" Smallwood asked the drill instructor.

"Nope," he answered, grabbing Uhernik by the arms from behind as he nudged him through the doorway, into the unknown. "You go first, Private."

"Jesus, how come I feel like I'm going down into a Viet Cong tunnel?" he asked, grabbing one of the long planks for a weapon.

"Make sure it's got big nails in it," suggested Zriny, smiling.

"You're gonna need 'em," confirmed Private Todd.

Within two days they had the place fit for human habitation again. The walls were repainted, the floors stripped clean and freshly coated with new wax, and the latrine was scoured free of circus-worthy fleas and other hopping critters.

"I don't wanna find no crabs running around this place!" ordered their platoon guide as he checked the bunk legs for cigarette butts. The men answered him with a barrage of toilet plungers and dirty rags.

"We're *all* just buck privates!" Todd reminded the reservist.

"OK, OK!" came the back-down, "I just want to keep the drill sergeants off our backs!"

"Don't worry about the DIs," said Todd. "They're too concerned with cramming our classes to be worried about spit and polish."

"You tell him!" Zriny cheered from up in his bunk. He had been studying hard for the following morning's quiz in Traffic Accident Investigation, and he flipped his thumb noisily through the thick training schedule for the platoon leader's benefit. "They expect us to remember all this crap?" he went on, "patrol procedures, cruiser mechanics and preventive maintenance, emergency equipment operation, traffic tickets and violators, narcotics investigation, route recon and map reading—hell, the list goes on and on! And that's just for this week!"

"I didn't study this hard in college," admitted Rick Taylor, one of the few "educated individuals" in the platoon.

"Yeah, I really get into this Finer Points of Directing Traffic chapter," Valters said sarcastically, slamming the MP manual shut and propping his head on an o.d. green pillow.

Bobby Ray, the comedian of the squad, danced himself into the troop quarters, a big smile on his face. "We finally finished the latrine!" he announced proudly. "Anyone wanna take a look at it?"

"That place grosses me out!" Zriny said disgustedly. "There aren't even any stalls in there! The idea of sitting across from another guy and staring him in the face while I take a shit just does not appeal to me." They all laughed at that one, surprised he had not gotten used to the lack of privacy during boot camp. "Face it: this place sucks!"

"I heard they used to keep Japanese POWs in these barracks," revealed Valters.

"I would have complained to the Geneva Convention," muttered Ray.

"I'm sure they did." Todd frowned as he started to sneak up behind Uhernik. The youngest member of the squad was perched in his bunk, examining some faded wallet photos.

Normally Todd's comment would have brought at least a chuckle from the more energetic recruits, but everyone was dead tired. After the morning run of two to four miles—depending on whether or not the drill sergeant in charge of PT got any pussy the night before—they were in the classrooms from seven a.m. to seven p.m. with a variety of grueling calisthenics before each meal. Contrary to how it had been in basic training, the evenings were usually their own, except for a surprise inspection every now and then, and a two-night bivouac every other weekend out in the swamplands and forest of Georgia.

"Whoooee! Who's the foxy lookin' cunt?" Todd grabbed the wallet out of Uhernik's hands and paraded it around in front of the other men. The ex-boxer half-expected the shorter, lighter recruit to protest, but Nick remained quietly in his bunk, impassive, only his icy, steel blue eyes following Todd. He realized that, although he didn't fear the bigger soldier, he was still no match for the older, more agile athlete. If he fought dirty, he was confident he could take Todd down without trouble, but he elected to endure the mild harassment. After all: they *were* classmates, and the brotherhood that had been instilled in them that first week at The School *was* all important to him. For the time being, he would calmly accept his fate. And wait for the appropriate time to retaliate. Don't get angry—get even. Payback was a bitch. Uhernik grinned, suddenly aware the Vietnamese way of thinking had rubbed off on him.

"Is she Japanese?" Valters and Ray had crowded in behind Todd.

"Where was this picture taken?" Smallwood asked.

"Saigon," Nick answered softly, bracing for the worst.

"Vietnamese! She's a genuine Honda Honey!" Todd exclaimed, his curiosity inflamed as he tossed the wallet back to its owner. "I'll bet you're the crazy motherfucker being shipped off to 'Nam!"

"He's got a twelve-month *contract* and everything!" Zriny

betrayed the secret. "Can you believe that? A goddamn contract!"

"For *Vietnam*?"

"A fucking *contract* for Vietnam?"

Uhernik went on to explain how he had been born there. How it wasn't the terrible place the news media made it out to be. How you could come to love the land and the people if one allowed himself to understand the situation.

"Born in the 'Nam?" Todd kept on him, though he was really beginning to like the kid. "How come your name isn't Phuc or Duc or something like that?"

"His parents are American, stupid," Zriny laughed, gulping too late as Todd popped him in the shoulder and sent him flying across the room.

"My father's a consular officer at the embassy. 'Uhernik' is Hungarian. It means, 'the soldier from Czechoslovakia.'"

"Soldier?" Todd challenged. "You ever kill any of them commies over there?"

The smile on the ex-boxer's face was ear to ear, but the question had a disheartening effect on Nick. For weeks he had pondered that exact problem: When the time came, would he be able to kill the enemy? Would he hesitate, or could he pull the trigger without fail?

His eyes fell to the floor, and he turned without answering, slid the wallet back into his pocket and slowly walked out of the room.

Torrential rains slammed into the camp over the next few weeks, and the men often spent their free time capturing dozens of monstrous leap frogs that blinked at them with sad, glazed eyes the size of olives as they floated by in the flooded canals. Private Cargill, the camp's practical joker, found the slimy creatures stuffed in his cot on more than one occasion.

On one of the religious holidays they trucked sixth platoon down to the post chapel and introduced them to "the God Squad." Uhernik had been a sometimes-practicing Catholic until he arrived at Fort Ord, California. Though he often found himself praying himself to sleep and asking the Lord to get him through just one more day of boot camp, the flag-cluttered chapel, bathed in o.d. green with a portrait of L.B.J. on the altar, was not his idea of the ideal place of worship. He just couldn't kneel convincingly and confess anything with the commander-in-chief's eyes staring down on him. It got worse at Fort Gordon.

They were greeted by three chaplains: a Catholic, a Southern Baptist and a Jew.

"Just call us the God Squad," laughed the priest who, after failing to get so much as a smile from the dozing audience, launched into his fifteen-minute sermon on the evils of prostitution and the various incurable strains of VD running rampant in nearby Augusta.

"At least use your army-supplied rubbers if you can't control yourself," added the Baptist preacher, who immediately roused the crowd of suddenly attentive GIs. "They come in an assortment of attractive colors: blue, red, green, black, white and pink. That's six. Don't forget: you rest on Sunday!"

The soldiers forced a round of applause as both men of God then argued at length over the morality of birth control and the use of rubbers by practicing Catholics. "Now you know why I abbreviate Southern Baptist: S.O.B.," laughed the priest as more and more men filed out of the chapel. He would be unable to salvage the sermon.

A few minutes later, before Drill Sergeant Flowers began another class on "search and seizure law," he instructed the recruits to bow their heads and say a prayer for the God Squad.

"One of these days they're gonna kill each other."

Everyone laughed for a change.

5. CHASING CURFEW DOWN TU DO STREET

Downtown Saigon

Pvt. Leroy Crowe eased the seven-round clip into the butt of his .45, careful not to dent the hollow point on top, then slammed it home until the chrome clicked in place. He grinned after sliding the pistol into the laminated holster and snapping the flap cover down, then motioned for Schramm to follow him from the barracks down to the headquarters building.

"I hate it when they order you over to HQ and neglect to tell you the reason." Schramm frowned. "You never know what you did wrong—they make you sweat it out, and you never know if you screwed up in the first place or if they're just bored and fuckin' with the privates."

"*Did* you do anything wrong?" Crowe asked, acting the part of veteran and senior partner even though he'd only been in the 'Nam a couple of months himself. "I didn't think you'd been here long enough to figure out how the brass plays mind games with the men on the street." He allowed himself an overconfident smirk.

"You're right." Schramm nodded his head stiffly, careful not to let the MP helmet slide off. It was tilted precariously on the edge of his forehead, and he had been having problems with the liner strap inside. "I was initiated in boot camp, remember?"

"You oughta get supply to issue you a new helmet liner. Your first chase'll see that one you got now flying off in some back alley. Then you'll never see it again. The whores snatch 'em up like cups of Saigon tea—they make numba one souvenirs!"

Schramm allowed himself a slight chuckle as he finished wiping down his own .45 with an o.d. green handkerchief then locked the empty chamber back. He took a soft-nosed cartridge from his pocket, slipped it carefully into the chamber then let the slide slam shut. He then inserted a seven-round magazine into the butt of the weapon and replaced it in his holster.

"What the hell you doing?" Crowe stopped in midstride, mouth agape at the method in which "his rook" had loaded his automatic. "You trying to blow your toes off?"

"Whatju talkin' 'bout?" Schramm said in his best black accent, the look on his face one of surprised innocence tainted by hurt feelings.

"Where the hell you get off chambering a round like that?"

"Christ, Leroy! Just 'cuz I'm a newbie don't mean I know nothing about firearms. Everyone knows an automatic with an empty chamber is useless in a sudden firefight—it takes too damn long to pull back the slide. And the chance you'll jam your first round is just too great—too much excitement playing games with your finger dexterity."

"My fuckin' *what*?"

"Dex—"

"And just who the hell is 'everyone?'" he interrupted Schramm. "No one ever told me all these little tidbits of gunlore!"

"Well, my brother taught me a lot about firearms. We used to jeep out to the cliffs outside my home town a lot . . . before he went off in the service."

"'Nam?"

"Yeah."

"Bummer."

"Yeah, KIA even." Schramm made the statement matter-of-factly, but in a whisper demanding respect for a fading memory.

"Double bummer."

"Yeah. He always told me you wasted your time carrying a .45 if you didn't have a hot load waiting in the chamber—ready for business."

"Well, I can understand that, but it sure seems awful dangerous. I'd be so preoccupied worrying about the damn thing going off that I wouldn't be able to concentrate on anything else—I mean, you didn't even put your safety on."

"Sure I did—but you just didn't notice. You get used to doing it with just a little flick of the thumb—not a long, drawn-out ceremony greased with sweat."

"Well, all I got to say is it's against regulations."

"I heard there were no rules in Saigon. That's why I came here." Schramm feigned disappointment in his frown.

"That's wishful thinking. There's rules and regs everywhere the Green Machine goes."

"Naw, not the 'Nam," Schramm goaded him on. "They told me that in Saigon you got to do your job—no bullshit attached. You weren't handcuffed by red tape. You didn't worry about the stupid rules, didn't do what the hypocrite's laws said—you did what was *right!*"

"Who told you all that?" Crowe placed his hands on his hips like the thirty-year-old liberals back on Sunday afternoon TV Schramm despised so much.

"The DIs back at Gordon, who else?"

"Aw, gimme a break. Everyone knows those drill sergeants are all just burnt-out street cops taking it easy in their last years before retirement. They're all out of touch."

"Well, I think you're wrong there," Schramm said, "but it don't really matter. You gonna let me carry eight slugs or not? I can't see another private pulling rank on me over something so trivial. What you gonna do when we get out in the field with them Airmobil crazies? You think *they* follow the rules?"

"Hey, get off my case, OK? So long as you don't skip a round up my ass I got no complaints. But first chance you get you might take your clips over to CC's down on Tu Do and get 'em chromed. It keeps the rust off—you know by now how humid this heat gets." Crowe turned to face him and tilted his customized belt buckle up at Schramm until the wide glare from the sun's reflection flashed in the other MP's eyes. "You can get yourself one of these goofy buckles for your web belt too. See mine—it says, "BATTLE FOR TAN SON NHUT, VIETNAM, JUNE 1967." Everyone's got one with something

59

or other on it. Just stray from obscene engravings or profanity. The PM frowns on that. Of course, you'll have one that's blank until you get into a firefight or something. 'Course some guys just put their home town on there, but you got more class if you can show you been in an actual shoot-out."

"Looks to me like that crap'd just attract snipers." Schramm was not impressed. "Sparkles like a beacon. You look like a goddamn highway patrolman or something with all your little brass trinkets."

"Well, I chuck most of 'em on graveyard shift."

"Yeah, I'll bet mother starlight bounces off you like a full-length mirror!"

"It makes for a little excitement on dull nights," Crowe admitted.

Schramm tired of harassing the white Arab and asked, "Whatta ya think Stryker's up to, calling us over to HQ like this? My first impression was that he was a good guy—didn't fuck with his troops. Now he goes and keeps me in suspense. I got enough headaches as it is."

"Yeah, me too."

"Oh, yeah? Like what, for instance?" Schramm didn't think Crowe's personal problems would interest him in the least, yet now the curiosity was as intense as the heat beating down on them.

"Aw, it feels like I'm pissin' crushed glass whenever I take a leak."

Schramm tried to hold it back but as they approached the headquarters building he ended up bent over with laughter. "Already? Christ, you just snuck her into your hooch last night! But I warned you. Why do you think Lydic calls her *sawtoi*? That's ARVN slang for clap trap! Burnin' already, huh? Man, you musta caught a mean dose!"

"Naw, I think it was Y-von. You know, the one from Thursday night, down at the meat market?"

"The one with so much makeup on they call her the vampire?"

"Unfortunately."

Schramm continued snickering as they mounted the steps to the 716th Admin offices. "You take the fuckin' ricecake,

Leroy." He shook his head back and forth feigning disgust and compassion with the same facial expression. "Gonna have to find you a steady cunt. One who'll take you home with her, walk on your back every night, fuck you silly, soap you down with perfumed bath bubbles, feed you exotic breakfasts every morning and lay out your toothbrush with the toothpaste already on it!"

"Naw, they don't do all that for ya." The challenge in Crowe's eyes betrayed hope.

"Sure, Thomas got me set up with a real pro only two weeks ago. She's burnt out and kinda old, but she'll do anything for me, 'cuz she don't wanna go back to the street. And I mean *any*thing!"

"How old is old?"

"Twenty-seven." Schramm lost his smile as he mentally subtracted his own age from hers.

"Yeah, that's pretty old," Crowe confirmed solemnly.

"I'm sure Thomas can fix you up too, if you'd like me to ask him. He's got all the right connections."

"Let Thomas fix him up with *what*?" Stryker confronted them at the top of the stairs. "My men aren't talkin' drugs, are they?" he grinned ruefully.

"We're talkin' *women*, Sarge." Schramm returned the smile, but Stryker's mouth dropped to a frown.

"Women, eh? That's *worse* than drugs!" and he thought back to the beautiful tarot-card reader currently sharing the room he rented down at the Miramar Hotel on Tu Do. She had "cut off his supply" the last few nights because he was spending so much time at Pershing Field training the rooks in the OJT program.

"What's worse," giggled Schramm, "is that he just caught—" But Crowe elbowed him and he fell silent.

"Caught what?" Stryker was intrigued. He folded his arms across his chest and leaned back to see if the story would impress him.

"Oh, just a case of the ass," Leroy muttered. "Can't figure these Oriental women out. Their way of thinking just blows my mind."

"Channel that thought below your lap, and you got it made,

61

my friend. The only way to keep these cunts happy is to treat the ladies like whores and the fuckin' whores like ladies!"

"Where have I heard *that* one before?" Crowe asked sarcastically.

"Where have you *been* before?" Stryker answered just as cynically. "It's the same across the globe, except that *here* the girls'd just as soon slice off your pecker as look at you." He stared down at Schramm in particular. "I wish all you newbies'd remember that."

"Hey, Sarge," he claimed defensively, "so long as I pay the ten dollar a month rent on the apartment, buy the soup and take her to the Rex cinema once a week, *my* old lady's all love and kisses!"

"Did you need us for something, Sarge?" Crowe changed the subject, bracing for the worst. He didn't think anybody had seen him and Broox blow up a dope pusher's Citroën Tuesday night, and it had been a week since they shot out the street lights on Thanh Mau.

"You clowns are scheduled to join up with the First Cav tomorrow," he reminded Leroy.

"Yeah, we tried to get the day off but Sergeant Richards said the PM disapproved our request—they don't cut you no slack around here anymore."

"Well, Lady Luck is riding with us on this one, boys. Got one Cpl. Alvin Kline just happens to be en route Saigon at this moment for his R&R from the First Cav unit you're headed to. The USO already reserved him a room at the Caravelle. Our CID agent in the field says Kline is one of the prime suspects in the attempted murders on Airmobil officers. Particularly our Moast the Ghost case.

"Beat feet back to the barracks and change into your civvies then mosey on down to the Caravelle before he arrives. Keep a low profile. I just want you to get a look at him so you'll know who you're dealing with in the boonies."

"No contact?" Crowe confirmed.

"No contact. Just a quick in and out. Make him, then split. Don't let *him* make *you*."

"What if I ain't got no civvies here at Pershing?" Schramm

asked with a I-done-fucked-up-again expression on his boyish face.

"What the hell you wear off duty?" Stryker grumbled, "your birthday suit?"

"Well, I carted everything down to my bungalow. Since you guys were sending me TDY into Injun territory I thought it'd be safer there. You know: out of the way."

"How long you say you've known this sweetheart of yours?" Stryker couldn't resist the taint of skepticism in his tone.

"Coupla weeks, Sarge, but—"

"Save your butts." He shook his head, imitating Crowe. "Just stop by home sweet home on your way to the Caravelle and change into something inconspicuous. And for Christsake don't wear one of those 'Feel safe tonight: Sleep with a cop' T-shirts Thomas has been selling."

"Number twenty-three Lam Son Square," Schramm told the taxi driver after he and Leroy climbed into the blue and yellow Renault Bluebird.

"You want boom-boom tonight, Joe?" The cabbie turned around to face them with a toothy smile and eyes hidden behind large black sunglasses. He made a tight circle with the fingers of his left hand then forced the middle finger on his right hand in and out roughly. "Numba one cherry girl! Guaranteed tightest pussy you ever have: only two thousand p."

"Four bucks?" Schramm responded incredulously.

"Include skull job!" The cabbie nodded his head up and down eagerly. "For five greenbacks I provide you with all-nighter: clean as a whistle—guaranteed!"

"Jesus, you carry a menu with you too, papa-san?" Schramm pulled out his wallet and peered inside dramatically, then feigned intense disappointment. "Aw, bummer, I only got a couple bucks on me, pops."

"No sweat, GI!" The cabbie's eyes brightened like novas about to explode as he took off the sunglasses. "Me have reasonable financing," and he swerved back over to the curb and pulled out a small pocket notebook. "You MPs are good risk—I discount your financing: fifty percent due on payday." He started writing furiously as though he were writing up a

63

loan application, quotes and all.

"How'd you know we were MPs?" Schramm's own eyes came alive with curiosity.

"Just take us to the Caravelle!" Crowe snapped from the back seat, interrupting their conversation. He already knew the answer: cabbies were notorious for their underworld connections. They knew all the *canh-sats* by face as well as the young Americans, despite the annual rotations back stateside. And as much time as the taxi drivers spent loitering outside the main gates of U.S. installations, it was not surprising they'd know all the uniformed cops on sight.

The cabbie frowned but calmly replaced his tattered notebook in its oily pocket and rocketed back into traffic, cutting a large truck off and forcing two other taxis to skid to a stop as he slid sideways through a congested intersection onto Lam Son.

"What a killjoy!" Schramm elbowed him playfully, but Crowe's thoughts were on the woman they had just left at the younger private's flat. He had seen her somewhere before, but he just couldn't place the face. Probably just one of the countless whores he had logged in and out of the meat market, he decided as the cab coasted up to the Caravelle's mixed French and Oriental design rear courtyard. Schramm reached out and petted one of the three guardian dragons at the compound entrance as the sedan sputtered to a stop, and Crowe wondered at the simple innocence his partner seemed to cling to despite his job and its hazards. Of course it could all be an act—a front, put out by the mind subconsciously as it struggled to absorb the constant bustle of activity and intense electricity that was Saigon, regardless of the hour.

Two women in bright miniskirts leaned against either arch of the hotel's back door, their alluring legs long and sleek, accenting their dark, exotic eyes. Crowe, the first to climb from the shiny taxi, noticed them both working their spell on him: trying to lock his eyes on theirs like a laser beam latching onto its target for the kill. He refused to play, concentrating instead on the cracks in the sidewalk, but their provocative smiles remained frozen in his mind. He was also seeing the woman with the long, black hair and the sheer nightgown they had left

64

back at Schramm's apartment.

Crowe could not believe it at first when they entered the modest bungalow together and the woman appeared to glide out slowly from a back room, casually pulling the thin robe around her naked shoulders, oblivious of Leroy's presence as she went straight to Schramm, kneeled before him, and started unzipping his pants.

He wasn't quite sure if it had all been staged just for him: the gorgeous woman falling to her knees in front of her man, firm thigh muscles accenting the tight haunches as she gently reached into his trousers, found what she was seeking, and started to bend her head forward slightly.

It had to have been an act. The way Schramm blushed and caught her by the shoulders, giggled with embarrassment as he lifted her back to her feet and quickly plopped his penis back into his pants, whispering just loud enough for Crowe to hear, "Not now, honey. Later. Tonight."

Yes, now that he thought back on it, it had to have been a joke. The look of disappointment on her face, the way she recovered from the near-tantrum so quickly and whirled around to greet him when she "realized" there was a third person present in the room. The way those firm breasts beneath the nightgown swayed ever-so-slightly as she turned to face him, the erect nipples jutting out against the see-through fabric.

"You buy me Saigon tea, Joe?" The prostitute with the seven gold bracelets on one arm winked at Leroy as he started up the steps toward the door.

"Some other time, ladies," he growled, wondering what had dropped him into the bad mood. The thought of leaving the excitement of Saigon for a harsh assignment in the boonies had been bothering him lately, sure, but now here he was showing hostility toward a very real part of that nightlife he so relished.

But did he enjoy the street that much, really? He was just like all the other MPs: constantly bitching about the whores ripping off the GIs, the equipment going out on you when you were in the middle of downtown where the taller buildings made your PR useless, the pollution and heat in the heart of the concrete jungle, intensified many times over that of the countryside beyond the wire.

"You numba ten mothafucka," the first girl answered back at him, her reasoning being, Why come to such a fancy hotel unless you wanted a good time? The woman beside her was on the verge of concluding Leroy was a "cheap Charlie" when Schramm floated up between them and put his arms around the shoulders of both hookers.

"Well, good evening, ladies." He beamed like a neon sign, announcing no cover charge and a good time till curfew could be had for all inside. "How 'bout escorting me and my buddy over to a table directly in front of the floor show? This place still got a psychedelic bottomless act where the dancers do it with a twenty-foot python?"

Automatically, as if on cue, both girls wrapped their slender arms around Schramm's waist and swayed their hips back and forth against his as they followed him into the establishment. Crowe looked back at the laughing trio with irritation in his eyes, despite the sensuous appearance of the smooth-legged women balanced almost precariously on their black high heels.

"You with *him*?" The older woman with long, crimson-colored fingernails motioned toward Leroy with a disapproving glare.

"Oh, he's OK, honey." Schramm's smile was contagious, and both girls imitated it, even if their sincerity was plastic. "Leroy's just on the rag tonight, that's all. Got a Dear Leroy letter from mama-san back in the World, you know what I mean?"

"From his mama-san?" The younger hooker's eyes grew wide as her mind slowly translated the English into Cholon-Chinese. "He get Dear John from his own mother?"

"Can you imagine that?" Schramm made his own eyes arch higher. "His own mother wrote him a shaft telegram disowning him for coming to your beautiful Saigon to napalm innocent children! Now wouldn't that ruin *your* evening?" Schramm insisted, wondering what other tall tales he could come up with to spice the conversation.

"The sarge told us to keep a low profile." Crowe frowned at the story as he held the doors open for the three. "Now why you wanna go talkin' all that horseshit?"

66

"You big spender, honey?" The older girl twirled her fingers around inside Schramm's "Fly the friendly skies of Laos" T-shirt until she found one of his nipples. She pinched it gently and grabbed his ass with her free hand. "For five thousand p you can have not one but both of us, all night," she whispered seductively into his ear while her fingers slowly caressed the back side of his jeans and came up holding his crotch.

Schramm looked over at Crowe and winked at the silent proposition but his smile faded as they entered the lobby of the Caravelle and there was no sound of music to greet them. Several old Asian hands, mostly burnt out French and British correspondents who covered the war from their balconies, sat around in deep lounge chairs, reading the latest issue of the *Saipan Post* or *Vietnam Guardian*. There was no sign of the bar stage he had expected.

"Maybe it was the Continental Palace," he muttered to himself, annoyed with his sudden lapse of memory. But they *had* been shoving so many addresses at him to memorize, and he *was* still a newbie in-country, wasn't he? There were just too many trouble spots to keep straight in his mind: bars, hotels, restaurants.

"Maybe *what* was the Continental?" Leroy had overheard him.

"Coulda sworn this joint had a flashy floor show." Schramm's eyes tightened and his face took on a strange twist as he searched his memory banks.

"I think you're thinking of the Bamboo Palace," Crowe started to suggest, "or the Monsoon nightclub over on Tu Do."

"We go upstairs now?" One of the girls smiled up at Schramm, anticipation a sparkle in her bottomless brown eyes.

"Chop, chop," Crowe corrected her, falling into his pidgin slang. "First, we sample the restaurant here." The older prostitute lapsed into an unrehearsed smile. It wasn't often she was treated to dinner at a fancy restaurant before hopping into the sack with her two-dollar joe.

A skinny waiter in black tights, his black, oily hair slicked back with invisible cream, scampered up to them and, after the briefest of disapproving frowns directed at the girls, motioned them toward a table in the far corner, deep within the cavernous room's shadows.

"Fuckin' faggots," Schramm whispered over to Leroy as they followed the waiter, imitating his slight swish between tables. "How come we can't get one of those cute bargirls over there to wait on us?"

"The location's perfect, anyway," Leroy replied. "From here we can watch the lobby entrance and the stairs both. You still got that personnel photograph of Kline?"

"No sweat. He should be a cinch to spot: short little fuck, crewcut, thin mustache, shrapnel scar on his left cheek." Schramm opened his menu and began scanning the seafood column, his favorite.

"You talk 'fuck'?" The younger prostitute smiled up at Schramm, winking a heavily penned eye.

"Just order your chop chop," Schramm said, smiling back, "and no crabs." He frowned at the inflated prices, "Too—"

"Oh! We no have crabs!" The younger woman slammed her menu shut as she threw a startled expression at the man. "Clean as whistle!" and she pursed her lips and blew out a stream of air that failed to make any noise.

Schramm rolled his eyeballs toward the ceiling in resignation and Leroy suggested they speak in Vietnamese. "You know neither of us talk sing-song," he answered, and the table fell silent for the next few minutes as everyone studied their menus a second time. Crowe felt like saying, "You get the impression they know that schmuck cabbie with the skin menu?" but he resisted the impulse, afraid it would just ignite more misunderstanding and wisecracks from the girls.

"May I take your order?" A slender waitress in thigh-length, tapered pantaloons and a glittering halter top had glided up to their table silently, and Schramm stared at her revealing bosom open-mouthed as Leroy ordered a plate of bo nuong la: a tender slab of beef, chopped into minute sections and wrapped in grape leaves then sprinkled with steaming pineapple cubes.

"Canh chua," the woman next to Crowe whispered her selection in the midst of a minute-long recitation of the latest street gossip, and Schramm recognized the informal title of the shrimp soup cooked with bean sprouts, sliced pineapple and celery, though he was lost in the rest of the whirlwind conversation.

"Might as well include a bottle of ruou de," Leroy added when she was finished, smiling for the first time as he ordered a quart of Vietnamese rice wine.

"Cha gio," the younger woman said anxiously, running her tongue along her lips as she surveyed the huge menu. Crowe knew cha gio was more an appetizer than a main course, consisting of small rolls filled with chopped vegetables, pork, noodles and crabmeat, deep fried in rice paper. "Bo bay mon," she pointed to another selection, this one being several sweet beef dishes, each prepared in a different way and spiced with contrasting traditional sauces. For dessert, the girl ordered chao tom, which was a favorite among the Saigonese: grilled sugar cane cubes rolled in tangy shrimp paste.

"Are you quite finished?" Leroy asked sarcastically as he mentally calculated her tab alone. If he and Schramm *did* bed her down later, she *was* going to earn that chao tom.

The girl didn't answer verbally, but the defiant grin told everyone at the table this was one whore who was going to dine like a lady for a change.

"Got any hamburgers?" Schramm asked loudly, and Crowe slid down in his chair a few inches, turning red.

"Grilled ham-cheese is only 'Merican dish we serve Caravelle." The waitress's tone was apologetic. "And Pepsi."

"OK." Schramm grimaced in mock indecision. "Make mine pho soup first, followed by com tay cam and some of that milky Vietnamese ice cream."

"Ca rem?" She smiled, already writing the sugary dessert down.

"Yeah, that's it, honey!" and Schramm watched with keen interest the way her graceful wrists flashed across the notepad. His favorite dish was com tay cam: a rice platter sprinkled with mushrooms, chicken and finely sliced twice-cooked pork, but as he stared at the swollen halter top above the flat tummy he grinned at the prospect of a more sumptuous midnight snack until the waitress noticed how he was inspecting her and graciously vanished in blushing retreat.

69

"Check out Sergeant Rock over there." Crowe motioned for Schramm to eyeball the narrow corridor leading from the lobby into the hotel restaurant. A tall, husky American in full combat gear, including an M-16 slung over his shoulder and a camouflage-covered helmet balanced atop his crew cut, was being escorted right toward their table.

"You think that's Kline?" Schramm whispered back needlessly: the girls were ignoring them, immersed in their own conversation about the countless meal combinations on the fancy menu.

"Naw, Kline's a little runt. This guy must top six feet, easy. Besides, they'd have made him check in his weapons and gear before he left his unit. They'd have sent him south in Class A's too."

"But he's wearing a First Cav combat patch," Schramm observed as the infantryman came to within a few feet of their table.

"Yeah," muttered Crowe as both men took to kissing the long folds of jet-black hair hiding the perfumed neck of the closest woman in an attempt to hide their faces from the grunt.

"Ooooohhh, what come over you?" The younger girl put her arms around Schramm, surprised at the sudden romantic behavior, while her friend playfully slapped Leroy and told him to behave while they were in public.

As he passed by, the soldier muttered, "Lousy REMFs," and cast both men a disapproving scowl.

"What did he say?" Schramm leaned over toward Crowe after the soldier was seated several tables away.

"Called us REMFs." Leroy frowned bitterly as he shook his head from side to side slowly, trying to control the unwarranted anger.

"What the hell is a REMF?" Schramm asked with a grin on his face, "Real Eagerly Mauling Females?" and he hugged the woman beside him again, running his fingers down to the inviting valley where her skirt was hiked up to her lap.

"Rear Echelon Mother Fucker," Crowe corrected him harshly.

"What?" the word exploded from Schramm's throat the same instant his fingers located the curly strands of pubic hair

70

between the smooth, muscular thighs.

"Settle down." Crowe reached over and placed a hand gently on his partner's shoulder, and the girl beside Schramm grew startled, afraid her trick was upset at the discovery she wore no panties beneath the miniskirt.

"Why I oughta go over and shove that M-16 up his ass," Schramm hissed, gritting his teeth as his fingers continued to explore the warm folds of flesh hidden beneath the tablecloth.

"It's not worth it," Crowe maintained. "The last thing we need now is a scene. Remember: low profile. Eyeball Kline then split, mission accomplished."

"Yeah, OK—whatever," Schramm sighed as his fingers became moist suddenly—at just the same time their waitress reappeared with bowls of soup and tiny dishes of the offensive-smelling nuoc mam sauce. One odor mingled with the other and nobody seemed to notice as he wiped his fingers on his napkin and poured everyone a glass of rice wine.

For the next few minutes, as they awaited the main course platters, the two MPs watched the variety of customers enter and leave the Caravelle: off-duty marine embassy guards with their heads shaved to the skin, foreign correspondents with their noses hollowed out by cocaine, little old men in Hong Kong suits peddling stolen watches and switchblades in tattered briefcases, shoeshine boys sneaking in to approach the old men in the lounge chairs only to be chased off by the limp-wristed porters, prostitutes in flashy hot pants loitering near the main doors, Chinese businessmen loaded down with file folders and Japanese cameras, and Australian tourists who still didn't know Saigon was part of the combat zone. But there was no sign of Corporal Kline as dusk approached.

"Thank you, dear," Schramm displayed his most lovable smile as the waitress returned to pour them all a refill of chrysanthemum tea. The young woman blushed, nodded her head slightly to acknowledge the statement and hurried to back away from the range of the candlelight flickering in the middle of the table. Schramm turned to Crowe and shook his own head slowly as the hot tea worked to chase away the dizzying effect brought on by the rice wine. "Too bad they make her wear that sexy outfit," he said. "She looks way too shy—innocent's the

71

word, to be wearing something that skimpy. She must catch hell from the drunks."

"Yeah, she looks like she'd be more at home tutoring school children or tending the rice fields," observed Leroy.

"*She* looks like a schoolgirl herself," the younger prostitute beside Schramm added, but her girlfriend laughed sarcastically at the remark and turned to face the man beside her.

"That 'schoolgirl' would lick your ass clean for five hundred piasters," she said softly, her tone bitter but matter-of-fact in its inflection and Leroy and Schramm both detected the jealousy in her narrow eyes.

"You didn't see that," Crowe warned as the waitress brushed up against the grim-looking infantryman and the soldier reached out and grabbed her by the waist, but Schramm was already rising to his feet when the soldier pulled the girl down onto his lap—his free hand latched onto a generous portion of her firm bottom, and she jumped back up with a shocked squeal, only to be restrained by the powerful American who then started to hug her.

"I think you've had a bit too much to drink." Schramm tapped the man on the shoulder, distracting him from trying to force his lips on hers. "Why don't you leave the young lady alone?"

"I haven't had *anything* to drink, yet," the soldier growled, turning to face Schramm as he released the waitress and pushed her down onto the floor. "Who the fuck are you anyway, punk?"

"Are you alright, miss?" Schramm ignored the man and stooped to help the waitress up, but was himself rammed down onto the polished teakwood as the soldier kicked him hard in the side with a heavy jungle boot.

Schramm felt the air forced from his chest as he crashed to the floor atop the girl, but the slight cry of pain that escaped her seemed to give his own body strength, and he forced his head up just in time to see the M-16 butt racing down to connect with his face.

Crowe did not know he could fly. One minute he was shaking his head at the waste of energy connected with rising to the rescue of a bargirl—the next he was racing to the aid of his

72

partner: feet first!

Crowe had practiced the drill in MP school only twice. In fact, the move was discouraged: too many recruits had broken their ankles or torn leg muscles charging their opponents with the flying boot kicks. Perhaps it was the rice wine, maybe the adrenalin, but before he knew it, the rook was airborne. And seconds later he had planted his heels in the man's chest and catapulted him end over end onto his back across several collapsing tables.

"Oh, no no no no!" The hotel manager came scurrying in amidst the crashing of plates and upending of tables. "You takey out to street! No fight here! You takey outside, or me call MP!"

The two prostitutes abandoned back at the corner table began a more than convincing act of hysterical screaming, and the younger one threw the bottle of rice wine at the proprietor—it missed by several feet and shattered a long mirror that ran the length of the west wall.

The infantryman forced himself to his knees, swinging his rifle up and around in the same movement, but Schramm was ready for him, letting fly a lateral wrist clip that caught the soldier in the throat.

Hot lead mixed with bright red tracers sprayed the ceiling as the M-16 discharged repeatedly, emptying an entire clip on automatic. The waitress at Schramm's feet let out a terrified scream, and the private was torn between rushing to her aid or turning to finish off the infantryman.

Soon a distraction of sirens and flashing lights pulling up in front of the Caravelle had captured Schramm's attention, and too late he realized the grunt was not down to stay: in fact, the man had Crowe balanced above his head in the grip of two mighty, clawlike fists, and was twirling him around in circles— gaining speed to heave the off-duty MP through the plate-glass windows in the front of the restaurant.

Schramm grabbed the empty rifle at the soldier's boots, then tossed it over his shoulder, away from the brawl, and tackled the infantryman around the waist, toppling the trio into more tables.

Sgt. Mark Stryker, one of the first military policemen

through the restaurant's swinging front doors, batted the M-16 down casually as it came flying his way, and then, quickly determining there were only three combatants involved, stepped aside to let his men break up the fight.

A few minutes later, he was only mildly shocked to find Schramm and Crowe at the bottom of the fracas.

"Up against the wall, douche bags!" Davis held in the grin as he ordered all three Americans to submit to a frisk. Broox and Thomas, also enjoying themselves, put a little more kick than usual into it as they slammed the prisoners' feet farther apart with their own boots. All the MPs on shift that evening had been briefed that the two rookies would be casing the Caravelle, and that should trouble break out, they were to be treated no different than the other scumbags—to protect their cover, of course.

"Where's your military ID?" Davis finished patting the grunt down but failed to find even a wallet in the man's pockets. "What unit you with?"

"Go screw yourself, nigger boy!" the infantryman replied, turning his head from the wall slightly to look Davis in the eyes. The private allowed himself a it's-gonna-be-one-of-those-nights grin as he glanced over at Broox and Thomas briefly then slammed the soldier's face back into the wall. A trickle of blood began to ooze down a large tapestry on the wall, making it look like the subdued mountain scenery had suddenly erupted into volcanic lava.

"I said, What unit you with?" Davis repeated in a soft whisper, though every MP in the room could feel his teeth biting his lower lip.

Schramm and Crowe strained to look over their left shoulders at the pat-down search, and Broox and Thomas, playing their part to the hilt, rammed the rookies' faces back into the wall roughly, causing even Stryker to wince.

"Don't you see the patch, mothafucker?" the soldier yelled. "First fuckin' Cavalry! Killed me ten dozen gooks this tour and I'd kill your black ass too, if you'd take off that badge and gun!"

Almost every MP in the room chuckled over that one, remembering somewhere, sometime in their illustrious past, when they had obliged a mouthy prisoner, took him into a back cell alone, and handed him a new face.

"What's your name?" Davis remained calm, ignoring the challenge for the time being.

"You want my name, you suck my cock," the soldier mumbled just soft enough for Davis to hear, and the MP lost control and slammed the grunt face-first into the opposite wall. As the prisoner went down, Davis brought a heavy boot back but was restrained by Stryker.

"Check his name tag," Stryker remarked matter-of-factly as he pushed Davis gently out of the way. The MP sergeant had no intention of taking the matter any further with the black private—he merely wanted to move the investigation along more quickly, and it was so much harder to interrogate a belligerent prisoner when he had a broken jaw.

Thomas bent down and grabbed the infantryman by the wrist, flipped the semiconscious grunt onto his back, and read off the name tag over the right chest pocket: "Saxon."

Stryker scanned the top page on his clipboard, smiled, and nodded his head. "AWOL, my friends. Twenty-nine days," and he turned to Davis. "Too bad, Craig: another day and he'd be on the hot sheets as a deserter!"

Davis returned the smile, then reached down and snapped the handcuffs on the prisoner. Broox moved over to help him drag the grunt to his feet.

"I ain't no goddamn deserter!" Saxon yelled, more at the waitress than anyone. Trying to save face, Stryker decided, almost wanting to understand. "I didn't run away—not under fire anyway! I left because Moast the Ghost was gonna get us all killed! And for what! For some lousy hill on which he could lean his promotion ladder? Some motherfuckin' hill Charlie'd just reclaim the next night?"

"Save it for somebody who gives a fuck," Thomas muttered, pushing the prisoner out toward the jeeps in the street.

"I ain't afraid of the VC!" Saxon screamed as they dragged him out through the swinging doors, kicking and biting. "I didn't desert my country! I just took the fight to Charlie Cong where it counts—in the tunnels! I been kickin' ass on my own for weeks now, don't you see? It was just time for a little Saigon

R&R. A little R&R."

"What a space cadet," Broox said with a laugh, but Stryker grew silent, thinking about what the soldier had said, wondering if there were others like him. Out in the jungle, hiding in the tunnels and the trees by day, ambushing the communists by night. Taking the war to Charlie on his own level—without the fancy helicopters, enormous firepower, and limitless reinforcements.

"Whatta we do 'bout these punks?" Broox grinned after Saxon was led out of the restaurant, past hearing range. "Solitary confinement?"

Stryker withdrew his night stick from its web-belt keeper and bounced it lightly off Schramm's head. "What am I gonna do with you two?" He shook his head from side to side, in good humor only because the disturbance had netted them an AWOL.

Stryker turned without waiting for an answer and started to walk back out to his jeep, and Crowe and Schramm slowly brought their hands down off the wall, ready to joke about the incident with their buddies, when Cpl. Alvin Kline walked into the restaurant.

The same instant, Stryker recognized the First Cavalry combat patch on the short man's uniform. He whirled around and ordered, "Lock 'em up, gentlemen! Disturbance and assault."

Cpl. Alvin Kline, loaded down with suitcases and a duffel bag, staggered sideways, out of the way, wide eyed, as Stryker brushed past him, businesslike, out into the street. The short corporal's head jerked to the left as the handcuffs closed with a sharp, metallic click across the wrists of the two men spread up against the wall.

A bewildered Alvin was still clutching his bags, trying to stay out of the way, as Schramm and Crowe were hustled past him, out into the night. "Welcome to Saigon," Thomas muttered to the infantryman in a bored tone as he and the last of the MPs departed the demolished Caravelle, hopped into their jeeps and disappeared down the street.

6. POPPING CAPS ON HILLTOP SIXTY-EIGHT

U.S. Army Military Police Academy Firing Range, Ft. Gordon, Georgia

He had been guarding the parking lot from cars all night. Armed with an empty M-16, the drill sergeants had dropped him off shortly after dusk and ordered him to keep the ten-acre stretch of blacktop free of vehicles so that the street-sweepers would have no trouble rolling in to clean it out at dawn. Typical army shit detail, but he didn't mind; it would give him some free time away from the hectic barracks life in which to read the letters from Saigon.

Nick Uhernik watched the first rays of sunlight splash red across the horizon and he could immediately feel the heat rushing toward him as it burnt away at the mist. He shut off the o.d. green flashlight and tucked away the letters from Angi back into his helmet, watching the sun creep above the treeline as he did so, wondering if his Vietnamese friends beyond the horizon, in the distant Far East were watching the same sun. Wasn't it setting on their western coastline just then, at that time of day?

He recalled all the times Angi had walked the beach at Vung Tau with him, hugging him in mock fright as the playful sea gulls dove down at them, stopping just short to scream out their greetings amidst a flapping of great wings. He could hear her voice clearly, even though she whispered against the crashing of the waves; she was telling him to stop and listen— could he hear the huge, orange sun hissing as it dipped into the sea, turning day into night and setting the ocean to boil at its edge?

Nick knew she'd be arranging her bed soon, stretching the mosquito net across the bamboo poles, just above the pillow. And since he had spent the entire night on guard duty, the drill sergeants would let him sleep too—and despite the ocean separating them, he'd meet her in his dreams.

"Hey, dreamer, jump in!" Andy Smallwood, the only black soldier in his platoon, had coasted up to him unnoticed.

"Where'd you steal the jeep?" Nick asked, forgetting the letters.

"They checked it out to you and me. They told me to come pick you up. Today's convoy duty!" His smile was ear to ear.

"But I just spent all night on guard duty," Nick protested, painfully aware there was nothing another simple private could do.

Smallwood only raised his hands in the air, helplessly, and began singing, "You're in the army now. . . ."

Nick stared at him in tired silence for several seconds, then shrugged his shoulders and tossed his rifle in the back of the jeep. "Tell me this don't suck, Andrew my man," he sighed, pulling his slender, underweight frame into the right seat. "You know this means I won't even get to throw up over the powdered eggs and oily coffee at the mess hall," and he climbed over into the back seat and went to sleep, the smog drifting in from the city reminding him of Saigon and bringing a smile to his face.

The two recruits returned to the barracks, got into their web gear and packs, then joined a sixty-jeep convoy headed for the rolling hills of Georgia.

"Only a couple weeks to go—" Smallwood checked his calendar watch and elbowed his partner awake—"and we're home free: graduation! Don't fuck it up by getting wrote up for sleepin' on duty. Like Sergeant Flowers always says, 'You snooze, you lose.'"

Nick laughed himself back straight in his seat. "Do you think he was really born with that name, or he had it legally changed just to freak the rooks out?"

Smallwood allowed himself a little chuckle. "Yeah, could ya

see some dude named Flowers tryin' to survive in the ghetto?"

"Really. Hey, bro, lay off my mama or I'm gonna hand you your head—I'm one bad dude."

"What yo' name, Mista Bad Dude?"

"Just call me Mista Flowers, my man!"

Both privates lapsed into unrestrained laughter and Smallwood allowed the jeep to stray across the center line as he bent over, clutching his belly.

"What the fuck's goin' on here?" Senior Drill Sergeant Mills had raced up beside their jeep and activated his siren with a blaring yelp as he coasted along on their left, ignoring oncoming traffic. "You rooks straighten up, or I swear I'll recycle your young asses and put you through this entire school again from day one! Got that?"

Uhernik swallowed the chuckle rising in his gut, but Smallwood, still feeling cocky, saluted the sergeant and grinned his acknowledgment.

Mills, fully aware his privates knew you didn't salute NCOs, ignored the disrespect and gunned his jeep until he had overtaken the lead vehicle and run several civilians off the road.

"See what we get for making fun of Sergeant Flowers?" Uhernik grinned despite the sincere attempt to remain stone-faced.

"Yeah, I guess he don't deserve it, neither. The man's one cool dude—really helped me out with my AI reports last week. But that Mills is another character altogether," and he hacked up some mucus and spit it out at the brown and gray countryside rolling swiftly past them.

"Hey, knock it off, Smallwood!" Several irate recruits in the jeep behind them made an exaggerated effort to lean over their windshield to wipe off what the wind had carried back.

Smallwood just waved, flashed them a toothy smile, and continued rattling on without interruption, "Anyway, like I said, coupla weeks and we'll be Ten-seventy-six our next duty station. The big time, real thing. Street patrol!"

"You know you love it here," Nick goaded him as they left the highway and started up a steep hill pockmarked with foxholes and "bomb" craters.

As the lead jeeps reached the top they were met by a platoon of "resisters," who unleashed a barrage of small arms fire and tear gas on the convoy, forcing a hasty and unplanned retreat back to the bottom of the hill.

The recruits regrouped under a thatch of spindly trees, posted a few perimeter guards, then discussed their counter-attack. The drill sergeants stayed out of the exercise completely, except to tell the men they had no air support to request and no ground reinforcements to radio for. They were on their own.

The men decided to split the convoy into three groups. Squad One would circle around the hill, while Uhernik and Smallwood's Squad Two would scale the hillside again, this time firing their jeep-mounted M-60 machine guns at the first sign of enemy contact. Squad Three would remain behind the treeline until the hill was secured, or the men in Squad Two sent up a smoke-flare call for help.

As soon as Squad One began taking "sniper fire," Squad Two advanced on the hill. Smallwood requested that Nick take the wheel of their jeep, complaining the last attempt up the hillside had "jarred his brains loose" and he would just as well enjoy jarring his arms loose this time with the huge M-60.

Halfway up the hill they were hit with more tear gas, just as their jeep dipped sideways into an abandoned foxhole, almost overturning. It was already in four-wheel drive, but Uhernik was losing traction, and then all four wheels were airborne and they were suddenly floating backwards, down upon the jeep behind them, driven by the ex-boxer, Barry Todd.

Barry's eyes grew wide with helpless fear at what was surely going to be a fatal collision, but his hands mysteriously took over at the last moment, swerving to one side as his mind was still preparing to shake hands with Mr. Death, and the jeep driven by Uhernik narrowly missed him and smashed into another trenchline instead.

"Jeeeeesus!" yelled Smallwood as he held onto his helmet with one hand and blasted away on the machine gun with the other.

"What the hell you shootin' at?" Nick laughed at their luck, the Article Fifteen reprimand and price tag for a new jeep still flashing before his eyes.

"Where the fuck'd you learn to drive?" he replied, still firing off hundreds of blanks at the moving bushes that dotted the scarred and blackened hillside.

On their second attempt, Squad Two captured the hill, took no prisoners, then were, in turn, captured by a full company of the enemy, who lay in wait for them beneath the hilltop in an elaborate "VC" tunnel system.

"OK," the drill sergeants gave up on them again. "Take twenty for lunch."

Uhernik sighed with relief at the break from gunning down all the American faces. With his M-16 still smoking, he joined Smallwood over at the training bleachers set up on the edge of the vast plateau that made up the four-acre hilltop, still wondering if the real Viet Cong would drop before his rifle sights so easy, and if their faces would carry the same shit-eating grins before they fell lifeless into the muck of the rice paddies.

The raid on Hill Sixty-eight was supposed to be a survival exercise, but after the recruits failed to trap any rabbits or snakes, the DIs made a big production of frowning, decided they were running behind schedule, then gave up all hope and trucked in a load of chickens, which the hungry rookies butchered, burnt and wolfed down.

After the feathered cuisine, they were jogged over to another hilltop and given a class on the .45-caliber automatic pistol.

"It accommodates seven rounds in the clip and one in the chamber," the instructor rambled on in a bored, unemotional Southern drawl. "Most duty stations allow only five. Combat zones are another story. You'll pick up on what the other guys carry." He held up a pistol for all to see. "Uncle Sam pays sixty-six dollars apiece. Take care of 'em!" He smiled, suddenly popping off eight rounds at a target fifty meters away. It flopped back, struck by the first bullet. "The maximum effective range of this cannon is twenty-five meters," he continued while Uhernik fingered his ringing ears, "but hot

81

dogs like me can bring down a running commie at fifty, no sweat!"

Another distant target popped up, then moved slowly down range on a pulley wire. The sergeant popped out the empty magazine, inserted a fresh clip, chambered another round and fired twice, knocking this latest target out of sight. There came a scattering of applause and murmurs of awe from the more naive recruits. "Do I have any potential hot dogs in the crowd?" His overconfident grin challenged the men crowding the bleachers.

"I'd rather have a .38 revolver," stated a man in the first row.

"How dare you!" the DI yelled. "Drop, slick! Knock me out seventy-five!" and the private dove to the ground and began the push-ups.

"This firearm will be your primary weapon during your career with the Military Police Corps. . . ." began another instructor.

"Career?" smirked Zriny.

"Corps?" objected one marine to another over the use of the word. Both men were out of earshot of the drill sergeants.

"It kicks back a little," continued the DI, "but it won't hurt you—so long as you keep your thumbs parallel to the slide, not up in the air like some cowboy."

"Yep—seen a couple rooks get their thumbs torn clean off when the slide snapped back upon discharge," agreed another instructor somberly.

"You guys are gonna come to love this little beauty!" the first sergeant said eagerly, popping off another clip at a target halfway up the closest hill. It went down immediately.

They handed out seventy bullets to each recruit, and then they checked out their pistols from an armory van that rolled up unannounced out of the gloom. They were issued red-wax ear plugs and sent out on the firing line, given a refresher course on how to load and operate the weapon, then told to insert a five-round magazine, chamber one bullet, and switch on the safety.

"Ready on the firing line?" asked a drill sergeant from a distant, safe tower. It was definitely out of range of their firearms. Most of the men raised a left hand into the air, meaning they were ready. Bobby Ray, who was left handed, raised his pistol into the air and shot a round into the sky.

"Holy shit!" yelled Zriny, diving to the ground.

"Hold your fire! Hold your fire!" came the amplified command from the tower loud-speakers. "Hold your fire!"

"Aw, fuck," muttered Bobby Ray as soon as he realized what he had done. "Why does this always happen to me?"

"Who's the turd-face that fired his weapon?" Two drill sergeants were running up to Ray.

"I thought he said, Fire!" explained Bobby, pulling heavily at the thick ear plugs in hope their bulk would provide him with an excuse, but the DIs were all over him, showing no compassion. Ray holstered his weapon and fell into the push-up position automatically. "One, drill sergeant, two, drill sergeant," he began to knock them out, counting in a loud, rasping voice that was laced with mental exhaustion.

The .45 was one of the biggest, most powerful handguns in the world, and the men held them pointed out at the targets rigidly, in fear of blowing off their toes if they didn't. After Bobby Ray completed his hundred punishment push-ups, he fell back into line and the recruits again awaited instructions from the tower.

"Get the impression we're in the yard of the state pen, with guard towers over every shoulder?" Smallwood whispered over to Uhernik as the drill sergeants slowly went from man to man, cautiously inspecting their weapons visually, without handling them.

"Yeah, with itchy trigger fingers on low-gauge shotguns."

"This man's got his safety off! This man's got his safety off!" cried a drill sergeant down at the end of the line. He snatched the pistol away from the recruit, and the privates all bent back, straining to see who got caught.

"Eyes on the firing line!" boomed the DI in the tower. "It's none of your goddamn business who fucked up!" The men flashed their faces back to the targets, but they could all hear an angry voice down at the end of the line cursing one of the recruits.

". . . Ten, drill sergeant, eleven, drill sergeant. . . ."

Pvt. Nick Uhernik could feel his arm getting heavy as the punishment push-ups were knocked out, but he imagined the weight was merely his slender Angi—he was carrying her through the smashing waves as they frolicked on the beach in Vietnam, and the pain went away.

"Ready on the line?" the tower control finally asked.

The men all raised their free hand. No shots rang out.

"Fire!" came the command, and Nick disengaged his safety with the flick of a thumb and jerked back on the trigger. The pistol discharged, a hot piece of empty brass flew back and bounced off his nose as the weapon recoiled, lifting his hand a few inches into the air but quickly falling back level, then a puff of silver smoke obscured the target.

Men on either side of him, relieved someone else had taken the plunge and fired first, were now jerking down on their triggers also. The reports were loud, but bouncing in harmlessly off his ear plugs, and a new feeling of excitement was crawling through Nick's fingers—as the smoke cleared slightly, he was pulling the trigger again and again. As a huge, gray cloud formed in front of the men it looked as if they were shooting at a wall of rising mist, the targets now completely hidden in the distance.

"Hold it, son, hold it," a drill sergeant was whispering into his ear. "Let the smoke clear so you can see what you're shooting at."

The target was still standing. Nick had not even winged it.

"Now take some deep breaths," he coached the private. "Rest your arm, breathe deeply, get a sight picture—use your damn sights, that's what they're there for. Then squeeze the trigger, gently, don't jerk it—squeeeeeeeeze."

Nick squeezed off a round and a white spot magically appeared in the center of the black silhouette. The target flopped down, then popped up again in a few seconds.

"That's it, son," the buck sergeant encouraged him on. "Squeeeeeeeeze it gently, like a whore's nipple."

The target went down again the second his pistol discharged, to the amazement of the recruits on either side of him. Nick turned to thank the drill sergeant, but the man had moved on to another rookie.

84

7. MONKEY HOUSE BLUES

Pershing Field Holding Cells, Saigon

Norman Saxon was still banging his face against the bars of cell block six when Stryker led Crowe and Schramm down the dimly lit corridor past him.

"Gonna kill you REMFs! Gonna kill you REMFs!" He reached out through the thick bars and almost latched onto Crowe's arm, but Stryker was quicker, knocking the man's fist down with his sap.

"Even put the goofy fuck in the pink slammer," Stryker muttered to his "prisoners" matter-of-factly as Saxon leaned up against the bars, drooling spit against the cold steel as he watched the two new inmates being led down to an end cell. "The shrinks over at Third Field Army Hospital suggested we paint one cubicle pink, especially for violent jerk-offs like Saxon there—was supposed to mellow 'em out mentally. But you think we could have such luck? As you can see: no chance. He's still as much of an asshole as when we brought him in here."

"I ain't no deserter! I ain't no deserter!" Saxon began screaming again, and he resumed ramming his face against the unyielding bars.

"I didn't say you were a deserter!" Stryker yelled back at him, "I said you were an *asshole*."

Saxon emitted a roar that could be heard in the street outside, and took to kicking the walls with his bare feet.

It was Stryker's intention to reinforce Crowe and

Schramm's cover by making the First Cavalry soldier think they were in as much trouble as himself and in no way connected with any law-enforcement entity. But as things stood now, he was beginning to feel the whole scam was a waste of time. Saxon had repeatedly tried to assault his captors on the way to the monkey house, and if that didn't earn him some hard time at the Long Binh stockade, some military judge would surely commit him to the psyche ward for observation on a mental health hold. Stryker was convinced he had hustled his two MPs out past Alvin Kline fast enough that the second First Cav soldier wouldn't be suspicious either.

"This place sucks!" Crowe gave the act his best as Stryker threw him against the bars of the last cubicle and kicked Schramm in on top of him.

"What's the goddamn charges?" Schramm hissed, pulling a mattress up off its metal cot and whirling it around at the sergeant.

Stryker slammed the door shut in time and jerked a fire hose from its rusted wall hook. "Settle your young ass down or I'll let both of you have it across the mouth with a jet spray of water!" He fought back the grin and the urge to turn on the pressure.

"You can shove that fuckin' hose up your ass, you faggot screw!" Crowe screamed. He couldn't remember the last time he was actually authorized to talk tough to one of his NCOs, especially Stryker—whose reputation as the meanest MP in Saigon was near legendary.

Schramm couldn't resist either. "I asked what the charges were, semen breath!" he yelled at the top of his lungs and the words echoing through the cell block merged with the sound of Saxon banging his chops against the bars again. "I demand a military lawyer—I know my rights!"

"Here's your rights," Stryker mumbled, surrendering to the urge himself. A powerful stream of highly pressurized water shot out at the two privates, knocking them both over the wooden toilet and bouncing them off the far wall onto the slick floor.

A few seconds later, as was common during every shift change, the on-going MPs dropped by the cell blocks behind the Pershing Field comm-shack to see who was making all the ruckus. And what would be necessary later to settle the prisoner down, be it shackles, tape across the mouth or a strait jacket. Usually strait jackets weren't found around Saigon, however, and a night stick, employed at just the right leverage and velocity, accomplished the task just as well.

When the four MPs from Charlie Company crowded into the doorway and saw Stryker hosing down two of his rooks with a satisfying smile, they could hardly have been blamed for blowing their cover.

"My turn!" Raul Schultz ran up, grabbed the hose from Stryker, and soon had Crowe sliding back and forth into the walls at the end of the jet spray. "Take that you bad, bad boy!" he laughed as the stocky private rolled back into the toilet and knocked it off its foundations. Schultz glanced back over a shoulder and grinned at Stryker. "What'd these morons do anyway to rate a night in the monkey house?" He turned the hose on Schramm, not waiting for an answer, and the rest of the MPs erupted into laughter and applause as the "prisoner" slid face-first under a cot, out of sight.

The smile faded from Stryker's face as he noticed Saxon out of the corner of his eye—the prisoner's expression and behavior was also changing as he watched the comedy unfold into drama then mystery in the cell block before him. Here were these cops treating two arrestees like longtime friends. The brutality he had expected failed to materialize. Instead, events were transpiring more like a drawn-out practical joke gone awry. It made Saxon grow quite silent as he took it all in, bewildered, and Stryker tensed, hoping the grunt had banged his senses into a mindless daze, unable to comprehend what he was hearing and seeing.

Two energetic MPs brushed through the crowd in the doorway, and the ex-Green Beret grimaced when he recognized Lydic and Schaeffer. The men weren't really cops anymore, in the literal sense of the title. They had once been damned good MPs, before their dedication was twisted inside-out by the job itself and their minds were sizzled beyond limit, like a fuse, melting in half under the stress of a power surge. Lydic had been working an undercover narcotics operation when the suspects had forced him to inject a normally lethal dose of heroin into his own system—the overdose fried his brain in the ethics and decision department, but left him otherwise mentally alert and intelligent; Schaeffer, on the other hand, had contracted rabies while answering a lousy vicious dog complaint, and though the resulting fever had also scrambled portions of his thinking process, PMO had allowed both men to stay on with the 716th in a maintenance capacity rather than send them back to duty stateside where they'd only die spiritually and end up on the psyche ward.

Stryker always had second thoughts about the two. He was totally against them being allowed to go about their duties in marked MP units but buckled under pressure from the men every time he tried to get them sent home. In fact, only the week before, when the compound was being plagued by a suspected VC sapper who harassed the wits of every soldier on guard duty by cutting down power poles, street signs and even guard towers with a noiseless hacksaw, Stryker unexpectedly solved the case of the midnight phantom by stumbling across Lydic and Schaeffer fleeing the scene of a tumbling tower— hacksaws slung over both their backs like M-16 rifles. They even had the gall to snatch Stryker's helmet off his head as they raced past him in the opposite direction.

When they were finally captured in downtown Cholon and brought before the provost marshal for a sanity hearing, Stryker was again outvoted. The brotherhood prevailed, Lydic and Schaeffer were given a few additional shots to mellow them out, and Pershing Field returned to normal.

When the "odd couple" brushed past the MPs in the doorway, it was for those reasons that Stryker began to sweat. Both men went straight for the cage at the end of the corridor, eyeballed the off-duty MPs inside, and commenced to bellowing like apes, bent over at the waist, knuckles dragging along on the concrete as they swayed from side to side imitating zoo animals who now were allowed to make fun of humans for a change.

Schaeffer jumped up toward the ceiling and latched onto the upper half of the bars as he reached in with his free hand and tried to grab Crowe, all the time uttering vulgar chimpanzee noises. Stryker frowned and placed his hands on his hips—so long as the two kept their mouths shut, things couldn't get much worse.

Until Lieutenant Slipka appeared in the doorway.

He peered over the helmets of the enlisted men, recognized Schramm and Crowe, and flew into a rage. "Get those MPs outta that cell!" he yelled, unaware of the situation. He glanced at his wrist watch, thinking they were assigned to relief shift. "They still got six hours left on their shift—an' I want 'em out on the street, earning their paycheck! Now!"

The cell block fell completely silent for a microsecond, then the quiet was shattered by Saxon. "I knew it!" he screamed, banging his head against the bars again. "You motherfucking pigs!" He glared in through the bars at Crowe and Schramm. "I knew you was the goddamn heat from the first! Fuckin'-A right! I knew it all along!" and an insane smile laced his cheeks as he erupted into hysterical laughter and continued slamming his swollen lips against the steel lining his cage.

"You must have been petrified." The woman on David Schramm's back flicked the long, black hair off her shoulders so that it hung down and brushed against his body.

It still bothered him, how well she spoke English, but he tried to ignore it for now and concentrated on how expertly her fingers worked the stiff muscles in his back, kneading just the right spots this way and that until the pain seemed to evaporate in the swirl of humid, muggy air sneaking in beneath the humming ceiling fan. "I told you—there was no reason to be scared; they were not really throwing me in jail, it was just an act to—"

"But *any* trip to the monkey house must surely be most unpleasant," she insisted, and as the massage brought him to the edge of drifting off, Dave wondered how many trips to the slammer *she* had endured over the years. How many *canh-sats* had stripped her naked for the interrogations. How many American backs she had walked to get this good. How many cocks she had sucked.

"Let me explain it to you again," he whispered, the mild

irritation in his voice coming through, but she gently touched her long, slender fingers against his lips and told him to rest.

"Be silent," she whispered softly in his ear, leaning down low so he could feel her breasts pressing against his back and smell the perfume on her throat.

"Right *there*," he nearly gasped as her finger tips found the sore spot in the small of his back and he reached out to turn up the volume on the cassette player. It was his favorite Vietnamese song, Thai Hien singing, "Em ben nha," about a woman separated from her child and her lover by the war and an ocean.

"And tomorrow you leave me for the jungle." She said it unemotionally, without pain or bitterness showing through, but was the sudden pressure in her fingers a sign she felt some anger, some loss? How many men had she already lost to the war?

"It's only temporary, Thuy," he said, wondering if in fact he spoke the truth.

"And temporary is how long?" She began rubbing the sides of his neck but the feeling was more dreamlike than anything, and even as he tried to concentrate on the insides of her smooth thighs pressing against his hips, the only sensation he could really feel were her tired, jaded eyes staring at the back of his head, trying to probe his thoughts. Though she had never left Saigon, Thuy possessed a worldly sophistication that both frightened and sheltered David. In her face he saw the pain of a thousand bitter women, yet in the depths of her eyes he often found a reflection that could only be his own innocence.

"I will return when the mission has ended." He spent several minutes assembling the words to form the sentence—his mind wanted to picture the sweet, soothing sing-song words of the Vietnamese lyrics instead.

"And what is so important a young policeman of your inexperience must be snatched away from me?" Did he detect a mocking smile?

"You know I can't discuss my job."

"You've told me about the street fights. You've told me about the bodies floating down the Saigon River. You've told

90

me about Barney going dinky-dau, and you've told me over and over about the day your seven friends died. What could be so secret that you, an E2, could not tell me?" She laced the question with insult more than hurt.

"It concerns the VC. It is not a police matter, therefore it is better we don't discuss it."

"And you fear perhaps I am VC? Or I talk to the VC? Or maybe my brothers are VC and I would warn them about something?"

"You told me you have no family." David turned slightly to face her, a sly grin on his face, and she slapped him lightly, forced his head back down and began "massaging" his shoulders with stinging karate chops. "Hey, settle down."

"Maybe *I* am Viet Cong." She spoke the words like an icy threat. "Even now I could be pulling out my straight razor to rip out your throat."

"I'm not worried." He kept his eyes closed as the massage softened along with his sudden passion. "My MP friends would track you down and cut off your breasts." The statement came out dryly, meant as a joke, but she went on, challenged by his jest.

"Even now I could be wiring a grenade to the both of us— like the whore over on Thanh Mau last night who learned her GI was leaving for the stateside. She pulled the pin and held on to him until the explosion killed them both. I could be contemplating that."

"Don't compare yourself with some whore, Thuy."

"But what do you consider me, my dear David? A Vietnamese maiden, praying for her high school wedding? A cherry girl, cautiously guarding her virginity?" He could feel the smile below the moist eyes.

"You are my woman."

"I am a slut," she said softly, her strong fingers maintaining an uninterrupted rhythm.

"You are *my* slut," he replied, refusing to start up the old arguments again.

"I am a bad girl. I sell myself to survive."

"And that makes you a bad girl?"

"I am nothing but a whore, a toy for foreigners."

91

"With your knowledge of English you could easily get a job as a translator somewhere—the embassy, or some travel agency."

"I am a whore," she repeated, "a *lazy* whore."

"How can I remain optimistic if you insist on looking at yourself that way?"

"Just tell me one thing, David." Her hands fell to his sides and she leaned down on his back, resting her lips against his ear. "Do you plan to return to me?"

"Don't talk crazy." He tried to turn over, but she braced her elbows against his ribs, threatening to tickle him if he didn't remain still.

"Ly saw you at the Caravelle this afternoon. You were with a Vietnamese girl. You were not in uniform, yet you told me you were at work today." She paused, waiting for an excuse.

"Word travels fast."

"We sluts stick together." He could feel her smile, but he could also feel her heart racing.

"It was part of the job. It's called undercover work."

"Yes, undercover. I know the term. Ly says you had your hand between her legs. You are very dedicated to your duty."

"Ly doesn't miss much."

Thuy sat up on his buttocks and hit him in the back of the head with her fist, but she was weak with clashing emotions and it didn't hurt him. "You don't deny this?" Her voice raised for the first time.

"Circumstances created a touchy situation." He grasped for big words, hoping they would slow her down as she struggled to translate them in her mind. He could tell her anger was rising with her voice, and that meant she would soon be thinking in Vietnamese again.

"Don't bullshit me," she said as he turned onto his back beneath her. The tears were starting to slide down her high cheekbones, onto his chest.

"It is one of my faults." He forced a smile, hoping the contrast would halt the tears—he couldn't stand to see her cry. "Even when I am with you, Thuy. Even when I am walking down through the flower gardens of Nguyen Hue with you— the most beautiful woman in Saigon—I will see another girl

92

approaching us, and my eyes will lock on hers, and I will see myself in bed with her. Even though my hand is in yours, my lust is chasing the stranger walking toward us. I see in her long, black hair and dark exotic eyes a new adventure, a new conquest . . . new emotions, new love."

"A new hole," she snarled, sounding almost as ugly as an American woman.

"I am sorry. It is an emotion I can't control. I tell you all this now because I care what you feel, what you think of me, and I want you to understand. *You* are the woman I love."

"Do not talk love to a whore you've known two lousy weeks!" she lashed out at him.

"In Saigon, love blossoms quickly. People do not have that much time."

"Talk to me of love after one year—not now," she whispered defiantly, leaning back to stretch as though she were getting bored. He watched her firm breasts jut out, the nipples still flat, unaroused. A year: her men always left on an annual basis.

"My weakness is raping beautiful women with my eyes," he admitted, "but I am faithful to you, Thuy. I will always come back to you." He pulled her back down slightly so that he could lick the edges of her nipples with his tongue. They quickly grew taut then erect and he pulled her down further, forcing her lips roughly onto his.

After several seconds she pulled away and laid the side of her face on his chest as she held onto him tightly. "Do you realize how many men have sweet-talked me into their hearts," she finally asked, "only to leave me later?"

"I will be back, Thuy. I promise."

"Can you imagine the thousands of promises my men have broken?"

"What can you do except trust me?" he answered, surprised at the sudden cracking in his own voice.

"If you don't come back soon, someone else will warm this bed. I have to survive," she said sadly, in a businesslike tone.

"There are three hundred dollars MPC in the same drawer you keep your scarf and picture album. There is also one of the gold coins my brother left me—now I leave it with you, for

93

'insurance': surely enough to support you like a queen for the next year." Thuy sat up again, surprised. She gazed over at the dresser, then looked back down at him in mild shock. "Wait for me," he said, "I do not wish to come home from the jungle and find another man in my bed."

Before she could answer, he forced her legs farther apart and plunged himself deep inside her. Her reply became a throaty gasp, and the room's darkness soon filled with the sound of her soul moaning in relief and ecstasy.

Seven blocks away, Pvt. Leroy Crowe allowed the woman to lead him up the dark stairwell. Her slender fingers, clasped tightly around his own, betrayed no hint of hostility, but he rested his free hand on the .38 in his belt nevertheless.

The stairwell was steep and dimly lit at the top by a single flickering blue fluorescent light, but with the beams from headlights down in the street below his eyes could follow along the smooth line of her firm thighs all the way up her dress. He still marvelled at the way these Asian women possessed such soft, hairless legs, and how the prostitutes often wore nothing beneath the miniskirts. With each step, he strained to see more as she climbed above him, until the curve of her bare haunches peeked down at him briefly then disappeared in the shadows again. A chuckle escaped him as he realized his efforts were a waste of time. Soon enough she'd be on the bed, completely stripped down for his pleasure, and there'd be little need for juvenile antics.

"What you laugh at, GI Joe?" Her high, birdlike voice was soiled beyond rescue by the offensive pidgin English.

Leroy didn't answer, remaining totally silent as she reached the third flight and inserted her tiny key in the padlock. He let her enter first, then brushed past, into the dark buffet, revolver drawn.

The bargirl giggled at the sight of him acting so cautious. "You think cowboy hide inside my closet, under my bed? Steal your money?"

Finding the room empty, Crowe holstered his weapon and closed the door against the night, hastily bolting it from inside. He pulled a small money roll from his sock and laid out five hundred piasters on the crimson-colored satin sheets.

The girl frowned as she stared down at the Vietnamese currency and rested her hands on her hips. "I am not worth more than one U.S. dollar?" she asked, embarrassment in her eyes. Crowe, short for an American, still towered over her dainty frame. His eyes fell to the healthy swell of her chest and he reconsidered, thinking back to the tight haunches he had seen climbing the steps. He laid another bill on the bed, trying to keep his memories on her muscular thighs, but his mind was racing back to a burning tenement weeks earlier and he was seeing a different Vietnamese woman, plunging over a fifth-floor stairwell railing to the concrete at his feet. He was beside Sergeant Stryker, and they were both staring down at her crumpled, broken form, ignoring the helpless, pleading eyes and concentrating instead on the long, sleek legs spread out in front of them, her ripe haunches propped up and inviting, despite the fractures and splattered blood.

"What you wait for, GI Joe?" The toy doll standing before him was speaking like a real woman, yet the sing-song voice was plastic, unreal, a fantasy. Leroy shook the flashback from his eyes and found that the bargirl had already unzipped her skirt and allowed it to fall to the floor. Was unfastening the halter top. Now it was free, tossed over a bedpost, her breasts springing out at him.

She laid a beach towel out on the cool sheets, as if to protect them from what was to come, and then she sat down on the edge of the bed and licked her lips with her tongue. The effect was truly sensuous, stimulating, but still lacked something and Leroy could not decide what was missing. "You like massage, Joe?" She smiled up at him, motioning with her fingers for him to join her on the bed.

"I like blowjob," he answered in a no-nonsense tone, unzipping his jeans, and the smile instantly faded from the girl's petite face.

"No suck nothing," she said with a determined, unyielding voice. "Numba ten!"

"Oh, no no no, honey," Leroy sat down on the bed beside her, sliding his jeans off onto the skirt on the floor. "Number one! Definitely number one! You like, for sure!"

"No!" The bargirl shook her head furiously. "No good!

95

Buddha dwell in head! Bad luck to lower head that way!"

Leroy reached down and pulled another five-hundred-p note from a pocket and placed it on the dark triangle between her legs.

"No!" she repeated, finality ringing with the refusal.

"How much?" he asked, fatigue clouding his eyes.

"Ten dollars!" she snapped, deciding without hesitation, and Leroy erupted into laughter, grabbed her by the long, silky hair and rammed her face down onto his crotch.

At first she resisted, but he easily forced her jaws apart and soon her mouth was stretched tight, stuffed to the throat, and as she started to gag he eased off, thinking for some reason about the legendary wench Stryker had told him about. She had this bad habit of bedding GIs down, then tearing off their erections with her teeth. Naw, that one couldn't be true.

Over the sobs, she was soon cooperating, allowing his calloused hands to slowly force her head up and down, endlessly, until she was dizzy and nauseous. And then it was over.

He threw her off, over against the wall, and she lay there panting for several minutes, out of breath, her hair and body lined with perspiration and fear, the semen drooling out the corner of her mouth onto the satin pillow.

Leroy started laughing softly after a siren, racing past in the street below, broke the tense silence in the room, and he reached over and slapped her on the buttocks. "Good job, my dear, good job," he muttered sarcastically. "Thank Buddha for you and your magic mouth!"

Still lying face down, unmoving, the girl forced out a trembling hand, palm up, and demanded in a shaky, cracking voice, "Ten dollars."

He jumped onto her back savagely, like a jungle beast leaping onto its prey, the rage exploding through his body as he mounted her from behind.

The neighbors ignored her screams—it was a common enough sound in that neighorhood after dark—and no one bothered to look out their windows after he shot her between the wild, petrified eyes and dumped her body down the stairwell, into the filthy gutter below.

8. MONSOON MEMORIES

Splinter Village, outside The School, Ft. Gordon, Georgia

"I'm getting tired of standing on that fucking box in the middle of an intersection waving traffic on!" complained MP recruit Jack Zriny as he rubbed his sore arms. "I feel like the whole world just keeps passing me by."

"Real original," laughed Smallwood.

"Aw, man! We got Riot Control again tomorrow," griped Todd, thumbing through the schedule.

"You gotta learn to direct traffic," the platoon guide told Zriny. "That's an important phase of being an MP."

"Aw, stick it!" the whole squad chimed in unison and Valters released a huge bubble of disrespectful gas as he attempted to spit shine his boots. He had spilled battery acid on them during traffic accident investigation class.

Sergeant Flowers skipped into the room, a broad smile on his dark face. "Load up, men!" he announced, "we're movin' out!"

"But we just got in from Bivouac!" complained Bobby Ray. "Aw, come on, Sarge! Give us a break."

"A platoon in Bravo Company just got shipped off to the riots in Germany," he said, smiling. "We're moving back into Brems Barracks!"

"Aw, Sarge," the men all groaned, proud of the dead WWII barracks they had brought back to life.

"I thought you clowns would be eager to get outta Splinter Village," he said, dropping the smile.

97

"But we worked so hard on this place, Sarge," Uhernik frowned.

"Drop, slick!" he yelled at the private. "Knock me out fifty! No, *all* you crybabies drop! Knock me out a hundred! This ain't a fucking summer camp! Knock me out *two* hundred, then move out!"

Brems Barracks.

Named for Patrick J. Brems, a military policeman who had been gunned down in Vietnam.

After they dragged all their gear back to the new complex, the DIs surprised all the men by allowing them a full twelve hours sleep, something unheard of at The School.

Then it was back to more classes.

Search & Apprehension, more hand-to-hand self-defense, detecting false IDs, traffic tickets and violators, more route recon and map reading, and of course, the "observation, description and identification of suspected criminal elements." Really, that's how the classes were titled. Uncle Sam would have it no other way.

During the second half of the academy, the recruits were sent through a mock court-martial, complete with a real judge and courtroom. Zriny and Uhernik combined talents to present evidence in an "assault on an MP" case. They lost.

"Your testimony was not convincing," the judge later told them.

"What were we to do?" they complained to a drill sergeant outside the courtroom. "Practice perjury?"

But the DI only laughed and shook his head, muttering, "You'll learn . . . in time," as he walked off down the hallway.

"Forms, forms and more forms!" griped Valters as he skimmed the week's study material. "If I knew police work invovled so much paper work I'd have become a damn tank driver or something."

"It takes computers to run tanks these days," commented Todd.

"I put in for tanks," Bobby Ray recalled. "Originally. I was too young to get into the MP academy, but I lucked out—at

98

least I think I lucked out. Anyway, they lowered the minimum age for MPs to eighteen while I was in my last few weeks of basic."

"I didn't want to be an MP," reflected Cargill, who had wandered in from the First Platoon barracks, "but us draftees never have any choice what we want to be. I wanted to get into radar, but no two-year man has access to those grapes."

"Aw, you'd just get out and go back home to be one of those goofy weather forecasters," Uhernik muttered.

"Yeah, they all wanna be side show comedians," commented Todd. "Fuckin' flakes."

"Someday I'm gonna be provost marshal," declared a grinning, confident Private Valters.

"All the way to the top, huh?" laughed Bobby Ray.

"You bet!" he replied. "This boy's gonna have stars on his shoulders."

"I was hoping for Green Beret," mused Smallwood, leafing through an adventure magazine. "That's why I chose Georgia. But they decided I was too skinny, and they stuck me in the MPs."

"Makes sense," said Bobby Ray. "Stick all the skinny guys like us in the MPs so they can go to the bar fights and get their asses kicked."

"Green Berets?" laughed Barry Todd. "Why would you want to go jumping out of perfectly good airplanes?"

"Airborne!" screamed Valters, leaping off his bunk to the ground. He threw a karate kick at a trash can, knocking it across the room and sending the lid bouncing out the open door. "Gung ho! Hardcore!"

"What about you, Todd?" Uhernik asked. "What do you want out of Today's Army?"

"He's gonna box himself to the top!" Valters raised a fist.

"I'm not sure what I want out of the Green Machine," admitted Barry. "Maybe I could get back into boxing and work my way up to something too."

"Armed forces ring champ!" suggested Zriny.

"Yeah, that could get me into the Olympics, maybe," agreed Barry, shaking his head but not taking all the talk really seriously.

"Why think so small?" said a smiling Bobby Ray. "You could take that loudmouth Clay, easy!"

"Champion of the world!" declared Valters, raising Barry's clenched fist into the air. The stocky man with the short, brown hair and the flat nose grinned awkwardly and the entire barracks cheered.

As Nick Uhernik watched the guys carry on, he thought back to the friends he had made in boot camp, back in California, and wondered how they were faring. They had become so close in such a short time, yet they hadn't even exchanged home addresses. He had even forgot where most of them would be going after Fort Ord. Perhaps it was just the mind's subconscious way of erecting a mental block against returning memories better left buried.

He found himself wandering through the mist back to Splinter Village one evening after their chow break. The place seemed so empty, almost haunted, at the lack of occupants. He walked back into his old barracks—it seemed to lean out from the fog at him as he arrived, as if in greeting—and sat down on the dusty rear steps. He started a letter to his parents back in Saigon, but was interrupted by a squadron of helicopters landing in the distance: troops on maneuvers, not yet the real thing. He usually came back to Splinter Village in search of some precious solitude from the other men and the noisy hustle and bustle that was Brems Barracks. This place had always been so peaceful.

Nick wrote about the training, the abrupt change in climate, the vast differences between his new American and his old Vietnamese friends. The letter was dry, impersonal, overly modest. He rewrote it twice to make sure there was no hint of suffering, hardship or homesickness. He didn't want his mother worrying needlessly.

He didn't worry about his father, who had served in the Korean War and knew his son would fulfill the family tradition of having at least one man from each generation soldier overseas. Boot camp and AIT would be the easy part. The bullets weren't real, and if they were, they were fired well above your helmet, intended more to scare than to kill you.

He sealed the letter and set it aside, then brought out the

photos of Angi. For the first time in his life he was feeling a pain in his heart at being separated from her so long. It was an emotion he had never felt for anyone else before—a strange, helpless torture that actually wrenched at his gut and made his chest ache right where his heart was. Heartache.

His heart actually ached. Was this the pain poets wrote about so often?

Another storm was rolling into Fort Gordon, and he rushed back into the old building just in time to miss a sheet of hail, and the thunder and lightning that always followed. He looked down at the pictures of Angi, recalling the skill with which she could make her dark eyes appear so sad over the smallest disagreement. The wind lashed out at the old building, and a finger of it slipped through the cracked windowpane, nearly tearing one of the wallet photos from his hand. The storm picked up, its gusts laughing at him with mournful cries that reminded him of the way the monsoons rolled into Saigon, lacing the city with heavy blankets of rolling mist and blinding downpours.

The humidity in the Georgia air made him see the warm, sticky nights they walked down the busy boulevards after watching Chinese war epics at the Le Loi cinema. He could see her face clearly now—over the last few weeks he had had trouble imagining the shape and contours of it, but he blamed that on the intense training and mental fatigue—and for the first time since leaving Saigon he suffered an empty hollowness that could only be homesickness.

It was also the first day since leaving Vietnam that he failed to write a letter back home to her, but the guilt he expected to flood over him vanished with the storm.

He watched the last big drops splash against the dirty, neglected windows, then found himself walking back to Brems Barracks in the drizzle.

9. DEATH WORE A CAMOUFLAGE CAPE

Ten kilometers west of Loi Tan hamlet

Pvt. David Schramm fought back the uncontrollable spasms of laughter that still racked his slender body, grabbing at his ribs and belly like invisible, tickling fingers, with only the slightest warning. He concentrated on the vibrations of the gunship's metal skin as the chopper skimmed low over the matted treetops, and tried to think about something serious: a Negro raping his crippled sister, an H-bomb falling on his home town—anything grim to keep the fits of laughter from returning. The helicopter crew was getting just a little bit peeved at his disturbing outbursts. They had already threatened to toss him out the side door twice if he didn't quiet down, and now he could feel another chuckle rising in his gut.

It was just that he had never seen one of the notorious Airmobil gunships in action before: strafing two *sampans* down on the lazy, winding river below . . . with cinder blocks!

The chopper dropped through a few more layers of the constantly shifting, hot, sticky air blanketing the jungle, and the lush green canopy's topmost branches snatched out like great, gnarled fingers, hoping to snag the huge bird's shiny skids at any moment. The sight of those "fingers" started him giggling again.

"Kick that dipshit out the window!" the co-pilot snarled back good-naturedly. The doorgunner added, "Out into the wild blue yonder," but so soft the men up front could only try to read his lips above the grinding whir of the rotors above.

Crowe was giving Dave an icy you-better-shut-the-fuck-up-or-they're-gonna-toss-us-both-out frown, but the private just couldn't get over the incident he had witnessed a few minutes earlier.

They had been following the Song Dong Na River south from their base camp at Nhon Co when the pilot, a twenty-nine-year-old warrant officer with two years in-country, first spotted the two narrow boats. "Yep, VC ching ching," the co-pilot had agreed as they caught the Vietnamese onboard heading for the cover of overhanging foliage at the first sound of the helicopter.

But it was too easy a kill to just zap them with a lightning spray of 7.62 tracers, though it was always great sport to watch the thatched covers over the center of *sampans* light up after the burning bullets burrowed deep into the dried palm fronds, sliced clean through anyone hiding inside, then sent bubble-laced tunnels out through the bottoms as they zigzagged toward the floor of the riverbed.

Yes, over the years, the First Cavalry grunts had found a more challenging way to bombard the scurrying *sampans.* Cinder blocks. And sometimes mere bricks, if no cement blocks could be found or the already maximum payload prohibited more weight.

Schramm would never forget how the doorgunner, a mellow enough man named Nelson, had remained silent behind his huge M-60 MG the entire trip, until the crew had spotted the dark, wooden boats. A grin suddenly creasing his features, the spec. 4 had hoisted the twenty-pound blocks from under the flak jacket he was sitting on, then peered dangerously out the side hatch, exposing the upper half of his torso to groundfire.

Satisfied he was not bombarding an innocent group of terrified fishermen (he had spotted the blue, red and gold VC flag long before the dinks had the presence of mind to pull it down their makeshift flagpole), Nelson carefully gauged their elevation above the Song Dong Na then, after anticipating the distance it would take for the cinder block to travel from the chopper to the water's surface, estimating their craft's speed, and crossing the fingers on his left hand into an obscene gesture, he delicately dropped the block of cement out

103

the hatch.

It missed by several yards, kerplunking into the swift water with a muffled splash that sent a forty-foot geyser of spray across both *sampans'* bows.

"What a sorry-ass wimp!" The pilot turned back and flipped Nelson the bird after the crew surveyed the near miss.

The co-pilot on his right also offered a retort to the doorgunner's performance, turning away from the controls as the craft raced dangerously close to the treeline. "Oughta deck your nearsighted ass a week's pay, Candy-Randy! Such a waste of ammo!"

Nelson grabbed up two cinder blocks this time, struggling to maintain his balance as the pilot banked sharply to the left, missing a line of leaning palms by scant inches as he swung the chopper around.

The doorgunner, held into the craft by a single bandolier tied to his web belt, perched himself on the edge of the doorwell as the gunship's nose dropped several meters and the green bird dove back down at the snakelike river.

"Hey, that's cheating!" one of the soldiers strapped in next to Schramm called out, but Nelson ignored him, tossing both blocks down at the same time.

The first projectile impacted between both boats, unleashing a monstrous wave that nearly capsized them, and the second crashed through the roof of the smaller craft, sending pieces of bark and splintered bone skyward in the bloody spray that exploded with the secondary splash.

"Well, I'll be a son of a . . . you got a Charlie Cong hiding inside!" The co-pilot slapped his hands together as they all watched the *sampan* halt in the center of the expanding ripples, oblivious to the wild current rushing by on either side. The bow of the craft began to slowly twirl around as the swash-turned-crater quickly refilled itself with swirling water, and in seconds the boat sank beneath the crimson waves.

"But you missed one!" Schramm's observation, made without thinking and meaning no insult, nevertheless wiped the satisfied grin from Nelson's face. The doorgunner grabbed the private by the front of his jungle fatigues and pulled him across the belly of the gunship until he landed on his knees against the last cinder block.

"OK, William Tell!" Nelson challenged the newbie as he folded his arms across his chest confidently. "Take your eagle eye and let's see you beat them apples!"

Schramm followed the man's pointed finger down to where the *sampan* had sunk, then swallowed hard as he looked back at Crowe. The fellow undercover cop just threw him a you-got-yourself-ass-deep-into-this-mess, get-yourself-out frown and leaned his head back against the vibrating metal skin, feeling for the bullet-hole rims that would massage his stiff neck—Leroy wasn't used to humping so much field gear.

"So here's one for Thuy," Dave groaned as he heaved the block down at the boat racing frantically for the tree cover along the banks.

"Beginner's luck," muttered Nelson as the chunk of cement crashed into the sturdy bow of the *sampan* and flipped it end over end out of the water, throwing the two occupants into the murky current.

"Now *that's* what I call job satisfaction!" Schramm turned and smiled back at Leroy after the gunship circled around for a final pass and the private was encouraged to finish off the panic-stricken swimmers with the big machine gun balanced precariously out the open side hatch.

Crowe's eyes watched the heavy lead pouring out the M 60's glowing muzzle. He watched the rounds rain down across the Song Dong Na—first slicing neat, parallel "railroad tracks" through the waves, then smashing into the meaty shoulders of both guerrillas. Both swimmers' backs caved in, then tore in half under the barrage, a bloody froth exploding forth as their backbones disintegrated beneath the unyielding bullets. Crowe's eyes were watching the arms and legs of one swimmer snap free and fly several yards from the torso as Schramm brought the barrel back into a second crisscrossing pattern he knew would finish off the black-pajama-clad commies.

The undercover MP, still strapped in against the trembling skin of the gunship, watched silently as the limbs, bloody and severed at the joints, spun around slowly as they drifted along with the current, but Leroy's mind was seeing a Saigon bargirl bounce unceremoniously down a filthy tenement stairwell, her

105

wrist still twitching slightly after the body came to rest in the gutter.

He bent forward slightly now, trying to watch the mutilated arm sink beneath the surface of the river as the chopper pilot took his craft back above the treeline and headed again for the mission's original destination. Crowe thought back to how he stood at the top of the stairs, hoping the woman would not look back up at him one last time, remembering the relief he felt when she didn't.

A few random sniper shots sang up at the gunship through the trees, and as the craft veered to the left sharply, its port side suddenly becoming its belly, Crowe's eyes took in the orange orb of the flat sun and the castlelike clouds threatening to swallow up his world, but his mind kept watching the bargirl at the bottom of the stairs. He would never forget how beautiful, how sensuous she looked, even in death—lying there, face-down in that sleazy, back alley gutter.

David Schramm held onto his helmet as the gunship swooped in on the firefight already in progress. Because of the time spent taking out the *sampans*, they had fallen back behind the rest of the squadron, and the first choppers down had encountered intense sniper fire from the treetops to the west.

Schramm's adrenalin was still flowing through his veins at high speed from the episode with the *sampans* when the first green tracers slammed through the helicopter's aft wall. Now, as the sizzling bullets peppered the space around him like bright, smoking lasers, he was sure the heart pounding to be free of his chest would explode.

"Incoming," the pilot muttered without emotion into his headphone as the gunship bounced across the landing zone and the VC mortars began walking up through the elephant grass toward them, bursting with fierce little fireballs that mushroomed out across the land then swirled away—like children being chased—as successive rounds impacted in their wake.

"Out! Out! Out!" Nelson was yelling at the two cherry replacements as he kept his machine gun spewing out its fury against the angry treeline. "Out!" he ordered the last of the

106

grunts as he jerked the big gun from side to side on its greased swivel, and Crowe struggled with the straps holding him back, remembering instantly the time he had chased the soldier in the stolen jeep for fifteen miles, only to be unable to release the seatbelt after the suspect stacked it up and fled the crash scene on foot—Leroy had been so excited that his shaking fingers could not operate the simple strap latch, and the jeep thief had gained a considerable lead on the rookie MP. He had captured the man in the end, after the punk ran down a dead-end alley and was too yellow to fight his way out, but now he was confronting tracer bullets that killed indiscriminately. And hot lead did not back down.

When two rounds bounced off the ammo cans at his feet and ricocheted about the cabin, he broke free—spurred on by the increase in activity in front of his face—and charged out through the doorway, landing on Schramm's back as both men stumbled into their first real battle with hostile forces.

"Motherfuck!" the complaint escaped the MP on the bottom like an accidental belch, and Nelson was immediately helping both men to their feet. He had jumped off the craft with the heavy M-60 cradled in his right arm, the last man in the squad out through the shaking hatch. Crowe thought it strange, at that moment, that the doorgunner would abandon his post just to aid two newbies—the private had not seen both pilots in the cramped cockpit sustain fatal chest wounds only seconds earlier. Moments later, a carefully placed shoulder-launched rocket would pierce that same cabin, separating the helicopter into two halves in a crackling sheet of flame that would rain down on several of the men. At the same time the craft's engine shaft would collapse, sending broken rotor blades slicing through the gun smoke, instantly killing a half dozen more.

Schramm watched the decapitated head roll past him in the mist. The ghastly sight propelled him even faster toward the gulley most of the soldiers were securing. It would not be the memory of the swollen, quivering tongue that would stay with him the rest of the day, but the startled, still-blinking eyes. Round eyes. American eyes. Blue eyes of a fellow soldier he had been joking with only minutes before the abrupt landing had deposited them all in living hell.

"Come on, damnit!" Crowe was tugging at his elbow, pulling him along with the flow of green uniforms, firing his rifle on full automatic from the hip.

Schramm tore his eyes from the battered head—it was now lying face-down in the muck, unmoving—and soon he was imitating his partner, spraying the treeline with his M-16, unsure if the snipers were squatting behind the short, thick mahogany stumps or perched high in the lithe, swaying bamboo.

A willy-peter shell exploded between the Americans and the edge of the jungle they were advancing on, sending bright, graceful arcs of sizzling white phosphorous showering down on the platoon. Schramm and Crowe both dove for the dikelike wall of earth that leaned out over the gulley and reinforced several interlocking blue-and-green-shaded rice paddies. The treeline was a hundred meters distant, and the paddies, most of them dried out and neglected for years, provided a slight buffer against an all-out sweep by the VC. At the least, it would be difficult, costing them precious time and manpower.

Schramm glanced over his right shoulder, saw the white phosphorous fall across three soldiers like a blanket of acid and felt the rest of their squad slam against the hillside on his left.

Crowe was really getting into it: popping up every few seconds, letting loose with a five-to-ten-round burst from his rifle, ducking, jumping back up, ducking again just in time, ejecting spent magazines, ramming fresh clips back into the bottom of the rifle, staggering his reactions now so the Cong couldn't second guess him and hand him his head.

"Lousy Moast the Ghost gonna account for this one," Nelson muttered out loud, promising himself the privilege of punishing the fool that had lead them into another hopeless situation. "Gonna cram my MG up his ass sideways. Gonna make it hurt! Gonna twist and shout, 'You done fucked up *again*, Mr. Moast!'" Nelson had lapsed into a jive accent, his voice rising with his anger, the tone changing to imitate Johnny Cash when the singer performed to a San Quentin prison audience and yelled, "You gonna die!" at the Boy Named Sue's father.

Nelson jumped up just then, planning to fire another belt of rounds at his enemy, but a single bullet from an AK high in the trees spun him around and slammed him back down in the grass.

"Oh yeeeeeeeeeesss!" Nelson was now mimicking a black gospel preacher as he sat up and fingered the smoking hole in his flak jacket. "Ole Moast the Ghost gonna *die* over this one! And yours truly, Candy-Randy gonna be suddenly ten grander richer!"

Nelson turned to face the eight soldiers who were already staring at him with calm, expressionless eyes. Even Crowe, half his ammo already exhausted, was now leaning against the earthen bank on his haunches, content to let the first phase of the battle run its course. Nobody cared to antagonize the VC tree apes any more than was necessary. They all knew—and Crowe and Schramm were learning—that all that was required now was to sit tight against the dike; let ole Mr. Charlie have his fun. He'd soon tire of his shooting gallery, or run out of rounds, or lose his guts and flee into the jungle and disappear into his tunnels, well aware a flock of Cobra gunships would soon race to the rescue. He'd have to beat feet and retreat if he didn't want a set of helicopter skids rammed up his ass.

Of course there was always the possibility they had been ambushed by some hard-core North Vietnamese regulars. Now they'd be bright enough to guess *these* were the only choppers flying the province that particular day. But then again, despite the storms clashing about on the horizon, and the mist creeping along the jungle floor, the weather was not all that bad. And that meant the possibility of the dreaded Phantom jets. Jumping out of the path of rolling napalm was definitely no party.

This latest mission deep into the heart of a traditional guerrilla sanctuary was the result of Captain Moast learning that the renegades who had looted the village of An Linh had been seen in the area in the last twelve hours. Therefore it was only fair that Moast the Ghost take his legion of deathships into hostile territory despite warnings the NVA battalions were massing in the area and rumors of an underground VC base camp in an intricate tunnel complex deep beneath Loi Tan.

"What you bums waitin' for?" Captain Moast himself came

109

charging over the hill behind Nelson's squad. The officer, followed by four troopers from his own helicopter, dove into the dirt wall beside Crowe and with one clean, smooth motion heaved a hand grenade out at the treeline. A sharp, cracking explosion along with twigs and dirt clods bounced back at them and an unearthly scream pierced the staccato rattle of gunfire from both sides then died abruptly.

"What's the goddamn holdup?" Moast repeated, slamming an open palm against Crowe's shoulder as though he expected the private to stand up and charge the treeline, ignoring the hail of lead that would eventually cut him down.

"We're already low on ammo!" Randy Nelson yelled over at the captain with anger in his tone and hatred burning the edges of his eyes. "This was supposed to be a fuckin' humanitarian mission to rescue some cunts from a two-bit bandito, yet you set us down in the middle of a lead-laced shit storm with eight lousy gunships! There must be ten thousand dinks out there, Moast!"

"Hey, so we lucked out and located Charlie in our back yard!" Moast grinned almost insanely. "Instead!"

Crowe and Schramm both eyed each other briefly, anticipating Nelson's next action, sure he was about to slice the officer in half with the M-60 at any moment. Neither MP relished the thought of trying to prevent such a murder, or trying to arrest the doorgunner with the huge MG afterwards. Their only concern at that second was survival. Living through what the enemy would throw at them until the Phantoms could swoop in and save them.

"Come on! I'll show you how it's done!" Moast, to the amazement of every man cowering alongside that dikewall, jumped to his feet and started up the steep slope.

Two rounds immediately caught his flak jacket in the chest, catapulting him end over end back down to the ground, where he landed on his back with a painful thud.

Crowe and Schramm did not move. Both men held their helmets down and froze while several mortars rained down on their position and two of the privates from the captain's chopper ran over to his side. Crowe's eyes slowly followed every move the grunts made: cautiously going down on one

110

knee on either side of their commander, shielding him from shrapnel that was no longer flying, lifting the dazed officer up to his knees then dragging him back over to the cover of the dike. Crowe made a mental note of the two men's name tags. They were now eliminated from the list of potential suspects in the bounty case.

Schramm's eyes were still tightly closed as the infantrymen dropped Captain Moast beside him, but his fingers were busy picking the tiny, burning pieces of shrapnel out of his scalp. His hair seemed to be lined with them, even with the helmet on, and several small rivulets of blood were beginning to trickle down his face and neck.

Schramm ran his thumb and forefinger together when he first felt the liquid oozing from beneath the pieces of metal. He knew it would be blood, had been taught at The School that scalp wounds bled a lot but were seldom serious—the superficial wounds anyway. Another solitary mortar round crashed in less than thirty yards from their position, and the shock wave bounced his eyeballs around in their sockets and popped open the lids. He found himself staring straight into the dazed eyes of Moast, his ashen face looking more ghostly than the legend surrounding him.

Schramm recoiled slightly at first, unprepared for such an encounter, even in the field, where the officers were known to sometimes share foxholes with their enlisted men. But then Schramm realized the officer's eyes were not staring back at him—merely gazing out at some other world, some other place only Moast the Ghost could see. Schramm's own eyes fell briefly to the man's chest, searching for wounds, but it looked as though the thick, fiberglas flak jacket had deflected the rounds and allowed only a painful set of bruises where the bullets had struck. A deep gash across the officer's forearm was refusing to shed much blood, and after finding no other obvious wounds, the private's eyes were drawn back to the captain's grim, stress-lined face. A long cut above his left eye, right at the scalp line, had spilled a layer of crimson across his brow and cheek, yet now the wound—probably caused by the same shrapnel Schramm was finding in his own hair—was magically clotting despite the heat and humidity, and the flow

111

of blood had ceased.

Schramm ignored the heavy, excited breathing of the men tensed around him, ignored the moaning of another private yards away who had caught a large chunk of white-hot shrapnel in the groin, ignored the incoming bullets and shells that seemed to be increasing by the minute. Instead he studied the eerie pools of thought swirling about in the depths of the captain's jungle-green eyes.

It was like Schramm was watching a flickering, poorly filmed home movie of the morning he and Crowe had first reported for duty with the First Cav. Moast always made a point of it to greet new incoming soldiers, especially newbie replacements brought in to recoup the unit's heavy casualty losses. Schramm would never forget how they had been choppered in to the base camp at Nhon Co on a Jolly Green Giant chinook with four other privates.

Moast, his jungle boots spit-shined and perfectly bloused below freshly creased trousers, had rushed up to them with long, businesslike strides and offered a welcoming handshake, his face a warm, fatherly ear-to-ear smile.

Schramm would remember till the day he died how he reached out and grasped the captain's hand tightly—after all, first impressions and that show of inner strength and confidence were all important—shook it heartily . . . and the captain's entire arm seemed to come off before his eyes!

Schramm's jaw had nearly dropped to the red clay as he stumbled back from the screaming officer, the mutilated arm still going up and down slowly as he continued to shake it, but becoming heavier now, colder, lifeless as he realized the puffy fingers clutching his own belonged to a dismembered Viet Cong arm.

Captain Moast, his own arm tied behind his back to give the appearance the private had wrenched the limb off, was rolling around on the ground, still yelling, "What a handshake! What a powerful fuckin' handshake! Man of iron, man of steel! Gonna put that superman out on point tonight! Gonna stick him out on perimeter and let him shake hands with Mr. Charlie! Gonna let him stick that powerful claw of his through the wire tonight and latch onto the bad bad VC! What yo' name, boy? You gonna get me a damn high body count this week, yes you are! What yo' name, soldier?"

Dozens of grubby, hardened combat vets, fresh from the jungle, lined the outskirts of the landing pad, and most of them erupted into wild laughter and applause when Schramm first jerked the arm loose, torn tendons and bloody ribbons of muscle still hanging from the end of it. Schramm's face flushed as red as the clay at his feet and a tide of anger and embarrassment welled up inside him until the nausea threatened to make him pass out, but then he caught the gleam in Moast's eye.

The captain was still sliding around in circles on the ground, refusing to end the practical joke until the private returned his all-forgiving grin: Schramm forgiving Moast for the dirty trick, and Moast forgiving Schramm for being a private.

Schramm had swallowed his pride and forced a smile, then walked over and handed the arm to Leroy, who promptly tossed it up into the invisible blades of the monstrous helicopter. A sudden spray of blood rained down on the new arrivals and veteran grunts alike, the chopper pilot began yelling obscenities down at Crowe, and a shocked, disgruntled infantryman raced out from the crowd, desperately searching for the arm he had so courageously liberated from its owner.

Later that same day Moast had taken the new men up in one of the Hueys for an aerial tour of the region. MACV had just dispatched another "attaboy" to his command for the sector's highest enemy body count, and that seemed to keep him in high spirits the entire afternoon—even to the point where he jokingly suggested Crowe, who had looked sullen and overly serious the entire day, take over the aircraft's controls for a little while; now that would surely chase the newbie private's scowl out the window. Crowe had been astonished an Airmobil captain would propose such a ridiculous idea—Leroy had no pilot training whatsoever, civilian or otherwise—but Schramm jumped at the opportunity, and soon the jungle was alive with a wild, droning creature, pouncing up and down out of sight between the palms, swooping low across terrified villages, diving down at stampeding water buffalo with short, jerking dips and plunging thrusts that, from a distance, made it look

113

like an enraged predator, serpent-winged—its black multieyed insectlike nose resembling a giant dragonfly's.

The extreme confidence the drill sergeants at The School had instilled in Schramm carried all the way over to Vietnam with him; he felt indestructible, like he could accomplish anything—was immortal. And surely capable of flying a simple whirlybird. Moast had carefully placed the private's steady, unshaking hands on the proper controls while they were still a thousand feet above the treetops, and within five minutes he had taken the craft down low and kissed the mist, flirting with Death and its hilltops, to the utter dismay of an angry, disheveled Leroy Crowe.

Schramm had repeatedly tried to land the Huey as he listened to that insane Moast's calm, almost robotlike instructions over his shoulder, but the closest he could come without destroying the craft was a bunny-hop maneuver through a rice paddy that sent half a dozen helmets sliding across the belly of the craft. . . .

"How's he doing, Private? Captain Moast—how's he doing?" A clay-caked lieutenant had crawled up to their position from one of the burning gunships, tearing Schramm's eyes and dreamlike fascination from the glassy, crystal-ball orbs of Moast the Ghost.

"I asked you, how's he doing?" the lieutenant repeated, but there was so much lead still flying and a constant roar of discharges and explosions that Schramm could only concentrate on the officer's face below the twig-lined mustache, squinting uncertainly as he tried to focus on the angry mouth and read the lips.

"He'll make it." Schramm could feel his own face stretching to form the words, knew what his reply had been even if he couldn't hear his own thoughts above the din of battle. "He's just stunned."

"Good. What about yourself, soldier?" The officer stared at Schramm but did not really let their eyes meet, and before the private could answer, a pancake-sized slab of shrapnel tore into the lieutenant's nose and mouth, ripping his face off and over the ruptured eye sockets like a great, invisible hand snatching the rubber mask off someone at a costume party. Schramm felt

114

the bile rising in his throat as the headless body remained on its hands and knees for a moment more, then flopped to the ground, twitching wildly in the blood-soaked clay.

"Let's go men! Let's get them yellow bastards!" One of the privates who had first accompanied Moast was now starting up the hillside to the top of the dike, not bothering to look back to make sure his confidence had rallied his comrades.

As if in reply, the blue sky above the soldier turned black with smoke and his entire world came alive with the deafening screams of turbojet engines as the fighter planes swooped low over the battlefield, unleashing their payload of deadly napalm.

Schramm caught the look of disbelief and terror on the soldier's face as he reached the top of the dike—and was swept off his feet by the flood of liquid fire. Crowe dove onto his partner just then, shielding him from the waterfall of napalm that cascaded down like gold jelly over the top of the dike, and both men knew without looking that the charred stump which fell across their backs was the charcoaled corpse of an infantryman who had kissed Mr. Death on the lips.

10. NIGHT OF NO MOON

Five klicks east of Vinh An, on the west banks of the Song Dong Na

Pvt. Leroy Crowe scratched at his right shoulder absent-mindedly, right where the First Cavalry Division combat patch just happened to be sewn on.

Naw, it couldn't be that infantry duty bothered him *that* much, so intensely, in fact, that, perhaps subconsciously, his shoulder missed the Eighteenth MP Brigade patch that *should* be there instead.

Another flare popped out into the black sky—the sergeant in charge of the perimeter guards was sending aloft two flares every ten minutes now to chase away the night.

"Ain't nothin' out there," Schramm whispered across their foxhole to him, but Crowe didn't answer, even after he detected the fear in his partner's voice. Instead, he just continued scratching at the patch, feeling gravely out of place on that plateau overlooking the Song Dong Na. Now and then he'd stretch up above the trenchline, trying to spot the sluggish river only twenty yards away, behind them. He'd try to locate the white flashes that were starlight reflecting in the ripples of current—the sight had almost a hypnotic effect on him, reminding him of the neon-lit flower festivals in the middle of Nguyen Hue street, back in the city.

Saigon. He thought he'd never miss her. Especially after the incident with the bargirl, and the haunting that seemed to follow him now. Vietnam. Land of so many war dead, so many wandering ghosts. He had assumed the boundless energy, the constant hum of activity, the electricity that was a city of three million exotics, would scare away any spirits that chased him; then he remembered how silent the capital fell after midnight curfew was clamped down across it, how quiet his empty room was in the wee hours of the morning—when he'd awake with a start from the nightmare, only to sit up and see *her* crumpled body staring at him from the corner shadows, her snarling face with its hollow, accusing eyes finally fading away with the first slivers of dawn.

A hand reached out from the dark and grabbed his arm, sending Crowe halfway out the foxhole, into the unknown.

"Hey, don't you agree?" It was Schramm, whispering harshly against the sound of another flare whooshing up toward the North Star. "It's just a fucking waste. Ain't a goddamn thing out there past the wire."

Crowe secreted himself back into his hole silently, refusing to answer, pulling his helmet and flak jacket in over him like a trap door, a spider retreating into its den.

"Nothin' but a bunch of snakes and gibbons and wild boars." Schramm paused to allow a comment from Leroy, but only a tired rasping emanated from the black corner he knew his partner to be huddled in. "And rain forest ghosts, wandering aimlessly through the bamboo," Dave added cryptically after a few seconds.

A tortured sigh filtered up through Leroy's "trap door," from his fortress of solitude below. Nothing more.

"Fuckin' snakes," Schramm repeated, slapping at the imaginary reptile he was positive just slithered across his feet. "This whole damn country's crawlin' with 'em. Ever hear of the Two-step viper, Leroy? Actually, it's known as a Bamboo Crete, but the GIs call it the Two-step viper. And you know why, Leroy? 'Cuz two steps after it gets ya, you're fuckin' dead!" Schramm struck out and pinched Crowe on the ankle, but his partner ignored him. Even the "Stick your viper up your ass" retort he expected from Leroy never came, and after some grunts a few foxholes over ordered him to quiet down, Schramm went back to watching the thick, muggy blackness move about in front of his eyes. He remained silent for a long time after that, even when the urge struck him to borrow

117

Leroy's survival knife to see if he could cut the ebony blanket before him like just so much shimmering jello—it was that thick!

Schramm settled back on his pile of sandbags and ignored the constantly shifting shadows out there, electing instead to try and count the stars overhead. There was no moon out tonight, making the brilliance even more radiant, and he searched for the Big Dipper, remembering painfully now how he had neglected his astronomy classes in high school and probably couldn't name a single constellation floating about out there. A shooting star fell boldly outside his field of vision—he barely caught sight of it out of the corner of his eye, and when he turned its way he noticed the dim, golden star that never twinkled, but seemed to move ever so slowly across the heavens, leaving the other pinpoints of light behind.

As he followed the satellite across space, Schramm thought back to Thuy, and how they often spent long hours out on her balcony, counting the falling stars. He'd never forget the disbelief on her face when she brought the moving light to his attention and he explained to her the star was man-made, a satellite launched from Florida by his fellow Americans.

She had been skeptical for days, until he brought her the *Time* magazine article from the PX newsstand. For all her sophistication and experience, Thuy had never heard of satellites—only of rockets that crashed down on Saigon now and then, making the nighttime with your lover a precious gamble. Clutching each other hours after curfew, when the first VC bombs went off, listening for that solitary missile that might land next door, or in the next neighborhood.

Thuy had studied the story silently for several minutes, and when David saw the first tear streak her face he half expected one of her laments on the hardships suffered by her people: all the poor, poverty-stricken, uneducated peasants his white fatboys had come ten thousand miles to "advise" on their civil war. Instead, she calmly traced her slender finger along the photograph of the launch pad in Florida and said, "How sad I come from people whose most important possession is their bicycle or their water buffalo. People who have lived their whole lives beyond the jungle—who have never seen Saigon,

118

or even a paved road. Yet your people have the power to own their own stars! How wonderful to come from such a land!

"Why do you come so far, to Vietnam, to fight in rice paddies, David?" she had asked him, genuinely puzzled.

He remembered his relief in her total innocence then. No sign of her words mocking his Americanism, his foreign adventure. The way she squatted on the balcony, ignoring the magazine now as she placed her chin in cupped fingers and gazed into his eyes, patiently, attentively awaiting his answer.

He had told her how he came to her country to use it merely as a stepping stone in furthering his law enforcement career. He was not political by nature, hadn't even investigated the makeup of her country's enemies, the philosophies of the guerrillas in the countryside, or the hang-ups of the college punks protesting in front of the White House. Those things did not interest him. Street violence did, and where else to battle snipers, terrorists and underworld gunmen at the tender age of eighteen but in the Pearl of the Orient, Saigon?

She had merely smiled when he outlined his honest, almost naive answer, ignoring the politics of it, or the lack of politics, completely, smiling at the subtle trace of evidence that she had latched on to such an idealistic, inexperienced cherry-boy. He'd never forget the almost defiant smile that replaced the frown below the tears when she rose easily to her feet after nearly an hour in the seemingly uncomfortable position, stretched the sinews in her firm, shapely thighs, then took him by the hand—led her young, durable lover back into the bedroom.

He wondered who she was with tonight, or if she was true to her word and sat alone on the teakwood floor of their bungalow, recounting the money he had left her, patiently awaiting his return from "his other mistress in that *jungle* out there."

Schramm shielded his right eye—the one he used for aiming—with his hand as the flare popped skyward and exploded well beyond the wire, taking several minutes to drift with its parachute along on the warm night breeze. He used his left eye to scan the rolling hills beyond the perimeter, but there were still no hordes of vicious Charlie Cong emerging from the

119

treeline at the edge of the jungle. After the flare bounced off a blackened tree stump and fizzled out, he reopened the right eye and could see in the night as if no flares had ever been launched. Now he closed his left eye so there'd be no contrasting shades of sight—the purple vision in the left eye was destroyed by the bright flare and would take several minutes to readjust.

As the reflections of the night of flares burned out in his retina, he thought back to the standoff that afternoon where the survivors of the platoon had been "saved" by the squadron of Phantoms and their napalm. His fingers still ached from the minor burns and blisters that had resulted when he snuffed out the jellylike liquid burning on Leroy's flak jacket. Most of the fiery tide that rolled out across the rice paddies at them had been forced back by the high dike walls, and only three Americans had been killed by their own planes. The VC had finally retreated after two dozen billowing fireballs took out over half their forces.

Captain Moast had gotten word the band of renegades who had looted the temple at An Linh and kidnapped the village chieftain's two daughters was sighted by one of the black bat SR-71 spy planes marching toward the Song Dong Na at a point five klicks north of Cau Ben Nom. And although his command had been nearly decimated by the enemy ambush, he ignored the obvious need for resupply and reinforcements. After the more seriously wounded troops were airlifted out by the unarmed slicks, Moast the Ghost force-marched his men after the bandits, refusing to glance one last time over at the smoldering ruins of the latest fleet of gunships he had lost on the ground.

At the edge of the battlefield they came across the three boys. Teen-agers actually, but all of them clutched what remained of their AK47 assault rifles in lifeless hands. Schramm held back the shudder that tore at his gut when one of the veteran grunts flopped over the youngest guerrilla and the Berkeley University T-shirt came to light. Some of the soldiers gathering around the trio of dead Cong were beginning to show the first signs of remorse until Moast went down on one knee and made a closer examination of the youth's black tire-tread Ho Chi Minh sandals.

"Yep," he said, "exact match. Don't you agree?"

One of the older enlisted men bent down to examine the tread pattern and nodded his head slowly. "Same bastard that zapped us north of Bu Tek Zong last week."

Moast looked up at Schramm and Crowe. "Been findin' this motherfucker's tracks after every ambush in this region. I'd guess he's responsible for killing ninety to a hundred white boys." Moast made the observation without hatred in his voice—more like he was a farmer tracking a wolf that had been killing off his defenseless cattle.

The remorse festering in his stomach left Schramm immediately.

Crowe had mysteriously produced a pocket camera just then, and several of the grunts took out their frustrations by taking snapshots of each other posing with their jungle boots poised dramatically on the ghoulish heads of the corpses. One soldier was innovative enought to stick his bayonet directly behind the body of one guerrilla, then pose leaning against the stock of the rifle so it appeared as if the sabre had been plunged deep into the communist's ribs. Moast would not stand for war atrocities, but that kind of good, clean fun was a boost for morale, and he was one hundred percent behind keeping a smile on his men's faces—even if those same men flipped him the bird the moment he turned his back.

"Where the hell'd you get that photo-taker?" Moast had cornered Crowe as the men lined up to have their moment of glory immortalized.

"Oh, my parents made me take it along, Cap."

"Made you?"

"Yes, sir, my pop insisted the 'Nam was a once in a lifetime opportunity. *My* war, if you will. He said I'd be nuts if I didn't keep a journal and take photos every now and then—for my grandchildren if nothing else."

"A journal." Moast's tone was of unmasked suspicion. "You mean like a diary?"

"Something like that, Captain."

"You ain't writin' a book about this unit, are you, son? I mean, you aren't recording what you see here, are you?"

Crowe tried not to reveal he was going on the defensive, but answered in a bored, unconcerned tone, "Naw, I said it was a suggestion, sir. I have enough trouble keeping track of my meal card as it is."

"Just don't wanna see none of my men takin' notes, that's all," the captain muttered under his breath, more to himself than anybody.

"Hey, check this out." One of the grunts had located a stiff-backed wallet-sized portrait photo in the dead youngster's calico pack.

"Awful morbid looking." One of the privates had snatched up the unsmiling, black and white picture.

"That's a funeral portrait," Moast told his men as they gathered around the body. "The dinks are real superstitious. They're afraid if they leave no likeness of themselves behind after death, then they lose contact with family, friends and mother earth itself—these people are real close to the land, you know," he said solemnly, failing to even notice all the words he chose to use in describing his enemy. The Vietnamese Kit Carson scout present, who often acted as interpreter when they were lucky enough to take prisoners, didn't even flinch at the derogatory label. To him, it was directed only at the Viet Cong or NVA, not all Orientals.

"That's funny," reflected another soldier, "I thought all these zips really shied away from cameras."

"What do I look like, a fuckin' schoolteacher?" The officer had tired of the questions and walked over behind a tree stump, going down on one knee and unslinging his rifle automatically at the sound of something approaching them down one of the jungle trails.

Schramm had been totally surprised when the three bicycles—their little handle-bar bells ringing merrily—came rolling around a bend in the tall reeds. On board were six prostitutes from nearby villages, colorfully costumed in bright sarongs and psychedelic hot pants. They had been drawn to the battlefield by the sound of gunfire.

Crowe and Schramm both refused to join the long lines that quickly formed and led down to a hastily erected lean-to a few meters off the trail's edge. At first Crowe suggested that their uncharacteristic (for a grunt) celibate behavior might make an already wary Captain Moast even more suspicious, but after they took a walk down to the lean-to and peeked in, Schramm was even more determined than ever to avoid the whores. One was so bored with her customers she sat propped up against the soldier's helmet, smoking a cigarettte during the intercourse while her girlfriend beside her blew huge, pink bubbles with her bubblegum.

An hour after the men had hiked their trousers back up and headed for the river, Nelson came across a Russian SKS rifle lying abandoned on the side of the trail. A prized war trophy, it was obviously booby-trapped, with several wires running out to grenades encircling the area and probably a bouncing-betty land mine or worse underneath the weapon.

"Let it lie," Moast had ordered. His mantle back in the World was already lined with two AK47s and a Khmer crossbow.

"But, Cap," Nelson had protested, "we leave it where it is, and some stupid village kid is gonna come by and get his face blown off, or some ARVNs gonna get lax and lose a whole squad."

But Moast would not budge.

"Or one of them fuckin' whores is gonna come across it and her tits are gonna land over in Laos. *Then* where will we be next time we gotta unload our nutmeg clear out here in the middle of nowhere?" another man commented.

Five minutes later, Nelson had the seven trip wires disconnected. He carefully slid his bayonet under the entire length of the rifle then, confident no other pins or detonators ran down into the ground, lifted his prize high in the air for all to see.

In the same exultant breath, the jubilant doorgunner threw the rifle down and was hopping around in front of the men, screaming at the top of his lungs, a ten-inch reed spider clinging to his fingers.

Moast had run over to the rifle, saw that the entire underside was rotted out and had been used by the huge tarantulalike arachnid to nest in, then sprinted over to his doorgunner and boldly slapped at the grotesque buggy-eyed creature with his bare hands.

But the spider refused to yield, tightening its hairy black and green legs around Nelson's fingers and increasing pressure on its stinging pincers, more frightened than angry, as the humans tried to bat it off.

Finally, taking their cue from some latent training they had slept through back at The School in Georgia, Crowe and Schramm together dragged Nelson over to a tree stump beside the discarded SKS and calmly dissected the creature to death with their switchblades.

Four kilometers later, their veteran interpreter, the Vietnamese scout, stumbled across a trenchful of urine-soaked punji sticks while walking point and had to be airlifted out by one of the medevac choppers. Schramm had watched silently while Moast argued with the helicopter crew—they seemed at first surprised then angered that the casualty was not an American wounded—then after several minutes they reluctantly lifted off with the ARVN. The pilots had recognized the scout for what he was: a communist turncoat who had gone over to the imperialists' side for money. Schramm wondered if the Asian would make it back to the field hospital or slip out the back door at five thousand feet.

It was shortly after reaching the river that they came across the two women. Tied to stakes that were driven deep into the sand banks, the chieftain's daughters lay naked on their backs, one half submerged in the murky river water, the other closer to land.

They had probably been there three or four days, and the one half submerged—the one with the sand crabs crawling out of her eye sockets—was already dead.

The rivers in Asia, especially the Song Dong Na, do strange things after dusk. Mainly, they rise several feet. And the renegades had positioned the younger girl's body right at the point they knew the waterline would rise to and remain until the moon set beyond the horizon. Almost like the ocean. Strange, but probably just the farmers upstream playing games with their shiny, new government-donated irrigation pumps.

Crowe and Schramm, as newbies to the unit, had been designated the task of cutting the mutilated corpse from its

124

bonds and slipping what had once been a blooming woman into an uncaring, o.d. green body bag.

Schramm didn't like carrying the empty body bags in his pack. It was just like humping the empty sandbags: wasted space and wasted energy. Perhaps having missed out on the pearls of wisdom of infantry training after boot camp, the necessities of such equipment were lost on him. He felt the body bags were a medic's responsibility, or at least should be kept on the medevac slicks, not out in the field with the grunts, where they were bad for morale. But he remained silent, impassive, unprotesting as Crowe held the bloated body under the shoulders from behind and he crossed her ripped and shredded arms over the flat, boy's chest—the kidnappers had hacked off her breasts while she was still alive with their machetes merely because her father was the wealthiest poor man among the peasants in their village—and struggled to stuff the body into the rubber-coated canvas.

Schramm watched glassy-eyed as two other men cut the older woman free—she couldn't have been over twenty—hesitated slightly as they hungrily ran their eyes up and down the curves of her body, then resignedly covered her shivering frame with a poncho liner. The girl was obviously suffering from shock, though her only physical injuries appeared to be severe sunburn and some irritated insect bites along the swell of her chest.

Moast decided the men would make camp right then and there, despite the poor strategic location, refusing to budge from the spot until he could have another interpreter flown in the next day so the girl, who spoke no English, could tell them more about the renegades who had kidnapped her. Especially their direction of travel after they had left her on the sand bar to die.

Schramm recalled how a gunship had managed to drop them a roll of concertina wire so that they could deploy a crude perimeter around the camp, yet was unable to locate a Vietnamese translator willing to be flown out to the middle of hostile territory so near to dark.

They had hastily deployed their LPs (Listening Posts) several hundred yards beyond the perimeter, deep within the

125

treeline itself, before the storm that had been lingering along the horizon all day moved in over the camp. Schramm could still hear Moast saying, "No, son, you don't dig in 'before the rains start.' Monsoons don't start. They arrive. Ain't you learned that by now?"

For a few seconds he could hear one of the grunts, somewhere down the line, playing a small transistor radio. Vietnamese music. And that surprised him. He didn't think anyone in the First Cavalry was impressed with dink sing-songs except himself. But the minor disturbance was reported to the C.O. fast enough, and soon the captain had rushed out to the perimeter and confiscated the radio; he'd have none of that rock & roll violating his regs governing nighttime silence.

And that surprised Schramm too. He knew, by now, that Moast was one crazy fool who disregarded most of the personal security measures laid out by his lieutenants, and that, sooner or later, his men would get brave again and roll a grenade into his path then disappear in the dark and the confusion.

Now that the melodic voice of Khanh Ly, singing Dem Viet-Nam, had been jerked off the airwaves and all he had left to listen to—to keep him awake while Leroy snoozed—was the horde of cicadas, nestled along the riverbanks and calling to each other with their shrill cricketlike music, Schramm reviewed mentally the statistics Stryker had read off to him and Leroy at their last briefing. Two hundred and forty army officers had been "fragged" by disenchanted soldiers in the last three years. Twenty-four were killed in the incidents, yet in only three cases was there sufficient evidence to warrant a thorough CID investigation, and no arrests were ever made.*

Another of the endless flares shot skyward, and as he followed its arc through the night with one eye the statistics faded from the muggy blackness before him. When the flare's parachute deployed, three of the four nylon guide wires snapped loose. As the smoking star fell prematurely to earth, its rotorlike fluttering noise reminded him of the choppers that

*Though actual statistics prior to 1969 are sketchy and incomplete, Congressional data reveals that, between 1969-1971, 730 officers were fragged. 83 died.

had medevaced their wounded out that day.

As planned earlier, Schramm had slipped a message canister aboard the slick, addressed to one of the medics at the evacuation hospital. The corpsman was actually a CID plant, working undercover on a narcotics theft and black-marketing racket, and the locked tube would draw no suspicious attention from the helicopter pilots. Medics in the field were using similar canisters all the time to request pain-killing drugs and placeboes.

In *his* canister, Schramm had scrawled a brief memo that would eventually be forwarded RUSH to a 716th command officer in Saigon. It read:

Have infiltrated target unit without snag. Suspect yet to return. No frag incidents yet, though victim officer definitely a space cadet that should be relieved of his command at all costs.

Spook 2

As he reflected on the message, Schramm, on second thought, hoped it didn't sound like "at all costs" meant the MP believed the efforts of the men trying to murder Moast should be condoned. He sincerely felt someone in authority, above the rank of captain, should review Moast the Ghost's casualty losses as opposed to his mission successes. And, to Schramm, mission accomplished did not mean capturing a lousy pockmarked hilltop only to abandon it the next day—at the cost of dozens of patriotic young American boys.

"Aw, fuck it," Schramm muttered aloud, as another flare popped forth from its tube. "Who gives a flying fuck what they think back at—"

"You say something?" Crowe's mental alarm clock had gone off just then, waking him at precisely the time he was scheduled to relieve his partner on watch.

"Oh, I was just thinking about the message I sent back to Puzzle Palace," he whispered, rising to his feet in shock now as the ghastly scene beneath the flare was slowly taking shape, registering in his tired, fuzzy mind. "Maybe they won't like the way I wrote it," he continued, spacing the words out now as he still failed to perceive what was appearing beyond the wire just then. "I mean . . . what are they gonna do? Send me to Vietnam?" he asked, his heart now beating wildly as his eyes focused on the shapes scurrying about under the flickering flarelight.

"And this *is* about as *Vietnam* as you can get," Crowe's own gasp was an incredulous intake of air as he rose to his feet, grabbing his rifle in the same movement.

"No shit," Schramm's voice cracked as it finally dawned on him what was transpiring beyond the perimeter. Several other soldiers must have seen the activity also, for a dozen more flares hastily shot skyward, illuminating the barren stretch of clay between the treeline and the edge of camp.

Hundreds of black-pajama-clad soldiers were rushing toward their position, bayonets gleaming in the ghostly, surrealistic light.

11. COP COLORS

Back at The School, Ft. Gordon, Georgia

During their last week at the academy, the recruits were put through a bivouac designed to weed out the wimps and show the DIs which men really wanted to wear the MP armband, which deserved it, and which could care less (draftees coasting through to their next duty station and eventual discharge). Two days of patrolling rolling hills, infiltrating behind "enemy lines," and practicing seek out and destroy missions in a mock Vietnamese village (the same adventures a liberal news media was labeling "SAD"), complete with booby traps, hidden weapons caches and exploding tear gas canisters just to keep things moving. They even "rescued" top-secret documents from a downed air force jet, braving thousands of blanks from snipers secreted in hidden tunnels.

The afternoons were often dedicated to target practice with their .45 automatic pistols.

"My gun keeps jamming, Sarge," a private complained one time.

"Drop! And knock me out fifty push-ups!" the drill sergeant snapped. Turning to the rest of the recruits, he held a pistol in the air and said, "I don't ever wanna hear the term 'gun' around here again! You pussies should know better!" and with his free hand he grabbed his crotch.

"Here we go again," whispered Zriny, shaking his head slowly.

The sergeant began waving the pistol in the air. "This is my weapon!" he yelled, then he shook at his crotch with the other hand. "This is my gun!" he referred to his penis, smiling, but the grin was sadistic, not friendly. "This is my weapon!" he repeated. "This is my gun!"

"This is my weapon!" the recruits all mimicked him. "This is my gun!"

"With this I kill people!" screamed the drill sergeant, waving the pistol again, then he pointed back at his crotch. "With *this* I have fun!"

"This is my weapon, this is my gun!" they yelled feverishly. "With this I kill people! With *this* I have fun!"

They spent the next half hour repeating the poem, until they had it right and the DIs were sure they knew their weapon from their gun.

"Class dismissed!" advised one of the sergeants, after the privates had become somewhat proficient in the care and handling of the twelve-gauge riot shotgun. The recruits started for the mess hall, a pleasant respite from the grinding rigor of the twelve and eighteen hour days, despite the slop splashed on their plates. They did their best to ignore the smell that was breakfast, lunch and dinner, content at having fifteen minutes free time to exchange rumors and GI gossip (though a strict rule at The School that no food be left over on their trays left little time for small talk).

"Private!" Sergeant Mills called over to recruit Uhernik, pointing a rigid finger, "you remain here!"

Zriny and Todd frowned, then walked out of the shotgun pit without their buddy. Valters made the sign of the cross, then gave Nick the thumbs up.

After all the men had left, Uhernik walked over to the DI and assumed the position of attention.

"Knock it off, Nick," he said, offering the soldier a cigar. "How come you're the only goofy fuck around here went and volunteered for the 'Nam?"

"I requested it, Sarge," he said modestly, knowing deep inside that if the man really cared that much he'd have scanned his 201 file and discovered the private was just returning home to Saigon. Instead he added, "That's where the action is, right?"

"That's what you want?" He frowned. "Action?"

"Well . . ." Uhernik hesitated slightly as the civilian with the plastic arm and leg appeared at the edge of the pit.

"I know," he smiled suddenly, looking up at Kip Mather with a warm nod, acknowledging the ex-sergeant's presence. "Not quite sure what you want, right? I know. I was the same way. I still am. Hell, I don't even know where I'll be a year from now."

"So you think I made a mistake?"

"It's not for me to say."

"My folks think I did." He caught the gleam in Kip's eye and decided to play the game of Only-son-going-off-to-war. "I guess they want me to go to college."

"Nobody wants their kid to go off to war."

"I just had to start my life, you know? I mean, I loved my family and all, my home town. But there's something waiting for me over there, can you understand? Something's calling me," he hammed it up. "I mean—does that sound crazy?"

"No," he laughed lightly, "you just got adventure in your blood."

"I don't know. I read a lot when I was a kid: faraway places and all that."

"You're *still* a kid, damnit."

"I'm a soldier," he protested softly, without showing disrespect.

"I didn't mean . . . You're a man." He nodded his head and blinked an eye. "But you guys are *all* kids to me. You're all my boys, that's all I meant. You can go spend five years in Nam and you'll still be *my* boys, 'cuz it was *I* taught you how to survive out on the streets of Danang, or Pleiku—"

"Or Saigon," Kip added with a knowing smile.

"Or Saigon—wherever you end up. Damnit, I just don't wanna think maybe you won't make it back. I almost thought we were done sending kids over there. Now, you come along. Why the hell you wanna go over and get jungle rot, anyway?"

Uhernik was thinking that this was not the way a gung-ho drill sergeant's supposed to be talking, but he ignored the lack

131

of encouragement and answered, "I don't want to get jungle rot. It's just that, I guess, well— I read a lot about distant lands and people: islands out in the Pacific, the dark continent of Africa. What could be more exciting then the steaming jungles of the Orient?"

Mills didn't answer. He was staring off into his own distance, perhaps recalling some long-forgotten battle, or Asian lady.

"I can see there's no explaining Vietnam to you," he finally said. "You'll just have to go over and find out for yourself." He reached into a shirt pocket and brought out a small, wrinkled manual. "Here." He shoved it over at Nick. "I dug through my soldier's trunk last night and located it."

"Guide to the Languages of Vietnam," the recruit read the cover.

"Who knows." Mills scratched his chin nervously, staring at the handbook. "It might even come in handy."

"Thanks, Sarge. I appreciate it. But do you really want to give it up? The impression I get from the other DIs is that any and everything brought back from the 'Nam is sacred, precious. You really want to part with it?"

Mills's eyes remained on the manual for several more seconds, then in a dreamy voice he finally said, "It's time I started getting rid of some of the memories," and started to walk off. "Oh, I just remembered why I held you over after class. Mr. Mather here wanted to speak with you." With a nod in Kip's direction, he was off again.

Nick and Kip exchanged forced smiles after they were left alone, like old friends who are brought together under tense circumstances after a long separation. Before coming to The School, the last time Nick had seen Kip was on Bis Ky Dong Street in Saigon, when he was a sergeant with the Decoy Squad. A whole man, tough as the younger rogues in his command. Now he was a civilian instructor at the academy, medically retired by the Army heirarchy—a constant reminder of what could go wrong in Saigon, on the street.

Mather had shown the recruit special attention throughout his first seven weeks at The School, without being obvious to the other students, and Uhernik had remained painfully distant, remote. Uncomfortable with a man he knew had changed both physically and mentally since their last meeting.

132

He convinced himself that first week they retired Kip that he would not spend the rest of the academy on a guilt trip, yet every time he saw Mather giving his Booby Traps class with those empty, lifeless eyes Nick found himself looking away, unable to accept the possibility his beloved Vietnam could so destroy a friend.

"I'm your new Southeast Asia tutor, till you graduate," he declared. "From now on, after the other recruits call it a night, you and me will be busy learning Vietnamese phrases, finding booby traps in the bush, and tuning you in to survival in the jungle, got that?"

"But . . ." There was already so much to learn, and it *was* "skate" week, the final phase of The School.

"No buts. If you've got it in your head to be a street cop in Saigon at least I'll rest easy knowing I did my best to get you through your tour over there. Got that? Do an old man a favor—humor me."

"OK, Sarge," he said. "I mean, mister. But you gettin' overtime for this?"

Mather just grinned, grabbed the booklet out of the recruit's hand and thumbed through it briefly. "Now," he said, ignoring the fact his student already spoke near-fluent Vietnamese, "*dung lai!*" and he raised his .45 for emphasis. "That means 'Halt!' in Vietnamese. Repeat it."

Uhernik's eyes followed the automatic pistol as it stopped level with his chest. At least Training Command had let Mather keep a mock weapon while he went from class to class. They had taken his honor, pride and half his body. But they had left him a toy gun.

"*Dung lai,*" the recruit repeated softly, fighting off the moisture clouding his eyes.

Georgia's night air was alive with pidgin Vietnamese all that week.

"Pass the salt," Valters asked one of the marines sitting across the chow table from him.

"Get it yourself, doggie!" came the reply, along with a bowl of "tossed" salad.

Meanwhile, ex-boxer Barry Todd was beginning to pour

some ketchup on his hamburger. The top fell off and the contents plopped onto his plate, covering everything. Barry looked up slowly, controlled rage in his narrow eyes as he scanned the men seated across from him. It was obvious the marines had sabotaged it!

Zriny, who was sitting next to Todd, began laughing at the husky private's predicament while he poured sugar into his coffee. Jack's top also fell off, depositing a pile of sugar into his cup which promptly spilled over into his lap.

Suddenly the mess hall was a combat zone of flying food and crashing plates. Tables were knocked over and chairs were transformed into weapons as more soldiers joined in on the melee.

The mess-hall sergeant, a tall, black weight-lifter with his head shaved bald, charged into the dining facility blowing a whistle in an attempt to restore order. Barry punched him out and deposited the hulk in a trash can.

Soon, the fight escalated outside to the parade field. "Where the hell are the drill sergeants?" Uhernik was wondering, trying to keep a low profile as a slice of pie slammed into the back of his head. Two marines were drop-kicking Zriny all over the place and Nick crawled under a long table, cherries sliding down the back of his crew cut as he emerged on the other side of the mess hall. He jumped onto the backs of the two bullies and all four recruits tumbled into the grease pit area of the kitchen.

Marines and GIs were flipping each other over their backs left and right—just as the DIs had taught them to—when the first MP cars pulled up, sirens blaring. It looked like a mass, unorganized hand-to-hand combat course gone berserk by the time the drill sergeants arrived.

It took an MP squad of riot dog handlers to break up the two biggest brawls, which resembled giant athletic contests in Europe where a huge ball is tossed back and forth on a soccer field—except in this case the "balls" were semi-conscious soldiers, the object of a comical game of "keep away" between the two services.

Sixth Platoon almost pulled stockade time over that one.

*   *   *

134

It was accepted, even expected, that the recruits would go for each other's throats during the last stages of the academy. After the battle in the mess hall, where they were allowed to exhaust their frustrations and personality conflicts without ending up in the slammer, the privates were hit from all sides by the DIs. In forty-eight hours, the drill sergeants had molded, shaped and beaten the dazed men into what they considered was the ideal military police rookie, their final product.

"Now, we'll see how long you little girls last out on the street!" Sergeant First Class Dolph grinned evilly. "You think *we* were mean motherfuckers, just wait till you try and collect your pension fighting the scumbags out in the *real* world every weekend, when the goddamn bars spill out into the streets!"

"You men'll do fine," Lieutenant Wilson followed Sergeant Dolph to the speaker's platform as the recruits stood at parade-rest in their Class-A's. "We've tried to instill in you the experience we, as military policemen, have gained following years behind the wheel of that patrol car. Now it's up to you. I'm confident you'll not tarnish the image, protected through four wars and numerous conflicts, of the MP corps."

First Sergeant Blalock took the podium. His huge form dwarfed the other men on the speaker's platform. "How you men doin' tonight?" He leaned against the podium and slowly ran his menacing eyes from one end of the formation to the other.

"Doing fine, First Sergeant," a scattering of tired privates answered uncertainly.

Blalock's knuckles went white with restrained fury and he repeated his question word for word, but this time in a thunderous roar. His grizzlylike frame seemed to grow to twice its size as the microphone replied with a frightened squeal of feedback. *"How you men doin' tonight?"*

Uhernik, who had been dozing on balanced heels, nearly somersaulted back to reality as privates on either side of him snapped to attention and yelled, "Doing fine, First Sergeant!"

"I can't hear you pantywaist wimps," he whispered softly into the microphone this time.

"Doing fine, First Sergeant!" they yelled again, adding a sharp double-boot stomp to punctuate the reply.

"That's better." He smiled warmly for the first time. "See these Crossed Pistols?" He pointed to the collar brass on his uniform. "They represent your chosen profession—draftees excluded: the Military Police of the United States Armed Forces. The MP armband also. Someday we'll probably be running around with badges too. Just like the cops on the outside. Well, whatever." He wiped at his nose briefly. Someday you men may find you owe your life to these instructors," and he waved a hand slowly in the direction of the drill sergeants, their tilted campaign hats hiding their unblinking eyes from the parade field spotlights. "Remember them: Sergeants Wuttke, Dolph, Denson, Mills, Williams, Sineath, Flowers, Carey and Craigmyle!"

"And Mather," Lieutenant Wilson's whisper was picked up and amplified by the microphone.

"And Mr. Kip Mather," the first sergeant corrected himself matter of factly and waved his other hand at the civilian in camouflage T-shirt and black calico trousers standing beside an MP jeep by himself, separated from the DIs by fifty feet of open space and light years of silent misery. Sergeant Blalock did not look directly at Mather, as if the civilian was painful evidence of what could go wrong in this line of work, and he ignored the scattering of applause from the recruits that followed the rare recognition.

"You don't realize it," Blalock continued, "but these sergeants have sweated *blood* over you—they've even got their goddamn *wives* on their backs, because they spend more time babysitting you in your barracks than at home!"

Nick couldn't help but notice Kip's eyes fall to the ground with the mention of wives. The recruit tried to ignore the sudden loss of proud smile on his friend's face, and he fought off the demon in his mind that tried to picture the crippled man with a young, healthy woman. "The prostitutes," the voice was laughing in his head, "even the prostitutes probably shy away from him."

"So," said a smiling Colonel Austin, their commanding officer, "the night you've all been waiting for. The night you ride with members of the 555th Military Police Company. Good luck, men. Tonight should decide if you stay with us in the MPs, or leave the service after your tour is up. I hope you find a love for the streets, as we have." The men surprised all the sergeants by cheering. They were all keyed up now, psyched for the challenge. "I'll see you again in a few days, at the graduation ceremonies."

Captain Hutter saluted the C.O., then took the stand. He took his .45 from his holster. "Men," he said, "it's the real thing now. You're going out on the street with real weapons, real bullets. But don't lose your head with eagerness. You're still in training—we call it OJT: on the job training." He raised his pistol, so all could see it.

"You know why they invented this heater?" he asked, referring to the ominous-looking .45 side arm. "Well, back in the days of the Moro Uprising, in the Philippines, we kept getting our boys massacred by drugged-up natives. So they built this baby because it's powerful enough to take your arm off." Nick resisted the impulse to see how Kip was reacting to the descriptive speech. "The natives were no longer restless," Hutter continued, "after our men became armed with this cannon. And we still use it—there's some two hundred and thirty-nine thousand left in the government supply system— because it's damned near indestructible. But, gentlemen, sometimes it does the job too well! So use common sense! If you shoot somebody with it, make sure it's a righteous shooting—because you're liable to shoot your objective, the guy behind him, and the building behind them both! I'm not trying to scare you—" he displayed his best fatherly smile—"I just want you aware of the power of your authority, and the power of the tools you'll someday use to enforce that authority.

"Your sergeants will lead you over to the MP station. Dismissed!"

In the armory of the provost marshal's office they were given the black helmets with the white MP emblazoned on them, assigned their .45 automatic pistols with five rounds per man, and issued the legendary armbands.

"You look alright!" praised a grinning Private Zriny after he fastened Nick's armband on tighter than he had originally attached it. "Fucking *stract!*" he decided, saluting his

137

fellow private.

"You don't look so bad yourself, MP." Nick smiled back, patting the butt of his .45 as he attached the keeper strap. "Yeah, it feels good," he said, testing the snugness of his pistol in its leather holster.

"Let's get out and kick some ass," decided Todd, flexing his biceps and trying to stretch the armband past its limitations. It would not tear.

"What, no night sticks?" Nick asked the desk sergeant a few minutes later.

"They're on back order," he replied sarcastically. "We been breaking too many over jarheads," he referred to the big brawl at the mess hall. "You don't need 'em anyway," he decided. "You all look like real *bad* hot dogs!" Then he rolled his eyes up to the top of his head and waved the recruits out of the building. "Go meet your rides next door, at the orderly room," he directed. "Get the fuck outta my sight!"

At first Uhernik was a bit disappointed when they took him out with a dozen other rookies and stuck them on post gates to check IDs and wave cars in and out, but then their escort explained that Gate 3, where Zriny and he were abandoned, had been the site—only months earlier—where an eighteen-year-old MP had been shot down by a passing car in the middle of the night.

"They never found his killer or killers," the Pfc. in the sleek MP cruiser lamented as he slowly drove off into the mist. "The poor guy lay bleeding in the street, until he died. Nobody stopped to help him."

The two rooks spent the next two hours with their hands on their gun butts, eyeing every passing car suspiciously. Around sunset, the duty officer stopped by and warned them that Fort Gordon's commanding general would be through any time, and that they were to stay on their feet and keep alert. "By the way, were you told about Private McKinley?" he asked.

"Private McKinley, sir?"

"The poor bastard that got ambushed here a couple months ago. Shot him in the back! Quite a shoot-out, from what I heard, so keep your eyes open." He pointed up at a weathered sign atop the guard shack that read: McKINLEY GATE.

Zriny looked up at the sign, wide eyed, then slowly back

138

down at the lieutenant. "Sir?"

"We don't want to have to name a gate after you two guys," the officer explained, then he signalled his Spec. 4 to drive off before the recruits could comment.

General Moore finally went through a different gate around 1900 hours and Desk Sergeant McCormick picked up the two rooks and started to return them to the MP station when a call for help came over the radio from an MP at a larceny scene on the other side of camp. McCormick activated the blue flashing lights of the sonic bar atop their Malibu but they had proceeded only a few blocks when other patrols already at the scene radioed in that the situation was under control.

"Cardinal rule number one," he told the attentive privates, "no matter what you're doing, when a brother MP calls for help, you drop it and fly balls-to-the-wind to his assistance!" Both rooks nodded their agreement, and Uhernik recalled the countless times he had been told, "You never desert your partner. Under any circumstances!"

They were diverted to a burglar alarm at the main PX store, and the sergeant punched the cruiser into overdrive and flicked the blue lights back on, ignoring the siren this time. "One of these days I'll get you back to the station," he said, grinning as they squealed around a corner, narrowly missing a group of black soldiers. "Fucking idiots!" he muttered.

McCormick doused his unit's headlights about a block away from the PX, then killed the engine and allowed the sedan to coast up to the rear parking lot.

They quickly checked the entire building, but found no break in. "Who wants to take the roof?" the sergeant asked. He noticed their astonished expressions. "Get used to it, boys. Cops spend half their careers wandering about rooftops after dark."

No burglars had chopped through the roof either, and the call was logged as a false alarm. Zriny bought the sergeant and Nick a cup of coffee at a cafe just outside the camp, and as they were leaving McCormick stated, "Thanks for the brew, kid, but one thing you gotta learn, the coffee's free. Some meals are half priced. Some of *them* are free too, but if you get that lucky, be sure and leave a big tip."

A long line of recruits crowded the MP station when they got back. "Jesus, we're never going to get the chance to go back out on the street," Zriny whispered over to Nick. They reluctantly joined the group sitting on benches beneath a long bulletin board cluttered with FBI bulletins and Wanted posters, and watched a Spec. 4 atop the raised Complaint platform answer phones and log reports.

A young Oriental girl walked in and stopped directly in front of Zriny. She was about nineteen, with long, sleek legs ending at the bottom of cut-off black jeans. Her breasts, full and taut, were hidden by long, silky black hair that fanned across her cherry-blossom halter top. She examined Nick briefly from the corner of dark, almost mysterious eyes, then spoke to Zriny. "I wish report stolen license plate," she said shyly, using broken English.

Jack pointed her over to the desk sergeant now climbing up to his throne, and she walked off with a grace that aroused every man in the room. "Now I know why you want to go to the Orient," he said with a grin, nudging Nick in the side. "You can probably buy two of her over there for half a paycheck; that's four juicy nipples to nurse you through the night."

Somehow the remark didn't set right with the other private, but he ignored it.

"She's Korean, or Japanese," observed Valters, a few soldiers down from them, "judging from the ample sway of that gorgeous chest. Nick's going a world away from there—where the cheekbones are higher and the rent's lower."

Nick started to ponder that comment when an MP sergeant walked into the room from off the street. The private's eyes immediately latched onto the combat patch on his right shoulder—the gold hatchets separated by a green dagger and stalks of bamboo, unit patch of the Eighteenth MP Brigade, Vietnam. His nametag read: Howe.

"I need one good man," he declared, looking straight at Uhernik. Everyone else froze, but Nick jumped to his feet. "Good," he said, "come on."

The slender rook followed the tall, muscular cop out to one of the o.d. green patrol cars lining the parking lot. "MILITARY POLICE" flashed out at him from the reflectorized door labels as he pulled on a handle. They got in. Into another world of shotgun racks, hot-sheet pads and steel flashlights, where the harsh radio speakers were crackling off garbled dispatches in military code.

"Haven't been on the street in three nights," Howe volunteered the admission, breaking the silence after a few minutes of cruising. "I feel good tonight—lucky. Might as well take a rook out on the bricks!" Uhernik's eyes were glued to the shoulder patch he was not yet authorized to wear. "Know your assignment, yet?" Howe grinned.

Nick pointed at the patch, remaining silent more out of reinforced academy respect than awe.

"Vietnam?" he sounded surprised. "I didn't know we were still sending recruits over there! Just us lifers and volunteers. From the MPs, anyway."

"Everybody keeps saying that," Uhernik wondered aloud. "I hope I'm not the only guy to get off the boat at Newport."

"Boat?" he laughed. "They'll probably send you over in a 747, drinks and all."

"That would be nice," he said, realizing he really didn't care if he disembarked alone or not. He was not, after all, going to a strange place. He felt suddenly embarrassed, but didn't know why.

"Just keep your head low." The sparkle in Howe's squint faded as he turned dead serious. "Those fuckin' helmets stand out a mile away. Lotta snipers over there."

In the short time they had, Sergeant Howe gave him a condensed version of his adventures overseas. He repeated certain pointers, until Nick found it easy to tell when he was talking man to man, MP to MP, or veteran training officer to green rookie.

"You get to love the street," he said, shining a spotlight down a narrow alley in search of prowlers. "And you get to hate it. You'll think about it when you're not on it, and you'll think about your old lady when you are. You'll wonder what she's doing while you're on patrol, and it'll eat away at your insides over the years until you're all fucked up. Physically and mentally." Howe had been an MP ten years. "You'll want to quit, hang up your holster after a while, so you take a vacation. Boston or Bangkok—hell, I don't know. Doesn't matter where you go. Every time you see a cop walking his beat, or a squad car scream by, your gut will turn just a little

141

bit. Until you can't wait to get back to the street.

"Your old lady will be on your back constantly, because of the shift work—the lonely nights she spends alone, at least you hope and pray she's alone. Could be she's crabby 'cuz the jerk she's screwin' on the side just left her for some younger, firmer jailbait. A lot of the guys get divorced. A lot of the guys give up the street. Some end up eating their .45 or—"

A sports car sped by in the opposite direction, its taillights burned out. Howe made a U-turn and pulled in behind the small vehicle after punching the 440 under the hood into overdrive for two blocks. "They tell you at the MP school you're a soldier first, a cop second. That's why so many guys put in their three or four years then go into civilian police work. Better pay, better equipment, better working conditions."

Sergeant Howe radioed in the car's license plate number to see if the vehicle was stolen or recently used in a crime. "So why do you stay in?" Nick asked.

"I ask myself that two or three times a week." He smiled. "For one thing, I'm getting too old to get into civilian police work. City departments usually freeze their hiring around the age of thirty-two. In ten more lousy years I can retire, anyway. At the tender age of forty-three—hell, still young enough to go be a county sheriff somewhere. But I think the real reason is because of what I saw in the 'Nam.

"A buddy of mine—a guy I served with in Saigon—got out and became a policeman in Chicago, really makin' the big bucks, you know? But he misses it. Can you believe that? He misses the MP corps. Writes me now and then and says he misses being a part of the corps overseas—American MPs in Vietnam. He says, sure Chicago's the big time, lotsa crime. But it don't compare to the mystique surrounding police work in the streets of Saigon, or Bangkok, or Seoul. They're the toughest beats, you know. The toughest beats in the world."

The dispatcher acknowledged that the car they were following was clear: no wants or warrants. "Ten-four, thanks," Howe said into the mike, activating his blue lights simultaneously with the other hand. "No taillights is a chickenshit traffic stop," he admitted, "but it gives you probable cause to detain these creeps and run a computer check on them. Might

142

come up with a warrant. I got a punk on a bank robbery warrant one time—and on a lousy failure to signal!"

The sports car was not pulling over so Howe hit the siren a couple of times. Three startled, black faces looked back at them. The car swerved over to the side of the road. Howe unsnapped his holster and cased his cruiser in behind the violator, offsetting his left front bumper slightly to protect him from passing traffic.

Sergeant Howe slowly walked up to the driver's door while Uhernik positioned himself behind the right rear corner of the car to cover his partner. A bright spotlight illuminated the vehicle's interior and blinded the occupants whenever they looked back. The driver and his two passengers all had their hands raised slightly in the air to show they were not armed. Two Atlanta policemen had killed a black car thief recently after the suspect had pointed a sawed-off shotgun at them and tensions between minorities and law officers were running high. Howe obtained ID cards and returned to the patrol car.

As they sat in the front seat again, awaiting computer checks, Howe repositioned the spotlight directly in the center of the rear window. "Don't ever give these dudes the edge," he said, "or they'll take it and shove it up your ass sideways. When you're walking back to your unit, never turn your back on them. Now don't get me wrong, but the majority of our violent crime suspects and arrestees are minorities—kind of ironic, huh?"

"Yeah, I guess," Uhernik said, realizing for the first time that the girl waiting for him back in Saigon might also be classified a minority. In America. He had never really thought about it that way. Then again, there just *had* to be more black Tyrone Washingtons running around the U.S.A. than white Nick Uherniks. "Their color don't matter to me," he finally told Howe. "I just hate punks, you know? The hoods. The 'bad guys' for lack of a better phrase. I'll arrest them if they're purple, if they break the law."

"Good attitude," Howe replied, "but it won't last long. The street is gonna turn you into one mean motherfucker, whether you like it or not. Accept reality; one year from now your values, your views and feelings will change drastically. You'll be called a pig so many times and shit on so many times and spit on so many times that it'll change you, man.

"The drill sergeants tell you 'pig' stands for pride, integrity and guts, right? Fine. If they wanna dish out that bullshit, good. It's not much comfort when you have to listen to the threats and the promises—the punks, they say they'll burn down your house and rape your wife when they get out of the slammer, you know? The drill sergeants don't have to take that crap in the classroom. We on the line can't tell our prisoners, 'Drop slick! And knock me out seventy-five!'" His little speech did not seek pity, but was given in a soft, unemotional tone meant to convey to his rookie partner just exactly what he was in for, all academy whitewashing aside.

"Car 5, your parties are clear," advised the dispatcher.

Howe acknowledged the metallic voice, then finished filling out his FI (field interview) cards. "And watch out for the news media," he continued. "Biggest bunch of jerks, wimps, liberal bleeding hearts and back-stabbing bloodsuckers you'll ever run across." He started laughing, recalling some past incident.

"One time, this broad from Augusta—TV newswoman, excuse me—well, she's giving me one shitload of bad press because I sticked some Puerto Rican loudmouth at a bar fight. So I invite her to ride with us one night, got it approved at the top and everything, but no TV cameras, OK?" Howe laughed again and the humor was not plastic.

"Well, it couldn't have worked out better! It's hot, so the windows are down. We're catching catcalls at every intersection, right? Pig this and pig that. All of 'em minorities. But I play it cool and ignore everything I hear. Real impressive, OK? Especially since this dame's trying to make me out to be a hothead. Well, I come across this guy with his car disabled along the side of the road. Just happens to be a black guy. So I get out to help him, and the jerk decks me! Right as I turn my back to fiddle with his engine—he catches me completely off guard! Claims I'm invading his fuckin' privacy!"

Nick cocked a skeptical eyebrow at him and Howe feigned indignation. "No, really! This jerkoff decks me, for Christ's sake—slams the fuckin' hood down on my head, then runs back toward my patrol car, waving a tire iron at my passenger. Probably thought she was a policewoman or something." Howe was now choking with laughter and reached over to pat his rook partner on the shoulder. "Now don't get me wrong again, Nick—I'm all for women's lib and all that crap, but did you ever try riding around with a *police*woman for eight hours when she's on the rag?" he asked seriously. "Jesus H., that's the moodiest partner you'll ever have. How can they be equal with all those woman problems draggin' them down like that?

"Anyway," he continued, "so this gorilla is smashing out my windshield with his tire iron, and the woman reporter is screaming her head off—really terrified. It was beautiful! Well, the guy cracked my helmet down the middle, right? So I'm stumblin' around in a daze trying to call for a backup on my PR, and up rolls a two-man car. Disarmed the guy and took him into custody without a scratch. Turned out to be an escapee from the nuthouse.

"Worked wonders on that TV newswoman! Nothing like an eight-hour shift to wake those spoiled jerks out of their nine-to-five rose-colored high-rise world. An eight-hour shift with us, I mean. Put these bleeding heart liberals out on the street to deal with the gutter scumbags they're so hip on liberating from oppression—the same gutter balls we deal with every day, and they open their fucking eyes! Works every time. It was great! Dumb broad even recommended me for an Army Commendation Medal."

"Did you get it?"

"Gimme a break." He laughed. "I'm an MP, remember? They don't give ArComs to MPs—everyone knows that. Fuck no, I didn't get it!"

A van full of white teen-agers drove up just then and three empty beer cans clattered to a stop beside the MP car.

"Yo' mama!" the enraged driver in the car Howe had pulled over flipped them the finger, evidently taking the blatant affront personally—the thought the beer can may have been an act of disrespect directed at the MP as an authority figure never crossing the black man's mind. Uhernik observed that Howe didn't seem to notice any of it.

As they returned to the car to give back the IDs, the driver directed a hate-laced stare at the MP private. The naive recruit thought to himself, "If looks could kill, they'd be shipping me home to Saigon in a box this very night," but stared back unflinching, though he was never quite sure afterwards what their eyes had been dueling about.

As they cruised the signal corps billets, Sergeant Howe checked his watch and remarked, "Quiet for a Friday. Must not be a full moon."

Just then the dispatcher keyed a special alarm tone on the radio—an unnerving shrill triple yelp—designed to get the attention of all the patrols. He gave an address that meant nothing to the private, then stated, "Family disturbance, possible firearms involved."

"Aw, shit," muttered Howe as he activated the sonic bar on the roof and squealed a U-turn. The siren's electronic wail drowned out the sound of the protesting tires. "That's an MP's house," he explained.

They started sliding on sand through one intersection, but Howe kept the snarling cruiser under control without batting an eye. At eighty mph he was suddenly giving his rook partner a class on defensive driving, showing him how to position his hands on the steering wheel during various maneuvers and teaching him how to anticipate hazardous situations blocks ahead.

They pulled up on the scene and found two other units, their blue roof lights rotating sluggishly because the motors were off, locked and parked partially up on the curb in front of the NCO housing cubicle the dispatcher had sent them to.

Howe left on his parking lights but turned off the engine and secured the unit before they started up the walk toward the front door. He eyed the other two patrol cars closely, disapproval clouding his expression as he searched for their unit numbers at a glance, as if to verify the identity of the drivers. "Don't ever leave 'em running," he advised Uhernik, "unless you've got an extra key and you lock it up. Too many joyriders lately getting a kick out of stealing patrol cars and ditching 'em off post—rolled one down a hill into the side wall of an X-rated movie house in Augusta last week." He pointed to the two units with the lazy flashing lights. "They'll probably have dead batteries when they come off this call." He frowned. "And all of it just to look a little more dramatic."

The two spec. 4s inside the residence seemed to have the

146

situation under control as Howe and Uhernik entered. The wife sat in the living room, complaining to the white MP, while her husband, a black MP sergeant currently off duty, had been led off into the kitchen by the other MP, who was also black. "Things usually cool down pretty quick when you separate the husband and wife," Howe whispered.

"Hello, Howe." The husband waved at the newcomers upon their entrance. "Everything's cool." He forced an embarrassed smile.

"I don't think we're needed here." Howe nodded to his fellow NCO and motioned Nick toward the door.

"The daughter called it in," the MP standing next to the wife advised them after they started out of the dwelling. "There was no weapon. She just figured we'd get here faster if a gun was mentioned."

Howe frowned again but said nothing, and they proceeded back to their car. The white MP was also leaving the call, and he met the sergeant outside just as he was getting into his unit.

"That crap really torks me off," the specialist fourth class was telling Sergeant Howe as he pointed back up toward the porch, where the two black MPs, one off duty and the other on, were spending a good two minutes exchanging their soul handshake. "Them niggers shouldn't be allowed to do that while in uniform," he complained.

Howe jumped back out of the patrol car and grabbed the spec. 4 gently by the front of his shirt, so no one else watching would notice. "Look, *friend*," Uhernik could overhear Howe, angry but controlled, as puzzlement fell over the recruit like a shroud. "I agree with you about that handshake nonsense—it torks me off more than you 'cuz they had the audacity to call it a 'dap,' which in Vietnamese means 'beautiful,' and to me it *ain't* fucking beautiful—and I'll speak to him about it later. But as long as you're in my squad, the man's an MP, not a nigger. Got that? You ain't white, and he ain't black, as far as I'm concerned. And I'm the fucking sergeant, right? We're MPs. Nothing more and nothing less. Not white. Not black. Just cops, just MPs."

"OK, OK," the other man was saying. He got back into his car, slammed the door shut, barely succeeded in starting the weak motor, then drove off recklessly into the night.

Howe exhaled a deep, painful sigh. "Now that little episode's gonna get all over the barracks and I'll look like a watermelon seed."

"A watermelon seed?" Uhernik frowned at the comparison.

"White on the outside, black on the inside."

"Oh."

They drove around in silence for a few minutes, while both men pondered over whether the right things had been said back at the last call. Now and then they'd stop along in the warehouse district and shake doorknobs, but they found nothing open.

"You think maybe I said the wrong things back there?" Howe finally asked.

"I'm still trying to figure out what you meant by watermelon seed. I thought they were black." Uhernik smiled, trying to lighten the mood that floated stagnant in the patrol car.

"Just answer the question, smartass. Ignore whatever I said a few minutes ago. Sometimes I get flustered when my men piss me off over stupid shit."

"It's not for me to say," Uhernik admitted how he felt, "but I *am* really getting tired of all this black power bullshit."

"That crap doesn't enter into it," he interrupted. "We— and I'm speaking as MPs—we ain't got anybody out there on the street to back us up but ourselves," he explained. "We gotta stick together! And the black MPs—they catch the worst of it! From both sides—their own 'people,' if you can call 'em that, and the street scum."

They cruised a few more blocks in silence before the buck sergeant went on. "Hell, maybe now that I'm back from 'Nam, I'll turn into a regular bigot like everyone else around here." His throat was going dry as they started back toward the MP station for shift change. "It's just that color don't mean much when you're sharing a foxhole with a black guy and the mortars are comin' in. Mr. Death and his hot shrapnel don't give a lizard's shit *what* color you are."

Two nights before graduation several of the men from Sixth Platoon found themselves lounging around the orderly room pool table, toasting beers to their favorite instructor.

148

Kep Mather raised his own can of Miller in response, then downed its entire contents to the cheers of the privates around him. Outside, a patient honking of a car horn, coming across as a mere tap every few seconds, went unnoticed among the group of recruits, and the MPs sitting outside finally hit the siren a couple times.

"Knock it off with that fuckin' siren!" barked a brave and swaying Zriny, leaning out the doorway into the foggy night. A strong beam of electric light splashed across his face and from the MP car's loudspeaker the driver's metallic voice penetrated the party atmosphere inside.

"Mister Kip Mather in there?"

"Who the fuck wants to know?" Valters had staggered up behind Zriny and leaned heavily over the smaller private as he poked his head out the doorway and tried to focus on the marked sedan sitting half on the sidewalk and half in the street.

Kip Mather's smile faded instantly when the loudspeaker announced that he had a visitor waiting in the car. "A visitor?" Mather's eyes searched those of his pupils uncertainly. He hadn't had a visitor or friend come to see him since they patched up the holes where his arm and leg had once been.

Mather, sure there was some mistake, started toward the door after hastily putting the beer can down— he was more concerned with restraining Zriny and Valters just then. One thing they didn't need the night before graduation was a disorderly conduct arrest.

Several of the intoxicated privates let out with whistles when the driver opened the back door and a slender woman with long, black hair stepped out, her anxiety-filled eyes darting about with apprehension at the sight of so many unruly soldiers.

A Vietnamese woman.

Mather lurched forward hesitantly on the porch outside the door, his glassy eyes struggling to focus on the beautiful woman with fog hiding her feet. He raised his arm slightly and the recruits automatically fell silent, sensing something special about this reunion. A tension in the air demanded respect.

"Hoa?" The name escaped Mather somewhat like a parakeet, surprised to find the cage left open. Its feathers rustled about in his throat.

"Kip?" The voice chirped at him like a frightened bird, free for the first time, yet terrified.

"Hoa? Is that you, Hoa?" His mind was racing back to that night in Third Field Army Hospital, hours before he was scheduled to leave Saigon. He could see the Vietnamese nun, her youthful face and untouched body almost completely hidden by the black robes. He was seeing the tears in her eyes, minutes after she had learned he was going home. Home to no one. After the weeks she had spent comforting him, holding his hand through the painful therapy, talking him out of his spells of depression. He was hearing her words an ocean away, "I'm so very sorry. . . . I'm sorry you have to come to Vietnam so this can happen to you. If I could take your place, if I could give you my limbs, or if I could. . . ." He was seeing the tough little saint, standing in that depressing hospital ward, at the moment her wall collapsed and she broke into sobs at the sight of his injuries and the proud way he endured the pain, the bitterness. The loneliness.

Kip Mather, just then, was seeing the sister in Saigon—the nun, forbidden fruit—holding him tightly to her bosom as they both broke down and cried. He was remembering—it was all flooding back now, hours of anguish compressed into a microsecond—how he felt when she held him with all her heart. It had been an unselfishness no one had forced on her— the way duty forced the nurses to smile at him despite the wounds, the ugliness. He was remembering the way he held the sister that night. Held *on* to her was more like it. Afraid to let go. Afraid she would be the last woman who would ever hold him again.

"Kip, how are you!" She was running to him now, excitement in her voice, the tears almost familiar as they streaked the smooth, mascara-free face. He caught her in his good arm, lifting her easily off the ground and swinging her to his chest to the cheers of his men.

The MPs inside the patrol car, caught up in the good cheer, sent the blue strobes on the roof flashing to punctuate the reunion, and as Mather suddenly saw himself twirling around—the smile on Hoa's face was of slow-motion happiness, the scene flickering before his eyes, and the meaning of every other frame was missing—the strobes shooting out against the blackness of night served to jolt his memory. He moved hastily to put the nun back on the ground.

"I'm so sorry, Sister Hoa," he was choking up on the apology, noticing for the first time that she was clad, not in religious robes, but a conservative Western-style dress. "Certainly no way to treat a nun, in public."

The men crowding around immediately sensed something was wrong and a tense silence closed in on the couple.

Hoa's anxious smile did not falter. "I not nun anymore, Kip-san!" she beamed, throwing her arms around his neck again. "And I not hypocrite anymore. I have to leave," she whispered the last few words into his ear, the tears still flowing from her eyes contrasting sharply with the waning smile, "I have to leave the sisterhood, for a while." Then her voice rose in an excited pitch again. "I come to visit you!"

Again, as if on cue, the recruits erupted into immodest applause. At the same time, they sensed their intrusion into the couple's privacy, and in small groups of two and three, they drifted off with the fog.

"Maybe you no go back Vietnam?" Mather's shift into pidgin English was automatic, both surprising and alarming him. As he took her hand and they started walking down the street, the walls of the Hotel Majestic rose up on one side and he could hear the Saigon river flowing free and wild down the block.

"No, I said I come to visit you." She squeezed tightly the hand of the only man she knew in America. "I sell everything for buy this dress and visa stamp."

"Just to come see me?" Kip feigned astonishment and she punched him slightly on the arm, ignoring the hollow plastic feeling that snapped back at her under the fabric of his shirt.

"I think I stay for a while," she answered and Kip stopped fighting the tears back.

"I think I'd like that, Hoa," he said. "I think I'd like that very much."

It seemed fitting the nasty drill sergeants would stick Barry Todd and Nick Uhernik out on guard duty two hours later. Even though it *was* the night before graduation.

Never enough sleep. Run 'em till they drop.

The depot they protected by walking unscheduled circles around was supposed to be full of machine guns bound for friendly forces in Cambodia, but around three a.m. they picked the locks out of boredom and found the entire string of structures completely empty.

"Damn busy work," Todd groaned at the discovery. "And I needed my beauty sleep for the parade tomorrow."

They crawled into the barracks shortly after sunrise, desperate for a few hours sleep before the lengthy preparation for graduation from the MP academy.

Most of the other men were already up, discussing the home towns they were soon to see again and the women that were waiting for them.

"I got Panama!" one of the privates was yelling as he bolted into the barracks. "The duty assignments are posted!"

The entire building cleared out in a matter of seconds. Except for those men whose assignments were promised them in writing before they enlisted.

"Guess I had better make my appearance." Uhernik pulled himself out of his rack. Only a close circle of friends actually knew he was going off to Vietnam, and it appeared, contrary to rumor control, he'd be the only recruit from their training cycle bound for Southeast Asia.

"Make his appearance?" Todd smirked to the man snoring in the bunk beside him. "Sounds like a fucking West Point wimp ramrodded into attending another officer's bash. 'Guess I had better make my appearance.' Christ."

"Germany?" one of the men crowding in front of the bulletin board was complaining already. "Aw, fuck! What did I do to deserve Germany?"

"Honolulu, here we come!" Two men were laughing and dancing with each other in tight circles on the edge of the shifting mob. As they moved off, others filled the gap, pressing in for a closer look.

"Where the hell is Fort Dix?" another set of men asked each other.

"Hey, Nick!" Bobby Ray was calling out to the white Saigonese. "All it says after your name is RVN. What the hell does that mean?"

"Where the hell is RVN?" Valters was demanding.

152

"What the hell is RVN?" another recruit echoed.

"Nick's the *only* one going to RVN," an observant Andy Smallwood remarked softly, his suspicions bouncing back at him as he "felt" the answer in the air, and the air was icing up, cold and grim.

"Who gives a damn?" grunted the man assigned to Hamburg. "It can't be as bad as Germany!"

"RVN means Republic of Vietnam, you turkey heads," muttered Sergeant Mills. "Now leave the goofy fuck-I-done-signed-up-for-hell alone so he can start sweatin' it out." But Mills chuckled knowingly.

All the nervous talk did not matter. It was lost on Nick just then. His mind's eye was watching Kip Mather. The night they sat alone in the orderly room, drinking beer, shooting pool, and watching *The World of Suzie Wong* on TV. Just after the recruit had admitted he was not sure that, when the time came, he could uphold the reputation of the MP corps and calmly ice his opponent.

Mather's eyes had avoided him as he chose his reply carefully, and they followed Nancy Kwan instead, as she danced gracefully through the Hong Kong bar scene with William Holden. Nick had no way of knowing Mather's eyes were actually seeing the face of a man running toward him in a Saigon back alley. The first man he had ever killed. A common side street hoodlum who didn't see the MP uniform, and took the American for an easy wallet toss.

Mather's eyes were seeing the Vietnamese cowboy's face disintegrate in front of three quickly fired hollow-point bullets when he said, "A man cannot anticipate how another man—even his partner—might react under fire. Even, as in our case, an instructor and his pupil. The street is not the classroom. The classroom is not the street. When I killed the cowboy attacking me on Tu Do Street, I thought I reacted perfectly—precisely as I had been trained. Yet if I had reacted properly when those whores lobbed the grenade in my lap, perhaps half my body would not be cold to the touch."

"You could not have anticipated," the obedient recruit had interrupted, rushing to the defense of a hollowed-out warrior.

"Don't! I have argued it out a thousand times in my own head: if this, if that. It no longer matters. I'm no longer the man I was, yet Saigon lives on in her own way, unchanged. You will come back to visit me in a year, and you will have changed also. Perhaps more than even myself. And you may not have even drawn your weapon in all that time. And Saigon—she will not even have noticed. Or cared, my friend. She laughs at us both, even at this moment."

The men standing in front of the bulletin board began congratulating each other on their assignments, but few of them made their way toward Nick to shake his hand. Talk of Vietnam, of war zones, made young privates with families nervous and uneasy.

"It just don't seem fair," complained Valters, "that you're the only one to go. How the fuck am I supposed to send you a postcard from goddamned Europe?"

"It's not that way," Nick finally defended Uncle Sam, even if he *was* hoping for company on the way over—friends, not total strangers. "I requested Vietnam."

After the graduation ceremonies, he climbed back into his bunk and settled back for a nap before the flight to Oakland and the overseas processing center.

Moments later, despite the exhaustion of eight weeks at The School, he awoke, soaked in sweat, from a nightmare of a Vietnamese girl tossing a grenade into his patrol jeep to the sound of bugles playing "Taps."

A silence and calm had settled over Fort Gordon with the sunset, and as he gazed at the photo of the Vietnamese girl in his wallet, he listened to the last of the music fade and die away into the night.

He sat up, seeking one last echo across the land, but there was none.

12. PARTNERS IN SPIRIT

Five klicks east of Vinh An, in the Republic of Vietnam

Crowe lurched forward and yanked on the wire with all his might, detonating the claymore anti-personnel mines with a tremendous explosion before he began spraying the perimeter with his rifle. Schramm had no idea what his partner was sighting-in on—they had both been blinded by the yellow-white flash that seemed to rip out the belly of the blackness in front of them—but he joined in, throwing five-round bursts from left to right, then right to left, level with the ground. He knew the ricochets—those rounds that didn't burrow into the clay—would remain, at most, a couple feet off the ground. And that meant a lucky thirty-round clip could take the legs out from under a good two dozen VC.

Tracers were whizzing in at them now. From all over. And *they* were damn sure bouncing a good six, ten, even twenty feet off the ground as they arced in from every direction. And red tracers were even slicing the thick air toward them. After he had been led to believe they'd be green. The VC used green tracers, they told him. Must be using captured ammo tonight, he decided, groping for more mags. Must be something about the makeup of the tracerhead that makes 'em bounce so high too. Damn, it was beautiful the way they smashed into the rocks or somebody's helmet a few foxholes down and splashed into a thousand fiery pieces. And there went a white one! Christ, I never heard of *white* tracers. Man, the way it glowed! First hanging there, almost suspended in air as it arcs toward

155

you, then before you know it there's a sizzling little fireball accelerating toward you at the speed of lightning.

Schramm realized just then that he was reviewing his own thoughts. Despite the intensity of the firefight—the exchange of firepower was increasing with each minute—it was like he was floating above the scene, coaching his every reaction. A neon sign was hanging motionless above even his consciousness, and the thoughts came not as mental images or blurred messages, but distinct words, spelled out letter by letter in bright neon, the sentences racing by faster and faster now on that great chalkboard in the sky.

"Corpsman!" a strained voice several meters down the line was yelling between mortar explosions. "Corpsman up!"

On the other side, an older soldier—one of the buck sergeants—was yelling even louder, in a low booming voice, "Through the wire! They're coming through the wire at Niner's!"

Schramm was laughing almost hysterically, popping up above the sandbags every few seconds to spray off another clip. He could feel his whole body shaking, but he honestly couldn't decide if it was fear or the adrenalin racking him. "Leroy! Leroy, do you hear all that?" he screamed. "Dinks in the wire! Guys winnin' their Purple Hearts!" He leaned over and jerked off another half dozen rounds, on semi-automatic this time, and several dirt clods kicked up in his face in response, causing him to duck back down behind the sandbags. "Ain't this fucking great, Leroy? We're finally in it, brother! We're finally in a fighting fucking war!"

"This sucks, stupid!" Leroy yelled back, resisting the urge to reach out and slap his partner silly. A whole collage of tracers skipped in on them, throwing multicolored fragments of lead throughout the bunker and Crowe clamped his hands over his helmet and flattened himself against the earth in a bone-shaking dive. He struck his jaw on an empty magazine on the way down, and for a moment he saw the darkness light up with more stars. It felt like half his teeth had been jarred loose.

"Oh, damn! I'm hit, Leroy! I'm hit!" Schramm was dancing around, holding the calf of his left leg. "They got me, Leroy! The bad bad VC got your man Schramm! Oh fuck, they got me

156

good, Leroy! Hurts like a motherfucker! I can see it now: Ole Schramm limpin' down home town U.S.A. with a cane! They got me, Leroy! They done got me bad!"

Leroy Crowe always envisioned that he'd see men die on the battlefield silently, with perhaps that look of loss and intense shock as the enemy bullet peeled back their scalp or popped a three-inch hole through their face. Or just the opposite: Men catching a slug in the chest or the belly, screaming out that last painful cry against death before collapsing in the trenches and gurgling out the last of their life in blood-soaked spittle.

Yet here was that goofy Schramm—probably caught a sliver from some ricochet in the fleshy part of his leg—causing him more mental grief than they could possibly dish out at a Hanoi Hilton franchise.

Crowe reached out and grabbed his partner by the ankle, knocking both legs out from under him just as another barrage of smoking lead tore into the tattered sandbags piled along the rim of the foxhole.

"Get your ass down, Dave! Christ, you're the weirdest jerkoff I ever seen in the 'Nam!" Crowe inspected the tear in Schramm's pants leg. "I never seen anybody just inviting disaster like you. Jesus!"

"Whatta ya think, Leroy?" Schramm was wide-eyed with excitement, "am I gonna make it? How bad is it, huh? Level with me, brother!"

"Don't look good," Leroy lied, amazed with himself at having the energy to joke about a situation that still saw walls of lead raining down on them.

"I can take it, Leroy! Tell me, brother: Do it rate a Purple Heart?"

Crowe pulled the bloody leg around so that he could see the wound better in the flickering light from the string of dim yellow flares floating past over them. Schramm struggled to shift his body around in the direction Leroy was tugging.

Leroy was thinking, "Hope it hurts. Hope this teaches you a lesson," as he pulled on the leg again, twisting slightly now.

A tremendous blast on the edge of the perimeter rolled across the line of foxholes, penetrating even to the floor of their shelter. Both men felt the earthen walls creak and

157

shudder. They both experienced the moment of helpless, freezing terror when the hole seemed on the verge of crashing in on them, suffocating them to death. They both felt more explosions shake the ground, closer, then farther away—on the other side of the concertina.

Green star clusters were bursting overhead, drifting with the breeze across the American fortress, signalling the enemy was confident they had captured the poorly defended encampment.

But then more searing concussions were lighting up the night, and it was as if the air was being sucked from their lungs.

"I can't breathe! I can't fuckin' breathe!" Crowe was gasping, holding an empty bandolier over his mouth and nose, positive the rolling napalm would pour into their grave at any second.

Another series of blasts electrified the air along every inch of their bodies, and Crowe was flipped onto his back.

"The leg, Leroy! The leg!" Schramm was yelling, oblivious to their world ending before their time, before their number was up. "What about the leg?"

Crowe wanted to answer that the limb would have to come off—that would shut him up—but his eyes were glued to the sky overhead. Waves of red tracers were arcing magnificently out over their tiny, insignificant hole, and green and white tracers were zipping back into camp, often like Fourth-of-July fountains. Sometimes the waves clashed directly above him and the resulting shower of glowing sparks was like a carefully planned laser light show gone berserk.

"The leg, Leroy! It's not my ticket home, is it?" he sounded sincere. Insane, but sincere. "I don't wanna go home, Leroy! This is where I belong: in a jungle of no moon, land of tracer light! This is what it's all about, brother!"

"Your leg's OK, hero." Leroy forced himself to sit up and he emptied his bandolier of its last magazine. "Just a splinter of lead—you lucked out, hot dog." Crowe grabbed his partner's leg again.

"What—"

"Just wanna bandage it, Dave," he said calmly, a new succession of devastating concussions bringing tears to his eyes. Something wet was rolling down both ear lobes. He

158

prayed it was not blood, hoped it was only sweat or melted wax.

"Just a splinter!" Schramm jerked his leg away. "Just a fucking splinter?" He backed up like a snake recoiling, the empty brass on the ground scraping harshly between his trousers and the dirt. He was rising to his feet, slamming a fresh clip into his M-16. "How the hell am I supposed to get my first Heart—my C.I.B.?"

Schramm spun around on his heels and swung the rifle down on the edge of the foxhole, jerking off five rounds rapidly before he even realized an enemy soldier's face was staring, wide eyed, into the muzzle.

The MP private froze in shocked horror as the guerrilla's nostrils flared open and burst, splitting the face down the middle in a gush of crimson that splashed back in Schramm's own face before the shattered skull flopped back, out of sight.

A sudden excitement, stirred by unearned confidence, rushed through his entire body, and a grin replaced the mask of fear across his face as he spotted another Viet Cong rushing toward him.

A voice inside his head was banging a giant brass gong against his conscience, telling him he should not enjoy it so much—asking him if he had heard the enemy soldier scream. And was that word—his last word uttered in agony before his death—was that his mother's name he screamed out? Was it the woman who had brought him into the world that he now thought about, moments before leaving it? Or was it his wife's name, or a girlfriend's? The voice was screaming at him now, louder even than the VC had screamed: *That man died shrieking for a woman, not out of fear for you or death. There is no pleasure in that!*

Another voice was drowning out the gong, yelling: *More! More! Kill more Cong!* And his brother's face flashed before his eyes—his brother, who had been missing in these jungles for years now. Finally he realized what Dennis had found in the Orient, why he never wanted to return to the States. Never *could* return to a homeland at peace. Schramm's M-16 suddenly ceased firing, burping hot lead; its empty chamber was locked open, hungry for more soft-nosed loads.

Still another voice was screaming at him through the fog,

and he ignored Leroy's call for caution as he groped around in the dirt for more magazines.

"We're out! That's it! We're fucking out of ammo, David!" his partner was yelling right next to his ear, trying to pull him down, smash him against the earth, keep him away from the endless rush of singing lead that rained in on them in an ever-increasing crescendo.

The VC sapper who had been charging toward their position rushed past, ignoring them as he tossed his satchel bomb toward a larger concentration of GIs and was promptly cut in half by a combined burst from a score of automatic rifles. Three Americans rose to catch or knock away the package—like baseball fans fighting to catch the home run ball—and the bomb detonated prematurely, throwing limp, lifeless bodies up through the thick gun smoke, end over end.

Schramm jerked his arm from Leroy's grasp and tore open his pack with shaking hands. He was startled to notice the fingers trembling as they fumbled with the straps—it was as if his head was detached from the rest of his body and he was watching the effort from above, through a thin, smoky mist. Another 60mm mortar impacted with a thunderous rolling explosion beside their foxhole, jarring the walls like an earthquake. Both men were somersaulted onto their backs again, but Schramm bounced to his feet, the claymore mine free of the rock-hard canvas bag and in his hands now.

"Salvation, Leroy! Gonna take out some more Cong before we go meet our Maker!" and he slammed the anti-personnel bomb down on the edge of their hole without even looking to make sure it was aimed away from them, armed it with a swiftness that took Crowe off guard, then detonated it just as a swarm of guerrillas rushed down on them.

Leroy was positive he had died. The blast that sent over seven hundred tiny steel balls roaring out in a sixty-degree arc also sent a white hot flash past his closed eyelids to the center of his brain, throwing him off the cliff of consciousness into a deep, dark pit.

Falling, falling, falling further into an all-encompassing blackness that was both as vast as the cosmos and as confining as a well shaft, but then the depths of the bottomless pit were glowing a soft, pulsing crimson again, then dull orange, then bright yellow.

When the shades of color returned to a white haze he was still lying on his back, eyes open, pupils darting back and forth, following the tracers overhead without seeing them.

Schramm was standing off to the side, preparing another claymore, laughing hysterically, challenging the VC with taunting obscenities and insults directed in pidgin Vietnamese at their ancestors. The curses could barely be heard above the deafening clamor of gunfire.

"No! Not another one!" Leroy pleaded with the madman— this fellow MP he thought he knew inside and out—struggling to his knees, reaching out to grab him.

Schramm, his face and chest covered with shimmering rivulets of blood, paused briefly and glared down at his old friend, the flashes from distant explosions throwing a macabre shade of light across his features. The insane laughter stopped, and he seemed to scrutinize Leroy with disquieting puzzlement in his eyes as he looked down at him sadly, restrained temporarily by their frayed strings of friendship.

The death mask Schramm wore seemed to freeze before him in contrast to the glowing tracers bouncing in all around him, and Crowe's sudden relief was shattered as he helplessly watched the man's hand slowly trip the detonator, setting off another blast that cut down every communist within fifty meters.

This time there was no glimmer of growing light at the bottom of the pit, and as he plummeted down through the blackness, Crowe watched the hole above him, and the tracers crisscrossing beyond it, growing rapidly smaller, until his body ran slick with sweat, afraid this time he might slam into the bottom and not return.

Schramm pushed himself up off the floor of the foxhole and tore his pack apart, desperately searching for more claymores, but it was empty except for the dented C-ration cans and compressed hammock. That's what he got for travelling so light, and he managed to chuckle at the self-rebuke.

He crawled over to Leroy's pack—Viet Cong were now vaulting over the top of their foxhole in their rush to saturate the camp—ripped it open with his K-bar and dumped the contents in the dirt: five M-26 grenades and a .45 pistol.

He sprang up suddenly, enraged the enemy would ignore him in their blatant arrogance, and grabbed the first set of sandals gliding past over his head.

A young guerrilla, his zeal for American blood smothered as he was caught and dragged back down into the foxhole, was half trampled by the swarm racing past him.

Schramm reached up and snatched hold of the soldier's short hair, tried to jerk his head back so he could cut out the man's throat, but the crew cut was slick with sweat and the Vietnamese slipped free.

Schramm wrapped his other arm around the VC's neck and pulled back hard, then rammed the blade into the guerrilla's belly, deep to the hilt, and when it slammed against backbone he jerked upward with all his might, ripping the man's chest open—spilling his hot, steaming intestines down onto the contorted face of an unmoving, uncaring Leroy Crowe.

Schramm whirled around, hammered the already dead guerrilla into the earthen wall and scooped up his falling AK47 in the same movement. He pulled the pins on two of the grenades and heaved them out of the hole, toward the concertina wire, then fell back to earth as he stuffed the .45 automatic hastily in under his belt. The dual explosions from the grenades were indistinguishable from the din of constant mortar blasts racking the camp, but he could hear the added screams somehow, and the extra twist of agony he had just tossed at Charlie bathed him in bittersweet satisfaction—content with fate, ready for death.

He checked the Soviet-made Kalashnikoff: the magazine was nearly full. And as he prepared to leap up out of his foxhole—yes, he would go out in a burst of glory, against a hail of lead, taking as many of them along with him as he could—there came a sudden change in the mugginess of the hot, sticky air blanketing the battlefield.

Rotors were thumping everywhere, swirling man-made whirlwinds through the mist as a fleet of CH47B Chinooks descended from the skies and hovered above the perimeter wire. The monstrous transport helicopters, held aloft by a pair of powerful dual rotors on front and rear, unleashed a barrage of minigun and Gatling fire that lit up the night and cut down the line of advancing guerrillas.

Everywhere Schramm looked there were smaller Cobra gunships darting about, zapping Charlie on the run, maneuvering like daredevils in and out through the stationary chopping blades of the larger "mothership" Chinooks.

He stood up straight, spun about, desperately searching for VC to hunt, intense disappointment shattering him at the sight of all their bodies already hung up in the wire.

Deprived of The Kill, the slaughter, anger welling up inside him, Schramm could feel the impulse, the uncontrollable urge to fire upon the choppers—to cut down the survivors, his own men. Kill anything that moved, breathed, lived.

His helpless, hopeless scream was heard by no one above the dull whirring thump of the rotors, and in desperation he raised his rifle sights at the closest helicopter then, without explanation, lowered the barrel and fired all the rounds off into the earth before beating the AK47 to pieces against the uncaring corpses piled up around his feet.

"Check out *that* crazy fucker," the pilot of one of the gunships muttered to his crew as he swung the Cobra around to face Schramm.

"Looks like he's getting out of hand," the co-pilot observed, scratching his chin nervously as he watched Schramm repeatedly bayonet one of the already dead VC guerrillas.

"Maybe I should zap his ass," the doorgunner suggested, "before he flips out and downs one of the choppers." The remark was made without emotion and offered the same way an exterminator would decide on how much rat poison to use.

"Naw, he done wasted the last of his ammo," the co-pilot decided. "Let him be." And the gunship whirled around and continued down the perimeter.

"That's one grunt they're gonna ship back in a strait jacket," the pilot said, grinning. "Done flipped out on the 'Nam."

"Yep," the doorgunner agreed, making a circular motion with his forefinger beside his temple. "Done flipped out on the 'Nam."

*   *   *

Leroy Crowe spent several seconds holding his breath after his eyes popped open and he felt the warmth of the rising sun beating down on the top of his head. Aware of the bustle of activity and movement all about him, he quickly reclosed his eyes and tried to survey what was transpiring from narrow slits. There was a chance he was not in VC hands, a POW—he could feel his limbs were not bound, restrained. Maybe they thought he was dead. The surface beneath him was bumpy, shifting. Maybe he was lying on a pile of bodies—dead Americans being bulldozed toward a mass grave.

"What a fucking mess."

"Yeah, I heard something like forty KIAs, two birds downed by heat-seeking missiles too."

The voices, in English, bathed him in warmth and relief as they faded away in the distance, travelling the other way.

He sat up, the smile on his face hurting like a smile shouldn't, sending pain tremors across his forehead. The two GIs carrying his stretcher stopped in midstride, and a medic leaned forward and pushed him back down flat on his back.

"Lie easy, brother," a reassuring voice pounded his eardrums like sledgehammers, the acuteness of his hearing suddenly worse than during a hangover, but he tried to concentrate on his hands and feet. He shifted his fingers and toes about—could feel them move but instantly recalled stories of battlefield casualties who had lost their limbs yet could still feel the phantom pain where there was nothing but empty space.

"My arms, my legs—" he choked, "why—"

"Relax," the medic's voice was softer, more distant this time, exuding confidence, reassurance, "just a concussion. Could turn serious, though, if you don't settle down."

"Yeah, we'll hafta call some REMF MP to bop you with his billy club!" one of the stretcher-bearers joked, and all three laughed.

Crowe frowned at the ripples of pain wavering behind his eyes—it made the blue, cloudless sky above shimmer and shift about like a stormy sea.

"My partner—my buddy, Schramm. What about Schramm?"

"Which one is he?" the medic asked the soldier at Leroy's feet. The man's tone worried Crowe. It sounded like the camp had really taken a beating and suffered numerous casualties.

"Skinny dude," Crowe said, ignoring the pain that stabbed at him each time he moved his jaws. "Wire-rimmed glasses, scraggly-ass mustache. Looks more like a peacenik than a grunt. You know the type." He groaned and let his head flop back down on the folded body-bag pillow.

"Yeah . . . I think that was the guy they took over to the CP for observation: got that crazy gleam in his eyes. Made the medics afraid he mighta flipped out on all the action last night."

"Gotta tattoo of a slanted pussy over his bellybutton?"

"That's the guy!" Crowe sat up again, hope in his voice.

"He made it smile for us," the medic laughed, "the tattoo. Grabbed the sides of his belly around the navel and squeezed it till it looked like a whore's cunt, furburger and all!"

"Yeah, he's got the hair on his chest trimmed down into an upside-down triangle above the tattoo!" the third corpsman added. "Kinda makes you wanna hump him right then and there."

"You faggot," the first GI jested, and they almost dropped Crowe in the mild horseplay that followed.

"That's him!" Crowe was ecstatic. "Then he's OK?"

"He'll survive," the medic replied sarcastically. "Took a couple dozen slivers of shrapnel in his face and chest—"

"And a chunk in his leg—"

"But he'll make it."

Crowe grabbed the sides of the stretcher and hopped out onto solid ground—started running back toward the command post, what was left of it. He ignored the protesting corpsmen.

"Hey, come back here, shithead!"

"That headache of yours gonna split wide open!" the senior medic yelled after him. The stretcher-bearers had already washed their hands of the "injured" soldier and continued calmly walking away, as if they still had a patient between them.

The man in charge resignedly put his hands on his hips and

165

shook his head. "Crazy grunts. The 'Nam's turnin' 'em into animals. Wild fuckin' animals," he muttered before turning to walk away and catch up with his co-workers.

As he ran toward the CP, Crowe noticed the work details dragging in Viet Cong bodies off the concertina wire. Piling up the dead guerrillas who had breached the perimeter defenses only to perish once inside the camp itself. Not only had victory eluded them, they had apparently been dealt a devastating blow, Crowe decided. It was not often the communists left their dead behind.

Reward posters were also hanging all over the stretch of barbed wire. A couple soldiers were carrying piles of them from the edge of the trenchline where they littered the foxholes, and he could see that many of the VC corpses had their pockets stuffed with the eye-catching bounties.

Crowe snatched one up as it floated past on the breeze and examined the grainy likeness of Capt. Louis Moast. He cocked an eyebrow at the reward: it had been boosted to twenty-five-thousand greenbacks.

Somebody wanted Moast the Ghost, bad.

As he neared the command post, Crowe caught sight of several ARVN interpreters gathered around the village chieftain's daughter. Still shivering under her blanket, she was jerking her head from side to side at all their questions, her terrified eyes glued to the ground at her feet.

He had wondered briefly, during the first stages of the firefight, how she was faring. That first glimpse of her the day before, tied down on her back in the sand, legs spread wide, had remained with him throughout the battle. He envisioned coming upon her alone in some future adventure, rescuing her from the rising river, nursing her battered and swollen body back to health, she finally allowing him down between her thighs to show her gratitude. But the scattered explosions always drove the image from his mind, replacing it with the haunting face of the woman he had murdered back in Saigon.

Crowe was not often bothered by things he had done wrong in his past, but the prostitute's ghost possessed the uncanny ability to appear when he least expected her—usually just after he was convinced he had exorcised her from his conscience. He now accepted the punishment that vivid flashbacks of that horrible, out-of-control evening would follow him forever to his grave.

As he glanced back down at the poster, Crowe was reminded of the first time he had seen one, back with Big Barney, north of Gia Dinh, at the bungled ambush attempt where the three VC had died after their grenade launcher blew up in their faces. It appeared to even *his* untrained eye that the same printing press had been used to produce both series of reward posters. The style differed slightly, but both displayed a noticeable chip at the edge of each capital letter T, and there were similar insulting phrases repeated in both, describing in exaggerated detail all that was wrong with the American soldier and his way of life.

Big Barney, from his isolation cell in the padded psyche ward, had written Crowe and Schramm letters telling them how the army was planning to discharge him as mentally unfit because of the suicide attempt. But that was fine, he had stated, so long as they weren't going to confine him to some state hospital stateside after all. Crowe dug through his pockets for the letter, failed to find it, then checked inside his helmet. Lost.

Gone were the pills the doctor back at Third Field had issued him too. And all that time he had suspected Y-Von of giving him the clap! The tests had finally showed he, along with several other men at Pershing Field, had only contracted an infection from rusty drinking water in the barracks—for once Saigon's girls of questionable virtue were not to blame.

He raced his fingers through his pockets again, but the bottle of pills was definitely gone. And the burning sensation had nearly subsided. He didn't relish his next visit to the latrine to find out if he was cured.

"Schramm!" Leroy yelled with genuine relief when he spotted his buddy strolling unescorted away from the CP. "Wait up!"

"So you made it," Dave observed quietly a few minutes later, as they started back toward their squad. The insanity that had danced in his eyes the night before had faded to a cunning twinkle, dulled by the heat waves pressing down on the camp's survivors.

"Yeah, but what happened to *you*?"

"Aw, they had me holed up in that bunker back there, waiting for the shrinks or something. When the guard bowed out to fall in line down where those Honda Honies parked and set up 'shop,' I just walked off. Time to quit sloughin' off and get back to work, you know?"

"Sure, roger that." Leroy grinned, trying to gauge how serious the man was by the depth of his smile. The attempt was next to impossible.

Just then four unarmed Huey helicopters roared in over the camp, their noisy rotors raising funnels of dust for minutes after they had set down on the southern edge of camp, just within the concertina perimeter.

"Replacements," Schramm decided, as several gun-toting infantrymen, in fresh uniforms and clean shaven, jumped down while the slicks were still hovering inches above the clay. Cpl. Alvin Kline, his big First Cav combat patch dwarfing his small arms, was among them. Schramm recognized the scar on the man's left cheek immediately, even before images of the grunt's startled face—in the aftermath of the Caravelle brawl—drifted back from the recesses of his memory.

An angry-looking soldier disembarked at Kline's side, and Crowe couldn't help thinking he'd seen that freckle-splashed face somewhere before. The redheaded grunt's eyes locked onto Schramm's briefly, sending out hostile vibes that put both MPs in a defensive posture, but just as quickly he was gone, herded off by a hand-clapping buck sergeant who looked restless and eager for action. Crowe couldn't help but notice the man's light complexion—the sun was going to do a mean job on him in no time. The E-2 rank made him look new in-country, yet there was an impatience, a sarcasm in the redhead's expression that labeled him a veteran. But veteran of exactly *what*, Crowe was unsure. The name tag, "CHRISTIANSEN," meant nothing to him.

As the replacements trotted in formation past Captain Moast and his advisors, who were huddled around charts and plastic-layered maps deciding the unit's next move, both Schramm and Crowe noticed the redhead, Christiansen, almost stumble over himself as he glared over at the legendary Ghost, straining for a better look. But the special attention seemed more out of hatred than awe, and Schramm made a mental note to keep a close eye on the new soldier.

Leroy had other ideas, however. "That one, right *there*!" He pointed at the nearest helicopter, its rotors now twirling more slowly, the motors idling.

"What about it?" Schramm replied without interest. His eyes were on the ARVNs still questioning the chieftain's uncooperative daughter. As they passed the group, he overheard her repeat the Vietnamese words for American: "*wa-ky*" and "*my*," then bow her head again as she retreated into her fantasy world, where there were no gruff men to question and harass her.

"I'm gettin' on *that* fuckin' chopper, amigo!" Crowe declared.

"Why?" Schramm just stared at the bird with a dazed, far off, almost bored expression.

"Because it's there, stupid!" and Crowe made a mountain-like gesture with his raised arms as if he were envisioning a climb up cloud-covered Mount Fuji.

"Naw . . ." Schramm just shook his head, as though Leroy's antics were a distraction better left back in Saigon.

Both men turned away and shielded their eyes from flying dust as a small Loach helicopter spiraled down into the camp. An officer in tiger-stripe fatigues jumped out and raced past them, toward Captain Moast and his entourage.

"Even better." Crowe winked at his partner. "That black beauty right there is just what the doctor ordered. It's time to bum a lift back to the base camp for hot meals and a shower. This boonies crap gets old fast."

"You volunteered for it," Schramm reminded him, and as Crowe placed his hands on the chopper's door latch, it swung open and a warrant officer leaned out and planted a .38 revolver against his nose. The pistol's cylinders were so close Leroy had to cross his eyes to verify hollow points were staring back at him through the open holes.

"You doggies weren't planning to skyjack my craft here, now were you?" The pilot grinned from behind green-tinted sunglasses and a neatly trimmed aviator's mustache. He looked eager to pull the trigger, regardless whether it was Mr. VC or a mutinous grunt in front of the barrel.

"Oh, no, siree! You got it all wrong, mister!" Crowe backed up slowly, placing each footfall carefully behind the other, but the pilot kept the pistol in his face as he cautiously stepped down from the craft and advanced onto the ground. "We were just hitchhikin'."

"We thought you were our ride back," Schramm said with little worry or concern in his voice and he shrugged his shoulders at the gun and turned to walk away.

"I don't believe you," the pilot replied, cocking the hammer back loudly, "I think you yellow bellies was deserting!"

Schramm whirled back around, nearly letting a heel fly up at the man's jaw, but he balked at the last moment. "I don't give a fuck *what* you think, mister!" he snarled, the tone daring the pilot to shoot.

"Let's mount up!" A voice from behind them broke the tension. It was Moast, waving his hands about as he urged exhausted soldiers up onto their feet. "We got word one of MACV's Buffalos spotted our bandit bastard a few miles over those hills. Secure and load up! We're movin' out in five!" and he scurried back into his makeshift command post, out of sight. The Buffalos he spoke of were usually called Buffalo Hunters—unmanned, low-flying drone aircraft equipped with cameras—but so many had crashed recently that the Ghost had left off the "hunter" designation.

The Loach pilot holstered his .38 and climbed back into the chopper. "Have a pleasant trip," he muttered at Schramm an instant before latching the door shut. Dave rushed up at the handle at the same moment; Crowe jumped over to restrain. The pilot grinned, brought the idling rotors into a powerful climb that took the craft up out of the MP's reach, nearly catching him with the skids as it leaped up almost vertically and blew a gust of dirt in his face. Schramm shook his fist at the pilot and unslung his M-16, but Leroy nudged him against the shoulder, motioned over toward the CP, and both men quickly lost interest in the Loach as they watched the red-head, Christiansen, run after Moast and disappear down into the bunker.

"Better check it out," Crowe decided. He had been suspicious of the man's look ever since watching him jump off the gunship, and even though Schramm said, "I hope he frags the son of a bitch," both men started toward the CP at a brisk trot.

The tremendous blast that catapulted Leroy back into his partner, knocking them both down into the dust, erupted without warning and they both sat stunned amid falling debris as pieces of the CP's sandbagged roof rained down across the camp.

"Christiansen done fucked up," Schramm grumbled, rubbing his sore shoulder, lacking the energy or desire to join the search for survivors.

"Yeah, took 'em both out," Crowe agreed. It never occurred to either MP that the explosion might have been caused by a descending projectile instead of a grenade from within.

That is, until the barrage of mortars began walking across the camp, following the initial adjustment round which had been right on target.

It was almost like an invisible monster was slowly lumbering through camp, his giant paws making puffs of smoke appear from craters marking his tracks.

Schramm watched starry-eyed as a trail of explosions caught three soldiers midway across the camp and lifted them up in the air with a lead-laced blast that propelled each man in a different direction. An arm landed at Crowe's feet, and he yelled at the sight of the gnarled fingers still twitching and the bloodied tendon hanging out from the severed bicep snapping back and forth like a live hot electrical wire.

"Down!" He wrapped his own arm around Dave's neck and tackled him as a sheet of tracers flashed by, leaving smoky trails through the space where they had just been standing.

Crowe forced his face up out of the dirt at the sound of the additional gunships sweeping into camp. On either side of him, men were slowly advancing in a cautious crouch, toward the CP bunker, out of some lost sense of loyalty or misplaced dedication to their captain. Just as many soldiers were headed the other way, toward the landing choppers, their M-16s

171

nevertheless at the ready, braced against hips, for Charlie was throwing hot metal at all sides of the camp now.

Crowe fought the warning bells clanging in his head—the ones that told him to stay face down, till it was all over. But this time, he knew, it would be over only when the VC had overrun the camp and every last American was dead or captured. As he pulled himself up to his hands and knees, he was suddenly recalling all those past times he had answered sniper calls down Thanh Mau alley, back in Saigon. He remembered the cold, shivering feeling that oozed down his backbone with each step deeper into the shadows: anticipating that fatal shot finally ringing out. Wondering if the sniper was up on one of a dozen rooftops or if he was level on the street with yourself. Wondering if you'd feel that bullet ram into your forehead, or the bridge of your nose, or right into your mouth, then burrow its way painfully through the protesting layers of bone only to splash about unrestrained in the gray, cheeselike brain matter.

These same feelings were racing through Crowe's head as he got to his feet and headed toward the CP. He hoped that fateful round would pound through his heart and, like breath and wind being knocked out of him, tear the life from him, out the gaping exit wound, painlessly, before his corpse could even crumple to the ground.

"Well I'll be a . . ." Schramm didn't finish the sentence, but only stared ahead at the bunker, dumbfounded, as a blackened and tattered Captain Moast emerged staggering from the bowels of the collapsed CP, holding a dazed, near-unconscious Christiansen in his arms.

An unexplainable energy coursed through their veins at the sight of Moast rising from the dead—an apparition, almost, gliding through the smoke and ashes toward them—and both Crowe and Schramm rushed over to the captain.

He dumped Christiansen into Leroy's arms and pointed toward the nearest helicopter. "Get this man on board!" Moast directed. "Him and me gonna have a little talk after this is all over."

Schramm, seconds later, had cleared a trail through the soldiers hustling to board the gunship, and he helped drag the unresponsive redheaded grunt up onto the craft. Crowe flipped the pilot a thumbs up, and as the gunship's rotors took on more power and began to lift the bird, Captain Moast appeared on the edge of the skids, fighting to keep his balance as he dove for the open hatch.

Several men grabbed him and pulled him in, and though the chopper had dipped precariously with the sudden, uncompensated weight, the pilot uttered some choice obscenities then quickly regained control and swung the craft around in a half loop that tossed all the soldiers on top of each other, against one wall.

Tracer rounds spun noiselessly up on either side of the chopper, their smoke trails close enough to touch, evidence they were not yet out of the thick of it.

"Where to, Cap?" The co-pilot turned back to stare at Moast with a questioning look in his eyes.

Moast still hung in the doorway, clinging to the support braces, the clouds spinning past behind him the same way storms avoid graveyards at the last minute—the breeze whipping at his short, blond hair, now greased back with sweat, making him look more ghoulish than ever.

"We swing around onto their left flank!" His eyes were alive like lightning bolts, anticipation dancing about in their depths. "Cut off their main force and drive them back into the river!"

"You mean go back down *there*?" the co-pilot asked incredulously, pointing down at the blanket of black that was thousands of enemy soldiers massing along the banks of the Song Dong Na.

"I'm not taking *this* bird down *there*!" the pilot muttered without looking back at Moast. "I don't like the odds."

"Pull back and live today, so's we can return to fight another day," one of the younger grunts said to Moast, but the statement was more a suggestion than anything.

"We're *all* gettin' low on ammo, Cap," another soldier reasoned, but Moast was bounding past them, up toward the front of the chopper. His .45 was out as he leaned through the narrow partition into the cabin. "Take this damn whirlybird down. Right now, soldier!" and he placed the automatic against the pilot's head.

"And if I don't?" the man responded calmly. "You gonna

blast me with your equalizer there? Then we go down for sure: numba one crash landing, Cap. That what you want?"

"If you don't take this bird down, the only thing that awaits you back at base is a court-martial and life at Leavenworth. That what *you* want, mister?"

The pilot turned to look at his co-pilot with an irritated scowl, and the other man whispered, "No one would ever convict you—not under these circumstances." But the pilot cut back on the power and swung the craft around, dove twice to strafe the lines of advancing Viet Cong while they waited for the other helicopters to rejoin them.

Then they descended in force, miniguns blazing.

Their gunship hadn't been on the ground ten seconds when the burst of rifle slugs caught Pvt. Leroy Crowe in the belly and slammed him back into a shocked David Schramm.

Two men had already jumped down onto the ground, but resistance was so intense they were scrambling back on board, and the pilot was shaking his head back and forth, angry at the waste, the stupidity of it all.

"Leroy! Leroy! Can ya hear me, buddy? Can you hear me, goddamnit?" Schramm was yelling against the scream of incoming rounds bouncing about the cabin, but, as he sat against the wall of the gunship with Leroy suddenly forced backwards into his arms by the fusilade, he knew it was all over. His fingers were already slick with what could only be most of his partner's sheared intestines, hanging out over his customized belt buckle from the pancake-sized stomach wound.

Even as he struggled to get out from under Crowe, more and more bold and daring guerrillas were rushing past the chopper, pausing a moment to spray two or three rounds into the craft before continuing on toward the river, and Schramm could feel additional slugs impacting against Leroy's already lifeless body.

Finally, Moast was dragging his dead partner off him, tossing him aside roughly, urging Schramm to "quit cowering behind corpses" and get out there and fight!

The MP gazed down at Leroy's crumpled body—his eyes still stared out at the battle, and Dave was wondering just then,

174

despite the clamor of bullets pounding against the walls of the gunship, if Leroy had felt much pain. If someone back home— a girlfriend, mother or someone close—had felt an unexplainable pull at their gut, or a haunting twinge at the moment of his death.

Schramm felt he was going to die in a few minutes. The look on Leroy's face told him the whole crew was probably going to perish before the sun had set on this firefight, but Schramm wanted to say something to Leroy before he left—before Leroy left for hell, and *he* left for the hell awaiting him outside the chopper hatch. He wanted to be alone with his buddy. Just for a minute—that last minute.

Schramm went down on one knee beside Crowe and laid a hand on his shoulder, was just beginning to look into the man's lifeless eyes, just beginning to see the reflection of a dead prostitute's haunting face grinning her final content, when Moast grabbed him by the hair.

"On your feet, soldier!" Moast was yelling. "Charlie's waiting out there for you!" But no sooner had the captain jerked Schramm up off his knees when the enraged doorgunner, Randy Nelson, pushed Dave back out of the way and propelled Moast the Ghost out the open hatch with a mighty kick.

Nelson calmly turned back to face the startled pilots, gave them the thumbs up and muttered, "OK, *now* you can take her up." Soon the helicopter's rotors were laboriously cutting through the hot, thick air, straining to lift the craft back up into the laughing clouds.

The last thing Schramm remembered seeing before closing his eyes against the cruelty of it all was Captain Moast, alone down on the ground, engaged in hand-to-hand combat with four guerrillas only half his size.

But awaiting their turn were a dozen more Viet Cong, nursing their smiles eagerly as they sat patiently atop the charred carcass of a burned-out First Cavalry Division gunship, lying on its side, half buried in the sandy crab-infested riverbanks of the Song Dong Na.

13. INITIATION INTO HELL'S ELITE

Saigon

Mount Fuji's snow-capped peak pierced the vast white layer of clouds and rose majestically to greet them as their Boeing 707 drifted lazily over the Japanese skyline in preparation for refueling at Yakota.

"What a sight!" one of the men across the aisle from Nick Uhernik exclaimed, and the tired private, the only MP graduate of The School aboard the flight, forced himself to leave his seat for a better view.

Fuji *was* a truly spectacular sight. It seemed to take the plane forever to fly past, so great was the mountain, and Nick suddenly wondered, as they descended into the clouds and the peak disappeared from view, if it might be the last beautiful thing he would see on earth.

The men were confined to the airport terminal in Yakota for the two-hour stopover, so Nick busied himself sending off large postcards of Tokyo to Angi, hoping they'd be in her mailbox the same day she escorted him home from the processing center.

He also found himself watching the faces of the other men he had joined at the overseas processing station in Oakland. About fifty of them had endured that endless week at the center, pulling repeated KP and maintenance duties. They underwent abuse from the sergeants that even rivaled the treatment they had received in boot camp. When it finally came, they all welcomed with a sigh of relief the PA

176

announcement that their flight manifest to Vietnam was ready.

Everyone was buying a Japanese newspaper. He watched the men's faces as they scanned the unintelligible headlines—the pictures told the story: the war in Vietnam raged on. He looked for fear in their faces, but saw only confusion and anxiety.

"We'll be arriving at Saigon's Tan Son Nhut Airport in about five hours," the pilot advised them as they climbed back toward the clouds. "That will be 5:25 p.m., the twentieth of June 1967," he joked for the benefit of the soldiers who had lost track of time during the eighteen-hour flight from California. "Now let's all synchronize our little watches." The humor was wearing thin.

He spent the next few hours mesmerized by the endless expanse of clouds, noticing they grew more fortresslike as the plane crossed over into Vietnamese air space. He was feeling a nausea in his gut—things were not right. It was not like he was returning home—it was like he was being hurtled headlong, out of control, into a tempest that was meant to devour him long before he ever saw Angi again. He was now seeing this flight, this descent into Saigon, not as a home-coming, but as all the men around him; as the start to a combat tour he might not survive. He was not an anxious Vietnamese, oblivious to the war raging on outside the capital, but an American, being flown at dizzying speed, toward a hostile and alien land.

"I guess this is it," the private next to him mumbled uneasily as the seat-belt sign chimed on and the aircraft began to meander down through the maze of snowy white castles that rose from the blanket of clouds. They both checked their watches, then nervously shook hands.

"I wonder if . . ." Nick started to say, but the intercom came on just then.

"Ladies and gentlemen—" the pilot had to be smiling—"let me be the first to welcome you to Vietnam."

Everyone looked around the plane for the ladies, but then the plane was banking sharply to the right. Nick stared out his window, searching. "Nothing," he whispered to the man beside him. Nothing, at first.

Then, slowly, the line of clouds dispersed and vast patches of lush, green jungle lay spread out below them, along

177

the coastline.

"Below you is Cam Ranh Bay," stated the pilot, a strange pride in his tone, and they stared down at the military installation that seemed so out of place in that dark, teeming forest. And then it disappeared beyond the treeline, and there was only jungle again.

They passed over a slight mountain range, then the plane suddenly dropped hundreds of feet, a descent that shocked all on board. "We musta got hit," somebody ventured a hushed guess.

"Nothing to worry about," the pilot was saying, "we're beginning our descent now, and we like to take it low and fast to discourage hostile ground fire—in case Charlie's watching. Nothing to worry about."

"Look, out there!" The man beside Nick was looking out the window, pointing toward two helicopter gunships that circled far below them, firing their automatic weapons down into the jungle.

"They must be chasin' some commies," the guy behind Nick was saying. "Damn, I'm watchin' my first genuine firefight, and I'm not even in it!"

"Better than the late-night network news," the pilot spoke over the intercom, anticipating their thoughts.

The choppers circled a small hamlet on the outskirts of Saigon, showering the treeline with tracers and crisscrossing each other's path below the thunderclouds that were rolling in from the angry South China Sea.

"They're really blastin' them fuckin' VC!" observed the seventeen-year-old in front of them, a smile from ear to ear. Then he sat back heavily in his seat and the grin disappeared. "I wonder if I'll be able to do that," he thought out loud, "be able to shoot and kill the enemy."

The same thought had been troubling Nick the last few months. It was something he often pondered late at night, as he stared up at the various ceilings he was coming to know all too well. Sure, he had busted heads on the pugal stick course, and "killed" a dozen dummies with his bayonet. But could he slay a human being? Even the dreaded and hated Viet Cong—the enemy he had been conditioned to gun down on sight and ask

178

questions about later? Kip Mather had assured him that, when the time came, it would be only him and the Cong. And when that time came, gut survival would take over, despite your morals or how you'd been brought up. Nobody turned the cheek in the jungle. It's just that some men had a slower gun hand.

Their plane was passing over the wide, muddy Mekong River, and still they had taken no hostile fire from the ground—at least none that they were made aware of. Rooftops of blackened tenements and bombed out housing projects were suddenly passing only a few hundred feet below their aircraft, and then, with a jarring triple bounce, they touched down at Tan Son Nhut.

Small groups of Vietnamese, squatting along the runways, conical straw hats hiding their faces from the plane passengers and the intense sun, worked on the bombed out portions of the tarmac. Nick felt strange, as if he were viewing his fellow countrymen for the first time. The Vietnamese ignored the jet as it raced by, but American GIs supervising the clean up crews leaned on buried shovels and grinned at its passing as they wiped sweat from their brow then spit at the dust.

As the craft pulled up to the control tower and slowed to a halt, jeeps full of U.S. and Vietnamese security forces drove up, forming a huge ring around the plane with their backs to the new arrivals—and their weapons pointed out at unseen eyes lurking beyond the sea of shimmering elephant grass. Some of the SPs kept their M-16s at hip level as they nervously scanned the free fire zone beyond the long, swaying fenceline of barbed concertina wire, while others left them slung upside-down over their drooping, sweat-soaked shoulders.

Air force policemen escorted a ladder truck up to the 707 and quickly swung open the craft's doors. Normally flight attendants accompanied the military contracted jets, even into South Vietnam, but on this trip their crew consisted only of the manpower necessary to operate the plane. A co-pilot stepped out into the aisle and began shaking hands. It had been a long, tiring flight, but nothing compared to the journeys earlier groups of GIs had made by boat, and the men realized this. They were thankful times had changed; you no longer

179

spent thirty days swimming about in the bowels of a vomit-filled barge, confined below deck on your voyage across the Pacific. The co-pilot stepped in front of Nick and took his hand in a strong, fatherly grasp. "Good luck!" he told every soldier. He did not smile.

The newbies were herded into long, green Army buses that had appeared beside the jet.

"Jesus," one man whispered to the soldier beside him, surprised at the wave of heat that rolled up the steps to greet them. It was akin to walking into a blast furnace!

Uhernik started to take his hat off, but an officer behind him said, "You'll get used to the climate, soldier." The major was grinning at the men's discomfort. An Airmobil cavalry combat patch was on his right shoulder. He had been here before. The rest of the privates were all wearing shiny new, almost metallic, green jungle fatigues that had been issued them in Oakland, and most felt very conspicuous with the E2 private chevrons on their collar, and no battle patch.

A formation of soldiers, some marching in front but most dancing in the rear, filed past their bus singing rude and vulgar cadences. They were led by a darkly tanned man, wearing buck sergeant stripes, who pointed to the buses, commanded, "Eyes right" to his men, then yelled, "Good luck, newbies!"

His men repeated after him, "Good luck, *newbies!*" but with less enthusiasm. They emphasized the term newbies for the replacements' benefit, then filed onto the same airplane the new men in-country had just off-loaded from.

"Must be their freedom bird back stateside," decided the major with the combat patch. "They made it through their Tour 365," he said, grinning, staring out at the little men in conical hats and speaking to nobody in particular. "I hope we do too."

The windows of the bus contained no glass, but were heavily screened, with a thick wire mesh on the outside. "To keep the grenades from bouncin' in on you," quipped the major.

Nick tested the strength in his fingers against the durability of the chicken wire by squeezing as hard as he could. The blisters on his hands from the monkey-bar course back in Georgia started to split and bleed, and his ring scraped against

180

the metal with a sad little screech, but the wire held firm. As the thin stream of blood started to ooze down the bars of the window, he squeezed the mesh again, rubbing the ring against the sudden silence of the ride. He could no longer hear the blaring Saigon traffic as the long bus swung around onto a crowded boulevard.

Sidewalk vendors selling melons and prostitutes riding sidesaddle on Honda motor scooters raced by in a blur as his mind's eye drifted beyond the jungled landscape to a world he had not yet entered. A three-wheeled cycle backfired in front of the bus and half the passengers dove to the floorboards, fearing their first mortar barrage.

"Was that a sniper?" someone at the front of the bus yelled at their Vietnamese driver. The old *papa-san* leaned back in his soiled, grease-caked seat, puffed huge smoke rings from a cheap cigar as he smiled back at the GI.

"You want girl, Joe?" the aging sometimes-pimp answered the soldier's terror-stricken face with another question.

Nick had not dropped to the floor with the rest of the men, but the sweat of fear was beginning to wet the back of his shirt—he had not even been assigned a helmet or weapon yet. And suddenly the streets of Saigon he so dearly loved—the same streets he and Angi had strolled down on countless occasions—now seemed transformed into a menacing dragon, coiled at the edge of the bamboo forest, preparing to strike out at him. Now that he wore a uniform.

"Hey, Joe!" A young boy was suddenly running alongside the bus, holding his hand out to Nick. "You gimme bubblegum!" he demanded.

One of the men beside him tried to spit at the kid, but the saliva got caught on the mesh and just dripped to the floor of the bus. "Fuck off, ya little bastard!" the soldier screamed, genuinely irritated by the boy. He had an airborne patch on his right shoulder. He had been here before, too.

The little kid skidded to a halt in the dusty road and flipped the Americans his finger. "Cheap Charlie!" he yelled, waving a fist to cover up the hurt in his eyes.

Nick tried to keep sight of the boy, but he soon disappeared down an alley crowded with cycles and overflowing

181

with pedestrians.

"Never trust the little jerks." The soldier grinned back at the men. "They'll sell you their sister for fifty bucks, or stick you in the back with your own bayonet while they snatch the watch off your wrist!"

Nick tried to ignore the man. He knew the kids weren't all that bad. None of the people were as bad as these "veterans" made them out to be.

He wondered about the VC, and if the spitting soldier would drive the small boy closer to them than to the "American side." He kept telling himself he despised communism, although he wasn't really sure what it was. They had never discussed it in high school, except to affirm that it was a bad, evil thing the Saigon government would not tolerate. Even in basic training, the DIs had avoided the subject though it was repeatedly drilled into your head that the Viet Cong were bad. That all communists were bad, bad, *bad*, and that your mission as a soldier—your mission so long as you were on God's good green Earth—was to kill, kill, kill *all* communists! "And in South Vietnam," the drill sergeants had all said, "you can't tell the good guys from the bad guys, so you consider them *all* bad. Especially if they're wearing black pajamas."

Nick scanned the streets bustling with activity beyond the windows. Half the women shopping in the sidewalk markets were wearing "black" pantaloons under their flowing *ao-dais*.

He stared at the ring again. They had let him keep it, and now it sparkled in the low Asian sun—the brilliant gold dragon dancing on one side and "U.S. ARMY—VIET NAM" emblazoned on the other. A star sapphire mystically changed shape inside the blue stone as he tapped his fingers along the cage. He almost felt like a prisoner.

Angi had sent him the ring as a present while he was still at The School: a gift bearing apologies while not quite losing face. At the way she had slammed the door in his face the night he left Vietnam.

Some of the drill sergeants had told him that all jewelry would be sealed in a plastic bag and kept till the end of his tour in a vault in Oakland, but they had let him keep it—nobody seemed to care how you looked in the 'Nam. Mirrored sunglasses, multicolored headbands, and tiger-claw necklaces adorned the bronzed vets he passed. Most seemed to be smiling—having a good time as they wandered along the crowded, tenement-packed streets. Or were they grinning about something he couldn't yet understand? Their eyes, it seemed, stared off at some past, distant battlefield.

The bus suddenly pulled to the right as a police jeep roared by at high speed, siren screaming, chasing a motor scooter. Its riders had just snatched the wrist watch off a GI as he walked among the sidewalk vendors. The thieves had ignored one of the many government checkpoints that dotted the intersections at regular intervals. The chase proceeded down a side alley, out of sight. Saigon traffic cops on foot waved the bus on, enduring layers of blue exhaust fumes that seemed to settle upon their white shirts right before the Americans' eyes.

Nick scanned the skies at the sound of approaching helicopters and spotted two choppers racing below the clouds. The gunships, oblivious to the goings-on of the city dwellers below, passed over the seething crowds and snarled traffic, en route to some storm of flying lead raging above the jungles along suburban Plantation Road.

Their bus entered an American compound, and the first sight he perceived—the first sight to register in his confused mind—was that of a squad of soldiers loading body bags onto a U.S. Army truck. He wondered if the dead were friendly forces, or VC sappers. Were casualties mixed for transport, or were the green bags even wasted on the enemy?

The cracked sign above the compound's heavily guarded entrance had read, CAMP ALPHA: WELCOME TO THE REPUBLIC OF VIETNAM.

His eyes searched the mass of Vietnamese crowded outside the main gate, hoping Angi might be among them—he had sent her a telegram giving his arrival date, but they had held his manifest over several days at the last minute so she would have found nobody here if she made the effort to greet him on his return to Saigon.

The bus pulled up to another processing center, and the men filed off into a concrete bunker, once used to house airplanes above ground, in alphabetical order. They were issued a mattress and sheets, then assigned a cement barracks, each of which held only about twenty men.

The newbies were rushed through a floorshow performance given by slender dancers of the Vietnamese band, Hammer, served a quick hamburger and beer, then ushered over to another processing bunker for midnight orientation.

A master sergeant in starched khakis and a chest full of Asian combat decorations gave the men tips intended to keep them out of the Saigon jails, briefly reviewed Viet culture and customs (you don't point the bottoms of your feet at them or call them with a whistle) and showed an ancient V.D.-Prevention film that fell apart every five minutes.

"You men will be here at Camp Alpha only a week or so." The sergeant smiled down at them from his teakwood podium. "Or until your units decide to come pick you up. Hopefully, I'll see you all a year from now, when you out-process through this very same camp!"

"What will *you* be doing here one *year* from now?" somebody in the back of the room joked loudly, assuming the veteran would be long gone from the 'Nam before then.

"Are you kidding?" he bellowed. "I love this fucking country! Gonna retire here someday!" Some of the men forced a laugh. They were all getting tired. The booze was wearing off—or taking effect. And Nick was taking a liking to this big career soldier towering over them all—even if his hair *was* ridiculously short. At least he wasn't bad-mouthing the country like everyone else. "By the way, how many potential MPs do I have in the room?"

Nick and a few others, destined for the 716th MP Battalion in Saigon, raised their hands proudly.

"Good, good." He smiled, patting the beaming men on the backs. "Guard duty calls."

The other men in the room broke out into laughter. Some even clapped. After a few seconds of painful embarrassment, the MPs forced smiles themselves, but Nick made it a point to memorize the sergeant's name tag. Perhaps he'd see him out on the street someday soon. Golden rule at The School: Don't get mad, get even.

*　　　*　　　*

A thick mist clung tight to Camp Alpha that night. Flares fought to burn through the haze, but, from where they stood watch, the dimly burning pyrotechnics just could not do the job.

"This is the creepiest fucking place I ever pulled guard duty."

"I heard talk they burned up a dozen sappers right on the wire there last year," another man whispered as they were marched out to their posts. "They say them VC ghosts still come around on foggy, moonless nights like this."

Nick listened to the privates scare each other and their talk humored him, but he was really concentrating on that afternoon, his third day at Camp Alpha, when he found Angi waiting for him at the main gate, on the other side of the concertina.

This was not how it was supposed to be, he told her as their tangled fingers were pulled apart by uncaring sergeants who yelled at him for breaching the security barricades and fraternizing with the local girls. There would be plenty of time for that once you got assigned to your unit, they had reprimanded him, but so long as you were at Camp Alpha, you were quarantined from the outside world—protected. It was all part of the numbers game. Nick had explained the situation to the NCOs, and after they guffawed in surprise and wonder, they tipped their helmets to Angi in apology but still dragged him away from the fenceline. Rules were rules, and he'd have plenty of time to rendezvous with his tealock after they issued him his armband and .45 at Pershing Field. Nick would never forget the hurt look in her eyes when she backed away from the barbed wire, turned and disappeared in the teeming crowd, without a single word of goodbye, forced to return home alone.

Now and then formations of faceless soldiers marched by: to the KP duty, trash detail, or other of the endless busy-work chores dreamed up by the Camp Alpha staff. As long as they wore U.S. uniforms, and were taller than five foot, the guards did not challenge them.

Despite the bad visibility—Nick was convinced God had it descend only over Camp Alpha—jets roared off from the air base at regular intervals, while others landed on separate runways, racing their engines against the silence of the night.

Now and then that silence was disrupted by the thunderclap of bombs dropping in the distance, and the flash of lightning that was actually artillery pounding enemy positions outside the capital.

During one of the five-minute periods of eerie silence, there came a sudden running of heavy jungle boots and an answering *craaaack*! from a large-caliber firearm.

"What was that?" an MP whispered over to Nick from his position twenty yards away. His voice carried across the void of fog despite the echo reverberating from the shot fired.

"I don't know," he answered honestly and the sound of several M-16s being nervously chambered filled the night.

"I need a medic! I need a medic!" a man was calling from out in the dark, about a hundred yards down the fenceline. "We've got a man shot!"

Nick started toward the call for help, but the sergeant of the guard, patrolling on foot a few hundred feet down the opposite direction yelled, "Maintain your post, MP!" In a few seconds he had run up to the private's position. "OK," he puffed, out of breath and unused to the humid heat, even at night. "*Now* you can go. With *me*. Let's check it out."

They arrived outside a cluster of privates who surrounded a second lieutenant on his back. The officer had sustained a rifle wound to the chest and a sickly, gurgling sound filled the air as he tried to breathe with lungs that were rapidly filling with fluid. "It was an accident! It was a goddamn accident!" cried one of the infantrymen who had been yanked from sleeping in the barracks to supplement the shortage of MPs patrolling the camp. "The jerk was sneaking up on me! Musta thought I was sleeping or goofin' off. I zapped him, man. I thought he was the fuckin' Cong! Really, I did."

"Jesus Christ," muttered the sergeant, forgetting for the moment that he himself was still a newbie, "you guys should know there aren't any VC out there! This guard duty is just horseshit—busy work! Any Charlies would have to get through the air force SPs way out on the perimeter first. There'd be a hell of a firefight before the enemy ever got to this joint! Hell, anybody call for an ambulance yet?"

Nick started back toward his post, feeling pleasantly relieved that he had not been the man who shot the butter-bar. The rest of the night passed quickly.

The wounded lieutenant was sent back stateside the next day, after less than a week in Saigon. His superiors pinned a Purple Heart on him and labeled the incident hostile action. They left out the word "enemy."

That same morning Nick was awakened by a corporal kicking his feet gently out of the rack. "Up and at 'em, *newbie!*" he yelled the official proclamation, "I just come over from Pershing Field with your orders from personnel. You're staying in good ole Saigon with the 716th Military Police Battalion!"

Nick tried to shake the sleep from his eyes, but they were shut tight and didn't want to open. He kept the o.d. green pillow clung tightly over his face. "Get lost!" he moaned, "I need a couple more hours sleep."

"Sleep?" the corporal asked incredulously, nudging the man beside him playfully. "Did he say sleep?"

"Sleep," Nick repeated. "Just got off guard duty. Before that me and that crazy medic from Third Field spent the afternoon toasting the strippers at the club . . . listening to Hammer . . . gettin' all fucked up. Show some mercy, brother."

"Mercy?" the company clerk scratched his blond afro for a moment.

"On your feet, soldier!" the spec. 4 beside the company clerk bellowed, but Uhernik didn't even flinch.

The corporal with the pet rat balanced delicately on his shoulder kicked at the newbie's feet again, harder this time. "What you think this is, boy? A fucking resort or something? I said you was assigned to the Super Troopers of the 716th! You should be proud!" he said almost sarcastically, mocking the private's chosen profession. In fact, they were fighting words, the way he said them. Nick flung back the sheets and jumped at the man.

He was still clothed from the waist down in his jungle fatigues and boots—too hyper to sleep in only his underwear his first week with the U.S. Army Vietnam Command. He took a swing at the corporal but found he still could not open his eyes.

"Jesus H. Christ!" Calvin Schaeffer sounded shocked, "lookee at you, boy!"

"Whatsa matter? Whatsa matter?" Nick demanded. He pulled his swollen eyes open and walked over to the latrine, stared into the mirror, and suddenly felt queasy.

His entire chest, face and arms were covered with little red dots. It looked like a terrible case of the measles.

"What the fuck?" He started to ask himself what could account for such a malady.

"That'll teach you to not use your mosquito net, newbie," the corporal laughed. "Them little bastards ate you alive last night. I'm sur-fuckin'-prised you got enough blood left to be walking around. Hope you been takin' your malaria pills."

"Yeah, thanks, pal," he said, pulling at his eyelids for a better examination. The bloodshot eyes matched the bite marks perfectly, causing all three men to erupt into laughter.

"Fuckin' newbies." Schaeffer laughed longest. "They never learn."

Nick wanted to tell both of them that he had been walking the streets of Saigon back when they were still teething, but he resisted the urge. Instead, he puzzled over the mosquito bites and decided it was because he had never used a mosquito net in the past. At home, he had always slept beneath a slowly twirling ceiling fan—and that kept the pests away. There were no fans in this barracks.

"You clowns MPs?" He noticed the Eighteenth Brigade patches on their shoulders, and after watching the bug-eyed rat look back down at him for several seconds, he looked away, repulsed.

"I'm your company clerk," Jake Drake introduced himself as he pulled an unwilling Gertrude off his shoulder and plopped her down in the middle of his curly locks. "This here is Cal Schaeffer. At one time a fine Saigon Commando."

"Now, all burnt out to hell," Schaeffer muttered, staring Nick straight in the eye.

"Got attacked by wild dogs," Drake continued.

"Got rabies up the ass," Schaeffer affirmed calmly, his story inviting a newbie's challenge, but Nick just shrugged his shoulders.

"Does your rat have a name?"

"She's not a rat," Drake snarled defensively, "she's Gertrude."

"Aren't you afraid she's gonna shit in your hair?"

Jake Drake just frowned and motioned for the recruit to gather up his gear. "We're already running late."

An MP in his midtwenties, wearing khakis, polished jump boots, the black helmet with white letters on it, and carrying a .45 on his web-gear belt, waved their jeep onto Pershing Field. The guy had a deep tan—something he definitely spent afternoons working on—and a muscular frame. He flashed a toothy smile beneath a bushy mustache as they flew by and yelled, "Welcome to the 'Nam!" He even saluted Nick personally, although he outranked the private by two grades.

"Who was *that* guy?" Nick asked the spec. 4 seated in front of him.

Schaeffer replied, "We got some good guys at this camp, and we got some bad guys at this camp. In fact, we got some real *bad* pricks at this place!" He stomped on the brakes, threw the jeep into reverse and squealed back up to the MP at the gate, coming to a stop in a cloud of dust right at the man's spit-shined toes.

"This is *Mister* Jeffrey Reilly," Drake introduced him to the newbie and Jeff gracefully tipped his helmet and bowed. "Now he's one of the *good* guys."

"I'm from Australia," said the grinning Reilly, as if his heritage alone put him in the good guy class. He slurred the name of the country with a deep, aristocratic accent that made Nick laugh automatically, just as the Aussie intended—Reilly had this way of blinking his eyes rapidly and wiggling his nose so that Nick was reminded of Bugs Bunny, the TV cartoon rabbit.

"Jeff's from Australia," Drake echoed the man sarcastically.

"He's from Australia," repeated Cal, so there would be no question in Nick's mind that the man was from Australia. They shook hands and Nick told him his name. He wanted to reply with an "I'm from Saigon" but instead said, "I'm

189

from Colorado."

"Oh, *another* American?" He frowned distastefully, though everyone present knew he was just joking. He squinted at Nick's name tag and began to scribble something on his clipboard as if he were adding another newbie to his shitlist. Cal put the jeep back in second gear and kicked up more dust.

"Jeff's wacko," he affirmed, "but the best friend you'll ever have."

"What's he got against Americans?" Nick laughed. "I mean, he's wearing an American uniform, isn't he? The guy's not in the Australian Army or anything like that, right?"

"Shit, he's as American as—"

"As apple pie."

"Right," laughed Schaeffer. "Just born and somewhat raised in Australia. Acts just like a friggin' kangaroo too, now and then. But a real good guy. He'll go on and on about being Australian, though, if you let 'im."

They passed through the center of camp, and Nick noticed older GIs with wedding rings on one hand escorting bar girls toward the outdoor theater with the other.

A dozen soldiers he assumed to be off-duty MPs wore cammo-shorts and burned beneath the setting sun around a volleyball net. A platoon of military policemen, half in khakis and half in jungle fatigues, awaited inspection beneath a leaning water tower.

A line of Vietnamese employees, mostly housegirls and secretaries, waited patiently for gate guards to inspect their handbags for stolen toilet paper and clock-radios. A young MP, high in a tower along the east perimeter, threw butterscotch candies down to a mob of cheering Vietnamese children on the other side of the barbed wire. Old mama-sans, their teeth black from chewing betel nut to kill the pain of decaying roots, smiled toothless smiles at passers-by as they administered spit-shines to a dozen sets of black jump boots. The American and Vietnamese anthems were played over the camp's loudspeaker system as numerous flags were lowered with the sunset. Old men wearing eerie face masks sprayed huge clouds of multicolored but mostly gray smoke at larger clouds of marauding mosquitoes, and the aroma of buttered popcorn clashed with the ominous bug repellents.

Schaeffer pointed out the orderly room to Nick, then raced off to the mess hall after his newbie got out of the jeep. The private checked his uniform, then made his way up the old wooden steps toward the crack of yellow light showing through the bamboo curtains.

Men lounging inside stopped playing pool and watching a shrapnel-riddled TV that hadn't worked in years to stare at him as he presented his orders to the E5 behind the Admin counter. The short, balding NCO with bulging eyes and a melancholy smile tossed the papers onto a desk and shoved a wine glass, filled with bourbon, into the newbie's hand. A water cooler burped in the back of the room, breaking the tense silence.

"Welcome to the 716th," an anonymous voice crackled from the other side of the pool table softly. A siren wailed mournfully in the distance.

A corporal, hauling a duffel bag over his shoulder, entered the room through a back door. "Mail call!" he announced, his tone demanding a respect and thanks that just didn't seem to exist in the room just then. Some of the men got up, hoping to hear their names. Others sat back, resigned to the fact they had never received any letters from "home" and never would.

"Lydic, Gomez, Adams, Oliveras," he called out, picking through the many envelopes. He stretched his arm out to men in the back of the cluster. "Bolen, Underwood. Another one for Oliveras. Sergeants Schell, Farthing and Johnson. One for Reilly, postmarked a whorehouse in Bangkok." Mild laughter. "Reilly? Where's Reilly?"

"He's out guarding the meat market," one of the pool sharks advised. "Or maybe *they're* guarding him!" More laughter, but more strained this time.

"Hey, I don't know anybody by the name of Mr. C.M. Hoo," one of the men protested to the mail clerk. He started to tear open the envelope that had been penned in green ink.

"Don't open it!" the E5 behind the counter was yelling directly into Nick's ears. The man opening the envelope looked up at Nick and their eyes met just as the newbie finished signing the company roster—he probably thought Nick was the one screaming at him.

"Letter bomb!" a veteran in the room couldn't conceal the fear coating his voice as he tried to sound bored with terrorism while diving under the pool table. The private continued to stare at Nick dumbfounded, still tearing the envelope slowly down the middle. Men started running away from him as the blast tore his face off and smeared blood across the front of the newbie's uniform and down onto the signature he had just placed on the roster.

The force of the blast knocked Nick backwards and to the floor. The explosion shattered his sunglasses and sent shards of plastic into his eyelids.

Some of the men were moaning as the smoke settled and the electricity came back on, illuminating the grisly scene. It would be the last time Nick kept his sunglasses on past sunset.

"How many we got hurt?" one of the buck sergeants was asking, but no one answered. They all hugged the floor, expecting more explosions, or a sapper attack at any moment. The moaning continued, though most of the men were uninjured. Nick felt at his eyes, afraid to open them. There was little blood.

"I said how many we got hurt?" the sergeant repeated, feeling around in the dense smoke. Sirens were approaching from the main gate and Comm shack.

"Just one, I think," someone said. "Gomez is out cold, but I can't find any bleeding. Kramer bought the farm—took his head clean off."

"Where the hell are you?" the sergeant asked, following the sound. "Someone hit the fan."

"The fan bought the farm too, Sarge," another man under the pool table muttered sarcastically.

"Where's that fuckin' rookie?" the E5 crouched down behind the counter whispered as though he expected VC through the door at any second.

"I think he's dead too," came the confident reply from a soldier huddled right next to the newbie.

"I'm OK," Nick said, his guts tied in knots. "I'm OK."

"Fucking letter bombs," the sergeant was muttering. "We warn you guys and we warn you guys: don't open *anything* with green ink on it until it's been checked by the EOD bomb

192

squad." He managed to locate the mail clerk in all the confusion of tangled arms and legs. "Why the hell wasn't that letter checked before it got this far?" he demanded. "Especially with green ink—the fucking VC are using *green* ink this month! And Mr. C.M. Hoo? Jesus Christ! Every MP in this room shoulda known that's the numba-one alias of Honorable asshole Ho Chi Minh!" He pushed the mail clerk out of his way.

"Hell, I don't know, Sarge!" The corporal busied himself trying to brush the scorched parts out of his uniofrm as he scampered around the room salvaging shredded letters. Most were now only scattered ashes.

"You OK, Gomez? You OK, Gomez?" One of the men was trying to gently slap the big MP back into reality.

"Cut that out!" snapped the sergeant. "The poor guy's probably got a concussion. You bums quit acting like little old ladies who've never been attacked before and start acting like the professionals I'm used to seeing around here—Christ, you're a fucking disgrace to the corps!"

The man holding Gomez in his arms began slapping him about again.

"I said cut that out!" the sergeant roared, and Nick thought how little it would surprise him if the NCO, already strained to the verge of cracking, drew his pistol and popped off one man's head just to keep him from aggravating another's concussion.

"Wait for the ambulance," someone else suggested.

Nick opened one eye at a time and found he could focus both on a motto that hung above the doorway: OF THE TROOPS AND FOR THE TROOPS. The thick layer of blood and human meat that covered the front of his uniform began dripping onto the floor as he got to one knee. "Mind if I get washed up?" he asked the sergeant. He refused to look down at the dead man at his feet and there was an urgency in his tone that said, *Let me out of this room before I cry and throw up in front of the men.* The smell was getting pretty strong, just for blood. Perhaps it was the stench of burnt flesh, too. He was unsure.

"Nobody's going *anywhere*! Till the investigators get photos of *everything*!" he yelled, pointing a finger directly at the newbie. He pushed Nick back into a bench, forcing him to sit down, then recoiled in disgust as his fingers sank into the clotted gore.

He sat on that bench for the next ten hours. Until the investigators took his statement and sent him off to the showers. It was the first time in his life he felt justified in crying, but the tears would not come.

"My name Diep," the housegirl told him the next morning. "Cost you five dollars all month. Fix your bed, change sheet, shine boots, wash clothes, and—"

"Wait a minute, wait a minute," Nick interrupted the young Vietnamese woman with the crooked smile. He pulled out a ten dollar bill. "This place was bookoo mess when I moved in. But you zapped it spotless somehow. This money's yours, just for getting rid of the crud that was clinging to those walls." He pointed to the once grimy and greasy screens covering the walls of the wooden two-story barracks; they were now immaculate. Diep had definitely surprised him. "Here's another five dollars for the rest of the month," he said. "Keep up the good work, and you'll get another five payday." He smiled broadly, swatting her pants as she passed.

She grabbed his hand just as the fingers started to deflate the billowing pantaloons. "No money, no honey." She smiled, pushing his hand away. She started to skip down the hallway defiantly, then stopped suddenly and walked slowly back toward him. She tilted her head down at an angle, then looked up at him warily from the corners of her narrow eyes.

Diep unbuttoned her blouse then took his hand cautiously and slipped it inside the silky shirt until the skin of his palms rubbed against erect nipples. She seemed soft as satin. A warmth raced through his body without warning—a disrespectful lust he had never felt with Angi. He felt his face turning red and he started to back off, taking slow steps, trying to appear busy and not taken by surprise and off guard. "I have to get over to the—"

She grabbed him by the front of his shirt and pulled him closer, and with her free hand she forced his fingers to squeeze down on the soft-as-satin breast until the erect nipple poked

194

through between two fingers. "For five more bucks, I give you numba one blowjob," she said without batting one of her long, black eyelashes. He could really feel his face blushing cherry-red now. Diep slipped her hand into his trousers, then struggled briefly with his belt. His pistol belt fell to the wooden floor with a loud clatter, just as Cal Schaeffer walked into the barracks.

"Oops!" he said, grinning, overreacting as he placed his hand over his mouth and rushed back out of the building. "So sorrrry about *that*, GI!" he exaggerated his embarrassment. Nick could hear the apology even outside the walls—it was meant more to get the attention of the other MPs who'd be sitting around the bottom-level stairs.

"What's *going on* up there?" some of them yelled up, but none came to investigate. A suggestive whisper produced a scattering of applause.

"I've really got to go," Nick told Diep, tightening his belt back up while she struggled to tear his pants off. "Maybe some other time."

They continued to wrestle on the floor for a few minutes after Diep flipped him over a bunk, his trousers now tangled around his knees. "Come on, MP!" she hissed loud enough for the whole camp to hear. "Show me how much man you are!"

Nick grabbed his pants and web belt and started for the door, but Diep tackled him again, and down they went. "I want you to *fuck me!*" she started yelling as he dove out the door and tumbled halfway down the stairs. "I want you to fuck me! Fuck me! Fuck me!" she screamed repeatedly as she chased after him.

"Go get him, Diep!" one of the men encouraged her on as the others rose to their feet and began applauding until half the battalion had gathered to watch. An MP jeep, cruising by on routine patrol, let out a couple siren whoops as the driver and his partner cheered, but Diep froze at all the attention, then flipped Nick an obscene gesture with the extended middle finger.

"Fuck *you*, cherry boy!" she yelled down at Nick as he ran around the corner of the barracks, still holding up his pants.

Then she turned around and stomped back into the building.

"I hear Diep's after your cherry," Reilly laughed at the newbie later, after he had made his way over to the main gate on foot.

"That broad's really hot to trot," Nick concluded, running his hand over his pistol to check for any dents or scratches it might have sustained when he dropped it earlier.

"Yeah, all these dinks are oversexed," he replied. "I'll bet she even told you, 'No money, no honey.'"

"How'd you know that?" He was genuinely surprised.

"They don't have much vocabulary, but they get straight to the point." He turned to check the ID cards of two GIs who were just staggering into camp, slightly intoxicated.

"Are we at Pershing Field?" the senior NCO slurred the question out in one long word.

"We must be," the other soldier chuckled. "Only Jeff Reilly runs the Pershing Field main gate, and ain't *nobody* could possibly be as ugly as this here motherfucker, except Jeff Reilly."

"Jeff Reilly, *sir!*" the first man corrected his partner.

"Roger that, Rodger," required another outburst of laughter.

"Yes, gentlemen," Reilly put an arm around both sergeants' shoulders. "You are at the right place. And at the right time." Jeff checked his watch for their benefit. "Just about curfew: you made it in under the wire."

The NCOs congratulated each other and stumbled off in the direction of the bowling alley, where they'd be able to mooch some free beer from the enlisted men.

"And where are *you* off to at this time of night?" Reilly asked the newbie in a big-brother voice.

"Oh, I thought I'd jog around the perimeter a couple times."

"You're not one of those creep elitist jog freaks, are ya?"

"Naw, I just thought it'd get me out of the area until Diep leaves for the night. That woman's unreal!"

Reilly pointed to one of the last three-wheeled cyclos sputtering off down the access road west of the gate. "She's

196

history, my friend. Long gone—took the last cyclo at the meat market. Your cherry's safe till morning. When she comes back." Jeff couldn't resist a little laugh himself.

"Well, I think I'll force a couple laps on myself, anyway. I think tonight it's gonna be a little difficult to get to sleep."

"Yeah, well, just watch your ass. There's a war going on out there," and he waved an arm against the dark. "Don't let them armchair warriors at Puzzle Palace fool you."

"Puzzle Palace?"

"MACV Headquarters. They try hard, but they usually don't know what's really going on outside the war room—what with all the inflated body counts from the field. Anyway, they claim it's safe to stroll beyond the city limits after sunset. I say horsefarts. Wherever there's an MP patrol, or a squad of *canh-sats* sure, but otherwise: Charlie rules the dark, my young friend. Maybe four, five years—if the Arvin ever finds its balls—they'll retake control of the nighttime. Until then, watch your ass."

"OK, so I'll make it *one* lap around the block."

"Outfuckinstanding. Now you're makin' sense."

Private Uhernik was thrown out of his bunk the next morning by the concussion of an M26 grenade exploding down at the end of the barracks. As he scrambled under the metal rack for protection and groped for his weapon, he watched two bare feet—a woman's—run past as he tried to shake the sleep from his eyes.

She got about ten feet down the hallway before being torn up in a hail of machine gunfire. Nick's eyes were glued to the scene: her arm was bent back under her body awkwardly and her hand was twitching about in death spasms. A thick, dark stream of blood was slowly creeping toward him, across the wooden floor of the barracks. It began seeping down through the cracks. "This has got to be a dream!" he told himself over and over.

Two sets of boots stomped heavily past his hiding place, and he tried harder to jar the stardust from his brain. "Fucking VC!" one of the soldiers yelled. The girl's hand was still twitching wildly.

"Is she dead?" the other one asked.

"She *will* be," his partner replied, placing his M-16 at the base of the woman's head then pulling the trigger. A burst of automatic fire severed her head and blood gushed out like a fountain. Bullets splintered through the floorboards and ricocheted about the rooms below.

"What the fuck is going on up there?" men screamed up the stairwell as they dove for cover and dodged hot, flying lead.

More MPs were arriving on foot, until the dead woman was surrounded. Nick crawled out from under his rack, unnoticed. One of the lieutenants pushed his way into the adrenalin-charged circle. "What the hell happened?" he demanded, receiving a reply of total silence.

"Fucking VC bitch tossed a frag at Reilly," someone finally volunteered the information. "Rolled it right under his goddamned bunk!"

Flames were crackling in the background. "OK—get that fire out before this whole barracks goes up!" the lieutenant directed two men as he turned the woman's body over. The mutilated skull, held on by a single strand of shredded neck muscle, flopped over with the rest of the torso only after the tendon grew taut and sprung it around at the last moment. "Holy shit," he muttered.

It was Diep, Nick's housegirl.

"You'll do just fine," Sergeant Mark Stryker slapped him on the back as they followed the cluster of MPs filing out of the Pershing Field briefing room, "You'll be riding with Oliveras tonight. He's a good cop—just keep his bordello inspections short."

Pvt. Nick Uhernik could still hear the tough buck sergeant's words of encouragement as they cruised down still another deserted boulevard of the quiet MACV annex, distributing cans of lukewarm Seven-Up to the MPs manning the static posts.

They had spent the first two hours of the eleven p.m. to eleven a.m. shift rounding up drunk GI stragglers downtown who were having trouble making their way back to camp before the curfew was clamped down on the city, but at one o'clock they were dispatched over to Thanh Mau Street on report of a rooftop sniper terrorizing the American-occupied apartment building in the neighborhood. They made no contact upon their arrival with ten other units, and the call was logged as unfounded.

Four additional complaints sent them back to the same area over the next two hours, but again Charlie Cong faded into the night, without challenge. Sergeant Stryker had finally assigned one of the Cholon patrols to stake out the area, and Uhernik's unit was diverted back to MACV for the hourly guardchecks.

Nick wanted to talk with Oliveras about the sniper calls. He wanted to ask the slender Puerto Rican with the Fu Manchu mustache what he had planned to do if they actually got into a firefight with the snipers. He wanted to ask the soft-spoken, normally cheerful MP if he had ever smoked Charlie before—what it felt like, did he hesitate, were there nightmares afterwards? But Oliveras was having a bad night (his girlfriend in Gia Dinh had discovered he also had a hoochmate in Cholon) and didn't seem up to small talk.

He found himself wishing Stryker had paired him with Reilly, as was originally scheduled on the duty roster, but Jeff was now on light duty for a while, recovering from the minor shrapnel wounds the housegirl's grenade had inflicted. Nick still intended to find out just what Reilly could have done to Diep to infuriate her to the point of trying to take him out with a frag.

"I love the way there's a constant ring of flares floating along the outskirts of the city." Nick opted for conversation as he pointed out the C130 parachuting the devices just below the blanket of stagnant clouds.

Oliveras held up a hand, motioning for silence as he turned up the radio in the back seat with his other. "Any unit vicinity of the Ped Gate, report for disturbance. No word on MP at that location. Does not answer his field phone. Units to respond, acknowledge."

Oliveras activated the dual red lights on the roof of the jeep and executed a sliding U-turn before punching down on the accelerator.

As they approached the dark, tree-enclosed pedestrian checkpoint, they detected a small group of American soldiers harassing the MP and his two militiamen. Oliveras gave the siren a short burst as the biggest soldier picked up one of the tiny Vietnamese guards and hurled him through the air, into a tangle of concertina wire.

The patrol jeep skidded up to the group sideways, just as another soldier pulled out a survival knife and charged the second Vietnamese. The MP assigned to the post attempted to disarm him, and the fight was on!

A third soldier pulled his knife and also charged, but Nick drew his .45 and aimed at his legs, yelling, "Halt! Military Police!" at the top of his lungs, exactly the way they taught him to do at The School.

The bluff failed to work, and he changed course directly for the rookie.

"You motherfuckers are *all* gonna die!" the soldier with the knife yelled, eyes bulging.

Uhernik fired two rounds, taking off most of the opposing soldier's right leg at the knee. The soldier cried out in agony, smashed down into the dirt full force, and came up with a pistol pointed at the newbie's chest.

The soldier fired once, but the round missed completely and lodged in the patrol jeep behind Uhernik.

The young MP took aim on his forehead as thoughts of all that training back at the academy rolled out at him like a flood of neon-laced directives. He could feel the drill sergeant leaning over his shoulder and breathing into his ear, "Take a slow, deep breath, and squeeeeeze that trigger soft and gentle, like a whore's nipple."

But now he was shaking like crazy and gulping in the hot night air. The sweat was rolling down into his eyes, and as they began to burn he was thinking, "What the hell am I doing? This is a goddamn American in front of me, not the VC!"

The wounded soldier struggled to bring up the pistol again and Uhernik squeezed off two more rounds just as the other man pulled the trigger. Nick's hollow-points tore off the top of the soldier's head, and the soldier's bullet caught Uhernik's flak jacket in the right shoulder, knocking him backwards and to the ground.

Then everything was suddenly quiet, except for the old papa-san who was still struggling to get out of the barbed wire atop the sagging fenceline. Oliveras held the other soldiers at bay with his rifle and Uhernik got up and ran over to the static post MP. He was repeatedly bashing the plastic stock of his M-16 into the unconscious soldier's face, yelling, "Fuckin' asshole! Fuckin' asshole!" over and over. Uhernik grabbed him by the collar and tried to pull him off, but he didn't have the energy left.

He stumbled over to the bunker and leaned against it until additional units arrived, reflecting on what he had just done, on who he had just killed. At his feet was the other militiaman. He was very dead, the American's survival knife sticking out of his lower back.

Nick tried to recall all the details of the shooting—they'd go over it for sure. Step by step. He'd have to prove he was justified. But it wouldn't come back to him.

Military Police jeeps were sliding up to the scene and squad sergeants were already snapping off photos. The duty officer had ordered the rookie into the back seat of a jeep and instructed him not to wander off. Uhernik stared at the dead American, now lying under a poncho liner, and tried to remember why he blew the man's face apart.

"Stupid jerk killed an American, just over a fuckin' gook," someone, off in the distance, said loudly, for his benefit. But he did not look up. It did not matter. They did not know—did not understand. They had not been there.

And now it was over.

He had killed a man. In street combat. And much later, as he walked off down the silent road toward the barracks after they had taken his statement, he still wondered if, when the time came, he could kill the enemy.

201

14. WARRIOR'S REUNION

One klick west of Phuoc Loc hamlet, South Vietnam

Capt. Louis Moast whirled around, bending at the waist as if to pick something up, and kicked out as hard as he could. The heel of his jungle boot, underlined with a steel plate to thwart punji stick boobytraps, connected with the guerrilla's jaw and slammed the man unconscious even before his limp body fell flat across the sharp elephant grass.

Another Viet Cong was on him that quick, laughing eagerly as he leaped from the lower branches of a tall tamarind tree onto the American officer's sore back. It was almost as if the little bastards were drawing straws, he thought, gambling at the honor to bring the big foreigner down. Though sweat burned at the corners of his eyes and blurred his vision, he could see how quickly they had surrounded him—had turned this game of death into a farce. They seemed to even hold no fear of the deadly gunships returning to save him. And Moast the Ghost, despite everything, held faith his men—some of them—would come to his rescue. At the last moment.

And if they didn't? If his Airmobil marauders abandoned him, then what? Well, that would be alright too—it'd be OK, because he'd just die his warrior's death in that blaze of glory they wrote about in all the soldiers' novels. No, he wouldn't die like some candle in the night. Like one of his favorite authors, Jack London, once wrote, he'd go out like some fiery comet, blazing bright.

And then he'd return and haunt this godforsaken jungle and

all its worthless tunnel-digging commies until the end of eternity!

Moast fell to one knee and rolled the Vietnamese off his back, finished the man off with a wrist blow to the throat. He had bashed his own chin against the knee during the maneuver—a sign he was losing his strength and coordination—and he was beginning to wonder how much longer he'd last before a collapse snuck up on him. Or they tired of the little game and finished him off. Already his chest was heaving with the exertion. Just the month before, one of his point men had suffered a heart attack during a forced march—and the grunt was only twenty-nine! Here *he* was approaching *thirty*-nine, taking on another teen-aged hard-core jungle fighter. How long before— Moast pushed the thought from his mind and met the next charging soldier with a roundhouse punch that decked the Oriental with a suddenness that left small puffs of dust along the outline of his body as he landed flat on his back.

This latest futile victory nevertheless sent a bolt of exhilaration arcing through his veins—almost a sense of immortality—that bolstered his confidence and even stirred him to mock the VC's inadequate sparring abilities; he motioned, in the disrespectful palms-up manner the Vietnemese reserve only for calling to dogs, for the tallest guerrilla to take his turn and enter "the ring."

Three soldiers charged him, and Moast went down under a painful flurry of fists and flying elbows.

A cheer and barrage of unfamilair obscenities went up from the soldiers encircling the combatants, but the sound of its insult only served to inspire the infantry officer. He would not surrender to them. And he would not go out without the toughest fight an American had ever given them.

As he kicked out with both feet and flailed about clumsily with his own bruised and battered knuckles that very thought kept bouncing back at him: Why didn't they take more pains to make him their prisoner? A U.S. Army captain—especially with a First Cav gunship patch on his shoulder—would be a prized catch, a showpiece and propaganda tool their superiors would amply award them for capturing alive. Just thinking of all the intelligence information they could torture out of him would be enough to excite any promotion-seeking communist cadre.

Maybe these guerrillas had been out in the field too long. Maybe they didn't care about presenting a live POW to the hot dogs in Hanoi. Dodging the relentless gunships day in and night out could transform any devoted Viet Cong into a crazed mad dog, bent only on avenging the deaths of the many comrades he had seen rocketed to bloody pieces by the prowling Cobras. Maybe they'd find enormous satisfaction— and soulful contentment, thank you—in simply tearing his limbs from his torso, one by one.

Moast fought the trio off, felt his heart pounding fiercely against his ribs, trying to burst from his chest. The clouds rolling in dark and ominous off the horizon were now spinning around above his head, and as he gave in to the dizziness and began a slow-motionlike tipping descent toward the ground, he felt the gun butt slam against the back of his head. The pain and impact were distant, reminding him of the night, thirty years earlier, when he had raided his sister's pajama party and the girl from next door had struck him from behind with a feather-light pillow, and now, as his nose flattened against the rotted, dead-smelling jungle floor, Moast found himself hoping the boys were just having some healthy VC fun—and that, maybe, he'd wake up in some POW camp with his elbows tied back together, suspended upside-down from the ceiling of a bamboo cage.

Something in his gut refused to allow the gunship captain to submit totally to his enemy. Though his entire body was numb and unfeeling, his senses seemed almost electrified—totally alive. He could "feel" the man with the rifle circling him cautiously, moving toward the top of his head, around to his right side, where the .45 automatic was holstered. Moast could taste the dust on his lips, hear the man breathing heavily above him, smell the sweat of fear and excitement in the air. All these clear, precise pictures of his environment fused in his mind, though his eyes remained shut and his limbs refused to move on command.

The guerrilla snarled down at the captain, muttering an

unintelligible obscenity as he chambered a round into his AK47.

It was that screeching grate of metal against metal that motivated the American back up on one knee, primed him to face death head on, face to face—not with a coward's bullet in the back. He would not be coldly executed with a round behind the ear.

Moast the Ghost drew his pistol, ignoring the chorus of cocking rifles that answered him. The tall one—he would take out the biggest of them first, then empty his last seven rounds at the rest.

"Drop it, GI," the tall devil suggested calmly, grinning his elitist smile below unfeeling, snakelike slits, but Moast's belligerent reply was drowned out by the roar of rotors exploding behind the Viet Cong.

The Cobra helicopter had circled around, banking sharply from the main body of the squadron as it kept low along the edge of the treeline and swooped up from the swath of valley cut through the jungle by the snakelike riverbed.

Moast spent only a microsecond fascinated by the sight of the monstrous predator slowly rising with the heat waves behind the hilltop most of the VC were clustered along. Then he flattened back out against the warm earth—moments before the gunship's nose cannon erupted with a lizard's tongue of flaming metal that latched onto the careless soldiers and tore them in two.

Moast felt the rush of air that flew behind the barrage of minigun fire. He felt the curls of heavy smoke blowing across the nape of his neck as the pilot directed a burst at the Cong standing beside him. He felt the men disintegrate mere inches from his head, felt a severed arm bounce off his back, felt a bucketful of intestines flop like slop onto him after the glowing tracers ripped the man's belly open and flung the top half of his body twenty yards away.

Moast the Ghost resisted the urge to look up and see if the man's bottom half was still standing, teetering on the brink of falling over. Instead, he curled up in a ball and giggled uncontrollably as the downblast from the landing chopper's rotors washed over him with new life: once again he had cheated Mr. Death, and the victory left a sweet taste in his mouth. A taste that reminded him of that woman back in the Tu Do Street brothel, back in the unreal neon world of downtown Saigon, back where the war outside the capital just didn't matter all that much.

He could taste the candy-sweet nipple, erect at the base of the firm, perfumed breast, but he could not picture the prostitute's face. Instead, he saw an MP helmet, staring down at him on the floor of the Happiness Bar. They were dragging him in again for taking down three marines bare handed, and the sergeant with the night stick was smiling and telling one of his men to escort the good captain across the street to the Caravelle.

The private was hoisting the officer up over his broad shoulders and saying something about, "Fucking grunts. Go AWOL to the big city and end up bananas on a barroom floor."

"Not their fault," he could even now hear the sergeant coming to his defense. "It's not them—it's Saigon. Something about this city make a man wanna do only one of two things: make love, or kill everyone in sight."

Someday he was gonna track that buck sergeant down and buy the man a drink.

Pvt. David Schramm wept openly as he watched the Huey chopper lift off, swing around in midair, then climb toward the rolling clouds, taking with it the body bag holding his partner. He watched the craft grow slowly distant, until it was only a black-green speck against the stormfront, but against the shifting screen of gray he was seeing Leroy's face. And it was a mask, empty of happiness, that had stared back at him these last few days.

Schramm had been unsuccessful in penetrating the barriers Crowe had set up after that last night in Saigon. Something had happened then. Something that had chased the humor from his friend. Something devastating Leroy had taken with him at death. Schramm would, perhaps, never know what had been troubling his partner these last few days, but he knew a surefire way to supplement the insurance payment the government would be sending his family—supplement it by twenty-five thousand dollars.

The undercover MP was certain the good Captain Moast had to go. Somehow the maniac had survived hand-to-hand combat with over a dozen VC—one of his loyal lieutenants had broke formation and doubled back to scoop him out of the shit—and after he stepped almost ghostlike off that gunship with the death's-head painted across its belly, his first objective was to coldcock Nelson. Not have the doorgunner arrested, or shot on the spot for kicking his captain out the open door hatch into the arms of the Cong. Just deck him flat. In front of the men, setting some kind of crazy example only Moast could appreciate.

Schramm had watched the captain swagger across the landing zone, larger than life. The private had considered lifting the barrel of his M-16 then and there: eliminating the cause of the platoon's problem. Let the blade fall before it was too late—cut out the cancer at its source. Before one of Moast the Ghost's escapades got the entire fleet wiped out.

But he lowered the rifle back down between his knees and fought the impulse. He had too much to live for—his career had only just begun. And it *was* a career in law enforcement. He wouldn't let a gung-ho grunt captain destroy his future, no matter how satisfying the man's death would be, or his integrity. Then again, he might look the other way when one of the officer's fellow grunts lobbed a frag at him. Even an undercover cop couldn't be everywhere all the time.

Schramm watched the captain disappear inside a hastily erected tent, just before the sheet of monsoon rain rolled across the temporary encampment. He watched the last unarmed helicopter lift off into the gale, loaded down with body bags, but there were still ten American corpses piled up on the ground, awaiting transport out.

Schramm ignored the rain slapping at his face like an insulted bar girl. He watched the water cascade off the poncho-covered bodies and form little brown pools in the clay. If they could endure the storm—if the weather was good enough for them, it was damn sure good enough for him.

Off in the distance, to his right, a vibration in the air caught his attention. It was a steady hum, punctuated at short intervals by a dull chopping noise—a beating at the thick, jungle air.

Choppers.

Their powerful, straining rotors had gotten Moast's attention too, for he and his lieutenants dashed out of the tent and pointed toward the squadron of seven craft.

"Damn," Moast muttered as he kicked at the mud. "I request more medevacs in here to lift out my dead and wounded, and they radio back no more slicks available till after this storm clears."

"Definitely Hueys, sir." One of the lieutenants was intently studying the craft with binoculars. "They appear unarmed."

"ARVN?"

"Unknown, sir. No markings whatsoever. They're blacked out."

"Probably airlifting some USO starlets up to Pleiku, for Christsakes," the captain muttered, his tone razor sharp. Then, after a moment of reflection, "Or might be an Agency bird, spookin' around."

"Why don't we just use our own Cobras to evacuate our casualties?" the other lieutenant asked carefully. He didn't want to appear cowardly in front of Moast, but the captain's actions just didn't seem proper ever since his rescue from the jaws of Death.

"Priorities, my young lieutenant, priorities," Moast explained without anger, his change in tone surprising both his subordinates. "Our most seriously wounded casualties went out on the first dust off. These brave warriors lying under their poncho liners are in no hurry to leave now."

"Sir?"

"The chase, lieutenant. We must proceed with the chase. If the trail gets too cold—and this damn rain isn't helping matters any—we'll never catch up to 'em," Moast stated.

"Them, sir?"

"The bandits, man. The bandits," the more disciplined lieutenant clarified the matter.

"Nelson!" the captain decided suddenly, blaring the doorgunner's name above the gusts of wind whipping at his face, "I want Nelson front and center! Now!"

In less than a minute, the lieutenants had located the insubordinate doorgunner and hustled him back to face his commander.

"You're my best machine gunner, Nelson." Moast beamed proudly, no hint of their earlier confrontations in his expression. "I want you aboard that Cobra over there in record time. These lieutenants here are gonna fly you up the asses of those Hueys over there. And if they can't convince whoever's piloting them slicks to divert from their course and land here in my friendly little camp, then *you're* gonna knock 'em out of the sky with your MG! Got that, soldier? I want them choppers down here, now. I want my dead airlifted out, now. I want the chase resumed, now."

"And you want your fucking ton of gold. Now!" The doorgunner frowned.

"Bandito booty is like a free fire zone, Nelson. It belongs to the strongest man who dares to take it. And we're gonna take it!"

"It belongs to those villagers back at—" Nelson began to argue.

"Horseshit!" Moast disagreed. "Them bastards are as commie as those assholes you made me fight off alongside the river back there! That makes their lousy temple gold up for grabs."

"To the mercenary with the most muscle," the loyal lieutenant added.

"Fuckin-A right!" Moast ended the discussion. "Now get that Cobra airborne! I want this show on the road!"

It took nearly twenty minutes for Nelson's chopper to overtake the squadron of Hueys. When the seven birds spotted the Cobra descending at them from the clouds, they spread apart like sparrows dodging a hungry hawk. The lieutenant piloting the sleek gunship was taken off guard by their evasive action. Within seconds, the Hueys on the edge of the formation had banked out sharply and disappeared out into the cloud cover, leaving only two craft in the center, directly in front of the Cobra.

The lieutenant stayed behind the closest bird, and after its pilot failed to respond to radio transmissions, he pulled up alongside the Huey and motioned for the pilot to descend.

Instead, the smaller craft dipped suddenly, swooped below the Cobra then lifted its nose, catching the wind in an abrupt climb that took it arcing out high at ten o'clock.

The lieutenant reacted automatically: he fired two rockets at the chopper still in front of him, then pulled off sharply in pursuit of the Huey racing for the nearest cloud.

"Take him out, Randy!" the lieutenant instructed the specialist, but Nelson's eyes remained on the projectiles roaring after the wildly swerving Huey, plumes of solid, silver smoke billowing from their shark-finned tails.

He watched the rockets both connect with the smaller helicopter's tail shaft, despite its desperate evasive maneuvers across the skies, and grimaced at the fireball erupting from the thunderous blast before he looked away and concentrated on the second bird. He failed to notice the heavy crates that fell with the shredded pieces of warped metal and shattered rotors.

"Did you have to dust him like that?" The co-pilot twisted his head back, searching for bodies floating toward earth amidst the debris. "We're gonna catch some godawful shit over this one."

"No markings," the pilot responded, "disregarding my directives: plenty of reasons."

"I don't know who these guys are," the co-pilot relented somewhat, seeing his point, "but they gotta be dirty. Why else would they try to elude us?"

"Maybe some ARVN general's private dope-smuggling operation," Nelson muttered as they closed in on the escaping Huey. There was no sign of the other five ships.

"OK, Randy," the pilot grinned. "Now I'm gonna pull up beside this turd, and if he don't comply, smoke his ass! Got that?"

"Maybe he should just work on disabling it, so we can find out what they got on board," the co-pilot suggested.

"Whatever."

They watched the grim expression on the Vietnamese pilot's face as he refused to descend and started, instead, to bank away from the Cobra. A soldier, dressed in black fatigues, appeared in the open hatch with an automatic rifle, and Nelson let loose with a burst from his 60 that caught the man below the knees across both legs, knocking his feet out from under him and forced him out—arms and eyes wide—into the vast space stretching out below the dueling aircraft.

Nelson fired another ten-round burst at the Huey's rotor assembly, and with a black puff of belching smoke, the helicopter quickly began losing altitude.

"OK," the pilot smiled back at his doorgunner, "hold off till our dink nurses her in for a landing then burp the feet out from under anyone trying to flee into the jungle."

"Roger that," Nelson whispered to himself, feeling intense job satisfaction as he tensed his fingers along the MG until his knuckles turned white.

The directive was unnecessary. The crash killed the four soldiers aboard and spread debris across a hundred yards of scorched mahogany stumps.

Because of the dense overgrowth and saberlike palms jutting up to grab at rotors, it was impossible to land close to the downed Huey. They hovered above the crash sight until the lieutenant with the binoculars could verify that the shiny objects spilling forth from the splintered crates were brand new M-16 automatic rifles, still in the protective oiled plastic wrappers.

"Christ, will you look at *that*," the co-pilot gasped dryly and pointed at the family of tigers that had bounded into the wreckage and were now fighting over the bodies.

Nelson watched one cat pull hungrily at an arm protruding from under the chopper's mangled fuselage until the limb tore free, splashing a crimson spray across the beast's orange and black stripes.

"Well, case closed," the pilot decided as he prepared to ascend above the treetops.

"Wait," Nelson flung his straps off and jerked the rescue rope ladder from its wall case.

"Wait what?" The pilot didn't waste mental energy masking his irritation.

"Can't let all this go to waste," he replied. "Can't leave here empty-handed. Aren't you curious about who *they* were? Where those munitions were destined for?"

"Fuck it. Don't mean nothin'," the pilot muttered.

"Those are real man-eaters down there," the co-pilot tried to reason with the doorgunner. "They like how you smell, friend."

"Shee-it, sir," he replied sarcastically, flinging the ladder out the hatch. "Don' mean nuttin'."

Nelson shimmied down the knotted rope and, using hand signals without looking up, directed the chopper closer in toward the smoldering belly of the Huey.

One tiger watched him briefly with glassy, bored eyes, but its brothers ignored the noisy craft hovering above them, choosing instead to concentrate on the chunks of meat cuddled between their massive paws.

Nelson slipped the machete from its calf sheath and hacked at the plastic tape covering the white markings until enough peeled free that he could memorize the original numbers. Then he motioned the pilot high above to drift a bit to the left—and he snatched up three rifles protruding from a fractured crate and slung them all over one shoulder.

That should do it, he thought, a serial number off the bird and the ID numbers off three M-16s should provide some clue for investigators if he could talk Moast into bringing CID in on the matter.

Nelson motioned for the co-pilot to start hoisting the rope ladder, but as the winch began slowly turning, he jumped down and ran toward the nearest tiger, firing his revolver from the hip while it was still in its holster.

The startled cat leaped back and tottered on its hind quarters just long enough for Nelson to probe the gnarled flesh of the dead Vietnamese until he found the bead chain imbedded in the blackened gore that was once a shredded throat. He yanked off the soldier's dog tags and raced back toward the rope ladder, the angry cat now hot on his heels.

He could feel the beast's hot breath on his ankles, but it was the deafening roar that sent him hurtling that last ten feet.

"Whooeeee! Look at that crazy fucker go!" the pilot laughed heartily as both officers watched Nelson shimmy up the ladder at high speed. The graceful cat jumped after him, and when its giant paw snagged one of the rifle slings and held on, the gunship jerked dangerously to one side under the added weight.

"Holy shit!" the co-pilot yelled as the craft swayed from side to side, but the other lieutenant fought the controls and kept the Cobra stable. Nelson abandoned the rifle his pursuer seemed to want so badly, and after the tiger fell back to earth he climbed the rest of the way up to the never-looked-so-good portal.

"You are one crazy sonofabitch!" The pilot did not look back as he pushed the rotors for more power and lifted the Cobra high and away from the pacing, circling Bengals.

"Oughta put you in for a medal." The co-pilot was breathing as hard as Nelson. "A Bronze Star, at the least!"

"Oughta airdrop his ass into the LBJ stockade, for pulling *that* stunt!" the pilot countered, but Nelson ignored both officers as he flipped the bloodied dog tags in and out of his fingers. He watched the tigers fade off in the shifting contrast of the multihued greens below and thought about Captain Moast. The man had cheated death so many times, but always came back for more.

Nelson was beginning to understand what drove Moast the Ghost to pursue that twilight demon that killed mortal men but only toyed with jungle warriors of the Orient.

"Crates full of automatic weapons, eh?" Captain Moast grilled them separately upon their return. "And you couldn't bring me back even one lousy helicopter intact?"

"Like I said," the loyal lieutenant repeated, "upon contact they scattered like they'd drilled just such an escape-and-evade maneuver a dozen times, sir."

"But they *were* only slicks, right? Unarmed. You met with no resistance?"

"Not really. They sent some schmuck out the side hatch to level small-arms fire at us, but that crazy Nelson took him out on the spot. Other than that, I saw no miniguns, rocket pods or heavy hardware."

"Fuckin' CIA must be up to something." Moast scratched at the stubble on his chin, contemplating the possibility, mildly upset with himself for having cursed an organization whose operations he fully backed. He had the utmost respect for the Agency. Even if they *had* turned down his employment application a decade earlier.

"It just don't figure," the lieutenant remarked. "Runnin' all them guns through the jungle in black choppers without markings."

"No big deal, Lieutenant," Moast dismissed the whole incident with the same brush of hands that beat back a cloud of drifting mosquitoes. "Probably running arms to some half-assed group of Freedom Fighters. I got more important things to worry about right now. Can't get no slicks in here till this afternoon, and—"

"But what if the CIA comes down hard on us over this one?" The lieutenant who had piloted the assaulting chopper swallowed hard at the prospect of taking on the Agency. Nobody ever won against them.

"Fuck it, Lieutenant. Don' mean nothin'."

Pvt. David Schramm watched the four Hueys float in on the hot breeze of dusk and touch down at the edge of the LZ he had helped hastily clear. Soldiers in freshly starched fatigues and brand new cammy helmet covers were leaping to the ground even before the skids plowed tracks in the wavering elephant grass.

Twenty-five replacements to recoup the unit's recent losses.

"Schramm!" the captain was yelling at a man whose thoughts were lost in the thump-thump-thump of whirring rotor blades pushing the tall-as-a-man grass flat. "Schramm! Help get them body bags aboard that first bird! I want those heroes on their way home, now!"

"Move it, man!" The loyal lieutenant slapped the back of his helmet roughly. Damn, he hated when they did that! He hated it back when the coach did it to psyche up his second-string teammates, and he hated it all through boot camp whenever the drill sergeants felt the recruits weren't hustling fast enough. But Schramm held back the impulse to deck the butter-bar and instead forced his canvas-wrapped feet to lift his exhausted body and rush, bent over, toward the Huey.

As they were hoisting the last of the dead aboard, Nelson trotted up and handed the two M-16s taken from the wreckage over to one of the crew members.

"What's this?" the co-pilot asked in an irritated tone, "I ain't haulin' your fuckin' war trophies back to the rear, troop!

214

We're already overweight as it is."

"It goes to the MPs in Saigon." Nelson gritted his teeth in a determined scowl that showed he meant business. He also handed the man a plastic map case containing something wrapped in an o.d. green handkerchief and a letter of explanation. "Or CID—your choice, bonzo. Whoever can trace that stuff and tell us what it's all about. And don't fuckin' chuck it out over the South China Sea, motherfucker." Nelson ignored the warrant officer's higher rank. "My boss, Moast the Ghost has taken a personal interest in this crap—so guard it with your ass unless you wanna suffer the wrath of one crazy never-say-die gut-eating warrior. You got that, sky-boy?"

Schramm hid the astonishment he felt at Randy Nelson's change in attitude and moved forward until it was obvious he wanted to say something.

"And what's *your* crisis, runt?" the crewman decided to take his hostilities out on the smaller soldier.

"I just wanted to add you might get him to sign for it, Randy," Schramm whispered nervously. "If you lose your chain-of-evidence, you got no case—whatever you got going here. Just thought I'd mention it. At least jot down his name or something."

"Who the fuck are you?" the warrant officer growled, "Batman or Robin?"

"Well . . ." Schramm grabbed his wrists like a boy working up the courage to ask a popular girl to dance for the first time. "I *did* take a little law back before I got drafted," he lied. "Just thought you should know. I figured since you're talking weapons, you must have somethin' heavy goin' down."

Nelson shot Schramm a who-you-trying-to-kid look, laced with mild suspicion, and the undercover MP shrugged his shoulders and turned to walk away.

Another chopper was setting down nearly in his path, and the first man to jump off almost crashed into the slender private. Schramm looked up, expecting to dodge several more highly motivated Airmobil types, and the sight of the trooper poised in the hatch beneath the screaming rotors made him freeze in his tracks.

Norman Saxon, the hate-filled barroom brawler they had jailed back in Saigon—the one man who could blow

Schramm's cover and identify him as a cop—glared down at the MP as if he had unexpectedly come across a long lost friend who owed him a lot of money.

Schramm glanced to the side, hiding his face from the enraged grunt, but Saxon was not deceived. He began jumping up and down, snarling like a pent-up attack dog preparing for the kill.

"What's the holdup?" a voice upset at the delay bellowed from deep inside the chopper. "Let's move it out!"

"Oh, I'm gonna move it out!" Saxon yelled as he slowly unslung his rifle and brought the sights down on Schramm's back. "I'm definitely gonna move it out!"

Schramm felt the hairs rise on the back of his neck, felt that chill just before serious injury that signaled intense danger. When he whirled around to face Saxon, his .45 was extended in his gun hand.

Before a single shot was fired, Saxon appeared to rise slightly off his feet, cartwheel sideways, then upside-down, then fly out of control out the chopper hatch, landing on his back in the clay with a jarring, muscle-tearing impact.

The giant form that replaced Saxon in the open doorway— the monster who had just hurled the troublemaker through the muggy Asian air—was none other than Big Barney Fairchild.

Schramm didn't think to wonder why the ex-MP wasn't back in some mental ward in Tokyo. He didn't stop to ask what the gentle giant was doing on a First Cavalry resupply chopper. Did he have rope burns on his neck? Where was the leg cast or the dishonorable discharge?

Schramm rushed past the unconscious form of Norman Saxon and yelled a greeting at the man who had taken him on his first town patrols—had catapulted through the trees with him that day their jeep was upended by the land mine. Big Barney hastily lowered his three-hundred-pound frame out the hatch and wrapped a brotherly hug around his old partner.

Seconds later, the first mortars rained down onto the camp, striking the chopper behind them and blowing it off its skids in a tremendous fireball that sent slivers of melted metal hundreds of yards in every direction.

15. SNATCHED FROM DEATH'S JAWS

Military Police Headquarters, Pershing Field Compound, Saigon

"Maybe you buy me Saigon tea tonight?" the slender Vietnamese woman with long, jet-black hair leaned into Sgt. Mark Stryker's patrol jeep and ran her fingers through the hair on his arm.

Stryker nervously glanced up the steps to the provost marshal's office then sighed and gave his partner a tired look that asked, "Can you believe this lady of questionable virtue has the gall to proposition a uniformed MP—right in front of headquarters?"

Pvt. Nick Uhernik knew he should respond with a chuckle, but instead he just shook his head and looked away.

"Who the hell signed you on-post, anyway?" Stryker trained his jungle-green eyes on the woman's attractive-like-diamonds face, knowing all too well diamonds could cut through nearly anything.

"Oh oh," Nick groaned as he spotted a captain leaving the PM's office. The officer locked onto Stryker's jeep like a guided missile, homing in fast but keeping a grin on his I-got-you-this-time expression.

"Sorry, honey—" the buck sergeant removed the woman's hand from his lap—"but duty calls," and he threw the jeep into reverse.

"But Reilly say—" the woman started to protest as she stumbled atop her black high heels out of the way of the spinning tires.

Stryker allowed himself a hearty laugh. "Reilly? I should have known he was behind this!"

The captain was now hustling down toward the jeep, two steps at a time. "Stryker!" he yelled, fully aware the husky NCO had seen him exit the bossman's palace, "hold up a minute!"

The MP sergeant emitted a painful sigh and pushed the clutch back in like it required valuable energy the entire battalion was short on just then. With a sad frown, he bent over and looked past Nick toward the Charlie Company captain. "Afternoon, Cap."

"What's so fuckin' good about it?" The reply was more playful than argumentative. He didn't give Stryker the chance to reply back, because everyone at Pershing knew the sergeant never prefaced any of his greetings with the word "good."

"Afternoon, sir," the private offered the mandatory salute from the vehicle's occupants, but the officer ignored him and locked eyes with Stryker.

"Glad I caught you," he said. "The colonel wants to see you bad. Right now. He just phoned dispatch to try and track you down."

"Yeah, how cozy-convenient I just happened to be loitering right outside." He cut the sarcasm short, and asked, "What's up?"

The captain glanced at Uhernik with mild annoyance in his eyes. "This man got a security clearance?" He sounded suspicious.

"Save the dramatics for the outdoor theater, Captain Harlow. All my rooks receive a secret clearance before they complete in-processing."

"Well, *this* is *Top* Secret," Harlow snapped. "Meet me inside, ASAP!" and he spun about-face and trotted up the stairs, back into the office.

"What would we do without them goofy officers?" Stryker nudged his partner good-naturedly, aware the captain's childish rebuke could scar a new man's attitude for the duration of his overseas tour.

"No sweat, Sarge." Nick's mind seemed preoccupied with something that had been bothering him all day, and Stryker

218

could sense his private would not be offended by a few minutes alone. "I'll wait out here in the jeep."

"Good man!" He slapped Nick on the shoulder and started up the steps behind the captain. "Probably just a *secret* mission to shovel doggy shit outta the ambassador's back yard."

The captain, halfway through the door, heard the remark and paused to throw an icy look back at Stryker, but just then harsh airhorn-type sirens located across the compound began sending out short, high-low blasts. Stryker halted in midstride, halfway up the steps. He turned to watch nearly a dozen military police jeeps, lights flashing and sirens screaming, race by and charge off in the direction of the main gate.

The sergeant automatically turned and started back toward his jeep. "Turn up the radio," he directed the private. "We musta missed something."

"Stryker! Get your ass back up here!" Captain Harlow bellowed impatiently. He knew his short, wiry frame was no match for the stocky buck sergeant, but he also knew that, as much as it went against his grain, Stryker respected rank and authority.

"What's with the alert sirens?" He pointed across camp to one of the airhorn devices mounted atop a guard tower. "Some kind of incoming? I didn't hear no rockets!"

"That's what this is all about. Now inside!"

Stryker watched another five MP units roar past, the men inside enjoying the Hot Code run, trying not to think what might lay waiting at the end of the trip. "But what about my men, Harlow? Where the hell are *my men* going without me?"

"Have you forgotten the new procedures already?" The captain was waving him up the stairs. "Those troopers are just running downtown to pick up the off-duty men shacking up in District Eight. It's their turn to man the assault tanks. Now get in here so I can tell you why we gotta break out the heavy hardware."

The V-100s were definitely heavy hardware, Stryker thought as he nodded for Uhernik to keep the engine running. Mounted with huge fifty-caliber machine guns and dual M-60s, the tanks utilized monstrous balloon tires instead of tracks and had been known to outrace the MP jeeps patrolling Plantation Road. The two assault tanks parked across from the main gate had menacing Thor and Captain America characters painted across their front armor, and had yet to be disabled by anything Charlie had to offer.

Nick Uhernik watched another straggler jeep—its four riders still snapping down helmets and flak jackets at high speed—slide past, and though that little elf demanding excitement tugged at his gut, he ignored the call to action and concentrated on a graceful magpie balanced high atop a telephone wire, stretched taut between guard towers instead.

She would spend several seconds casually preening her long black and white feathers before fluttering over to scream at one of the irritating alert sirens, wings flapping their territorial warning. But the siren would continue its high-low fog-hornlike blasts, and the magpie would retreat for a few minutes to ponder the hopeless situation, her neck feathers ruffled in anger.

Her grace and perseverance reminded him of Angi again. He had signed out of camp the day before to visit her, but her parents kept him outside the front door—the first time they had ever done that—and maintained steadfastly that she was away from home, visiting an aunt. He knew this to be an untruth; her motor scooter was still leaning between the tamarind trees out back. Christ, they were treating him like a common GI, an outcast, ostracized from family and friends that fateful day he chose to enlist in the foreigner's army. Nick knew he could brush past Angi's father with little effort—hell, The School had taught him how to bust down doors—but a show of force would only serve to tarnish the respect he had built up with her hard-to-impress parents over the years. He hoped she was just simmering over the poor treatment she had received trying to visit him at Camp Alpha's in-processing center, and that she hadn't found herself another boyfriend while he was an ocean away in America.

"Hey, Joe." The bar girl had drifted over to his side of the jeep. "Maybe you buy me Saigon tea? Before all hell break loose and boom-boom start?" She ran her long, slender fingers up the hair on his forearm, and instead of feeling lust or pleasure, it was as if he were seeing her through the twilight of

220

a jungle encampment and a deadly snake was slithering up his wrist.

"Christ, woman!" he snapped, pulling his arm away, "can't you hear them sirens? That means some kind of trouble! You'd best get home—under cover." And then he smiled for the first time. "Or under the covers, whatever you're best at."

"I have no home." Her expression grew sad and a bit overly dramatic. "I sleep with your MP friends. Or I sleep in the gutter." Her words had a bitter finality, but as Nick examined her expensive clothes and new high heels, he found himself doubting her sincerity.

"Maybe you should go back, visit Jeff," he finally said, realizing for the first time that the massive air-raid sirens downtown had never activated to mingle with the camp's warning system. He wasn't sure what it all meant, except that all must be quiet in Saigon while something that smelled of death and danger was cooking at Pershing Field.

"Jeff sign in many beautiful girl," she whispered, as if betraying a solemn trust. "His weakness is long, silky hair and healthy chest." She cupped her silicone-enlarged breasts in her hands and propped them up at Nick. The private's shocked eyes flashed around nervously, but it appeared no one important was watching—only a few slightly amused house-girls, who were ignoring the sirens and busily completing their daily quota of laundry. "He never can remember every girl he let in—we all love him too much!"

Nick pulled out a military payment certificate, grimaced at the 1950s-style blonde stenciled across the brown bill, and handed it over to the prostitute. "Here. Go buy yourself a hamburger or a hot dog—just get the fuck outta my hair."

She snatched the currency up before he could change his mind. "You numba one MP, Joe!" She planted a juicy kiss across his lips and was off before he could protest.

Most of the camp was covered with round, one- and two-inch rocks, and as he watched her sexy bottom sway back and forth enticingly as she maneuvered over the obstacles with her high heels, he envisioned a solitary mortar shell landing on her as she reached the middle of the barren compound, ripping her body in half and lobbing one of those juicy melons in his lap.

221

But the hooker made it to the clubhouse without incident and disappeared inside without ever looking back at the rookie MP.

Inside the PM's office, Mark Stryker hesitated at the sight of eight other sergeants, two lieutenants and a squad of Vietnamese National Policemen huddled around a large easel-supported map. The men all turned to stare at him for the interruption, but Captain Harlow dashed the tension aside with a casual wave of his hand. "OK, everyone's present," he said. "The mechanics are firing up the assault tanks, and—" a wall shaking blast of thunder rolled across the camp and sheets of heavy rain from the storm that had been rushing toward Saigon all afternoon suddenly fell from the skies, rattling the window screens and drumming along the roof noisily. A warm, penetrating mist arrived on the heels of the downpour.

"Oh, great!" Harlow waved his fist back at the laughing thunder. "All I need now is monsoon flooding—I was hoping we could beat feet up north before the rains hit."

"Up north, sir?" Stryker cocked an eyebrow at the captain.

"Here's the low-down, Sergeant." Harlow waved a black night stick at the five-by-five map as though it were a magic wand with the power to set everything straight. Stryker could feel one of his migraines coming on and he sat down on the edge of the PM's pool table. "Elements of the First Cav are pinned down here, in the vicinity of Phuoc Loc. If you think the rain sounds tough out here now, it's reported to be cousin to a hurricane up north. The First Cav unit is socked in by the storm and surrounded on three sides by some lousy Cong who got lucky. Took out every chopper on the ground. The closest reinforcements, north of their location, at Nhon Co, were sent up to Duc An to help repulse an unforecasted NVA push across the Cambodian frontier."

"Kind of unforecasted like this thunderstorm, you mean?" One of the sergeants grinned, ready for a mission back to the jungle. He wore a combat infantry badge over his heart that hadn't been humored in two years.

"Sounds like a grunt matter to me." One of the lieutenants frowned. "You're talking about sending our entire alert force thirty miles outside Saigon just to rescue some hotdog

222

Airmobil types."

"Only half the force," Harlow corrected him quickly. "The rest of the men off-duty will be confined to MACV and Pershing for the duration of the mission, and the downtown patrols and static posts will be only slightly affected by the cut in manpower."

"Still sounds to me like it's none of our affair. What do them fuckin' grunts ever do for us except come into town on their R&Rs and tear up the bars and wrestle my men? I say screw 'em: it's not *our* problem."

"The PM has authorized this mission for two reasons, gentlemen," Harlow addressed the entire group, ignoring his lieutenant's apparent cowardice at venturing outside the capital. "Two of our men, Schramm and Crowe, are presently fighting side by side those First Cav infantrymen in an undercover capacity, and secondly, General Harding has personally asked that the PM dispatch the 716th north. He's unable to send resupply choppers in due to the weather and—"

"And since we, the 716th MP Battalion, are the main armed force charged with protecting the Saigon military region, it's the least we could do." Stryker stood up and stretched his powerful arms, arcing his back like a cat getting ready to set out on its nightly hunting foray.

"Something like that." The captain returned his sergeant's knowing smile. "General Harding has been a longtime friend to the MPs here. I don't really know why—he's never asked for any favors before. Maybe he just likes cops.

"Another thing. Maybe it's coincidence, we don't know yet. But Schramm or somebody up north sent down two rifles, the serial number off an aircraft, and some dog tags coated with blood. We checked them out, and the results are speculative at best, since the note attached to the items was a bit confusing.

"Anyway, the M-16s checked out to be hot. Stolen along with two thousand other automatic weapons last week from a warehouse at MACV annex. The aircraft markings belonged to one of eight choppers mysteriously missing since last month from Tan Son Nhut. And the dog tags come back on a Capt. Ng Van Cao."

"Cao," one of the *canh-sats* scratched his temple. "The name sounds familiar, Dai Uy."

"It should." The captain grinned almost devilishly. "Cao was the general's personal interpreter. Didn't report for work this morning."

"This could get interesting." One of the buck sergeants in the room began twisting at his mustache with two stubby fingers.

"What did the note say?" Stryker searched for a common denominator.

"Like I said, not much to it." But the captain carefully took a photocopy from a thick file folder and read it quickly:

Saigon Commandos,

Greetings from never-never land. Enclosed are two of many firesticks retrieved from a downed bird that was loaded down with many more of same. Markings of mystery bird also attached as are dog tags of pilot. Recovery efforts stymied by hungry Bengals. Crash sight coordinates listed below. Good luck on this who-done-it, but more important: why?

Duc when it counts,
—the Doorgunner

"Hungry Bengals?" The reluctant lieutenant seemed even more hesitant at committing his platoon.

"That *is* the jungle calling to ya out there." Stryker smiled down at the officer and walked over to the map. He looked at Captain Harlow. "What's the plan, honch?"

Glad to be getting down to business after dispensing with small talk, Harlow began handing out xeroxed briefing sheets. Already the air outside the room was alive with the anxious rumblings of a dozen assault tanks, lined up at the main gate, ready to roll. "Alright, gentlemen. We take Highway 16 up to Ap Dong Sac, then trailblaze east the last seven miles to Phuoc Loc."

"That's mighty bad country out there." The sergeant with the C.I.B. sewn on his chest looked only mildly worried. "Entire fields of wait-a-minute vines."

224

"Lotta anti-tank trenches left over from the French-Viet Minh war," Stryker added.

"Boobytraps up the ass, too," the other lieutenant, who had been silent thus far, finally spoke up. "And it's raining water buffaloes and elephants out there, Cap. What makes you think we can even get north of Gia Dinh in this storm?"

"'Cuz we're the 716th, goddamnit! The 716th kicks ass, wherever it goes, remember? No one ever said we were confined to the city. Don't forget our motto—"

The lieutenant whispered to the sergeant next to him as he took his seat quietly, "The jerk's a bozo. Gonna get us all killed, chasing that major's oak leaf."

"We're cops, Cap," another sergeant sounded off. "We're used to fighting snipers on rooftops, not guerrillas in trees."

"You clowns drill for this sort of thing every other day." The captain remained patient, but the red in his cheeks was a sign his anger was boiling over. "You can take your V-100s out there and bend the lousy palm trees right over—ram some fifty-cal barrels right up Charlie's ass!"

"It'd be better to go up Highway 24 to Xa Song Be," the man standing beside Stryker volunteered, "then follow the banks up the Song Dong Na river and veer west straight into the battle."

"Negative," Harlow remained firm. "The last radio transmissions out of Captain Moast's camp warned Charlie was dug in along the north, east and south perimeters. That means the only way in is from Highway 16, to the west. End of discussion: we head east from Route 16."

"Move out!" Stryker clapped his hands together, taking his cue from Harlow, ignoring the wary college-softened lieutenants.

"One final thing," the captain raised his voice to be heard above the clamor of men hustling for the door, "these *canh-sats* are accompanying you. They speak the lingo, and will expedite any delays encountered at the check points—the PFs aren't used to seeing MPs in full combat gear racing through Gia Dinh on V-100s. They'll be jittery."

"Just so they stay out of the way!" Stryker grinned with confidence. "The PFs, that is. The *canh-sats* I welcome aboard anytime," and he offered his hand to the nearest Saigon policeman.

"Sgt. Hoang Khoa is in charge of the *canh-sats*," Harlow mentioned as the roomful of cops squeezed out the narrow doorway, eager to ride the assault tanks into adventure. "Officer Jon Toi is his second in command."

"Just in case." The smile remained on Stryker's face as he in turn grasped Toi's handshake warmly. The two men had been through more than a couple close calls in the past.

"Just in case," the captain affirmed loudly, ignorant of the bad luck generated by mentioning things that *might* go wrong.

Stryker searched Jon Toi's eyes for some sign of reluctance, some hesitation to partake in the mission. He knew the *canh-sat* was a devoted family man who seemed much more at home helping Lan in the kitchen than trying to keep up with gung-ho MPs in the bush. He had been decorated for bravery in the street on numerous occasions and had nothing to prove to anybody. But Stryker found only that look of determination he always saw when the men found themselves on the verge of a tight situation and knew not all of them would be coming back. Toi slapped the MP sergeant on the back and said, "After you, Mark," as he waved the big American through the archway. "When this is all over, you owe me a drink."

Stryker playfully grabbed the *canh-sat* by the biceps from behind and jettisoned him through the door. "You always come first in my book, Officer Jon! And when we *both* notch this mission in our gun butts, I'll buy you and Lan a ten-course meal at the Continental Palace!"

"A simple Singapore sling would do nicely." Toi dodged the tossed canteen just in time.

Outside, Pvt. Nick Uhernik watched the first of the V-100s start chugging powerfully toward the gate like menacing super tanks.

"Chase down that tub on the end!" Stryker's eyes locked onto Nick's as he hustled down the steps toward their jeep. His finger pointed to the last V-100 just beginning to coast downhill at the convoy's tail. "We're heading north, Nicky-baby! Strap into your gear and hold onto your ass! Right now we need this jeep to discuss strategy. I'll get with you later, partner. Before the air is humid with heavy metal!"

Feeling no betrayal, disappointment or inconvenience at all—in fact, feeling no emotions whatsoever—Uhernik scooped up his gear and trotted off after the assault tank.

As Stryker watched his partner sprint to catch up with the convoy, he marvelled at how well the private had been coping with the shoot-out only days earlier. After all, it was the 'Nam, and you weren't allocated mandatory "mental health" days off just because you iced a fellow human being. It *was* a combat zone, for Christ's sake! No pampering like you got stateside after a righteous shooting. He was going to have to quit calling the kid his "favorite rookie." The title just didn't apply anymore. But what bothered Stryker more was that the newbie didn't talk about the incident. Or the repercussions the incident was having on his life, post-gunbattle. Most of the guys had quit snubbing him for dusting a round-eye—Stryker had seen to that—especially the guys who counted, the true professionals, the street cops who understood. But all it took was one wise guy and his loudmouth, off-the-cuff remark to twist the knife a little deeper. Hell, Stryker couldn't be expected to be everywhere, all the time, big-brothering the rook till his tour 365 ended. And there *was* something still bothering the man. If only Stryker could get him to talk. That's what partners were for. Sometimes you got closer, mentally, than wives did. Sure, just get him started talking. Then they'd burst like a flood through a torn-down dam, until you fear they'll never shut up. But that's what partners were for, too.

Nick was beginning to quickly tire of the game. Every time he was about to jump on, the tractor-tired tank sped up again, teasing his patience. One more time, he decided, and I'm gonna unload a thirty-rounder up his exhaust pipes.

A grinning Jeff Reilly popped out of the driver's forward hatch and turned to wave the private aboard. "Come on, cherry-boy! Bust balls! You can make it!"

"Who's driving this crate, *you*?" Nick began to speed up, despite common sense telling him to pick another tank. He whipped his heavy pack over to the other shoulder, the shift of weight nearly throwing him off balance as his footing struggled awkwardly to compensate for it.

Reilly raised both hands in the air and the V-100 began to drift toward the edge of the roadway. "Who else?" he beamed.

The newbie private—for he would be a newbie the next five months—grabbed onto a handhold and hoisted himself up into the reargunner's cubicle. He zipped up his flak jacket and strapped down his helmet, finally feeling the exhilaration and pride as the convoy rumbled past the envious security men at the main gate. He scanned the faces of the admiring women gathered inside the meat market bleachers and felt the invulnerable cockiness only a warrior racing to battle knows.

Every ounce of that superhuman strength and courage drained from his body, however, as their assault tank roared out through the Pershing Field barricades and he spotted Angi's startled, innocent face among those of compound employees waiting in line to be signed onto the installation.

Big Barney scooped up the skinny Schramm in one arm and hustled him over to the nearest foxhole as another set of mortars exploded across the camp, erupting with terrific splashes across craters already flooded with rain water.

"So *this* is combat," Fairchild screamed with delight as he slid in on top of the frail Schramm, already half drowned in mud.

"Welcome to the real war," his old partner grimaced as he struggled to squeeze out from under the three-hundred-pounder. They were soon back to back, eyeballing the perimeter from beneath the edge of helmet rims, neither man caring to acknowledge a single mortar could just as easily choose to descend straight down into their laps.

"You're the last man I expected to meet in the boonies." Barney revealed the warmth of reunited friendship in his voice. "What'd you do back at Pershing to get transferred to a grunt unit?"

Schramm hesitated compromising his cover, even for the sake of an old partner, and he resisted the urge to spill it all out. Instead, he asked, "What brings *you* out to Phuoc Loc? A resort town it ain't!"

"Aw, those crazy jerkoffs back in Saigon threatened to discharge me if I didn't attend a shrink session in Long Binh. Typical army snafu: they trusted me. Out-processed my ass from the 716th and cut me orders for the reorientation brigade at LBJ. On the way to my flight I just scrambled my 201 file around a little to make it look like I re-enlisted for the First Cav. OJT training, the whole bit. You know how easy it is to forge crap into your transfer ledger. They bought it without question. After all, who'd be crazy enough to forge documents sending him straight into a combat zone?"

Except a crazy man, thought Schramm. There was still no sign of a VC ground attack, though small-arms fire was erupting at scattered points on the opposite side of camp. Mortars were now raining down on them with such intensity the two men were forced to yell their conversation against the noisy barrage, while the other soldiers kept their faces buried flat against the earthen floors of their foxholes.

"What about your leg?" the question slipped from Schramm before he could stop it, "where's the cast?"

"Oh, you heard about that." Fairchild tried but could not bury the embarrassment beneath his tone. He wanted to tell Dave about the suicide attempt. Wanted to tell him why he backed out on the only honorable way: his MP service weapon against his temple. Wanted to tell him how degrading it felt to be told you were being sent home to a psyche ward without any medals, without self-esteem, cheated of the pride of serving your homeland loyally. He wanted to tell Dave how the guilt was eating away at him—the guilt of abandoning all those fellow cops back at the Gia Dinh ambush, the guilt of that simple act of turning the volume control down on the radio— the radio they called for help over. He wanted to confess about how he no longer possessed the strength to attempt another suicide, to end the daily—and nightly—mental anguish at seeing the ghost images of all his dead friends. Wanted to admit the only decent way to end it all was to volunteer for gunship combat and let the Cong finish the job. Honorably. Instead, he said, "I ripped it off myself. Was only a hairline fracture anyway. And you know there's no way they'd let me out in the boonies with a cast holding me back." He shielded his eyes from the wind-swept rain, trying to gauge Schramm's reaction.

"Must be awful painful." Schramm hugged the ground as two mortars walked past their foxhole, impacting with a stinging blast on either edge of the trenchline.

"What?" Fairchild had temporarily lost his hearing, and when Schramm repeated the question and couldn't hear his own words above the ringing sensation, he concentrated on outlasting the barrage without the small talk.

Schramm could feel the sudden vibrations in the earthen walls that had signalled, in the past, a large mass of soldiers rushing toward their position. Fairchild was already up and leaning against the lip of their foxhole, spraying bursts of lead out along the wire.

Big Barney turned to glance down at his buddy, screamed words the smaller man could not hear. "Charlie in the wire!" Schramm read his lips.

He slammed up against the bull of a soldier and fanned an entire clip out at the wall of black uniforms advancing on their position through the misty rain.

Fifty yards to their right, where the helicopter was now only a smoldering pile of twisted metal and fiberglas, a dazed Norman Saxon was rising to one knee, directly facing the charging Cong. When he opened his eyes and focused on the wall of enemy soldiers, his legs almost magically propelled his frayed torso—it suffered from several torn back muscles sustained when Big Barney heaved the man out of the chopper—backwards away from the advancing menace. Several of the daring VC fired rifle-grenades on the run as this new irresistible target presented itself, and when one of the projectiles crashed through Saxon's teeth and penetrated halfway through the back of his throat, Schramm tried to close his eyes against the ghastly scene. His motor reflexes refused to respond, and for the rest of his life—which at this point didn't seem to extend beyond the hour—he would carry that crimson image in the recesses of his troubled mind: the captured M79 round, slightly larger than an egg, detonated even before the smashing impact could fling Saxon's surprised body to the ground, and spears of blue-silver light exploded like star rays from the back of his skull before the residual blast completely beheaded the man.

By dusk, as the downpour intensified and visibility fell to a few dozen meters, the lead tanks of the rescue convoy had maneuvered through the old French armor barricades crisscrossing the jungle east of Highway 16's nearly impassable loose-gravel surface and growled to a halt atop a tree-shrouded plateau overlooking the village of Phuoc Loc.

The convoy had doused its yellow-shaded fog lights as the luminescence that was Saigon faded behind them, and before rolling into that last valley west of Phuoc Loc only a few roadside huts, boasting flickering lanterns, gave hint something strange was amiss in Phuoc Thanh province. Yet even these sleeping hamlets were so sparse the darkness seemed to swallow up the two companies of military policemen.

Explosions ahead grew louder and louder before they had reached that plateau, and now and then they shivered against the unusual cold as the horizon lit up, hot and glowing. Once three flares popped high above them, in the distance, and one broke free from its 'chute and plummeted to the ground. "Just like a falling star," mused an MP standing braced rigid against the big MG in the back of one of the gun jeeps. His driver didn't hear the words for his concentration was centered on the unexpected foxhole-sized potholes that would appear along the edges of the jungle trail around every other corner. The gunner's hands tightened on the M-60 handles with each jarring bounce of the vehicle's chassis, his knuckles white with pressure. He had been standing the whole trip so far—he was ready to take the exam.

Several times dull thuds and sharp twangs smacked the sides of the vehicles in the convoy, and the men were never sure if the noise was a result of a VC bullet or just stones thrown up by their spinning tires. None of the MPs were so naive as to think they could proceed unnoticed along a rain-forest trail after dark with a dozen V-100 engines grumbling against the strain of the uphill climb. And if messengers hostile to the Saigon regime didn't beat the convoy to its destination, no one doubted strong resistance would await them during their

231

descent down the hillside through Phuoc Loc village.

And then they were there.

Harlow pulled the convoy up a hundred meters from the ridgeline overlooking the battlefield, and the men were allowed to scamper over to peer down on the scene after perimeter guards and several LPs were deployed.

Now and then powerful whirlwind gusts forced the sheets of thick rain aside like some haunted opera house curtains and the soldiers could view the cluster of lanterns, candles and bonfires that was Phuòc Loc. Beyond the community of several hundred patriotic Vietnamese the battle raged. Constant flashes of light, similar to endless lines of bulbs suspended above a used-car lot, marked the east wall of guerrillas, and the responding discharges from the Americans seemed pitifully small in comparison.

The MPs atop the plateau struggled to repress the oohs and ahs as a cluster of flares popped above the firefight and began floating toward the far treeline. They watched as hot, pink tracers from the Airmobil perimeter knocked a sniper from a tree one hundred feet up, then a brilliant white phosphorous shell burst halfway across the camp, showering a bunker with sparkling chunks of solid acid that trailed silver smoke plumes. One of the glowing particles set off a whole batch of golden flares, and as they rocketed skyward haphazardly, an eerie glow was cast across the mist-blanketed valley.

"When do we move?" Reilly sidestepped the chain of command and approached Captain Harlow.

"Daybreak," he muttered, irritated conversation was distracting him from his outdated, inaccurate maps.

"Daybreak?" Reilly all but swallowed his bubblegum. "Those poor fuckers are already down to tossing spitballs at the Cong. I say we move out now, Cap!"

Harlow finally looked up from the penlight's dim glow, but his eyes lanced out past the spec. 4, searching for Stryker. "This *your* man?" He didn't bother masking his irritation.

Stryker, sensing anger in the air, had already started toward the informal command post setup beside one of the towering assault tanks—two rain ponchos had been tied together and stretched out between the tank's MG barrels and a jeep's canvas top beside it. "What's he gone and done now?" The sergeant managed a grim smile despite his agitation and the drizzle. There was no hint of stress in his voice.

"Trying to tell me how to run this goddamn outfit," Harlow snapped. "Can't you stick him out on a listening post somewhere?"

"I was just tellin' the cap I think we should move now." Reilly went on the defensive though his tone was unchanged. "Or the only way Schramm and Crowe are goin' back to Saigon is in a box, Sarge."

Stryker tended to agree with the soldier in front of him, but instead he said, "We roll tomorrow, Jeff. Racing down through that ville right now would be just too risky. Sergeant Farthing is getting together a recon squad now to check out our opposition. I suggest you pick one of those solo foxholes and find yourself a partner. It's gonna be a long night."

"Just plain suicide," Harlow agreed. "Mounting a rescue in the dark, over unfamiliar terrain. You'd be branding the men a suicide squad."

Reilly kicked at the mud and started for the perimeter, muttering something about, "What the hell you give us assault tanks for if we can't crash the party, rockin' and rollin'."

Private Uhernik blinked his eyes several times. Then he slowly closed them for a few seconds and popped them back open. Then he held one closed while he peered about with the other open. "I swear I can't see a goddamn thing out there," he whispered to the man beside him in the foxhole. "It's dark as black velvet—gives me the creeps, man."

"Cloud cover blockin' out the starlight," explained Jeff Reilly.

"Well, nobody ever told me war had to get so creepy. I wasn't warned when I enlisted that *there'd be nights like this.*"

"Combat hurls shades of fantasy at you the likes of which you'll never see back in the 'real world' of the civilian," Jeff mused softly and Nick envisioned him painting a cemetery landscape on an easel leaning against the other side of the foxhole. Jeff's tone changed to a cold rebuff when he said,

233

"What you complaining about anyway? We haven't even been fired on yet." The sky cracked a white flash at them.

"Shhhhh," Nick whispered harshly. "Did you see that?"

"I mean to tell ya." Reilly was ignoring him. "When the shit hits, you'll know it, brother. There'll be—"

"Shut up, dildo-breath—there it is again!"

Reilly turned to face the same direction his partner was looking and he held his rifle against his chest, the muzzle sheltered from the rain by his poncho liner.

Now and then the darkness had been sliced apart by sizzling bolts of lightning overhead, and as another one lit up the perimeter, this time Jeff saw it too.

His exclamation of disbelief—at seeing the naked girl racing past them fifty yards away—was drowned out by the thunderclap that followed the flickering glow of light. Then all was black again.

Their foxhole was on the northernmost edge of the perimeter, twenty-five meters out from the nearest pair of MPs, and as the two giggling men cursed their powers of suggestion, Nick finally said, "Maybe we should call it in."

"Are you kidding?" Reilly was adamant. "There weren't no pussy dartin' about out there, buddy. Just Mother Nature playin' tricks on our eyes. You wanna get us sent back to some psyche ward to join Big Barney?"

Both MPs remained rigid and silent for the next few minutes, secretly praying another bolt of lightning would enact a replay, across the vast motion-picture screen in front of them, of naked girls jogging back and forth out in the middle of the jungle.

When the triple blast of lightning threw a frozen, timeless spider's web of light in front of them, there was no mistaking the two maidens smiling in their direction from a distance. One girl was carefully maneuvering up a hillside wearing nothing but high heels, her full breasts swaying from side to side as she picked her way over the more slippery rocks. The other woman, about twenty-five yards away now, was jogging—as if in slow motion—directly toward their position, her large, upturned breasts bouncing up and down with each step. Both dreamlike images were Vietnamese, with their long hair coiled atop their heads and rain water glistening off their curves.

Then the night was total blackness again, and the thunder prohibited them from listening for falling rocks or modest laughter that just had to accompany those devilish smiles.

"Did you see what I saw?" Nick asked skeptically. "I mean . . . I mean . . ."

"Yeah, I saw 'em, goddamnit—just shut the fuck up and see what happens next. Maybe they'll hop in our hole so I can hop in theirs!"

But Nick groped about in the dark for the field phone. "I'm calling it in." His breathing had increased, more out of fear of the unknown than any kind of lust. He had heard too many stories from his childhood friends beside Vung Tau beach campfires about war zone ghosts that included innocent village maidens who just happened to get caught in the crossfire. "Stryker should know about this."

Reilly wrestled the phone from him. "Be cool, brother," he hissed, and Nick laughed out loud at the image flashing before him: Jeff Reilly, black aborigine from down under, complete with nose ring and lip bone.

"Really, Jeff! We better call it in. This can only mean nothing but trouble."

"Bullshit. It's just a couple cherry-girls from down in that village frolicking about in the rainfall: didn't you ever go skinny-dippin' in the dark? Well, this is how they get their jollies in the boonies!" Another bolt of lightning revealed the girls had joined hands and were now running away, around a small hillside. "See! They're beatin' feet! Come on, before it's too late!"

"But . . . but . . ." But Jeff was scrambling out of the foxhole, was long gone in fact. Nick placed the field mike against his lips and whispered, "Charlie Papa, this is Lima Papa Niner. Request an Echo-Five our location." He hesitated before deciding how to word the situation. "We got chicks in the sticks! Over, out."

He then felt about the foxhole, relieved when he failed to locate more than one M-16—Reilly had taken his along. He slung his own rifle upside-down under the poncho liner strapped across his shoulders and took out his .45 pistol before

235

climbing out of the mud pool.

Each time lightning cracked overhead he felt vulnerable to a sniper or ambush, but before he could go down on one knee or duck behind a stump, it was dark again. Reilly was nowhere in sight, but in no time he had sprinted up to the small hill behind which he was sure the two women had disappeared.

He ran with all his might now, careful not to slip in the pools of rain water or slick clay, abandoning all rules of caution and procedure they had drilled into him back at The School.

The far side of the hill was an interwoven network of tangled trees and vines, and when he rounded the first corner in the green tunnel leading through the suddenly dry maze, he found his heels skidding up to a wall of rifle barrels, pointed at his chest.

Reilly was a few feet away, his hands raised carefully to shoulder level. He slowly glanced over at Nick, wiggled his nose Bugs Bunny style, then muttered, "Sorry, partner."

"Silence!" a tall white man, flanked on either side by burly Orientals, commanded in a hoarse, strained voice. His face was masked with a dark mustache and beard that covered his throat and dangled across a cartridge-wrapped chest. His long, black hair was pulled back in a pony-tail. A dozen other men were standing around in various combinations of peasant garb, and the two naked maidens were now partially hidden beyond a wall of trees. They cast hostile scowls and icy eyes at the MPs from their jungle dressing-room as they hastily donned simple sarong skirts and black calico blouses. It was now obvious the two women had never known the intruders were observing their horseplay in the lightning storm.

"Who the hell are you bozos?" Reilly lashed back at the renegade American with the AK47, and the latter sprang forward at the challenge and smashed the stock of his rifle against the senior MP's jaw.

"I ask the questions around here!" The leader of the group, a barrel-chested Vietnamese, emerged from the shadows and leaned over Jeff. The MP lay on his haunches, rubbing his jaw and staring unafraid back up at the only Occidental in the group. "My name is Kam Ping!" He smiled proudly, expecting the name would impress the strangers. "I am master of all who

236

come and go in this region. Welcome!" and he held his arms out like a jolly Buddha, anticipating a reverent embrace.

Nick guessed the man weighed close to two hundred pounds, large for an Asian. His head was shaved bald, contrasting with the long Fu Manchu mustache that dropped below his chin. His chest was also crisscrossed with ammo belts, but beneath them was a flashy, beaded muscle shirt that clashed with his jungle environment. His trousers were tiger-striped fatigues, tapered above black sandals. "Are you VC?" the MP private asked softly, his voice refusing to crack as all eyes shifted off his partner.

"VC?" the wide man looked to his followers and the surprise on his face demanded astonished laughter from them. "Me VC? I'm Kam Ping!" he repeated.

"I'm sorry, Mr. *Kam Ping*," Reilly spat the name out sarcastically, "but we never heard of you before!"

The white gunman with the long beard rushed forward again and threw a kick at Jeff's face, but he knocked it away and rose to one knee. A shadowlike form flew through the air from the trees to their left, impacting with a shoulder kick that sent the disrespectful soldier tumbling again. Kam Ping went down on one knee beside the groaning American and touched the patch on his shoulder. Then he looked back up to the white man with the AK47 cradled in his arms. "This emblem. What does it mean?"

"It means watch your ass, boss." He also bent down for a closer examination. "That's an MP patch—Eighteenth Brigade."

"Police?" Kam Ping wrinkled his eyebrows in confusion. "Why police come my jungle?"

The American placed his rifle against Reilly's head. "I say smoke him. Smoke 'em both! They mean nothing but trouble!"

Kam Ping rose a hand to protest the execution and Nick was just beginning to lunge at the gunman when dozens of M-16 charging handles slid forward in the trees beyond the half-naked maidens. The sound of rounds being slammed into rifle chambers was so loud that the cumbersome Kam Ping, startled by the sudden noise, slipped forward onto his face.

"Military police!" Stryker's voice had never sounded so

237

good, and Nick rushed forward and grabbed the AK from the American's hands, whirling the stock around to butt-stroke the man in the nose. He went down heavily, the nostrils rammed into the fractured splinters of bone.

The single lantern that had illuminated the secret jungle camp was knocked slightly by several of the MPs that swarmed in to disarm the Vietnamese, and as the source of dim, yellow light swayed back and forth, seductive shadows played across the curves of the one woman who remained defiantly topless in front of the foreigners.

"Man, am I glad to see you, Sarge!" Nick's voice greeted the reinforcements, but his eyes scanned the edges of the camp in search of other hidden sentries. They came to rest on the women standing rigid in the shadows, and for once they lost their goddesslike arrogance and he feared they would spring off into the rain forest like frightened deer.

Stryker walked up to the bear of an Oriental crouching at the private's feet and kicked him back over onto the ground. "What's your excuse for living, scumbag?" he gritted his teeth and hissed the question.

"My name Kam Ping! Lord of all I survey!"

"Well, survey this!" came the answer, and the MP sergeant rammed another boot heel against the man's forehead. Turning to face the unconscious American, Stryker asked, "What's *his* story?"

"Probably a deserter." Reilly had regained his footing and was anxious to learn the gang's story. "They're definitely not commies, Mark. Something about 'em, though. This jerkoff here don't do much talkin'. Just likes to throw his weapon out at people," and Reilly held off the impulse to kick the man's teeth in.

"Check him for dog tags," Stryker directed after they were unable to locate a wallet on the man. His pockets were jammed with bullets.

"Nothing," the spec. 4 ran his fingers inside the man's collar.

"Check his ankles."

Reilly jerked the bottom of the man's trousers out from the jungle boots and had barely begun searching when he said,

"Bingo!" He produced a single metal tag with a bead chain wrapped through it and tore it off. His eyes grew wide when he read the name to himself.

"Well?" Stryker's tone sounded impatient for the first time that night.

"Schramm. Sgt. Dennis Schramm. Serial number 52248704. Roman Catholic. Blood B Positive."

"Schramm?" Half the MPs present showed their surprise.

"Dave's long-lost MIA brother," Stryker concluded. "Musta got disenchanted with the U.S. Army's way of doing things. Deserted. Took his own little war to the jungles, minus all the MACV rules, hypocricies and restrictions. The only reg was: Hit Charlie where it hurts. To hell with the hilltops, highways and plastic DMZ. Concentrate on the jungle trails—the supply routes south. Am I right, Mr. Ping?" Stryker took the small pocket notebook from his waterproof documents case beneath his shirt and thumbed through the stained and crumbling pages until he came to the Oriental's name. "Kam Ping. Notorious bandit ringleader."

Ping nodded proudly at the introduction.

"But that's really just a front, Mr. Ping, now, isn't it? Your little band of renegade Arvin deserters only seems to strike terror into the hearts of suspected Viet Cong villages—never the hamlets loyal to the Saigon government. Aren't you really all just a sorry-assed complement of amateur Freedom Fighters who happen to drag off a virgin peasant girl now and then? All in the name of the cause, of course."

"Of course." Ping nodded with a broad smile. "The government forces do it all the time. So do the communists. One must consider morale. I must keep my warriors happy!"

Stryker flinched at the casual use of the word "warrior" then glanced over at the two women staring back at him through the bamboo branches and waving leaves. He wondered briefly if they were being held against their will, then dismissed the suspicion—they ignored too many chances to escape. "You loot temples now and then, don't you, Mr. Ping? According to my notes here, gold leaf from Buddhist shrines is one of your favorite ways to finance your military operations."

The smile faded from Kam Ping's face and he avoided

239

Stryker's eyes.

"In fact," Stryker continued, "I do believe you might have a considerable amount of compresed gold leaf stashed right in this very camp. And I'll just bet you were planning to trade it off for a couple thousand automatic rifles that never made it to the exchange site." Stryker was thinking about the helicopter crash, and the two M-16s "the doorgunner" had sent back to Saigon for analysis. He turned to face one of the MPs at the edge of the camp. "Check down that ravine for any vehicles. I want 'em torn to pieces till we find something that glitters like a temple dome!"

"I can see a couple jeeps from here, Sarge." The MP slung his rifle over his shoulder casually and took two men with him down into the leech-infested gully.

Stryker turned back to Kam Ping. "I want to know who supplied those automatic weapons to you, my friend, and I want to know now." The MP sergeant's voice was calm but powerfully forceful.

Kam Ping just laughed in reply. It was a nervous chuckle, intended to hide the frog fighting to get out of his throat. "My heavens, but I don't have the slightest idea what you're talking about."

"Well, I think if we pluck out a couple of your fingernails, it'll loosen your tongue. But first"—he turned to face Craig Davis, the only black MP in the group—"set those women over there free!"

Ping laughed again, this time more confidently, and said, "They are not captives, my dear sergeant. They belong to me. The younger one is my niece, my sister's daughter." He beamed proudly. "And the one I shall slap soon if she does not cover up her body is *my* oldest daughter."

"I suspect I could take a set of vice grips from one of the V-100 maintenance boxes over there and hang you by your balls, yet you still wouldn't tell me where the gold is." Stryker grinned cunningly.

"I would say you are very probably correct, Sergeant." Ping grinned right back at him, a sudden pride and confidence twinkling in his dull brown eyes.

"That's what I thought. Well, you see that big buck nigger standing over there?" He pointed back at Davis, whose broad smile seemed to flash across the dark face each time he chewed at the four sticks of bubblegum in his mouth. The black MP scratched his chin in amusement as he wondered what Stryker was up to. With the other hand he rubbed at an itch in his crotch.

Kam Ping's smile faded again as he visually inspected the husky Davis.

"Well, since you won't talk, I guess I'm just gonna have to hand your daughter there—the one with the defiant snarl blemishing the otherwise beautiful face—I'm gonna have to hand her over to Davis till you talk. Now she's gonna bare more than her chest, and I'm hereby turning my back on the liberties Davis takes out behind the trees there. If I know my man Craig, he's gonna pop her cherry from here to Hanoi.

"But just to make sure he don't split her legs up the middle, I'll delegate our clowns from the Decoy Squad over there to chaperone the young couple. I guarantee you: They're *real good* at working undercover!"

Kam Ping didn't waver. "She will sacrifice what she must for the struggle," he completed the statement painfully.

"Broox, Thomas, Bryant and Sergeant Richards!" Stryker yelled just loud enough so the names would not carry past the camp perimeter. "Follow Davis and the woman there down behind those trees. See to it she's a groaner, if you know what I mean." He winked his true order.

As Bryant grabbed the slender woman by an elbow and whirled her around to face Davis, Nick's eyes were glued to the amber breasts swaying from side to side and he found himself wishing he could watch.

"Thought you were gonna have *my* job," Tim Bryant winked at Nick as he nodded toward the woman. "Eat your heart out, rook."

A few minutes later, after Davis and the Decoy Squad circled around through the trees and returned to their foxholes several hundred meters away, Kam Ping winced in torment as a girl, deep in the heart of the rain forest, screamed repeatedly above the howling storm.

"So that's how I got stuck ass-backwards out here in the

middle of nowhere." David Schramm had just completed telling Big Barney about the undercover operation. For some unaccountable reason, the Cong had pulled back hours earlier, just as they appeared on the verge of successfully overrunning the camp, and the MP had spent the cherished silence bringing Fairchild up to date on current events.

"And what about Crowe?"

"Leroy's dead," he cut in swiftly, but matter-of-factly.

Fairchild swallowed hard, unsure how to react. He hadn't known the man that well, and it sounded like their foxhole was the only one holding a conversation. The rest of the men—what was left of them—appeared huddled in silence, whispering encouragement, listening for the enemy they knew to be lurking less than a football field away, beyond the treeline.

The two former partners ignored the code of silence, continued their chatter through the night, stopping only when one of the wounded yelled in tortured half-sentences against the constant downpour. Sometimes it was hard to tell if the injured man was American or communist.

"How'd he buy it?" Big Barney finally asked and Schramm waited several seconds until he could control his rage.

"There was no reason for it." He fought back the onrush of tears that came every time he relived the death of a friend, held tightly in his arms. "Moast the Ghost gonna be hauntin' graveyards sometime soon."

"Why do you say that?"

"I'm beginning to understand why he's got a bounty of twenty-five grand on his head. When a SAD mission is headed by Moast, lotsa young white boys are probably gonna roast."

Fairchild whirled around on his side of the foxhole. "What was that?" he whispered for the first time, abandoning the loud, unconcerned tone both men had been using for the last hour, daring Charlie to try and silence them. Neither of them really cared anymore what consequences their carelessness provoked.

There was activity nearby. *Inside* the camp.

A figure, cloaked in the shadows and shapeless images that abound in the dark, was crawling up toward Captain Moast's bunker. Schramm and Fairchild immediately put aside their dislike for the Airmobil officer, totally forgetting the way they had taken turns insulting him throughout the night. Something in their system, in their gut—perhaps the cop and ex-cop in their blood—spurred them on to take some sort of action.

"Do you think it's someone trying to collect the bounty?" Fairchild whispered so close to Dave's ear he could feel the heat.

"I'd bet a month's pay on it." Schramm was slowly lifting his rifle out of the foxhole, preparing to sneak up on the steadily moving apparition. "Now if the Cong don't take offense to me doin' a little old-fashioned police work, this case should be closed in a flash."

The human slithering along the earth like a snake in the grass made his way around to the rear of the sunken command post—a section of helicopter fuselage had been rolled into a trench and covered with sandbags and it now served as the CP—with the two men from Foxhole Five right behind him.

"OK, freeze!" Schramm's voice meant business and the fluid-limbed shadow knew it. He slowly removed a hand from his flak jacket.

Fairchild planted a heavy boot down on the soldier's back and reached into the body armor, expecting to come up with a grenade. All he found was a flashlight, U.S. Army issue.

Schramm grabbed an arm and tossed the American over on his back, stuck his rifle muzzle up one of the man's nostrils. "Pat him down, Barney."

Fairchild read off the man's name tag. "Nelson. Don't mean nothin' to me."

"He's the doorgunner. Considerable p.c. to go after the Ghost." Schramm helped the E4 roughly to his feet. "Right, Randy?"

"What's this 'p.c.' crap?" Nelson raised his voice indignantly. "What the hell kinda college-boy words you usin' on me now, newbie? What's goin' on, anyway? You guys undercover oinkers or something?"

Schramm pulled out an ID card none of them could read in the dark and muttered, "716th MPs, Candy Randy. I'm taking you in."

Nelson laughed loudly, stirring several men back at the

perimeter to pop off nervous discharges into the night. "On what charges?"

"Criminal attempt, homicide, for starters. I'll add on others as we go along."

Nelson folded massive forearms across a strong chest. "So I'm under apprehension. You're takin' me in for questioning?"

"That's right."

The doorgunner chuckled defiantly. "You and whose army?"

"Just me," Schramm answered calmly. His hand automatically went for his night stick, then he remembered it wasn't there.

Nelson waved his arm at the tree leaves being whipped by isolated sheets of warm rain. "Look around you, boy. This is grunt territory. The jungle. *My* domain! Not Tu Do Street. I don't see any neon-lit massage parlors. I don't see any street-corner prostitutes."

Fairchild wrapped a powerful choke-hold around the doorgunner's throat. "Consider yourself under arrest." He chuckled this time, tightening down on the windpipe until the soldier's body began to go limp. Big Barney hadn't said those words in a long time. It felt good.

"Think again!" a voice from behind them shot through the dark. They spun around to face Alvin Kline. He had his rifle trained on Schramm's face.

"You're making a big fucking mistake, asshole." Fairchild's voice expressed restrained fury.

"Release him," Kline directed, and with the same breath he tossed a small, metallic object through the air toward Schramm. The slender MP, lithe with tension, alert as a jungle cat, lashed out and caught the grenade without taking his eyes from Kline's. "Now pull the pin. Roll it down into the bunker."

"You're crazy," came Schramm's whispered reply.

Kline slowly brought his rifle up to his shoulder, taking careful, deliberate aim on the man across from him. "Do it. Now. Or you're good as dead. Dead as Moast the Ghost."

"No way, sport. You're gonna have to come up with another

plan," the MP private tried without success to keep the buried fear from escaping dry-edged up his throat, shading each word with uncertainty.

Kline's right elbow went up and his shoulder muscles tightened noticeably, and Schramm could already feel the bullet splitting his face down the middle. But there was no blinding flash. No discharge. Only a rifle butt flying through the thick, muggy air, connecting with the back of the gunman's head, batting him unconscious while he was still swaying jelly-kneed on his feet.

After Kline crumpled to the ground, Schramm flipped on the flashlight they had taken off Nelson and played a beam of green, subdued light across the grim, no-nonsense features of the newcomer.

"Get that damn light out of my face!" The redheaded soldier jerked an open hand in front of his eyes. It was Christiansen, Schramm's number two suspect in the attempted murders.

"We owe you one, dude." Fairchild showed a toothy smile, but he shifted to the side, cleverly positioning Nelson between the two of them like a human shield until he could determine exactly what was going down.

A flare from the perimeter posts soared overhead suddenly, and every man ducked except one. Schramm was not so easily impressed. He kept his own rifle at the ready when he asked, "The question is: why? Aren't you part of this crowd?"

Christiansen produced a small watertight case from inside his boot and flipped it open. A gold CID badge sparkled in the flickering light from the drifting flare.

Fairchild dropped Nelson heavily in the mud and reached forward, but Christiansen instinctively stepped back. "Yeah, well you can have them cast in downtown Saigon for less than a basement blowjob. Don't mean nothin'."

"Take my word for it." Christiansen smiled slyly. "It's real." He slid a laminated ID card out from beneath the shield and tossed it over to Schramm. It verified he was a crime investigator with the U.S. Army CID Command—equivalent to a police detective back in The World, though Schramm knew all too well you could forge any document on Earth in the back alley shops of Tu Do Street also.

"So why's a CID dick masquerading around an Airmobil unit in a grunt's monkey suit?"

"Same reason you are, Dave. It's just that the all-powerful back at MACV got a little shook by your message canister—the one in which you stated Captain Moast needed to be relieved of his command *at all costs*."

"What'd I tell ya?" Schramm glanced over at Big Barney.

"Well, they were getting real nervous," Christiansen continued. "Afraid you might forget priorities and take matters into your own hands."

"I'd say survival is one of my top priorities," Schramm cut in. "This Moast the Ghost is a madman. I've seen more soldiers from his unit die in the last seven days than I've seen in—"

"Regardless, I'm here to set you straight. Or back you up, whichever. My report will show you've not strayed from your mission. After all, you *did* just capture this man as he was sneaking up to the CP—"

"Armed with a lousy flashlight," Fairchild interrupted.

"And you *did* force the rat to take the bait: we got Kline here red-handed, in the act. On top of menacing charges."

"Well, I just hope your report shows how irresponsible this Moast is. Crowe's dead, you know. Caught a belly wound the size of your helmet, landing in a hot LZ—for no fucking reason."

"I'm sorry, Dave."

"No fucking reason!" Schramm fought back the tears that came every time he recalled the helpless feeling he had experienced as the spray of bullets punched at the corpse in his arms, over and over, like a blood-crazed boxer the referee couldn't pull off. He had prayed both that Crowe's body would block the killing rounds and at the same time let some through to snatch his partner along for the ride down hell's rollercoaster. "I just hope you can see what it's like here! I hope you write it up the way it is!"

"No sweat, brother. The word was out, even before I choppered into this unit: Moast will soon be relieved of his command. At General Harding's request, personally," Christiansen revealed.

"Soon, you say. Soon. How many more grunts are gonna

have to die before the bimbos back at Puzzle Palace get off their lazy duffs and—"

The question was left unanswered as all three men went down into an automatic crouch. There came an eerie fluttering in the air and Schramm reached out and snatched up a soggy piece of paper that was floating lazily down through the black mist. Soon, hundreds of other leaflets were saturating the camp as well as the treeline beyond the perimeter, and the ghostly silence that had prevailed most of the last two hours was broken by the dull hacking of rotors high in the oppressive blanket of clouds.

"More bounty posters on Moast." Schramm played a beam from the green flashlight across the fuzzy features of the First Cav captain.

"The reward's gone up to thirty thousand dollars," Big Barney observed dryly.

"You may not get a chance to write that report." Schramm smiled though he knew he should be frowning.

Christiansen read his thoughts. "Yeah, them VC out there are going to read the latest gossip rag here and pull the plug on this camp till they can march our beloved leader's head atop a bamboo spear down Phuoc Loc's main path."

A sudden tension in the air signalled to the men that the helicopter was returning for another pass.

"We oughta spray the sky with tracers." Big Barney indicated the general direction the sound was coming from. "Tracers look beautiful climbing through the mist—we could send up a hot, glowing arc that'd bring that tub down rikky-tik!"

"Yeah, they can't send us no slicks 'cuz of the weather," Schramm complained, "yet some fool rogue in a stolen gunship can find the balls to drop toilet paper on us through this flush of a storm."

"You hit the pecker on the headjob." Fairchild nodded up and down stupidly. "Phuoc Loc: toilet of the Orient."

"Listen." Christiansen held up a hand which faded in the sudden darkness when Schramm doused the flashlight. "It's stationary. The damn chopper's just sittin' up there about eleven o'clock, hovering."

"You think it's gonna land?"

"Christ, I wish we could see up through the mist." The rain had ebbed somewhat, but high winds were still whipping through camp with such force it was often difficult to hear the whir of powerful dual-rotors overhead.

"Come on!" Christiansen was suddenly back on his feet, heading for the other side of the CP.

"What is it?" Fairchild was in no mood to play cat and mouse games, but his question was answered the instant they rounded the captain's bunker.

A rope ladder was hanging down through the mist—almost like something straight out of "Jack and the Beanstalk." Visibility was so bad, the men were not quite sure of what they were seeing until they practically stumbled over the man who was crawling along on the ground toward them.

Christiansen and Fairchild both dove for the man's arms, but the shadow-cloaked phantom sprang off the ground like an angry mongoose, leaving the already battle-weary soldiers, hampered by heavy field gear, tangled in the mud.

Schramm tackled the intruder's legs and wrestled him back down just long enough to conclude the man was not any communist infiltrator, but a stocky, well-built Caucasian, strong enough to not only fend off his blows but to also heave the MP through the air, into the side of the command post.

"Get him!" both Christiansen and Fairchild yelled simultaneously as they struggled to regain their footing and chase the man down, but the intruder dashed past the CP, spraying the entrance with submachine gunfire, then lobbed two fragmentation grenades in after the bullets.

The dual explosions sent sandbags flying and shredded sheets of aircraft metal cartwheeling across camp. When Schramm, Christiansen and Fairchild recovered from the concussion and momentary loss of bearing, the helicopter was gone and it was raining again.

Schramm opened his clenched fist slowly after confirming he still had all his limbs, vital organs and valued organs. A cloth C.I.B. decoration—the prized combat infantryman's badge— torn from the intruder's uniform, lay soaked in the palm of his hand. Christiansen and Fairchild rushed past and descended into Moast's bunker. A few moments later he could hear Big Barney yell, "Corpsman up! At the CP! Corpsman up!"

Moast the Ghost revealed that he was still mortal and not a ghost at all—he could bleed like his men. Suffering from multiple shrapnel wounds, he was hastily treated by the medics, then moved to a secret foxhole after the grinning soldiers of his command were ordered to keep their eyes glued out on the perimeter, wide open for Charlie. MACV could still not provide an airlift out of the besieged fortress. Chopper flights were now airborne on a voluntary basis only, due to the weather, and no one cared to brave thunder, lightning *and* the VC just for he-done-brought-it-upon-himself Moast the Ghost.

The two lieutenants who shared the CP shelter with Moast were dead. One had lost his head and half his chest to the burst of steel-jacketed bullets. The other had survived the assault unscathed—except for a single, pea-sized splinter of shrapnel from the frags that had pierced his heart and severed the aorta.

The maps, captured documents and PRC-25 portable radio-pack that had cluttered the ammo-box tables in the CP were now a shambles.

Five minutes after Moast was secreted in his new bunker, the Viet Cong launched another mortar attack. Old Mr. Charlie could buy a lot of *nuoc-mam* with thirty thousand greenbacks, and he knew it.

16. THEY DON'T GIVE MPs PURPLE HEARTS

LZ Firecracker, outside Phuoc Loc hamlet

Pvt. Nick Uhernik squinted against the downpour, but he had not yet learned squinting won't help you much in the dark.

The soldier in front of him was walking too fast—he could barely see the small, glowing patch up ahead as it changed from shimmering blue to hazy green each time it bobbed up and down with the man's footfalls.

The MPs had taken chunks of the glowing flora from logs filled with rotting phosphorous and rubbed the substance onto small pieces of tape sticking to the back of each man's helmet. The result was an eerie centipedelike creature that bobbed up and down through the shifting mist, but it could only be seen from the rear, and it helped to prevent the column from getting lost or separated.

The mission of the two nine-man squads was to prepare an L-shaped ambush far out beyond the encircled camp's northeast perimeter—to catch the retreating Charlie once the monstrous V-100s rolled into view—and they had been humping for two hours. Another hour and it would be dawn.

The column was resigned to the probability they'd only be coming to the rescue of a camp already violated by the enemy and littered with dead men—especially now that they could hear another mortar barrage showering in across the perimeter—but Sergeant Richards kept the MPs motivated with hushed whispers of the Brotherhood, and the long shot Schramm and Crowe—they still were unaware Leroy's life had been snuffed out ages ago—might be pulled out heroes. So long as the NCOs led the charge, their MPs would follow.

Stryker would be in command of the assault tanks, and the Saigon policemen, Jon Toi and Hoang Khoa, agreed to direct the gunjeeps in after the Cong defenses were rammed and beaten back. Toi was not known for his downtown driving skills, but Khoa was a notorious hot-rodder from way back, and since Stryker had put his most experienced men on the ambush patrol, he felt Khoa was his best bet when it came to scooping up the dead and wounded.

Captain Harlow and his lieutenants agreed it would be wisest for them to supervise the operation from the top of the plateau, by PR handsets—granted, they'd have a bird's eye view if the rain clouds would only fall back—and though they were determined to take the entire valley back from the enemy and out of terrorist hands, Stryker finally convinced them it would be safer to plan for a rescue attempt should they have to strike hard, penetrate, then make a hasty retreat. The important thing was plucking out survivors. After the storm cleared, MACV could call in Arty, the Cavalry and all of SOG to mop up shop if they wanted.

Uhernik could still see Stryker's clever smile when the Chinaman, Kam Ping, driven half crazy by the moaning child down in the woods, broke down and revealed where the ton of gold leaf was buried. In fact, Stryker had been practically standing on it the whole time. But the MP sergeant wasn't the only one surprised. Self-styled Emperor Ping was in for a stinging shock himself when the Americans allowed him to hustle down toward the now-ecstatic screams.

The black MP, Davis, had never touched the rebellious daughter. And the Decoy Squad had circled back toward the jeeps moments after disappearing into the trees. Reilly had planned to hand the defiant woman a few piaster notes every other minute, so long as she'd wail like the wind. Speaking no English, with a greed for money inbred, she abandoned all modesty and complied with the sign language and guttural coaching, ignorant of the reasons behind the weird behavior. So long as the American held out the wrinkled currency notes, she'd snatch them up, assembly-linelike, and utter animal-sounding whimpers that gradually increased in intensity along with the storm. One thing led to another, and by the time papa-san slid up on scene, the melon-chested maiden was straddled atop a delirious Jeff Reilly, her legs spread wide, the groans authentic, and soggy piaster notes scattered amongst the swaying bamboo.

The newbie private—amazed he could daydream even under these circumstances—was jarred back to reality when the lead man in the foot column jumped back a few feet as a young panther leapt across the trail and disappeared within the tangled brush. A flare hanging low in the sky gradually fizzled out, and as the shadows returned to the land, Nick could just barely see her.

Green eyes glowing softly behind the reeds, she ignored the soldiers as she moved cautiously in search of smaller prey and seemed oblivious to the exploding mortars falling within one hundred yards of her hunting grounds.

"Stupid cat has just *got* to be shellshocked," whispered Reilly, more out of admiration than anything else, but Nick barely heard him. They were now within sight of the target treeline, and the closer they got, the greater the chance became that they'd catch some of the 81 mike-mike projectiles the Americans were now lobbing back at Charlie.

"Just like the good ole days back at Pershing," Nick whispered back to Reilly as he gestured toward the tracers arcing back and forth along the circle of concertina wire.

"Huh?"

"Just a short jog, Jeff. One lap around the perimeter, and we'll call it a night," he forced a grin.

"Outfuckingstanding."

Pvt. David Schramm did not see the exploding projectile that whistled in on their foxhole and ripped out Big Barney's heart. He didn't hear the blast send chunks of smoking metal through the gentle giant's chest, for the explosion knocked out his hearing entirely. All he knew was that he was flat on his back in the mud and that he had to roll Big Barney off him to breathe. He did not think about praising the three-hundred-pounder's bulk for deflecting the shrapnel, did not consider thanking the man with grateful tears for saving his life—for at times like that you rarely talked to dead men—but he sensed Fairchild was at peace. That he had not died horribly after all. That Big Barney would have wanted it this way all along.

Charlie had liberated Big Barney from his self-imposed torture chamber, and the man's thick eyebrows—always creased with worry and guilt in the past—now seemed to take on a relieved smile, even if the lips didn't.

Schramm did not hear the ghostly bugles and the shrieking battle cries as the VC charged across the lines of concertina wire. All he knew was that instinct forced him to spring up, told him to empty his clip at the horde of black-pajama-clad guerrillas rushing toward him.

Now on his feet, it seemed strange that the enemy soldier twenty feet away had shot at him three times, seemingly without a sound.

The ringing in Schramm's ears was replaced by a silent void, and then the three bullets were punching his chest, slamming him back off his feet, down into the mud atop Fairchild. The guerrilla's face—as horrified as his own—was fresh in his mind; he could even see the AK barrel smoking, crystal clear but with no noise accompanying the kicking discharge.

The Vietnamese who had shot him hurtled over the foxhole—he could see the soles of his sandals clear as an enlarged photo—and dropped a grenade down in on top of the MP.

Schramm was powerless to move. He was petrified, paralyzed with fear yet at the same time bursting with rage—knowing any second that terrible rush of overpowering, all-encompassing pain would flash through his chest, drag him down to hell.

The grenade bounced down behind Fairchild, but the muffled explosion still sent hundreds of metal fragments stabbing through his body like a handful of pitchforks until he oozed blood like a crimson sponge.

Another guerrilla—this one was grinning with the taste of death on his lips—slid to a halt on the edge of the foxhole and peered down at the American. Though his chest felt like a sizzling soldering iron had been plunged through it three times, Schramm sensed the communist staring down at him, and he held his breath, motionless, feigning death. But then he could feel the razor-sharp bayonet pressing against his stomach, just above the customized belt buckle. The guerrilla grumbled something in VC slang and Schramm could feel the warm, nauseating spittle splash across his forehead an instant before the bayonet was slowly, firmly pushed clean through his belly. It went in like a hot knife through butter, felt like a burning wire being stitched through his guts. Then the Vietnamese was jerking the blade out, was jumping toward the next foxhole, soggy dirt clods knocked down in Schramm's face by his heels.

Schramm opened his eyes and could see shades of pink and orange spreading across a water-colored sky. It never occurred to him dawn was breaking—he had read somewhere that Japanese warriors saw a blazing red sun at their moment of chosen death, perhaps he was experiencing those same sensations now. He was still deaf, or the roar of assault tanks rumbling down the hillside toward the beleaguered encampment would have told him help had finally arrived—his fellow military policemen were turning back the tide, had the Cong on the run, their thunderous fifty-caliber machine guns not only kicking up rocks at their fleeing heels, but ripping ankles completely off.

Stryker's fleet of tanks crushed as many guerrillas under the huge tractor tires as they gunned down. Upon emerging from the cover of the jungle, four V-100s had veered to the right when reaching the perimeter, four more veered left and proceeded halfway around the camp until further venture would create a dangerous crossfire. The final four armored vehicles skidded to a halt at the base of the hill and began picking off Vietnamese soldiers who had taken refuge in foxholes laced with the mutilated bodies of dead Americans.

Schramm could sense a power cresting like a wave toward the edge of his foxhole. He could feel a warmth in the air that was pleasant, comforting—not like the heat of the jungle, the tropics—and when he saw Reilly's face and Davis's face, and the faces of the Decoy Squad peering down at him from the lip of his grave he knew that warmth was friendship, that his brothers had come, that they hadn't let him down after all. Schramm removed his cupped hand from his belly, tried to ignore the sight of all their smiles fading when he reached out to shake hands and the fountain of blood gushed out at them.

"It's OK, buddy! Hang on, you're gonna make it!" *It was that FNG—fucking new guy. What was his name? Right, the soldier from Czechoslovakia.*

"Thuy! Think of Thuy, brother! She's waiting for ya back in ol' Saigontown. Don't check out on us now!" *It was Reilly, the mellow clown. Funny how he lost his Australian accent whenever he looked death in the eye. Always thinking about women. Take care of her for me, Jeff. I know who you're speaking of. After all, I left my heart in Saigon, pal. We all left our hearts in Saigon, didn't we?*

"Your brother, Dave! We found your brother! Roaming the jungles, greasin' Charlie on his own, freelancin'. Your brother's alive, Dave!" *That'd have to be Richards. Such a card! Always jokin' around. Sorry, Gary. Can't see you guys anymore. Falling'. . . falling, Thuy. I remember what we had, I feel the love we shared, even here, even in this suffocating tomb, but I just can't picture your face, honey . . . I just can't see you anymore.*

Schramm could hear them now, high above him, distant, as if he had sunk to the bottom of a black pit. And then he was floating above them, looking down, watching the tops of their heads. Frowning at how the skinny kid lying on his back in the foxhole looked so familiar.

Reilly held onto Schramm's hand for several more minutes, ignoring the stray rounds that still whizzed and zinged in about them from different directions. He stared into the MP's eyes, but knew there was no one inside, looking out. "Your brother's safe now, Dave. He's back home. A little confused, a little wild, a little angry. But he's not missing-in-action anymore. They're takin' him back to Saigon right now, Dave. Can you hear me, partner?"

Schramm knew the warmth of friendship settling over him like a shroud would see him through whatever was to come. He knew his brothers had not abandoned him to the Cong. He knew that they were standing all around him right now—had not forsaken him after all. The realization that his brothers were there, even if they were helpless to save him, made it easier for Schramm to close his eyes, knowing he'd never open them again.

An endless hail of lead was peppering the ground around Captain Moast's foxhole. With the dawn came a lull in the storm and clouds along the horizon were swiftly clearing up. The added light gave the snipers in the treetops an advantage. They had Moast the Ghost pinned down.

The section of palms they had climbed up into—as much to allow their retreating comrades time to escape as to die a glorious death for Uncle Ho—was protected in the rear by a steep hillside, and the far slope was an inaccessible cliff wall that hung out over the river.

No way for the MPs—without the proper equipment—to circle around behind them. But no way for the Cong to escape either. Suicide, whether they inflicted it or sustained it, was the only way out, the only road home.

"I say blast them palms till they fall over!" suggested Reilly, after the ambush squads realized most of the guerrillas fled southwest, back toward the village, and moved up to assist the tank crews.

"Hell, give 'em Moast, if that's what they want," muttered Richards as he crouched beside the armor-plated belly of one of the towering V-100s. "And let's get back to the Caravelle for a beer."

Stryker ignored his fellow buck sergeant's grim humor and low-crawled over to one of the gunjeeps nestled safely behind the line of assault tanks.

"You hot dogs ready for a little contact?" he stared directly at Khoa, the senior *canh-sat.*

"No," Toi answered instead, his tone so soft Stryker couldn't tell if he was serious.

"We could sweat it out, wait for the storm to clear, let Charlie rebuild their wedge till the cavalry swoops in on their gunships and takes 'em out—and risk letting Moast bleed to death."

"Or we could earn our combat pay and run a couple

gunjeeps down in there and snatch his ass."

"*You* get combat pay." Toi stared back at the ex-Green Beret wide-eyed. "*We* don't get shit."

"I say take your best shot." Khoa's grin radiated confidence, impatience. "Let's finish our job."

"All right." Stryker didn't pause to allow Toi a redress. "At first I thought about running a V-100 down there and scoopin' him up under protection of all that armor. But the ground's too soggy. Even with the balloon tires, chances are they'd sink like rhinos in quicksand before they even got close to the target location—too much rain lately. Too much flooding from the river.

"Our jeeps aren't much better, but with four-wheel drive we can probably maintain enough speed to slide through just about anything."

"The terrain is too cramped for the tanks anyway," Khoa observed. "Too many clay outcroppings that you can't just ram out of the way. Not enough room to turn around if we hit a tight spot."

"We'll use two vehicles," Stryker decided. "Unit One will be me and Khoa—we'll slide in to scoop up Moast, regardless of how bad he's injured. Unit Two will be you Toi, and my cherry-boy rook over there—you clowns'll run cover circles around the target zone, spraying the treeline with 7.62 tracer. Make sure it's *all* hot stuff—burn Charlie right outta his palm fronds if all else fails."

Stryker was thinking back to what a drill sergeant had told him while he was an MP academy recruit, years earlier. The DI had once been in a similar situation: a half mile of straight road lay ahead of him, and he decided that the fastest way to travel from Point A to Point B was simply to "duck and go like hell!" Primitive, but sometimes effective. The gunner on his jeep had ducked too, not firing a shot, and the VC had let them go right by without any trouble.

Stryker doubted it would work so smoothly for them, but he had few other options. Khoa gunned the jeep and they started down the hillside toward the line of blood-soaked foxholes.

Stryker's eyes were pointed down over Khoa's shoulders, watching the vehicle's speedometer instead of the treeline. "What am I expecting?" he reprimanded himself, "a traffic cop to step out from the bushes and hand me a speeding ticket?" But their speed *was* crucial, and when the dial registered slightly past forty mph he kept his hand jammed down on the automatic four-wheel drive lever, fearing it might pop out under the grinding strain.

At fifty mph the bullet came crashing through the windshield. Stryker went wild with the M-60, hopping back all the way into the rear seat, abandoning the lever. The roar was deafening. They were going too fast for him to take aim effectively on any hidden targets, and as the hostile fire increased his inner doubts began to rapidly multiply and he wanted to turn back. For the first time in his life, he wanted to bow out, chuck it in the trash. Taking calculated risks was one thing. Inviting suicide was another.

He wanted to race back to Saigon atop the V-100, get smashed at Mimi's bar, watch a French porno flick in Cholon dubbed in Chinese, suck on salt-covered pineapple cubes . . . but his calloused hands kept the big gun rattling till the bouncing brass filled the jeep's insides and littered the field all around them in a sparkling rainbow of browns and golds and dirty coppers.

Khoa was probably thinking the same thoughts, but in Vietnamese—Stryker could see his hands were frozen to the steering wheel and his foot was glued to the floorboard.

The bunker at the edge of the perimeter, once so distant, was suddenly growing bigger and coming closer and closer far too quickly. Khoa had to smash down on the brakes to avoid hitting the bodies piled up around it.

The skid alone took them fifty feet past the target spot, and as sheets of slimy mud splashed out from under the tires Khoa was forcing the protesting gears into reverse. Dirt flew as the wheels spun deep down past the loose topsoil and the jeep growled angrily, finally moving backwards toward the trench-line.

Stryker could hear the motor from the other gunjeep racing back and forth, laying down cover fire. He could distinguish

Uhernik's barking M-60 from the walloping fifty cals blasting back at the assault tanks, rumbling idle now in a wagon-trainlike circle.

Suddenly the area was a whirlwind of mud and, surprisingly, dust. Multihued shades of dust from white to dark red. Leaves and twigs and branches rose in a giant deafening gust, and for a long ten seconds none of the men in the gunjeeps could see two feet in front of them because of the funnel.

A helicopter!

It seemed impossible, but a chopper was coming right down on top of them. It sported U.S. markings, was one of theirs, but suddenly a machine gunburst showered down on the hood of their jeep, and they all scrambled for cover, abandoning the disabled vehicle. Stryker couldn't believe it: one of their own gunships was firing on them! Khoa stayed with the jeep, hitting the red lights and siren button, but the electrical power was fading and the strobes did not reply. Uhernik was yelling over the PA loudspeaker mounted in the grille, "Military police! Military police! You are firing on friendly forces! You are firing on friendly for—"

The rain of lead stopped, and the nose of the Huey dropped as its power increased. The rotors began slapping at the air and reeds were flying about and cutting through their thin uniforms like long green swords. And then it was gone.

"Well, how do you like that shit!" Toi was saying. "I don't believe what I just saw!"

The helicopter returned in a few seconds and buzzed back and forth over their location, then hovered directly over the foxholes and began to lower a weighted rope ladder that still flapped about wildly in the downblast of the rotorwash. Toi's gunjeep coasted up to the side of Stryker's and all four men remained silent, disheartened. The MP sergeant scrambled out from under the chassis of his jeep and was preparing to jump into the other vehicle.

"Oh hell!" the rook was suddenly yelling above the shrill, mechanical whining of the gunship overhead. "Khoa! Khoa!"

Stryker turned to find the Saigon policeman lying in the back of their jeep in a pool of blood. Whether he had taken a burst of slugs from the American chopper or the Viet Cong snipers, they didn't know. Other *canh-sats* were running up from cover, sprinting down to them from the tanks, and crowding over his limp figure, and then Uhernik was throwing down his flak jacket, tearing off his fatigue top, stuffing his T-shirt into the open chest wound and yelling, "He's still alive goddamnit! Let's move it out of here!" And they were carrying Khoa over to the other jeep and throwing out all kinds of gear to make room for everyone. The bullets from the doorgunner's M-60 had rendered Stryker's jeep totally useless.

Toi jumped behind the wheel and threw the vehicle into gear, and then they were racing back up the gentle sloping hillside, trying to hold onto their helmets, weapons and Khoa all at the same time.

Stryker looked back just long enough to see the weak, bewildered captain scrambling up the rope ladder, missing several rungs, sliding down a few feet, pulling himself back up painfully slow this time. When he got to the halfway point, the chopper began receiving intense sniper fire, and as the sparks flashed off the bottoms of the metal skids and the bullets pounded the thin underbelly of the craft, the officer lost his balance and fell back into the raging jungle. The Huey banked sharply and disappeared into the mist.

Toi fired madly with his pistol as he steered with the other hand and was therefore unable to shift out of first gear. Still, their speed was soon a roaring thirty mph as the engine screamed and pulled them up out of the crossfire. The four men—even the semiconscious Khoa—were firing their weapons into the trees and brush and anything that moved, and then their tires were only rims and the jeep was smoking heavily.

Somehow they made it to the top of the hill, and like memories of some past schoolyard king-of-the-hill, Toi jumped to the ground and began waving his pistol in the air and hopping up and down like a wild man. He released a crude volley of profanity at the enemy and their mothers, and then he fired the remainder of his clip, but he was well out of handgun range.

One of the *canh-sats* attempted to raise a medical evacuation helicopter on the radio, but the ARVN choppers were not answering, and the Americans refused to land for a wounded Vietnamese.

"Who's in that fuckin' bird, anyway?" Stryker grabbed the binoculars from Sergeant Farthing and searched the blanket of clouds.

"It had U.S. markings, for sure," confirmed Richards.

"You realize we're gonna have to try it all again," Stryker advised Toi.

"Are you dinky-dau?" he asked in a half scream, looking up from Khoa. "Do you want to end up looking like this?" He pointed at the blood gushing from the soaked T-shirt. "No officer worth that much, Mark."

But the men all realized there wasn't much choice. Neither the jeep or any of the V-100s could make it back to Saigon in time to save Khoa. "If that damn fall didn't kill him, then *I* will when I get my hands on him." Stryker gritted his teeth, referring to Moast.

The air was now one solid, chopping vibration as a formation of helicopters flew past at treetop level, like giant, winged grasshoppers.

"Try to raise them on the net," Stryker told the radio operator, and he made a feeble, unsuccessful attempt. Soon the helicopters disappeared within the maze of clouds, and only the faint whirring of the rotors remained.

"We've got to get a dust-off for Khoa," decided Toi as he replaced the clotted, makeshift bandage with empty ammo bandoliers. "He's lost far too much blood to last through the day."

The *canh-sats* at the radio began to speak in excited tones, and Stryker ran over to see who they had raised. The voice in the static became stronger, just as a second wave of helicopters appeared to the west. Stryker grabbed the mike and began requesting a medevac. "We have a full-bird colonel with a head wound!" he was yelling against the static. "Advise when you want smoke! Bookoo Victor Charlie to your Whiskey!"

Within minutes the choppers were circling their position, and one of the men from the Decoy Squad popped a yellow smoke bomb, the only color they had, to signal wind direction and the best LZ. Toi had already told them the wind speed, that

261

there were no pole-wire boobytraps; then one of the Hueys dove down through the treetops, slid in with an abrupt sideways stop, its doorgunner blasting away at the treeline to the west.

Stryker and two other MPs were running toward its narrow skids, their pistols drawn, ignoring the sniper rounds that *pinged* in around them. Three *canh-sats* helped surround the craft—had their rifles at the American pilot's throat before he could pull out his revolver or lift off. The doorgunner, used to the insanity of Vietnam, didn't even resist, but simply threw the MG handles up at the ceiling of the craft so that the barrel clanged against the bottom of the open hatch.

"Now we got us a wounded 'gook' here that needs help bad!" Stryker yelled sarcastically, pulling back his .45's hammer with his thumb for special effect. "And if you assholes don't cooperate and get him back to Saigon, me and Mr. Colt here gonna do such a job on your face even your mother won't recognize you when I'm through!"

The warrant officer shrugged, as though bored and only slightly annoyed, and motioned for the *canh-sats* to haul the wounded "soldier" aboard. A tall, gray-haired officer brushed past the stone-faced doorgunner and stepped down from the back of the craft, his head held aloft confidently as he rushed over toward Stryker.

"Afternoon, General Harding," the MP sergeant gave a brief salute without looking directly at the man. "Welcome to the party."

"Looks like you got your hands full on this one, Stryker. But did you have to go pulling your cap pistols on my driver over there?" He wrinkled his nose at the sight of the *canh-sat* bleeding all over the ground at his feet. Stryker didn't answer immediately, and the general went on, "Anyway, thought I'd drop in and offer my help."

"That's a rog, sir—appreciate it." Stryker busied himself helping haul Khoa into the slick.

"Where's your C.O.?"

Stryker pointed up at the plateau rising from the mist behind them with his chin and said nothing. Harding just cleared his throat and shook his head.

Christiansen, still wearing E2 chevrons, emerged from the half circle of soldiers forming around the flamboyant brigadier and walked right up to Harding.

Half of the assault tanks had moved in closer to the besieged perimeter and were cutting the palm trees to shreds. The helicopter circling overhead made several dives at the carpet of thick jungle beyond the treeline, and Stryker could sense its pilot was nervously waiting for the bird on the ground to lift off.

Christiansen started to say something to the general, but then Stryker was yelling for the pilot to take her away. The pilot, in turn, was staring nervously at Harding, his expression asking if the general planned to stay on the ground or would be boarding. Harding gave the thumbs-up signal and before they knew it, the chopper was airborne again.

"They'll probably throw him out over Vung Tau," whispered Uhernik as his eyes squinted to follow the speck he could hardly see any longer. One of the *canh-sats* walked over to the Americans and asked in broken English if they thought Khoa would make it. Stryker couldn't provide an honest answer, but everyone knew his chances were not good. They'd be a lot better if he'd been choppered out earlier.

Stryker picked up a branch and smoothed out the clay before him. "OK," he said, making two large X's on the waterlogged map, "we're here, and the other friendlies are here. The commies are here, and here, and probably all throughout here. Moast the Ghost, or what's left of him, is over here. Now if we—"

Just then the roar of two monstrous CH-53 helicopters descended from the treetops and hovered above the foxholes beside the riverbank, throwing up a storm of dust and twigs. Four ropes dropped to the ground and within seconds two American soldiers rapelled to the ground from the "hell hole" in the bottom of the giant twin-rotored craft and dove for the sandbagged shelters.

Doorgunners on either side blasted away at the sniper-infested treeline, while the second chopper flew small circles around the area, peppering the jungle with a thousand bullets.

"Jesus H. Chhhrrrist!" One of the *canh-sats* was all charged

263

up with awe as Americans reappeared beneath the dangling ropes, supporting the wounded infantry captain and a second soldier. One of the troopers waved his hand in the air, and with a burst of power that sent a handful of birds shrieking and flapping away in flight, the helicopter slowly rose. The hundred feet of rope between the craft and the men soon tautened and they were jerked off their feet into the misty air.

"Well, will you look at that bullshit," Stryker laughed as the small huddle of bodies, looking like an upside-down parachute suspended from silver wires, slowly grew smaller and smaller. "Reminds me of the time . . ." But he caught himself and refrained from discussing his Special Forces days. He didn't want his men getting bored—and worse, skeptical, of the war stories he so rarely reminisced about. What his men thought about him behind his back was important to Stryker. And he knew real soldiers didn't think much of bullshitters and egotists.

"You'd think they were making a movie or something," one of the Decoy MPs mused.

With their arms around each other's shoulders, the group spun about in circles and was soon hoisted up into the bottom haze of the lowest clouds. The only sign that remained of its sister ship was the faint chopping of unseen rotors, pounding the air high above the light drizzle.

"Outfuckinstanding," came a whisper in the crowd of cops dressed like grunts, and Stryker knew the compliment just had to come from his favorite kangaroo killer, Reilly.

The Chinook appeared to shudder briefly as it labored slowly higher and higher, skipping along the bottom of the gray blanket hiding the sun. It was still only a few hundred feet above the battlefield, and the men began taking bets on whether it would clear the clouds with the added weight, now twirling around on the suspended lines beneath it, wildly out of control.

A squad of ragged-looking MPs was rushing up toward the circle of assault tanks, carrying four critically wounded infantrymen over their shoulders—there were no other survivors. The VC, what were left of them, were melting into the rain forest, down into their hidden tunnels.

Stryker was casually briefing the general on the current situation—something about regaining control of the camp finally, so long as Charlie didn't rebound with another wave—but Christiansen didn't hear the conversation. His eyes were glued to the faded, discolored rectangle on General Harding's uniform. Right over his heart. Where a combat infantryman's badge patch had recently been torn off.

"You've done a fine job." Harding was patting one of the weary *canh-sats* on the back, a gesture the Vietnamese don't appreciate.

Christiansen glanced down at the shredded C.I.B. patch in the palm of his hand, the single item of evidence Schramm had left him before his untimely death. He clenched his fist, unsure why a brigadier general would go to such lengths to cancel one of his captain's tickets. Why not just wait for the brass hats at MACV to straighten out the red tape and jerk Moast's commission? He couldn't understand why a career soldier with Harding's distinguished reputation would risk it all to take out a renegade officer. It had to be something personal, not professional. It surely was not concern for the grunts dying in the field, under Moast the Ghost's command.

Grunts dying in the field . . .

Christiansen had been staying close to the general as he rushed about energetically, congratulating the men on a mission that'd be full of medals in the end, regardless of who actually executed the rescue itself. "The support troops were vital in the case. The support troops were vital." He beamed proudly, like a father on the sidelines. Christiansen halted in his tracks as his mind flashed back to the distressing vision.

Grunts dying in the field . . .

The undercover CID agent swallowed the prepared statement where he intended to lay his badge on Harding, place him under arrest, handcuff him in front of the exhausted survivors.

Christiansen thought of Schramm. How the man had perished because of an uncaring officer's bloodlust. Was it the desire to succeed, to bounce up that military career ladder in record time that motivated the captain to so criminally disregard his men's safety? Or was it some twisted, demonic contest with Charlie, where not God but the jungle judged the victor?

No, regardless of the brigadier's reasons for going after one of his subordinates, Christiansen would not act. He would not allow Moast the Ghost to win another battle with MACV, only to return to the field to lead another fresh company of young Americans to their death. Christiansen crumpled the C.I.B. patch up in his fist and stuffed it down a pocket, turned to walk away.

Captain Moast's rescue chopper was now penetrating the bottom layer of clouds, fading away like a bad dream.

WHOOOOOOOSH!

The men circled around just in time to see the surface-to-air heat-seeking missile, its thick trail of gray smoke billowing out behind it, swiftly climbing the skyline toward the Chinook.

One of the wounded infantrymen lying under a V-100 cheered as the projectile smashed into the huge craft, filling the clouds with spiraling debris and smoldering bodies. It did not register in his confused, bitter mind yet that Moast the Ghost had just caused the deaths of another dozen soldiers.

"Get two assault tanks down there!" Stryker angrily directed, pointing at the section of jungle from where the rocket had been launched. "Right now! I want some Cong heads on my belt within an hour!"

The Decoy Squad and the unit's rookies eagerly climbed up into the closest V-100, and it was soon lumbering noisily down toward the treeline, deck guns blasting away long before any targets or even suspicious bushes presented themselves.

"Probably no survivors." Harding's binoculars were trained on the corpses fluttering back to green, hostile mother earth. "But I'll get some flyboys out there to check on it anyway." He started off toward one of the jeep radios.

"Hold it, *sir*." Stryker blocked the general's path with a thick, rigid forearm. Christiansen jerked his eyes up from the ground where they had been buried, suddenly interested in the proceedings.

Harding turned to flash the NCO a stinging glare at the unprecedented physical contact. "Yes, Sergeant."

Stryker turned to Richards, a few feet away. "Gary, take

care of that. Get on the box and have some gunships *di-di-mau* down there to round up the dead. I want a count. Verify it with ATC. I don't want anymore American MIAs roaming this stretch of jungle." He turned back to Harding.

The general's face was flushed crimson at having been kept waiting. "General Harding," Stryker said as he grabbed the man's left wrist with his right hand and whirled the brigadier around. Handcuffs were snapped down on the wrists in a blink of eyes half the GI spectators missed. Just as quickly, the stocky MP had relieved Harding of the pearl-handled .45 on his hip before he said, "I'm placing you under apprehension at this time."

"What's the meaning of this, *Sergeant*? What's the charge?"

"We'll start with running guns to a gang of bandits. Does the name Kam Ping ring a bell? He fancies himself this area's self-appointed emperor."

Harding swallowed hard.

"Then there's criminal attempt homicide, assaulting a military policeman, misappropriation of government property, conspiracy. . . , Do you want me to go on?" The muscles in Harding's cheeks shifted about as he struggled to hold in his anger.

"Kam Ping has given us quite a testimonial," the sergeant went on anyway, "about your deal to supply him with over two thousand *stolen* automatic weapons in exchange for Vietnamese gold—the 24K variety. The Saigon government will love to hear about this one, *General*." Stryker paused to relish the moment before he continued.

"I haven't pieced it all together yet, but I'd wager a month's pay *you*, sir, are the man behind the thirty thousand dollar bounty on Captain Moast."

"Me!" The general's eyes flew wide, but the act fooled no one standing behind Stryker.

"Moast has been a stick in your spokes from day one. First, his obsession with tracking down—unbeknownst to him—your gold supplier, Ping the Chinaman, and second, he foiled your gun-running operation by chasing down the rifle-laden choppers on his own volition.

"The same day the fleet of helicopters disappeared from Tan

Son Nhut your name was logged in on a back-gate SP's access roster. And of course your personal interpreter, Captain Cao, was caught dead-handed, with the stolen M-16s. In one of the stolen choppers." Stryker finally grinned, but it was with pride and not satisfaction—he had remembered all the clues without having to consult his pocket notebook, which was lost in the mad minute trying to rescue Moast with the gunjeeps.

"All circumstantial evidence, Stryker. You'll never prove any of it in court." Harding's facial color had deepened—was now red as a cherry.

"Oh, I'll prove it, General. Eventually the pieces of the puzzle will all fall in place. I won't leave this lousy jungle till I'm satisfied you rate a reduction to E1 grade and a twenty-year term at the LBJ stockade." *Hope I'll be here in Vietnam twenty more years*, Stryker chuckled to himself.

"You'll regret this, Stryker!" I've got friends in high *How many times had he heard that one before....* "I'll have you walking a foot beat in Cholon before this is all over!"

Of course the general had no way of knowing Cholon held a special place in Mark's heart.

"Whatsa matter, General? You don't make enough money as it is? Greed forced you to pan a little on the side? At the expense of all the innocent lives that were lost over a few lousy rifles?"

"I'll see you in court, Stryker! You haven't got a case on me!"

"You have the right to remain silent."

Christiansen smiled, suddenly feeling a flood of inner satisfaction. He was glad now that he had not tossed the C.I.B. patch in the mud. Perhaps Private Schramm had not died in vain, for nothing, after all.

Third Field Army Hospital, Saigon

"I'm sorry," the nurse with the blond permanent piled atop her head issued the insincere apology in a Southern drawl. "Officer Khoa is not allowed any visitors at this time. He needs his rest."

Stryker brushed past her with an impatient wave and led the

two dozen military policemen into the crowded cubicle. Officer Toi was back in full dress uniform, on guard duty at his friend's bedside, his feet propped up on the railing, chair tilted back, eyes closed.

Reilly kicked the *canh-sat's* chair out from under him, and above the laughter and applause from his fellow MPs announced, "It's time to party!" Each man from the Decoy Squad produced a bottle of rare champagne, and Raunchy Raul from Bravo Company whipped the rain poncho off the shortest "soldier" in the room, revealing the sexiest call girl the Majestic Hotel had to offer.

"He can't drink *that* stuff!" the top-heavy nurse with the swollen hips ignored the prostitute and forced her way past the unauthorized visitors again, reaching for the liquor. "He's got a belly wound, for Christsake!"

"Get that cunt outta here!" Sergeant Richards directed, and soon Davis and Uhernik were carrying the kicking nurse back into the dimly lit corridor.

"You can't do this!" she screamed. "You'll be in deep trouble, soldier!"

"Call a cop, lady," Davis suggested, and he wrapped an arm around Nick and slipped him back into the tiny private room.

Thomas and Bryant had just succeeded in waking the heavily sedated Khoa, and Broox was sitting on Toi's shoulders, tickling his ribs with one hand, pouring a bottle of champagne over his head with the other.

Thirty minutes later, with the door securely barricaded and Pershing Field refusing to send sober MPs over, the men scattered about Khoa's battered frame found themselves leaning on each other and trying to hold back the tears that come from friendship and loyalty.

It had always been that way. They leaned on each other— counted on each other out in the street where you could pull no punches: your brother cops were all you had. And the excessive drinking after the missions—especially when a man was lost—allowed the tears to flow more easily, often beyond control.

The following morning, when the informal critique and the cleansing of terrible memories had run its course—when the

269

MPs were all ready to leave—Officer Jon Toi held up a hand and asked Khoa a question in rapid Vietnamese.

The glassy-eyed policeman smiled proudly, slowly shook his head up and down, and Toi unbuttoned his shirt and pulled out a thin, plastic map case. From the container he drew a folded section of bright cloth—a small Vietnamese flag, barely the size of a helmet: three horizontal red stripes on a saffron field. A single bullet hole marred the gold background, symbol of Vietnamese ancestral earth. It was one of the flags Stryker had attached to his jeep's whip radio antenna.

"I give this to you, Mark," the weak Saigon police sergeant reached out and took the flag from Toi then handed it to the American. "It is not much, compared to saving my life as you did, but it is all I can offer just now in the way of thanks. Perhaps you can look at it some time in your future and be reminded of the bond formed between all of us today. A bond that, I know now, can never die."

Then he ran his eyes from man to man, surveying every MP in the room personally. He spoke to Sergeant Stryker, but his words were directed at everyone.

"I want to thank you for leaving your beloved country to come to my Vietnam to help my people and my land. You are truly the best friend a warrior—" the smile brightened—"and a cop could ask for. I often wonder what brings men like you to such a place as this . . ." But the sentence trailed off unfinished, and the smile faded slightly as his voice became a whisper and Khoa fought the pain in his chest. They clasped hands and he strained to keep his eyes locked on Stryker's. "Someday, you will return to U.S.A., but I will always remember your kindness, and I will tell my children about you. It will not mean anything to them, but I will tell them anyway, and I will enjoy telling them."

McLEANE'S RANGERS
by John Darby

#1: BOUGAINVILLE BREAKOUT (1207, $2.50)
Even the Marines call on McLeane's Rangers, the toughest,
meanest, and best fighting unit in the Pacific. Their first adventure
pits the Rangers against the entire Japanese garrison in Bougainville. The target—an ammo depot invulnerable to American air
attack . . . and the release of a spy.

#2: TARGET RABAUL (1271, $2.50)
Rabaul—it was one of the keys to the control of the Pacific and the
Japanese had a lock on it. When nothing else worked, the Allies
called on their most formidable weapon—McLeane's Rangers, the
fearless jungle fighters who didn't know the meaning of the word
quit!

#3: HELL ON HILL 457 (1343, $2.50)
McLeane and his men make a daring parachute drop in the middle
of a heavily fortified Jap position. And the Japs are dug in so deep
in a mountain pass fortress that McLeane may have to blow the
entire pass to rubble—and his men in the bargain!

*Available wherever paperbacks are sold, or order direct from the
Publisher. Send cover price plus 50¢ per copy for mailing and
handling to Zebra Books, 475 Park Avenue South, New York, N.Y.
10016. DO NOT SEND CASH.*